THE
DEATHS
AND
AFTERLIFE
OF
ALEISTER
CROWLEY

To Clementine, Laszlo & Heather

THE
DEATHS
AND
AFTERLIFE
 ## OF
ALEISTER
CROWLEY

IAN THORNTON

unbound

First published in 2019

Unbound
6th Floor Mutual House, 70 Conduit Street, London W1S 2GF
www.unbound.com

Text Design by Ellipsis, Glasgow

A CIP record for this book is available from the British Library

ISBN 978-1-78352-783-0 (trade paperback)
ISBN 978-1-78352-784-7 (ebook)
ISBN 978-1-78352-795-3 (limited edition hardback)

Printed and bound in Great Britain by Clays Ltd, Elcograf S.p.A.

1 3 5 7 9 8 6 4 2

Contents

PART ONE

Farmer Manzo: Old man, I'm worried. The village girls will go crazy over the samurai. If the samurai touch them, all hell will break loose.

Gisaku: Bandits are coming, you fool. Your head is on the block and all you think of are your whiskers?

Kikuchiyo: Use your balls, if you've got any!

– *Seven Samurai*

Prologue

I slept with faith and found a corpse in my arms on
awakening;

I drank and danced all night with doubt and found
her a virgin in the morning.

– Aleister Crowley

They used to call me the most evil man in the world.

The fools said that I was more influential than Jesus.
They reckoned I had seduced thousands of women, and even
more young men. They claimed I was a friend of Hitler and a
rabid lover of a burgeoning Prussia, and then a vile and eager
Germany. Some snaggle-toothed and half-baked buffoons said
I advocated rape, paedophilia and black magic. They hypothesised, with little regard for fact, that I sacrificed children and
dined with a vermillion Satan.

My name is Aleister Crowley, *The Great Beast*. 666. And I
am here to tell you the truth.

You see, wouldn't you want to do just that, if instead of
being blamed for trying to torch the twentieth century, you
had really only ever been responsible, in large parts, for rescu-
ing it.

And what is the point of busting an infernal gut to save a
generation, if one then sits by, lights a girthy and corpulent
cigar, scratches oneself around the well-cut trouser and

watches meekly as quite preventable mischief and horror ensues? Yes, there was adultery, but adultery does not imply marriage, no more than whoredom implies commerce.

You see, the truth is that I was the greatest spy of the twentieth century. The lies were all necessary, as they had been for that other great Englishman, The Scarlet Pimpernel.

For the longest time I could not care less about the conjecture that surrounded my unrivallable degeneracies. So why pipe up now after all these years? I shall get to that almost immediately.

In 1947, I faked my own death in that Sussex seaside town, where the destiny of England was forged, and where I larked as a green-knee'd boy. Hastings.

My life up until that year has its own documentation, partly laid out by me through fact, fiction and myth, and partly by others of varying states of bluster and of a precipitously sliding scale of talent. The factual regurgitation is of tiny consequence and is little more than shoddy typing and juvenile tittle-tattle. It is that lowest and most self-serving bar of memoir. One was even too long in the tooth for it back then. How many times must I tell them that my admission to killing children only referred to the near constant masturbation of my youthhood, my uncoupled ejaculate, my lonesome and spilled seed?

Now, I sit here in a meadow in Shangri-La. My home has been the elevated bliss of this Himalayan mountain lair for almost all the last seven decades. I breathe the thin and life-preserving air that most consider to be mere myth. And yet I am into my fifteenth decade. I feel quite fine.

But I must return.

First, however, I must enter into another personal brawl with Death, for He may take me in the mountain pass and turn me to dust as my true age is exposed, just as He has done to so many others. But I itch to fight that fucker one last time before I return to my boys and my girls in Cambridge to save the World for good.

It is 2024. There is a Final Conflict brewing across the world, one between Good and Evil. This is not the simplified fight of white and black that stained much of my life, one of God versus Satan. This is a fight between the Beauty and the Horror within man.

My own true Will has always been to champion the freedom of Man's spirit, so that he or she can fulfil all dreams and ambitions. This is what I call the Will.

Most of us are built to love and create and soar. Yet there are evil leaders with false smiles who aim to take the freedoms I have heralded for decades. Mean governments and willing police with billy clubs aim to orchestrate and synchronise a global *coup d'état* across the once-free world. Between them, they know of it as The Crackdown.

But they – those leaders, even in former bastions of decency like London, Paris, Washington – have not reckoned for this Beast's return. I shall have my Revolution where woman and man shall revel in love and an orgy of their own true destiny.

Only a god such as I can spark the people into an insurgency to keep them and their children free from a totalitarian world. And if I don't do it now, it will be too late. And I also have a promise to keep to my great friend, Mr Churchill.

I don't know how it will happen. I just know I have to return.

Perhaps, they were never really waiting for Christ's Second Coming. Perhaps, it was I, who shall lead them to The Promised Land.

And this is why I have written this opus. There may be nothing left of me seconds after I leave here, and the story of the fullest of lives known to this scabrous race called Mankind shall be left to the whispers of those mean and lying bastards. I shan't let that happen either.

And so you hold my Last Testament. It is the tale of a life, whose status could only have been maintained with a closed mouth. Given that any man of distinction really should have rumours about him, this Scarlet Pimpernel, this saviour of mankind, will now tell all.

> The common defect of all mystical systems previous to that of the Aeon whose Law is Thelema is that there has been no place for Laughter.
>
>   – Aleister Crowley

One

The Father, The Son & The Ghost

Love is the only principle that makes life tolerable.
— Aleister Crowley

I sit in an ancient amphitheatre cut into the slopes of the valley, weeping willows below and above, a stone wall of pungent, bloomed white gardenia to our right, a meadow of daisies and horseflies to the left as this man looks out across his adopted and quite beloved homeland. The morning is unreasonably beautiful. It would be a shame to leave this sanctuary, especially given that the odds of returning are so slim.

I breathe in deeply and gratefully, while I observe with immeasurable fondness the humble decency of this, the most unchallenged, the most unchallengeable and surely the finest spot on the planet. Shangri-La.

On the flanks are sweeping stone terraces dotted with some young children of touching and eviscerating beauty. Behind me on the hillside, higher up, are many more rows, reaching to even more rarefied air. This crucible possesses a soothing tranquillity and palpable serenity. It is used for their Buddhist ceremonies, for performances and song by young and old. I have many happy memories here.

The knowledge, smiles and serenity of all of those here lend weight to Buddhism. A logical mind rightfully struggles with reincarnation, but one finds it easy to forgive them.

Adorned in my sack-cloth simplicity, I look at the skies and tell three young lasses of shaven head, who eye me with reverence as they pass, 'The taking of pleasure in such minutiae might only be achieved by a man who is at peace with his world. Remember, we are the blue-lidded daughters of Sunset; we are the naked brilliance of the voluptuous night-sky.'

They giggle and shuffle off.

I digress! Let us speak vastly important nonsense and then let us visit those depraved and vulgar young goats of mine.

1.1 HOLY

You have *all* seen me before. There I am on the cover of Sergeant Pepper, back row, second from the far left between Sri Yukteswar Giri and Mae West. My fine boy John knew precisely who the puppeteer of that frazzled century was.

There was surely a time when I would have boasted that you are only here because of my intentional nudges on the axis of the twentieth century, as I squeezed and fondled her centre of gravity. Those days of bluster are largely over. I shall instead approach the claim from a more modest position. Without my meddling as part of British Intelligence, sometimes intentional, sometimes utterly cack-handed, it is perhaps possible none of us would be here. I only bring this up as, since I may or may not have interfered with history that allowed the very specific conditions for this, our world to be, we might as well get the pronunciation of my name right. Crowley. It rhymes with Holy.

And it was not always Aleister. As a boy, I was Alick, though when I barrelled into this realm, on October the twelfth 1875, I was to be baptised, under the Lord's font water, Alexander Edward Crowley.

I was born in one of those sturdy town houses in Clarendon Square, number thirty, in the Cotswolds town of Royal Leamington Spa, where the miraculous waters from font, tap or stream, allegedly healed and cured as if one were in the presence of a Christ. That Nazarene and I would have been marvellous chums; I so adored Him as a boy. I wonder whether I would have been dumbstruck, like the sodden autograph hunter at the stage door, had we met? Perhaps I might have been, for the minutest of moments, and long before even He would have chance to peer into my eyes of coal black in search of a soul. My father spoke of Him with much reverence and respect, but also with the proximity of a mindful and nurturing elder brother, who would shield us from any harm, as the days of pristine youth sparkled and the midges danced at dusk, until the final strides of another ambrosial day tripped over a gnarled, tangerine sun.

Or at least, that is how I recall them. Though these early years will always suffer from the patchiness of a childhood memory, it is naturally occurring in the atomic structure of the life story. Please bear this in mind as we hone in on the adult days, where I am able to tell you the exact slant of a morning shadow with the precision of a sundial. Some details shall always be meticulous, however. Papa, for example.

My father was Edward, a tall, handsome, lithe, dark-eyed brute with fine teeth and cheekbones like spanners in a sock. He carried a married tang of light oak from his subtle cologne and a stark, almost medical, soap. He was in his forties when I arrived. He was already retired. He had inherited a vast fortune from his family's shares in a London brewery, Crowley's Alton Ales. The rhythmic and perpetual soaking to the back teeth of pie-eyed and staggering swathes of the population of

London in his family's underwhelming booze allowed my dear father to do the great Lord's work at his leisure, though Papa chose to do it quite tirelessly. We went from village to village with gusto, as we spread the joy of our Gospel. I was a plump little boy, so father was convinced the exercise and the fresh air were good for me.

We relished the different accents that the countryside would bring. If Professor Higgins in Shaw's *Pygmalion* could locate the birthplace or current street of residence of a chap outside a West End theatre, then Father was equally as capable with the wretches and bumpkins of the Midlands, the Cotswolds and the eastern edges of the West Country. When he dozed after a meagre lunch under Gloucestershire or Warwickshire trees, I read the Bible, Longfellow's 'Excelsior' or *Martin Rattler Adventures of a Boy in the Forests of Brazil* by R. M. Ballantyne. He taught me, as a school would have, but without the harshness of those vicious martinets in charge.

Father had been born into the Quakers. As a young man he left them over a minor difference of opinion in the Scriptures.

He became a Plymouth Brethren until he then splintered from the main corps of that lot as well. The differences become minute at this stage, and barely worth considering, but for the record, 2 Corinthians was the bone of contention. His interpretation was at the core of his disagreement with the Plymouths. The issue was with whom one was permitted to eat. Father believed we should be allowed to dine with the poor, the uneducated, the unfortunates and the lepers; the Plymouths did not. We were now to be known as the *Exclusive Brethren.*

I would mimic such strops and such splintering with my own religious pursuits many decades later.

Our lengthy and daily exertion of saving souls, from hamlet to village to town, aided the maintenance of Father's fine physique, but only seemed to aggravate my fat ankles and force my chubby toad neck to sweat like a squeezed teabag. When we were not marching in search of the next door upon which to rap or seeking some poor soul trimming his lawn or awaiting his tennis partner in the park, he would be preaching and I would be stood erect by his side, not permitted to slouch or shuffle from foot to foot. I listened to the word of God. In my heavy black suit cut of the same cloth as his, and with the same heavy application of starch on my upright collar, I believed myself to be the happiest and freest boy in England. I did not see the inside of a school until I was eight years old.

I was a hard-boiled and applied lad, fascinated by the truth of evidence and proof, though this was still submerged by the wonder I saw in my old man and in the Scriptures. Once as we traipsed through a field to the next village, my father advised I circumnavigate a clump of over-green and erect nettles. I pushed him on why I ought to be so concerned.

'Will you learn by experience or will you take my word for it?'

'Learn by experience, of course, Father,' I said before I dived in.

1.2 THREE DEATHS AT THE CIRCUS

Yet I was disciplined. I read the Bible with a ferocity that made my father joyous. I remember reading as early as the age of four, and this can be bookmarked by history, as January the first 1880 was the final Leamington Fair to welcome in the Maximus de Paris Rouge circus. We had slipped through the ropes to the rear of the burlesque caravans, under the busy washing lines, past the steaming backs of the munching ponies of sagged spine, and through the thick and pungent brewed clouds of marvel from the pots of the cackling pink elephantine cooking ladies, as ecstatic in bawdy and ribald song as any man or urchin had likely ever witnessed.

There we found our unwitting prey: a plump lion-tamer and a weak-willed elephant master in their nightly preparation. Father approached to sell to them both a penny pamphlet on that wildly mild January evening, the eighth day of Christmas. For such an early memory, the image is a strong one, though it may be have been prodded and embellished first by my dear father, Edward, and then by me over the years, for it seems so full and vibrant to this day.

'Why are you doing that?' Papa asked the first chap with the large cat, as he moved the crown of his head along the beast's teeth and gum.

'Well, I am training my lion. I must.'

'And then?'

'Err . . . I do it to survive tonight.'

'And then?'

'What? To be alive to collect my Friday wage.'

'And then?'

'Ummm . . .'

'And then?'

This continued until the poor man was faced with the absolute futility of life and the inevitability of a lonely death. The fellow was called Gerald de Montneuf-Baton, a fancy name for someone of such a broad and lowly Bristolian twang. Gerald risked his neck for glory each evening and, at least it seemed, was firm friends with his charge, an elderly lioness in the finest fettle and teeth of pearled brilliance. Within a minute of having engaged with my father, this fleshy man, shirtless but with his suit trouser on, was nose-to-nose with his eternal damnation. The elephant master, known only as Small Man, nodded along, unable to counter my Edward's well-used gambits.

The will of the corpulent entertainer, Gerald, was then broken by Father. The pair handed over a coin each, to everyone's relief. We all then sat down on a large Arabian rug on a bank of grass outside the towering Big Top, and we chatted.

Unlike the Plymouth Brethren, we, the *Exclusive Brethren,* allowed ourselves to sit and eat with such unfortunates. We believed their ignorance and commonness gave them the excuse to be unholy and to err. We preferred gypsies and freaks to our own kind, who should know better. This was the Christ's way, after all; He who adored whores, thieves and cripples alike. And so, being supine with circus trainers was permitted, but almost never with others of our ilk. And so began my lifetime of apparently inexplicable contradictions that puzzled and angered a prudish (or at least, hypocritical) England.

As I pestered the trio, with careful measure and timeliness, to allow me to see the circus freaks who were accompanying the troupe for the first time, Father cut me off and told me to read to our new friends from his favourite passage of the 1611 King James Bible: Genesis 5. My belligerence was minimal then, but I read instead from my own favourite text, the Book of Revelations. I could sense the wonder that came from the circus pair, and I could feel my father's stare as I spoke the sacred words.

I hold this against you: You have forsaken the love you had at first.

I know your deeds; you have a reputation of being alive, but you are dead. Wake up! Strengthen what remains and is about to die.

I also remember with absolute clarity the wonder Father appeared to broadcast. But it was nothing compared to the lengthened and then renewed gasps that came from our two gullible pals, as I continued to narrate, but did not turn the page.

> After this I looked, and behold, a great multitude that no one could number, from every nation, from all tribes and peoples and languages, standing before the throne and before the Lamb, clothed in white robes, with palm branches in their hands.

Instead, I closed my eyes and the words poured out.

> I saw another mighty angel come down from heaven, clothed with a cloud: and a rainbow was upon his head, and his face was as it were the sun, and his feet as pillars of fire: And he had in his hand a little book open: and he set his right foot upon the sea, and his left foot on the earth, And cried with a loud voice, as when a lion roareth: and when he had cried, seven thunders uttered their voices.

And poured out. Until the written words of the Revelations came to their inevitable conclusion.

> And if any man shall take away from the words of the book of this prophecy, God shall take away his part out of the book of life, and out of the holy city, and from the things which are written in this book. He which testifieth these things saith, Surely I come quickly. Amen. Even so, come, Lord Jesus.
> The grace of our Lord Jesus Christ be with you all. Amen.

The pause continued, until my father eventually broke the silence, with a bellowed, 'Amen.' Gerald and Small Man followed with a staggered amen too. The lioness roared, the elephant defecated vast barrels of filth with a disturbingly pleasant musk.

We would perhaps see the circus again, but never in the town of Leamington, for that night there was a death in the ring, and their licence was revoked. We stared as the lioness sunk her teeth into Gerald's neck, almost apologetically. Within the hour, we heard the ensuing bullet as we walked away towards Clarendon Square. Oddly, there was a second one. I saw my father tilt his head as this rang out. We looked at each other.

'I told him so,' said Father. 'I did hint at such matters.'

Father regularly told me that he was always right, though I struggled to see precisely how in this instance.

The actual explanation was a far more logical one, for in having interrupted the training of the lioness, Gerald had also forgotten to feed his largely loving, but unforgivingly habitual darling. A comment by the veterinarian in the *Royal Leamington Gazette*, and picked up on the news wires by *Giuseppe Chiriani's La Hippodromo Mysteriosa*, the circus owners' own bi-monthly pamphlet to which we later subscribed and purchased all back copies, was that the poor beast's ravenous state was magnified by the presence of a vast and billeted tapeworm in her guts. It had appeared from the deceased lioness's rear, just as the old girl was being euthanised, and deserved a bullet all to itself, so chubby and worryingly agile was it. All trainers and owners of animals were now advised to seek the advice of a professional to keep their beasts worm-free and therefore to prevent such capricious mood swings from the animals, of jungle and plain, whose impeccable behaviour was the main reason tickets were sold.

1.3 DEATH AT HOME

It was to be a time of death. On the twenty-ninth day of

February, my sister, Grace Elisabeth Crowley was still-born. I was quite unaware of the scale of such an event but, with hindsight, it became quite clear that the impact of this would resonate across my world. Many times, perhaps twenty or thirty, I was taken, at the insistence of Mother, to see her corpse. Most things are confusing to the young, and are only explained with age. The perversion of these visits (or what later seemed perverted to me) seemed quite natural to me then, as a boy of four in short trousers that revealed the wide girth of my miserable ankles. I was more bothered about my physical defect than the slab of greying pink coldness in front of me. But as an adult, this has only led me to wonder at the lack of decent logic and the hollow sickness of those who would have this done. The room was frigid with a whiff of a spiky and unpleasant chemical, its hideousness partially abated by tangy Indian incense, procured by the caseload through mail order from Fortnum & Mason in Piccadilly, as if this would mask the indecency. I recall my late sister's marbled and translucent skin. One could see through several layers now, blue veins that bulged out from patches of grey. I had to sit and stare at this installation for hours, while repeating the Lord's words from the Scriptures.

This was all the malevolent work of my vile mother. She was full of such tricks. As a small boy, I recall her mental abuse. Like the typical abuser, the horror takes place in private, and the tortured is threatened to never speak of the 'secret'. I was told and perpetually reminded that she was a *clairvoyante*. This was not just her supposed ability to forecast the future, but she said she knew of my dark intentions and wicked thoughts as a young boy; a scared wretch barely able to go through the night without pissing himself.

Deuteronomy 18:9–14 tells us to condemn such sorcery:

*

When you enter the land which the LORD your God gives you, you shall not learn to imitate the detestable things of those nations.

There shall not be found among you anyone who makes his son or his daughter pass through the fire, one who uses divination, one who practices witchcraft, or one who interprets omens, or a sorcerer, or one who casts a spell,

Or a medium, or a spiritist, or one who calls up the dead.

For whoever does these things is detestable to the LORD; and because of these detestable things the LORD your God will drive them out before you.

You shall be blameless before the LORD your God.

For those nations, which you shall dispossess, listen to those who practise witchcraft and to diviners, but as for you, the LORD your God has not allowed you to do so.

Thus, the Bible condemns clairvoyance in all forms. The text brands it (and such misplaced claims to it) as evil. They would have burned her at the stake as a witch. So, with her Brethren piety in the company of others, this made her a clear hypocrite, a state so rank that even a very small boy such as I spotted it and gagged. And *she* had the nerve to call *me* The Beast, though this may well have been proof of her talent, for that is precisely what I became.

She and I were flighty. We were unbroken stallion and nervous rider. And when this happens, each party simply gets worse and rapidly so. They say that the wild dog and the dark-skinned gent rarely get on, for the canine sees only a pronounced contrast in the whites of the eyes and the prism of nature translates this as aggression. This perception is magnified when the fellow is scared and further pins back his eye-lids. The hound only sees danger – and off we go with a vicious circle of misunderstanding, anxiety and terror, when they really should be sound chums. Well, so it was (sort of) between Mother and young Alick.

Mother made the error of underestimating me. She thought her bullying and lying lecturing would box, crush and break me, and that I, silent and cowed, would be hers. But I knew that all I had to do was to tell Papa of her witchcraft, something she had not predicted, and no longer would she be such a *clairvoyante*. Q.E.D.

Her future and mine were both in MY hands. I kept my counsel for now.

Mother constantly spoke of cutting one's coat in accordance with one's cloth, but I would teach her that she ought to have cut it in accordance with the size of the man, in this case, a very young boy, her transgressive spawn. Do what thy wilt.

After weeks of these morbid gatherings around my disintegrating sibling, and as the furnishings at home receded to almost nothing, I remember that we left Clarendon Square. I did not know we would not return, but I suspect I might have thought some form of change was coming. And so began a year of my life that has never been documented. I guess those spa waters were not so special, not so potent after all, for they could not save my dear Grace, aged zero. Perhaps I should have been shocked, or at least grateful, that the decaying mite was not bundled up in swaddling or in a picnic basket of cherry-red gingham and brought along for the ride. From the raised voices that I could hear from my room, I knew that Mother and Father were troubled. I sensed from the bellowing down the cavernous halls that he was repulsed by her behaviour around Grace.

Our intended destination was Redhill, Surrey, one of those affluent and burgeoning villages to the south of London. The journey from Royal Leamington Spa is ninety-three miles as the crow flies. Yes, there is the complex majesty of London in the way, but my journey took thirteen months, daffodils blooming as we left and perishing as we arrived at that vast mansion of arched hallways, billiard table lawns, stacked libraries of arcane treasures, lavish and mossy frog ponds, and musty greenhouses of unworldly orchids, tennis racquets and croquet hoops.

My year in the wilderness was quite unintended. Father had intended a two-day dog-leg, a release valve, and a brief but sacred rustication, more intended as a bow to the Nazarene's forty days in the desert. I shall explain very shortly, but we got marvellously sidetracked that year. There were answers to be found, I was told. If that is what Edward Crowley said, then it was as robust as the Gospel to his young Alick.

By the time we arrived in Surrey in that glorious May of 1881, the days of the daily schlepp of that father-and-son double act, annoying the natives with the advent of a doom, avoided only by handing over a penny for a leaf of reasonably pleasant paper stock (my father did not need the penny, of course) were over.

We had travelled instead through a phantasmagoric prism, a kaleidoscope of the vastest of boyhood joys. I know my father agreed on the sunniness of both of our souls throughout that year. Even my ankles appeared to become less grotesque by a fraction, marginally thinner even, and my frog neck less moist by a sliver. Oh! the blessed mind is so playful, so willing to lark.

But how did all of this happen?

Well, I shall start with the day that the first issue of *Giuseppe Chiriani's La Hippodromo Mysteriosa* landed on the checked tiles in the airy hallway of 30, Clarendon Square. The mat was already gone, packed away after Grace's death with the desks, chairs, tables and beds, so we were close to departure. Father, always so measured and disciplined, appeared to canter in uncharacteristic fashion, in the cerise, teal and lemon light cast by the stained glass in the heavy oak door, warming in the spring sunshine.

He turned to see me watching him, and slowed marginally, but only before he grinned like I had never seen him smile before. He beckoned for me to come to him. I walked to him, and he lowered himself to his knees, and swept me up as I approached. His embrace was firm and intentional. He loosened his grip and spoke at a volume that was unnecessary given my proximity, as if he needed to say it in something more than a whisper for his own peace of mind.

'Be ready for eight o' clock, Alick. We have something we must do today.'

'Yes, sir.'

'Oh! and son. You had better have a small overnight bag with you. Bring your Book and the chess set. We shall head up to London* alone, you and I.'

'Yes, sir.'

1.4 A DAY (AND MORE) WITH THE YEOMANRY

We were on the 8.34 train from Royal Leamington to London Marylebone. We would rejoin the unwitting world in a morsel over one year from now. I am sure I heard my father guffaw, as the whistle blew and we moved down the train. We took the last two seats in the First Class car. In the rush, we had not noticed the lofty uniformed company of soldiers, in whose presence we now were. Most of the troops stared at these two civilian interlopers, some through monocles, others from a single eye next to a patched or glass one. There were

---

* I have always cherished the idiosyncratic English way of going up to London, no matter of the direction, and down to the country, again with no regard for compass. We should do more of this as a nation.

those who did not stare, for they were blind. They all wore the same uniform: red and blue with white piping. The blind ones had chums who whispered to them, each line met with a tiny acknowledging nod.

Other than the hushed reporting of our arrival, these soldiers remained absolutely silent. They all seemed to regard Father and me, even though some turned their heads to marvel at the English countryside, particularly verdant, pleasant and blooming in the Cotswolds in May. We were within a daily pamphlet traipse of Stratford-upon-Avon to the west and Warwick Castle to the east of the rattling track. The cradle of security and peace appeared quite contrary, even to this unseasoned lad, to where these poor souls had been. They maintained the orderliness, the restraint and the unity of a battalion. It was as if the Boers might appear at our next stop of Banbury station, the Zulu might attack with a vicious pincer movement from between the sleepy morning anglers on the lush banks of the Cherwell.

Once Banbury had been safely traversed, their silently appointed spokesman, who was stationed directly across from me, leaned forward, and addressed me. He had a shock of carrot hair, abundant freckles, a nose upon which one might have hung a Homburg, ears smaller than mine with a lining of soft ginger fluff, and magnificent eyes of summer-frog green. His smile betrayed the likelihood that he might have suffered from bullies as a boy, which cannot have been long ago by the elevated pitch of his supremely friendly voice, which I was seconds away from hearing for the first time, and which stays with me to this day. I could not stop looking at him.

'Good morning, sir!'

I sensed my father's approval, and I was rarely wrong on such a matter.

'Good morning, sir!'

'I am Captain Orr of the Warwickshire Yeomanry. How do you do?'

'How do you do? I am Alick. And this is my father.'

With no dog collar, there was no obvious clue that Father was a religious man.

'How do you do, sir?'

'How do you do, Captain Orr? I am Edward Crowley.'

'A pleasure to meet you both. I see you possess a chess-board. As we say in the Yeomanry, "Gleaming!"' He had a soft Midlands lilt, but spoke at a volume so that even those who might be hard of hearing in the unit could hear above the din of the train, the tracks and the hum of the warm breeze pervading from the open windows.

'Would you care for a game, sir?' I spoke without thinking, yet my father did not correct me.

'Very much,' the captain replied. 'I should warn you, however, that we play as a unit.'

'Well, so do we,' said my father barely allowing the soldier to complete his final word.

'So be it. Remember that whoever said that the white queen is mightier than the sword, has never encountered the Orange Boers of Kapuitshuit before breakfast.' The unit laughed as one, for even those who were receiving an audible transcription from their guide were aware of Orr's bluster before the sentence was finished.

'But at least, are we permitted to know the names of OUR enemy today, please?' Father asked.

'Yeo-man-reeeee!' Orr shouted.

The unit then presented themselves with an astonishing rhythm and precision. The order was clearly not alphabetical, nor was it by rank, it seemed to Father when we later debriefed, post combat.

Fairfax! Runciman! Trench! Guinness! Byron! Fanny! Talbot! Vane! Coote! Ball!

'How do you do, sirs?' Father and I said together.

I set up the board, before holding a black pawn in my right hand, a white one in the left.

'Major Fairfax!' yelled Captain Orr.

'The boy's left hand,' replied Major Fairfax, even though he was clearly blind, and should not have known I was holding two pieces before my sternum.

'We are white, lads.'

And, to a unified and synchronised bawl of 'God Save the Queen' off we went. Orr moved first, and yelled his opening gambit to the battalion. Then he screamed my reply. Then each turn thereafter, an initial Sicilian defence, was the responsibility of the other ten to shout their move in the precise order they had announced themselves to Father and to me, punctuated by Orr informing them all of our move.

A couple of them could see the board. The blind ones chuckled, the others purred and stared out at the villages, the steeples, the ponds, the sparrows and the wood pigeons, the orchards, and the farms, or above to the soft royal blue, speckled with thin and unthreatening balls of fluffed and woolled cloud.

The soldiers barely skipped a military marched beat in belting out a seemingly faultless defence, followed by a sturdy consolidation prior to the relentless grinding down of a stunned preacher and his astonished son. Father could not bear fools or shamsters, and was notoriously difficult, some might say impossible, to please. He was also an excellent chess player, so, when checkmate came seventy-seven moves into the mammoth conflict, he would not rest after a solitary game. I urged him on. Such was the alacrity and efficiency of the soldiers' game, they chalked an eighth victory without reply, as we slowed through the outer limits of the capital. They might even have pushed a ninth by the time we trundled into the shade, dust and endless romance of Marylebone Station.

We all disembarked with far less efficiency than their mobility on the chessboard. Father insisted the chaps join us in the Station Hotel for luncheon. We were an odd lot, as we moved from platform seven through the marbled halls and towards the bright sunlight and the potent marvels of that thrumming city at large. Orr, when he unravelled his full frame, stood at almost seven feet; all the more impressive to a tiny and unathletic scamp with fat ankles and a fleshy neck. Two fellows were lifted into wheelchairs, three, without sight it seemed, were walked by comrades. They moved as one; amorphous and shapeless perhaps, but still with a strong military understanding and camaraderie.

It was still middish morning, but some of the men had become excited at the possibility of a drink from the bar on the broad terrace, so pleasant on that May morning. Crowley's Alton Ales were being served, though not one of the squadron took one, preferring instead small glasses of liquid that made them wince upon imbibing. How odd, I thought.

Father took Orr to one side at the bottom of the railed steps into the pleasant station gardens, wrapped in a quadrangle of honeysuckle, scarlet roses and tulip trees. He appeared to be making his usual move to his small case to access his pamphlets, when he stopped, and Orr began to speak instead, moving his face closer, and with a thoroughly unthreatening intensity, to my father's. Orr seemed to soothe and disarm him, and the pitch on the Lord's behalf was seemingly over before it had begun. Then after several minutes of apparently protracted and unrelated questioning from my father, the two sat down on the lower steps. My father did not even sweep detritus from the stone. For the first time in my life, I saw Edward Crowley accept a cigarette, take a light, smoke and then shut up, unable to counter. I can barely communicate my excitement all these decades later such was the profundity of how my father was jack-knifed by this quiet-ish Orr chap. The unstoppable force had lost out to the immovable object.

After several minutes, my father turned his head towards me. He knew I would be eagerly awaiting his gaze, and extended his palm an inch towards the pavement, where the remnants of his cigarette now fumed wilfully. He lowered his eyelids. I knew we would discuss fully later. I must, for now, remain quiet. Little boys, after all, should be seen, and not heard.

I sat at the far end of the long dining table to my father. He looked at me from time to time, and smiled, while he held my gaze. He spoke with each of the men within his sphere, privates and officers alike. All importance leant to rank seemed to have been eradicated, not by him, but by the soldiers. I could barely wait to have my father to myself, so as to discover what he had learned.

In my mind, I turned to the Scriptures to remind me of the value of passivity, even temper and grit. I whispered Ecclesiastes 7:8–9:

> Better is the end of a thing than the beginning thereof: and the patient in spirit is better than the proud in spirit.
>
> Be not hasty in thy spirit to be angry: for anger resteth in the bosom of fools.

And from Revelations 14:12

> Here is the patience of the Saints: here are they that keep the commandments of God, and the faith of Jesus.

*

And so that day, I taught myself meditation and the Tantra, without having a name for either process but with the very precise prompting of the Lord.

I recall, next, sitting with father on that same lower step, where he had smoked and listened, by the wrought-iron railing under the stars; two soldiers now slept in their luncheon chairs, adequately covered in tartan blankets, while from three vast windows of lemon-yellow light on high, military bawdiness filled the chorus while my father shielded my ears from the verse. The men's song and laughter seemed to fill the cavernous chambers of generous luxury, and rush in rhythmic waves across the delicately gas-lit London streets, along which gentlemen and hansom cabs flitted to and from private club, sumptuous dining, the anticipation of small children past bedtime and illicit love affairs. The joy from on high seemed to mean far more coming from the blind, the infirm, and their fraternal carers from the battlefield than it would were it to come from a regular crowd of revellers.

This was the moment I took to speak to him, as I had wished. Of Mother.

'Sir, I must tell you something.'

'Yes, son.'

'It is a matter that concerns Mother, sir. Something is horribly wrong . . .'

'Speak of it. Speak of it all.'

And I did thus, telling of Mother's bullying, claims of clairvoyance, sorcery and even branding me as The Beast. Aided by the relief of my confessed secret, I even added in her most recent gem of blaming me for the stillness of my icy and decaying sister.

I am convinced this was the moment that he became determined to elongate our hours and days in the wilderness into weeks and months. He betrayed no venom or disappointment in his eyes but, within twenty-four hours, I would see him hover over the writing of a lengthy letter that I knew to be to her. He seemed to relish the process and would drop it with a proud vigour into a pillar box the next day before planting a firm and determined kiss on the crown of my head.

As I stared at the stars above that night in Marylebone, Father spoke, finally. For his son and heir, his thoughtful words seemed to join together the bright points in the heavens into a pattern that would set this boy on a path of righteousness.

'What Captain Orr told me today is a magical thing, my boy. And it affects you and me.'

I waited, while he chose his words, seemingly fearful I would not grasp it all.

'These men are not the Warwickshire Yeomanry, Alick. Well, one is. The other ten are prisoners of war. They are Dutch. Boers. I am sure they would have engaged a Zulu, had it been at all possible. Trench, Vane, Fanny and Coote still go by their real names. The others have converted to the English Army. They seem to have seen the light,' and he laughed like I had never seen him do so.

He then took a deep breath, and settled himself. I knew he would elaborate.

'They are remarkably similar to you and me. They are travelling salesmen, if you will. They are spreading their word. They are paid well by our government to travel around the country, to barracks and military academies and give lengthy presentations on this and that, before revealing at the end of the programme precisely who they are. The audience shall learn the most valuable lesson any of us may learn. First, to look upon life and men with an intensity – and secondly, to presume *nothing*.'

He stared at me to see if I understood.

'Father. They only want to see the good in our fellow man.'*

My father closed his eyes for several seconds, and when he opened them, there was a definite dampness, as he swallowed and ruffled my hair.

'It is only by doing this,' Father continued, 'that the world shall understand God's work. Do you follow me, my boy?'

I think I nodded. He told me later that I nodded.

'Captain Orr kindly invited us to move with them from town to town, and it seems only right, given the way things are.'

I believe he was referring to my sister. And now, my mother.

He then said, 'We have much in common, and they can teach you much.'

On this point, he was correct, for that summer, short trousers, fat ankles and all, was the first time I witnessed many revelations, such as the majestic effects of opium on them; one of the few perks those poor, mangled lads could enjoy. 'Gleaming,' was how the men, known to themselves as *The Legion*, described almost everything. I would one day see how and why the world seemed this way to them, for the poppy in all her forms, well, she is a true marvel.

The men were in London to attend the annual Harrow versus Eton cricket match at Lord's. The Dutch are an odd lot, and the barometer of this is that they adore cricket. It is even quite feasible that the summer game originated in the province

---

* *This part was true, though they were merciless when it came to the intolerance, the bloated mystery and the foolishness of the Prussians they had encountered in South West Africa and back in Holland. Their only exceptions to their distaste of Germanics were Ludwig van Beethoven and Johann Sebastian Bach, whose cantatas were a supreme favourite of Coote, the trumpeter. The Prussians, they would reveal, have an Achilles heel. It is not women, neither opium nor gold. It is not even traditional power. It goes deeper and darker, and would be pivotal in my life's work. The Occult.*

of lower Holland. It was certain, it seemed, that the central reason all the prisoners were still in England, even though hostilities in Africa had ceased, was that they could not imagine leaving the cricket field.

The day after their excesses in Marylebone, they billeted themselves in a Camden military academy hostel that shared a high stone wall with the chimpanzee enclosure, that vortex of mischief, in London Zoo. The soldiers insisted that Father and I join them. We did so with no fuss.

It was now their turn to insist upon luncheon in the rear of the property, where Orr was almost tall enough to shake hands with the frisky caged rogues from our own back gardens. He could almost touch their digits, barely brushing chimp finger fuzz, in a playful echo of Michelangelo's *Creation of Adam*.

Before we ate, Father and I strolled on the small lawns, and he explained, now in more detail, how the men had been given a special dispensation by Sir George Pomeroy Colley of the British Army to pose as our own soldiers. Our military had always been a stuffy and inflexible machine. But there were the occasional bright and thoughtful fellows, visionaries you might say, such as Colley and the Yeomanry who saw that the business of warfare was about to change in the next century. Soldiering would soon become a far more complex business, and deception might be the key to victory. The day of the gentleman would one day end. To lose a war through honour would be a crime, punishable by the loss of Empire.

He did not need to remind me of Genesis 3.

Now the serpent was more crafty than any of the wild animals the Lord God had made. He said to the woman, 'Did God really say, "You must not eat from any tree in the garden"?'

*

Perhaps, the British Army's was not such a progressive and pioneering idea after all, for deception has a lengthy past. What was certainly a strange military stratagem, however, was the adoption of preacher and son, and this process was now well underway.

1.5 A BOY'S OWN INSIGHT TO OPIUM AND CHIMPS

And so began that lost year, centred in the city of London in a garden elevated by the sweet whiff of smoked opium, the frequent visits of women who were most certainly not soldiers (quite unknown to my father, I believe) and friendly chimps. Yes, Father and I again traipsed from borough to borough spreading the good news, but it was marvellously punctuated by and cosseted with the company of the most bizarre set of teachers and comrades, smiling through their aches and hardships.

That year informed me of much. The soldiers taught me that the unfortunate, disenfranchised and misunderstood were to be heralded. I had learned from sister Grace that death might be lauded. I knew I could not live without my father. And that our common foe, the Germans, were penetrable, as well as a source of malleable fun and such reward. Quite vitally, I found out that sometimes one's identity must be kept secret in order to preserve one's own value to a nation and beyond. I knew that summers and friends were abundant and the greatest fun of all.

And so we travelled across England with these marvellous men until Father had a vision. He thought it would be worthwhile to visit his favourite travelling circus, the Maximus de Paris Rouge, which would soon arrive on London's northern hillock below Alexandra Palace.

It was here on the fifteenth of February 1881 where Father

would be struck down on a soapbox in the middle of Deuteronomy 7:15.

And the Lord will take away from you all sickness,
and none of the evil diseases of Egypt, which you knew, will
he inflict on you,
but he will lay them on all who hate you.

His tongue simply stopped working. I now know this was the first sign I would see of the cancer that would take him from me, and forever change my life. According to a humbler god than I, this perhaps allowed for the squeezing, fondling and moving of that centre of gravity of the twentieth century, thus allowing you all to exist.

But why would the Lord take, of all things, that organ of his own Good Word? Why would he interfere with my bliss and cause such pain to this great man over his next six truly horrific years? Yes, I still believed in God and the Devil, but now, for the first time, I asked myself, as I thought of men in black who one day soon would be dropping my dear, dear Papa into the earth, 'Which one was which?'

And so now we resolved to return to *her*. To Emily Bertha Bishop, my cunt of a mother, in whose charge I would be left to fester and weep and rot.

We spoke of the imagined wrath she must have brewed at our disappearance. This was when Father held both of my shoulders on the day we crossed the Thames, came nose to nose with me until I could smell the rising illness in his mouth and whispered, 'All shall be well, my boy.'

He then laughed as loud as I had ever heard him, but sadly, laughter is not always the best medicine, and was quite useless here.

And so began my own Anno Domini, my year zero, as I invoked the spirit of the Dracule in denouncing *Them*.

'Fuck you, Jesus. *Why* have you forsaken me?'

'The people who have really made history are the martyrs.'
– Aleister Crowley

Chapter 2

It Rhymed with Unholy

I did not hate God or Christ. Merely the God and Christ
of the people I hated. The Christianity of hypocrisy and
cruelty was not true Christianity.

– Aleister Crowley

*It is rare to receive a letter these days. I am brought the
saddest news of grotesque importance that changes everything. I steady myself. I am aware I must leave now for England.
The Crackdown may now be imminent.*

*There is chit-chat there, of a disturbing kind. Gossip is
nothing new, of course.*

*I was once faced with a charge of treason against, and of
spying for the enemies of England, during the Great War. I
rejected with all my being such an absurd and monstrous
accusation. It was so ludicrous that it might only have been
hypothesised by the hare-brained, the limp of spirit and the
viciously under-informed. They have now had their turn, and
their woeful charges are nothing more than any squinting and
imbecilic clod might have read in yesterday's* Evening Standard
or Daily Mail *over the shoulder of some sweaty villain or
briefcased buffoon on the Northern Line or at any time over*

the last hundred years. As decades of perfumed summers slipped by, I sat while these oafs expounded upon their clumsy and boyish fibs, and instead I thought of Sunday mornings with dear friends on the Embankment or in Cambridge, with temporary and numbered acquaintances in broad Mayfair beds and alone, ecstatic and barefoot in the zoo.

But this chit-chat is different. It will be hard to leave here. Such a decision, after all, is very likely to kill me, as that vortex exposes my real age and I turn to dust.

Twelve hours to go.

2.1 NEW FRIENDS

It is important too, to note, if it were not made clear already, that this confession seeks not to repeat the well-publicised deeds and professionally authored achievements of my life, nor the rumour, though that might be challenged. There will be the acknowledgements of certain cornerstones and touchstones, of unavoidable nodes and markers in my life. My revelations shall mention those of note to me, but I shall not labour on what has already taken up a sagging shelf. We shall concern ourselves with the stuff that very few know. I shall connect the dots, yoke and couple the stars in my skies, and examine the previously private black matter between. There is little time for anything but.

It was Mother who first called me The Beast. I would teach *her*. Yet it was an inauspicious path to revenge, as I now grew breasts to accompany the matching horrors of my fat ankles and plump neck.

The succubus was waiting for us. Father and I reluctantly arrived in Redhill with a bearded, young doctor wearing gargantuan spectacles and who possessed sparkling eyes. The doctor, a Professor Horace Dandylyon, was, Father had assured me, pre-eminent in his field of oral cancer, and was a good friend of Captain Orr. He was, what I later found out to be, a wunderkind in his field. (It takes one to know one, they say.)

We had been firmly escorted by a muscly Amazon filly of a nurse, who smelled of delicious, crisp apples and gardenia, laughed out loud to herself with a perversely timed regularity and had tubbier ankles than mine. It was a pleasant combin ation, and just bizarre enough, aided by the strength of her teal-tinged stare, to inspire a warm confidence. She always wore maroon and cream. Her name was Prudence Venus-Coshe.

I was fascinated by this engaging pair from the very first moments. They both kept their eyes on me as the grown-ups, including them, chatted in the carriage. I sensed they were speaking to me without the use of any words, so intent was their benevolent stare.

'Don't worry, young fellow. Don't worry, young fellow. Please,' I seemed to hear, above all the other din. It was the sort of stunt Christ* might have pulled off.

The carriage drew up on the soft gravel on the wide drive to the house. My new home was intimidating in size and splendour: well pointed, lush, mostly covered with verdant Boston ivy and blessed with the cooing of wood pigeons that could not be heard on the approach and so seemingly came with the house, providing an enclosed and private concert. My year of joy might have been over, drawn in by that lengthy shepherding crook of the mean and niggardly penny-pinching false god on high, but the birds revelled on. At least now I knew how

---

* *'Jesus perceived their thoughts' – Luke 5:22. 'He knew their thoughts' – Luke 6:8. 'Jesus knew their thoughts' – Matthew 12:25.*

they felt when they soared and glided. I knew that I would take flight again, for freedoms and friendships were intoxicating drugs.

I recalled 2 Corinthians 4:18; that horror, like joy, would pass.

> While we look not at the things which are seen, but at the things which are not seen: for the things which are seen are temporal; but the things which are not seen are eternal.

Neither Papa nor I acknowledged the brooding horror of Mother, swaddled still in black, in the arches at the front of the vast property. Father wore a thick scarf around his neck, and was encouraged not to speak. The doctor said nothing to Emily Bertha Bishop, barely registering a flicker, as he led my father up the two stones steps and into the colossal hallway.

As I passed her, I said quite audibly so as to let her know that I was not – and would not – be cowed by her, 'I shall wager five bob that you did not see *that* coming, Mother dear!' The half-expected prod from my father to let me know that I had overstepped a boundary did not come.

The nurse gave Mother a wide berth, sensing as would a wild hound that something was crooked in this creature that had given birth to me. The effect of Mother's mean eyes, too close together to be trusted, set amid unnourished pale skin, and slitted to minimise the escape of greeting, warmth or affection, was a chilling one. Yet, for now, I did not feel alone as I walked into the house that smelled of recently turned sunflowers and would hold pockets of pleasant times for me, but only when within arm's reach of Father and these two new proxied protectors, Dr Dandylyon and Prudence.

*

Later that same morning, I saw from the shadows of one of the large and darkened hallways, the doctor and Mother arguing in one of the libraries. I heard them, as they clashed.

'I shall have you struck off for malpractice, Dandylyon!'

'It is Dr Dandylyon to you, ma'am. And please do. I shall give you the address of the Medical Association myself. You shall be doing me a favour. And please spell my name correctly when you write to them. They are as inefficient as you are unwelcoming, and I would not want any delay in their ending this forsaken career of mine.'

He spelled out his name.

'It is a thoroughly silly name.'

'Careful, madam! I put you on notice now. It means lion's teeth in French. I firmly advise that you do not force me to bare mine while I am making your poor husband comfortable. He only has two years to live, you do know?'

I had already heard a similar prediction, though this was to be a miscalculation. He would last far longer. Father's stubbornness was a worthy trait to inherit. His mulishness stood me in good stead many times, as obstinacy is a fine central tenet in the formation of any religion, as it is for a world-class spy.

Mother gulped, rouged and stormed out past me, knocking me violently as she did so, only my fat ankles seemed to aid me in keeping stable and upright.

Dandylyon walked to me with a firm and purposeful measure, leaned down, placed his slim, hard-skinned left hand on my shoulder. He said nothing, but he did smile at me. It was most comforting, prompting me to honesty.

I said, 'Please do not leave me with her.'

'We shan't. We have a friend in common in Captain Orr, and this makes you my chum. Tell me, Alick. Have you heard your father ever speak of "masonry"?'

'I have not, sir.'

He chuckled, and squeezed my shoulder, before bringing my forehead to his and saying, 'Be strong. I am your friend.'

'Yes, sir.'

'Good. Good. You are a fine lad. We shall get along just fine. Look in your pocket when I am gone.'

He walked off. When he had disappeared out onto the vast back lawns, I pushed my hand into the right pocket of my trouser. There was nothing there. Then I checked the left one, and there, deep in the material, which was a snug fit to my leg, was a cold metal object that chilled my fingertips. I grabbed it between my knuckles and drew it out, feeling the sturdy object against my thigh as I did, begging the question of how on earth it had got there. It was a winged beast with lengthy jaws and troubling horns in a circular pendant-type amulet, measuring perhaps three inches across. It was what I know now to be a Baphomet Talisman, an artefact of the Wiccan, intended to protect the weak or to comfort the troubled.

I still stood on the spot where I had eavesdropped on Dandylyon's conversation with Mother. It was as if an experienced Shaftesbury Avenue theatre director were in tight control of the whole scene, for just as the doctor left the stage to my right, it was now Prudence's turn to approach me from the left with her own version of benevolence. She came to me, and knelt so that our eyes were level. She was measured and precise.

'I have a marvellous idea,' she said. 'Want to come for a walk with me? I propose that we are utterly nosy, and see what this dusty old manor has to offer in the way of fun.'

I nodded, as I pushed Dandylyon's artefact back into my pocket. Once it was where I had found it, the nurse placed the palm of her hand on my high inner thigh and caressed the cold shape. It delighted her, it seemed, as she paused, gripped ever so tightly, before removing her hand, which she then used to ruffle my hair.

'Come. Let's start with the wonders of nature outside. It looks like we may be treated to a warm shower.' And she raised a single eyebrow in quite thrilling mischief.

Prudence carried with her a broad medical briefcase that she held, with utmost care, in two hands, keeping it level as though she were holding a tray of lemonades filled to the brim. We headed outside and she seemed quite meticulous in counting her steps from the imposing arches of the rear doors. She appeared to be guided by the sun, for she seemed to stride in relation to its position in the sky. The nurse picked a spot out by an oak tree and next to an ivied brick wall. It felt like she was following in her mind the directions to buried treasure, for she stopped quite deliberately, and said, 'This is perfect, young Alick.'

As she sat and placed the doctor's case on the lawn, she gestured that I sit down as well.

'Yes, ma'am.'

'Please call me Prudence. In return, I shall drop the *young*. And you can be Alick. So much more civilised, don't you think?'

She grinned and held out her right hand to shake on it, and as she did so, two courting sparrows descended to land on her arm. The most surprising thing I remember is that she was not shocked or dismayed in the slightest. Her eyelids dropped in minuscule, but quite obvious, ecstasy. The birdsong from the cooing wood pigeons above I can hear clearly now in my mind. My senses were spiked, and I knew not why. I knew I was thrilled by it, and appeared to be witnessing nature as I had never seen her before, despite those glorious days with Papa. A flirting hummingbird sashayed around us, and I knew, for some reason, she was a female. The branches of the oak and the top of the high garden wall were lined with starlings, jackdaws and magpies, all staring as if watching that theatre play.

Prudence smiled, revealing marvellous teeth, and this produced an even more pleasant overall effect, for her features were feminine and engaging. She had large green eyes, fine cheekbones and lips as plump as Amalfi figs. She leaned to open the briefcase, as the sparrows took flight. With absolute care, she removed an object. It was a small glass box with a lock on the top, which she opened with a deft touch. She then removed what appeared to be an ancient volume from the glass, as her reverence continued.

'This is a special book that will help us to settle in to a new chapter in our lives, Alick. I want you to remember this. For ever.'

'What is it?'

'It is very, very, very old. It is priceless. And it will one day belong to you.'

A feral cat minced around the sunflowers, then sat beside the oak, and looked upon the scene, indifferent to the birds. Bees made loud noises, and all seem to rotate around this magnificent woman.

'It is called *The Tibetan Book of the Dead*. This has been in my family for centuries. They have been quite wicked thieves for aeons, you know. And this will be yours one day, because I see your future with joy. The reason for this joy is that I see you – and for several lifetimes have seen you – as my own son. We must now bless this sacred ground as your new home.'

I sat silent and adored, as Prudence continued to look at me, as she recited words I presumed came from the text she held.

O nobly-born, that which is called death being come to
    thee now, resolve thus:
'O this now is the hour of death.
By taking advantage of this death, I will so act,
For the good of all sentient beings,
Peopling the illimitable expanse of the heavens,
As to obtain the Perfect Buddhahood,
By resolving on love and compassion towards them,
And by directing my entire effort to the Sole Perfection.'

At her prompting, we then repeated the spell in five equi-distant spots around the grounds that Prudence had clearly predetermined in her mind, so precise appeared the co-ordinates.

'Alas! When the Uncertain Experiencing of Reality is
    dawning upon me here,
With every thought of fear or terror or awe for all
    apparitional appearances set aside,
May I recognise whatever visions appear, as the
    reflections of mine own consciousness;
May I know to be of the nature of apparitions in the
    Bardo;
When at this all-important moment of opportunity of
    achieving a great end,
May I not fear the bands of Peaceful and Wrathful
    Deities, mine own thought-forms.'

Prudence kissed me with a surprising heat on my crown, as that feral cat rubbed the back of its neck passionately on my chunky left ankle, and I heard naught but revelling and frolic-some birds.

2.2 Trinkets & Doped-Up Lads

I was a young boy, and took in Dandylyon's and Prudence's every word as if it were the god's honest truth. I loved to hear from their treasure trove of stories of how they knew each other from their family histories, and also how they had then been introduced to my own family. They both repeated the general trajectory of the tale many, many times, though each time they seemed to take flight of fancy and weave in new subplots. Though they told me hundreds of episodes of how both of their familial lines had stuck together throughout the centuries, I shall give only a flavour of them here. That they would weave such fables (as I believed them to be) for me meant the world to this scared lad, for this was a barometer of their dedication to my battered, young spirit. In doing so, they brought magic and wonder back into my world.

I recall the general thread to be something, as follows:

Dandylyon's professional path of medicine had always seemed determined from childhood, as he came from a lengthy line of society physicians, who had treated the ailments of aristocracy and royalty for many eras. It had become accepted within his family that any boys would follow a similar career path. Given the proclivity towards incest and inbreeding in those lofty social worlds, the procession of Dr Dandylyons throughout the ages witnessed many twisted and malformed types, the kind to confuse any regular doctor. He was always quite fortunate in that he was in possession of the secret notes and unpublished works of his antecedents, as well as a magnificent network of contacts. His vocation, like his father's and his father's father's, was therefore really the path of least resistance.

Horace Dandylyon's forefathers had served kings and queens for centuries. One Dandylyon had attempted to treat Henry's syphilis before the monarch exploded by the maze at

Hampton Court. Another had written prodigiously of Mad George's arousal in his own defecate. One had even treated Boadicea with a mild calendula in her undergarments, in order to quell her preternatural libido. This was seen, by her counsel and her doctor, as crucial if she were to keep the respect of her armies, as it was believed by Dandylyon the Elder that her tendency to visit the fellows in the barracks by night was undermining her authority. If the truth be known, the administering of her nightly lustful desires was having precisely the opposite effect on the impressed and motivated troops, such was her enthusiasm and physical magnetism.[*]

And it was through Boadicea that, according to the pair of them, a first-century Dandylyon had first become acquainted with the ancestral line of the first Prudence. She was a young servant to the rebel queen, dressed in maroon and cream, and had one afternoon, by a forest camp, seduced a quack doctor of large beard, and the pair had formed a sexual union that ought to have impressed the beasts of the forest. Post-coitus, they agreed on their goal to protect Boadicea by preventing her evening visits to the soldiers. Prudence had her own ideas as to how to stop Boadicea, for she was a practising and quite brilliant witch.

The rebellion led by Boadicea to oust the Romans from Britain had a profound effect on Prudence, who from then on in used her magic to urge revolution of all kinds. As did all the Prudences yet to come. On the night of victory over the invaders, she cast a spell that she swore would last thousands of years. Her wish was that there would always be a Dandylyon and a Prudence, in unison, close to power in England.

---

[*] *I remember them telling me not to worry too much about this part of the story. I know now it was a required element of their histories, for throughout they were telling me the truth. These were not fairy tales.*

They wed and had two children, a Dandylyon and a Prudence, who then began their own dynasties of bearded surgeons on his side and attentive witches on hers. She was a magnificent witch too, for in those days only the truly special ones covered their tracks, hypnotised those who might present danger, and hence survived.

Prudence's line had then continued to meddle in witchcraft, the perfect foil to the Dandylyons' science over the years. In my boyhood, this modern-day Prudence must have told me of a thousand spells and invocations that her maternal line had cast. She confessed to their role of the dominatrix throughout the ages, and how they had all conducted a pilgrimage to the oceans every single spring to sing to the mermaids, urging them to continue to be ever-generous in their attentions to lonely sailors. The mermaids always sang back, assuring the Prudences that they would always honour a wayward shipman, no matter how putrid was his breath or unwelcoming was his groin.

It should be noted that an eleventh-century Prudence had narrowly avoided being bricked in at Glamis Castle in Scotland, the royal household of King Malcolm, himself the basis for the legend of Macbeth. One of those three witches was a Prudence, and she set a curse upon Glamis, and this shall become pivotal in my own story. Please bear with me.

There was also a direct impact on my own life from the Dandylyons, young Horace too, for all the latter-day ones had studied at King's College, London and Trinity College, Cambridge, beating down a path for me and my own studies, for I became his surrogate boy, but, again, more of this soon.

Dandylyon's own father had become acquainted with one Edward Crowley (my papa) and his father in the moneyed circles of England's pioneering Industrial Revolution. These were now the days when serving the aristocrats and royalty was no longer enough, for power was shifting into the ownership of mills, factories, shipping lines, manufacturing, mining and raw-material grabs in Africa and Asia, and beer brewing for the grubby and pie-eyed masses in London, a market dominated by Crowley's Alton Ales.

And so came into my life, magic and wonder, beards and maroon. Dandylyon and Prudence. Palaces and witches. Kings, queens and mermaids. Utter sensations.

Dandylyon and Prudence took rooms in the house, and kept me company often. Dandylyon loved to play chess and backgammon, and told me long stories of his feats of mountaineering. He told me of his days as a student doctor in India, Ceylon, Rangoon and China, and his mastering of the techniques of yoga and meditation. I told him that I had already asserted a similar discipline in the gardens of a Marylebone hotel to suppress my excitement one morning the previous May. This thrilled him. He showed me how to play billiards and snooker, while he taught me German (from Berlin) and Macau Cantonese. He insisted on the importance of the intonations of Cantonese and how they were, in principle, a mirror image of the angles that made one a champion in billiards. He was often plied with the fine sherry that Father kept stocked for him when we played. The drink seemed to change him quite amusingly throughout the evening.

The pair of them spoke to me of Father's illness more than Papa himself was able. The impression of what they told me was absorbed over several chats. They said that Father would leave me one day, and go to Heaven. I dismissed this, of course. I recall the look between doctor and nurse, when they realised the usual line was not a digestible one. They shifted gears, offering instead a warm and soft landing for this scared

child. They did this by extending friendship, time and understanding. Either Prudence or Dandylyon was always there for
me, night or day. I stayed with Papa on a chaise longue, reading to him late into many nights, often until we both slept.
Mother was nowhere, unless there was vitriol or nastiness to
dish out. The pair made every effort, it seemed, to ensure I was
never lonely, afraid or sad, but rather surrounded by grown-
ups who cared.

From what I now know of them, the doctor must have been
in his late twenties, and she too. They appeared old to me,
of course, and this was exaggerated by the reverence in which
he seemed to be held both by Papa and the small squadron
of other, far older, medical types who came to visit and who
kept vigil.

On many days and in all seasons, we walked the countryside and satellite hamlets of Redhill, over the parks and
through the woods. They schooled me in nature, mathematics,
science, and in the basics of medical care. We played tennis,
Prudence with more agility than the thoroughly enthusiastic,
but lanky, ungainly and windmilling Dandylyon, on the lawn
courts of the tennis club at the end of our lane. His hair
flopped on his face, and then his hand swept it back, jerkily
and well meaning, scratching and grooming his beard in the
same movement. The combination made for an endearing
sight, for either he was not conscious of his lack of coordina-
tion or simply cared not. I liked this immediately. We flew
kites with gusto on the downs, and hid from sudden storms.
They never told me we had to go home, but instead they
waited for me to tire. We chose books from the library and
took turns to read them to each other. When Mother fell ill
from time to time, they made sure she was comfortable, nothing more. After I became ill with the scarlet fever, Dandylyon
stayed by my side with the dedication not only of a physician,

but also a parent. I recall that his sleeves were always rolled up with a precision that meant they never needed fixing. When he had to sleep, Prudence was devoted and purposeful in my febrile flushes and heated delirium. Yet I know I was not in a daze when that committed, benevolent and faithful lady went beyond duty. I have heard since of the practice of plump-lipped Victorian nursemaids, able to calm baby boys in such a thoughtful manner, and quite acceptable in some Asian cultures for mothers too. My nurse soothed me thus with the fine generosity of medical fellatio. I was pacified from that vicious illness at its zenith by a lengthy and tender nursing, some might consider ill-measured. Since that hot afternoon, I may have, in my mind, added Prudence's enjoyment to what may have been simply a perfunctory act, a kind and humanitarian gesture. Perhaps I may have not.

I recall the grey and soggy day, lit only it seemed from the inside of the house, that Dandylyon and I properly discussed his interest in a strange world where spells, nature and science appeared to meet. It was as if the moroseness of the day outside had forced the truth out of him, and like a squeezed pustule, out it popped. That day and then over time, he showed me many books that he always brought along in his medical bag. They were tales of magic and friendly witches. He showed me pendants, miniature trident wands, helmets, necklaces, and small trinket boxes. The books contained pages of images of beasts, grotesques and incantations. He explained each, and left me with many toys from his lessons, but when he gave me my first silver pentagram, he was earnest in his assertion that this was no plaything. She was also nothing of which to be afraid. She required only reverence and respect, and her rewards would be a bounty over the years. I still have her today.

In Papa's chamber one mid-morning, I told Prudence and Dandylyon of our days with Orr and The Legion. They smiled, as I regaled them with tales of our year around England and London, sweet, clouded evenings by that Camden chimp cage, Coote trumpeting at our pals across the wall. Father often sat silent throughout, prompting from time to time with a scribbled note for me to tell the story of the day of the tornado at Sandhurst. Or with the nuns on Brighton Pier. Or when the Yeomanry changed the clock in the Cambridge University dressing rooms at Henley, commandeered their boat and raced in their place in the regatta, a coxed eight with two blind men, a legless fellow and a seven-foot-tall ginger type screaming the team home, before rowing on to the nearest bankside ale house. Papa was discouraged from speaking, but remained a perpetual and willing conversationalist with his small bell and sketchpad and ink nib to deliver his input. It was hard for him to prevent his laughter some afternoons though, as he began to see humour in sadness, as well as the more obvious pathos in comedy.

I thought of my Yeomanry pals every day. I resolved to write to the battalion at their Camden digs, and they replied with a typical promptness and rhythm. Of course they did. By return, I enquired as to when they could visit, and they came on the first Sunday of each month for two years.

Of course, Dandylyon knew of their dependency on opium, and aided them with their pain. Father was now also reliant on morphine. Many times, I saw Dandylyon take the narcotic himself, and I then sat among them as they shut up, apart from the murmurs of truncated gibberish of ecstasy. They appeared to be as happy as I had once been with Prudence on my centre at the height of my fever.

I remember the day that Father and I had subscribed to that old circus pamphlet, now to be mailed to our new address. I now wrote care of their classifieds to the Maximus de Paris Rouge circus, apologising to Small Man both for our sudden departure from the gradients of Alexandra Park that night when Father fell silent and also the unintended loss of his pal, Gerald, back in Royal Leamington Spa. I updated Small Man on most of my news (details of the drugs, thoughtful Prudence and the vicious bitch who bore me and whom I rarely saw were all omitted). I invited him to visit Redhill were the circus ever to visit Clapham Common or Goodwood for the annual horse race meet. I mentioned my friend Dandylyon, but offered no hint of the translation of his name from French for fear of disrespecting poor, late Gerald. Gerald was now likely fodder for worms of a different kind to the chunky critter that had caused the tamer's shocking death below the gasping trapeze girls and only feet from the weeping midgets.

I told Dandylyon of Small Man, and the doctor was as generous as ever. He procured a vast stash of worming tablets to forward to the circus in honour of the former lion-tamer. Such small gestures were perhaps quite pivotal in establishing my developing world view that those who followed Christ were barely able to speak a word to me, never mind a tender one, while the unorthodox were kind and overflowing with benediction. Father, largely still in his rooms, remained neutral and silent on all such matters now. I sat with him many days, reading to him from Ballantyne and Longfellow, never the Bible. I read stories that I had written and from the less controversial texts I was being exposed to by his physician.

And I would one day receive a reply from Small Man. By this time, Father would be long gone. In this thrilling correspondence, Small Man would kindly offer his services and that of his elephant should I ever need some *muscle*, but I rush ahead.

2.3 A FADING FATHER'S ADVICE

And so, it is generally assumed and written that I was an innocent boy until I tarnished a maid in mother's bed at the age of fourteen, quickly followed by the contracting of gonorrhoea from a prostitute.[*] These milestones are fair yardsticks and barometers to measure one's progress and battle scars, of course, but they ignore the events from the age of seven onwards, yards from the alleged strictness of the Brethren, when I witnessed military subterfuge; slow deaths; monstrous and abhorrent parenting; daily drug use; vast alcohol consumption; meddled, as any fortunate urchin in my position would, with the occult and its accompanying pornographic sketches of bestiality and orgy, and relished that rarest of treats for a prepubescent ragamuffin: benevolent oral sex from a plump-lipped tigress with the most humanitarian bent. Looking back, it was obvious how I would turn out. One really did not require the subtlety of the runes or the crux of the tarot to predict the trajectory of *The Beast*.

My life descended into true sadness on the first day of September 1883, when weeks before my eighth birthday, Mother got her way and I was sent away from Father, Dandylyon, Prudence and my home to boarding school across the town in Redhill. Boarding school is a vile enough punishment, but to endure it when one's vast family house and fading parent are in the same small town is savage and perverse. At the news, I was sure that my ankles bloated, my neck too, though worse was the source of bullying from day one. My mighty bosom forced worrying second glances in the showers from the other boys.

---

[*] *Though which delicious lass was the guilty party, and had gladdened me with her diseased sauce, cannot be fathomed from where I write. To attempt to guess would be daft, even if I knew their names, given the masses of rollicking mares of all ages, through whom I was ploughing.*

On the day I left home, as I hid my utter desperation, I was taken in to see Papa. I had not heard him speak for two years, and I would never hear him speak again after that day. He read to me from chapter nine of Genesis. It was the part when Noah survives the flood, plants a vineyard, gets drunk on the crop, and, in his intoxication, loses his clothes. His three sons, Ham, Shem and Japheth witness this and cover their father's middle with a cloak.

'Son, never let anyone touch you there.'

'I swear upon the holy Bible and the greatness of the Father, the Son and the Holy Spirit that I shall never allow this to happen, sir.'

I thought I saw Prudence shuffle ever so minutely. Was it guilt, embarrassment or even excitement? I now ponder. I was convinced that Dandylyon smiled at her.

2.4 A Death and then the Desecration of Tomb & Scripture

From late 1883 to 1885, there were two years of evangelical boarding school, under a malevolent arse called H. T. Habershon. This was a time that was beyond vile. The procession of schools I was forced to attend were all of a type, just different geographical coordinates upon which to be kicked and punched and probed. Habershon was one of those martinets I mentioned, dark in spirit from his own physical horror. He had a broad neck, bulbous eyes, peeling rosacea, sausage fingers, sweaty pits and teeth like a Dickensian cemetery; all leaning at odds, chipped and unwelcoming. He ruled with a violence that drained into the psyche of the establishment. It was hell on earth. I prayed for his death and when it happened, I recall believing for the first time in the existence of what Dandylyon had referred to as the power of the Will. If only now, I thought, I could exert the same influence on my physical appearance. If I could wish Habershon dead, then could I also shrink my tits? This would be a challenge I would surmount in good time, but first, following the brief joy of my schoolmaster's demise, I had another preparatory school to endure. My new tutor, one Reverend Henry d'Arcy Champney was a brute and a sadist too, but at least, in the scorching early autumn of 1885, I saw for the first time the city that would witness my eventual blooming. My esteemed and beloved Cambridge.

Mother, Habershon and Champney were the antithesis of human kind. We all would have benefited significantly from their immediate death. I have since, and with precision, copulated, micturated, farted, invoked spirits and shat on all of their tombs, they would be thrilled to learn. Herein lies a lesson never imparted on those tedious chalkboards or forced to learn courtesy of a whip or a strap or a cane:

Be extremely careful as to whom you hurt.

There is little need to touch upon the horror of these days. I suspect that most have experienced the lows of schooling and the roughest discipline. All the clichés are true, so I need not go over the well-trodden turf of forced sodomy and ice cold showers. At 51 Bateman Street, Cambridge, however, beneath the preached evil of the Reverend Champney, I saw a Spanish Inquisitor, who might well have relished in the use of the rack on these petrified souls, these still hairless boys, who ought to be playing snakes and ladders with mother. Cricket, the sporting delight of the English schoolboy, was allowed, but we were not even permitted by the sick bastard to score runs, for it was feared that the competition might encourage unchecked desire in the lads. When the boys were beaten, they were not even beaten on the buttocks for the fear that it would spark a youthful excitement in them. I considered an early letter to Small Man to come with the trumpeting cavalry.

I recall with joy the time the police removed Champney from Bateman Street in cuffs. It was not for the buggery he engaged in with his students, however.[*] It was for an unwelcome intrusion of a completely different hue. It was before the general election, the last day of June 1886, when he was carted off by three large-footed officers. Lord Salisbury's Tories would defeat the previous administration of Gladstone's Liberal Whigs in such a resounding victory, that it was of little importance outside of our ward that all of the ballots had been destroyed during a midnight break-in. The interloper did not leave, the court was later told, until after 6 a.m. when all of the ballot papers had been altered. Would-be voters were, apparently, to have had no choice as to their preferred candidate, for all of the papers now had four boxes to tick, each of which sat next to the words, 'I vote for Jesus Christ.'

Champney was given a suspended sentence and a manly handshake by a judge, who seemed to admire the deed far more than the election officials or the competing candidates, who had to delay their victory or defeat speeches by seventy-two hours. I was, indeed, surrounded by arses.

My misery under his putrid tutelage continued and straddled the day in March 1887 when Dandylyon and Prudence (to the precipitous intrigue of some boys) appeared at the school gates with news of the death of my hero, my friend, my father. It was no surprise for I had had a precise vision of the scene the previous night, as I half-slept. Now I was, in effect, an orphan, but I would like to be clear that I would never

---

[*] *At this time, I was not even good enough to be buggered by this tasteless imbecile, not considered up to snuff. This was the kind of clod I was forced to bear.*

wish to be perceived as a victim of my circumstances, nor would I ever apportion blame. I see each of the unfortunate events that I reveal as quite marvellous opportunities, or as wheels of fortune that sculpted me and allowed me to flourish into the *Great* Beast. I wish this opinion to be placed quite firmly on the record, for they allowed for a quite magical life. Those who wished to help me as a boy will be delighted with my gratitude, while those who looked to hurt me will be annoyed to a similar degree. Both were fine fuel to me. Such is life.

I understood from a sudden increase in Champney's snide remarks about spoiled brats and vile rich kids that he presumed that I had inherited my father's wealth. And so the frequency of punishments accelerated, and their severity peaked too. I am rather sure that these thrashings were the cause of my misbehaving, rather than the results of it.

I must have been flourishing physically, for I was finally sodomised for the first time by my headmaster. I informed Dandylyon's office in Pimlico by smuggled letter, and the doctor had me withdrawn from the school on the premise that I had developed albuminuria.* He did this unilaterally, and then told Mother of the sexual assault. She was unconcerned by it, he told me much later.

Her response seemed to corroborate this, as she shipped me off to more schools; first Malvern (1887) and then Tonbridge (1888) – the names are unimportant, the dates too, for they may as well all have been one corner of hell for a little boy who just wanted to walk the countryside with his now-departed father. Oh how those days seemed distant and from

---

* *An unhealthy level of protein, likely hereditary, and a likely clue to kidney disease. Known also to cause bloating of the ankles, throat and mammaries.*

a different sphere. At least I knew happiness and how it felt. And it strengthened my resolve to find it once more. And so, these schools were to me a requisite stage, I knew the horror would pass. These schools were architecturally pleasant, cornerstones of the revered English school system. Yet when each ancient and ivied corner spells a new beating or molestation, it is hard to appreciate the finer points of any establishment, regardless of its physical splendour or high reputation among those idly rich parents.

My only fun during those miserable days was the amusement and solace extracted during religious studies, as I would show a knowledge as polished as that of the learned teachers. I was able to repeat the Scriptures from the beginning of the Bible to the end without once glancing at the page. I could pinpoint any verse or chapter. I was viewed as a freak and a prodigy, but they were all falling for my master plan. I drew them in, convincing them of my freakish level of knowledge and giving myself a real authority. I was patient, though it hurt to give credence to the Bible. When I began to point out the scores of chronic and infuriatingly childish inconsistencies within the Scriptures (my favourite was the nonsense of the three days in a cave grave and the resurrection), the belittled professors would sanction mental and physical torture on me from the other boys. My measured and tactical response was to smoke cigarettes, and to practise incessant and uncomfortably energetic masturbation. I would exhibit the same zeal that I had in mastering the Scriptures in disobeying them. And I would hit the scholars and their god where it hurt most. I would sin against their cherished Holy Ghost. *That* would show *them*.

2.5 The Cavalry

In the spring of 1889, reports of my new mischievous

scholarly pursuits in Tonbridge reached Mother. So this time, I was packed off to a personal Brethren tutor by the sea in Eastbourne. As with my introduction to Cambridge, there was now a chink of light, directly and gratefully received from her meddling, for I was permitted to enrol in chemistry classes at the college there, and so piqued my intrigue in alchemy. This trajectory of turning shit into gold was, after all, one I had attempted ever since the days of Dandylyon and Prudence in Redhill, but now here were the precise practicalities of the treasured process and the gateway to the sciences, which in turn would one day soon take me back to my true home of Cambridge.

With the vast vacuum created by the evacuating of my brains of the stale defecate known as the Scriptures, my unshackled mental capacity soared exponentially. I was able now to play chess blindfolded as I had once witnessed as a boy on a May train carriage from the Cotswolds to Marylebone. At school, I gained minimal respect from this party piece, but respect all the same. It was a start, but one that seemed to coincide with the thrust into puberty; as my ankles trimmed, appearing almost normal, and for the first time, finally a hint of real definition in my jaw bones through the toad-flesh of my neck and chin. My right tit seemed to be firmer, some variable I simply had to put down to the inexhaustible use of my right hand on my tool thrice daily at an absolute minimum. I therefore began to self-pollute intermittently with my left hand, and the results upon my left udder seemed to be almost instantaneous, perhaps a direct consequence of the extra exertion of the less skilled, slightly wayward grip. Perhaps, the flimsy myth that two wrongs do not a right make had been debunked. I knew that there were benefits to be had from self-abuse and sinning. This process of renewal and change deserved a renaming of the boy. I was

now to be Alec. It was June the first 1889, and the Ugly Duck-
ling had fucked off.

Through all of the bullying, I had maintained a stoic calm.
I knew I would have to bear this torture in order to make this
man whole. Such an approach might rightly lead to accusations of sadomasochism, and quite rightly so.

This theory of mine is solid, for I could have ended the
torture from the boys and masters with one letter to Camden.
I never did this. A friend called Dandylyon did, however, and
when the Warwickshire Yeomanry appeared in the centre of
Eastbourne to swoop on five particularly cruel bullies, the
misery I suffered at school was over.* The masters, too,
relented, so I suspect a military manoeuvre across the school
grounds to visit the teachers that same day. I was then even
asked for my opinion on my own schooling: what would I
most enjoy as my studies of choice? I responded, 'Mountain-
climbing.'

I had of late been reading prodigiously on the subject
of mountaineering, obsessed as little boys can be. The two
climbing books I adored the most were, first, Thackeray's
son-in-law, Sir Leslie Stephens' *Playground of Europe* (Long-
mans, London, 1871) and, also, Albert Frederick Mummery's
My Climbs in the Alps and Caucasus (T. F. Unwin, London;
Scribner, New York, 1895). They were my two new bibles, and
I took them across the south and east of England with me, as
I was given a regular pass out of school. This was made all the
more fun as I was convinced that Mother knew nothing of
this. Crikey, she would have been livid.

In July of 1889 during the summer holidays, Mother moved

---

* *Of course, the Yeomanry were more than up to the task, but Dandylyon
later confessed that he had resisted Prudence's mischievous pleas to also recruit
Small Man and his willing elephant to scare the hell out of my young
persecutors.*

from Redhill closer to London, to the suburb of Streatham to be with her brother, Tom Bishop. Tom was an equal horror to Mother, and he took it upon himself to direct my education that summer when I was in his care. But once back at school and once the boys of The Legion had stuck their beaks in, and acquainted themselves with my tutors' headmasters, I was a free boy. Orr had developed into a sturdy beast to do justice to that once-lanky frame. I had my own minders now, uniformed and broadcasting enough military menace to scare the hell out of anyone I wished to intimidate, even if that intimidation just allowed me to be treated like a human being. The power was, of course, a potent drug, with which I knew I had to exhibit self-restraint, such was my love and respect for the men. Before long, other drugs like cocaine and heroin would be my less-respected servants. They would be mine to boss around, like a soggy-eyed and perpetually disappointed dog that sees its owner aroused and with his trousers down, but who can say nothing.

2.6 Ascendant Child

On long spring and summer days, I was now excused from hell. For now, my grand climbing passion was Beachy Head. The fantastic beauty of the cliffs can never be understood by anyone who has not grappled them, especially that obeliskian spike, the Devil's Chimney with its twin crests, the Tooth and the Needle. Beachy Head offers rock problems as varied, interesting and picturesque as any cliffs in the world. Chalk is probably the most dangerous and difficult of all kinds of rock. One can hardly ever be sure that any given hold is secure. In wet weather the chalk forms a paste that clogs the boots and makes a foothold impossible. But for all of that, many of my happiest days were spent on that face. The Yeomanry often came with picnic blankets, booze and opium, though, by this time, their number had dwindled to eight. Fairfax, Runciman and Coote had passed away, the result of slow descents and drug dependency from their combat injuries. Coote's trumpet was carried always in their memory. It was Orr who became my best friend from the unorthodox troop, and we wrote to each other twice weekly. I sensed he saw me as a son. I saw him and Dandylyon as fathers, supremely fine ones too.

I was a young boy, zipping around the south-east of England on trains, given leave from my schools, writing poetry in fields of daisies, weeds and daffodils, practising yoga on solitary hillsides and climbing the steepest rock faces in the region, all of which were around Beachy Head. I struggled to find more difficult ways of conquering them, for although they were not even considered mountains, it barely matters where one falls two hundred feet onto sharp rock, never mind the presence of an angry sea below. The result is the same.

When the same illness of albuminuria, with which I had been diagnosed by Dandylyon, took the life of my father's brother Jonathan on September the thirteenth 1889, Mother showed minimal concern that I might be next to die. Instead, her measured opinion was that I was to be forced to cycle to godforsaken Torquay in the west of England, a trip of a couple of hundred miles. This wisdom landed me with the whooping cough when I collapsed twenty miles outside of London, but my convalescence was with the best tutor yet. James Archibald Douglas was a twenty-five-year-old teacher of arts and philosophy from the northern industrial city of Sheffield. I had heard northerners were a different and queer lot. Quite marvellous they were too, as it turned out. Indeed, Douglas was certainly a far cry from the morons and dummies with whom I had been saddled to date. Douglas smoked and drank, and revelled in the company of ladies. My tutor showed me how to play cards and would have taught me billiards had I not unfurled the skills and dexterities, manual and geometrical, taught to me by Dandylyon on the slate baize in the snooker room in Redhill. He attempted to teach me that these vices were permitted, if one was able to enjoy them in moderation. It was a fair attempt, I suppose, and one perhaps I might have heeded were I not the Great Beast and a greedy drug and sex fiend. Douglas taught me sense and manhood, and I shall not easily forget my debt to him. I suspected that Douglas had been planted by either Orr or Dandylyon. Or my precious Prudence, of course.

As proficient as Douglas was in deceiving Mother and Uncle Tom, it was not long before I was brought home to live in Drayton Gardens, Streatham with them. When Tom caught me with cigarettes, he lectured me lengthily on the Two Wicked Kings, the twin evils of *drin-king* and *smo-king*. He had recently written an article for *Boys' Magazine* on this very subject and was keen to share his wisdoms.

'Alec, my lad.'

I was NOT his lad.

'Yes, Uncle?'

'Do you know of the two wicked kings?'

I stared and said nothing.

'Drin-king and smo-king?' he said.

He did not know that I had read his article.

'But, Uncle, you have forgotten to mention a third, the most dangerous and deadly of them all.'

Uncle Tom was confounded, and I did not give him the benefit of my wisdom, as to whether that third was wan-king or fuc-king. The riddle must have stayed with him, for a week later I was punished and locked in my room for three days. The twit need not have worried about my keeping myself busy, as I further sculpted my left tit through admirable exhaustion.

*

1889 was a pivotal year. Adolf was born, for one. I was thirteen for the most part of it. There were rumours of my being
able to recite the Bible and win seven games of chess blindfolded. Yet I was far prouder of a level of yoga that allowed
me one thrilling day to fellate myself. It should always be
noted that while this remains the unholy grail of the young
boy, in this quite lonely but intriguing scenario, the fellater
also must fellate. This never bothered me. In truth, it spiked
the whole experience towards a delicious exponential, and I
rarely left my room. The filthy and glorious chrysalis was
about to reveal himself.

Indeed, I had now bloomed to such a degree that Mother's
gamesome maid flirted with me, leaving trails of a girlish perfume in her wake, and made it clear she found me desirable.
One Sunday I faked an illness to keep me from the furnace of
church, and I took her to my pious mother's bed. Dandylyon
later spoke of Oedipus. This felt like it was far more than just
another victory, this one was soggy, marvellous and spirited,
over the oppression of the preachers and those vicious texts.

This tale is no secret, but still worthy of a mention, a yard-
stick of how far I had come and the level of disregard I had
for the institutions of Church and Mother, as well as the fuel-
ling joy of getting my own way over both. Mother still bristled
in my presence, but like a hollow and unevolved lover, she
hated my absence (for she could not bully me), but the thought
of my freedom and happiness elsewhere drove her to distraction.

The maid then told Mother of our frenzied coupling, in an
attempt to secure a higher wage. I confessed to the lesser
charge of being at the tobacconist's with some local lads at the
time, and the lovely, and quite mauve, scrubber was dismissed.
I was bothered by this, though. And I wrote of it at the time
in my diary.

First, we have a charming girl driven to attempt blackmail, next a boy forced to the unmanly duplicity in order to exercise his natural rights with impunity, and incidentally to a woman for whom he had nothing but the friendliest feelings. As long as sexual relations are complicated by religious, social and financial considerations, so long they will cause all kinds of cowardly, dishonourable and disgusting behaviour.

The whole episode unravelled, however, in my favour, with no help from soldier, mercenary, midget or elephant. With an absolute joy, I discovered that my mischief could no longer be tolerated in the family home, so it was time to move on again, and wherever I landed for the next four years, my protectors would likely find leverage to continue my fun and my own choice of learning: yoga, mountaineering, chess, military history and strategy, Russian, German, Cantonese, poetry, pornography, the classics and of course, science. I was nineteen years of age when I completed my studies in chemistry at King's College, London, and thereby passed the scholarship to Trinity College in Cambridge.

2.7 BLOSSOM

It was 1895 when I joined the Scottish Mountaineering Club. The clique-ish English would not have me, so I made do with an alternative as I did with Satan to the Lord. I had conquered the Alps with ease. I had not just straddled and sat upon the precipitous peaks of the Matterhorn, Trift, Jungfrau, Mönch and Wetterhorn, but I drank champagne upon them all. When I rested my arse upon the top of the Eiger, I had done so with bare feet for a bet. I could never resist a wager with a fool, from whom I separated two hundred pounds in cash when we all got to back to Berne.

I was unstoppable. Or I certainly felt it.

The world was about to hear from me, as the century approached its end. Victoria ruled. Hitler was just six; Rasputin twenty-six, and already excelling in waggery and roguishness. The Legion still boarded in Camden by a largely new cartload of chimps. Small Man was regularly worming his elephant somewhere on that sturdiest of sceptr'd rocks in the sea – my England. Mother was still a cunt. Prudence was as astonishing as ever, and Dandylyon visited me often and now, free from any harshness such interest might have provoked in my juvenile schools, the doctor began to speak for the first time in years of the misunderstood and ill-lit arts. It was truly time to blossom.

The Occult beckoned.

And shortly after we took the train from Liverpool Street to Cambridge that sodden night in October, just two days after my twentieth birthday, now ignored and released by the raggedy monstrous goblin of a parent in Streatham, the three of us would dine at George's before I was introduced to the magic of cocaine. Prudence obliged us both with her generosity, and we all invoked a new spirit. Well, it was a new spirit to me. Absolute liberty.

Chapter 3

Кембридж, Россия
Cambridge, Russia

The burden of caught clap. How sore it is!
A burden of sad shameful suffering,
The bitter bastard of a bloody kiss,
The Parthian arrow poisoned from Love's sling!
Lo, sweet Lord Christ, thou knowest how sore a thing
Is a cock crooked and consumed of fire
Shooting out venomous sap that hath a sting!
This is the end of every man's desire.

– 'A Ballad of Burdens',
from *White Stains* – Aleister Crowley

If I am to die in the mountain pass, it must be pointed out now that I have always believed that Black Magic is suicidal. In boxing, one may fight according to the Queensberry Rules or one might do the other thing. I approve of some kinds of magic and not others. I disbelieve in the form known as Black Magic, which is not only foul and abominable, but, for the most part, criminal. To begin with, the basis of all Black Magic is that utter stupidity of selfishness which cares nothing for the rights of others. People built thus are naturally quite unscrupulous. In many cases, Black Magic is an attempt to commit a crime without provoking the harshness of the law. The almost main instrument of Black Magic is murder, either for inheritance or some other purpose, but to gain personally out of it.

I have always preferred to use the power of the mind, the power of suggestion, the strength of the drugs, the magnetism of the flamboyant leader, the variants of nature and THEN a well-measured mixture of the flimsiness of others' minds to be moulded and then harness the power of their own brain, like the well-set cement in the kiln to hold unholy water.

Eleven hours to go.

3.1 AND I SAW GHOSTS OF GREAT MEN

I moved into my university residence at 16 St John's Street, the breadth of a well-hung cat's cock hair from King's College and Bridge Street, a fraction farther from where it was intended that I study, Trinity College. Quite vitally, I had discretionary access to fifty thousand in pounds sterling from Papa's estate. I was free, twenty and white.

We started this tale by settling on the correct pronunciation of my name, and I moved into Cambridge with a similar intention. I was no longer Alexander, Alick or Alec. I needed something that would reflect my blooming and my metamorphosis into the world. Crowley is a name with its roots in Ireland, and, in those love-flecked days, we of a poetic bent were celebrating much that was Gaelic. So, I would now be Aleister, the Celtic translation of my birth name. This snake was undressing, layer by layer, and by luncheon on my first day, I had also made it very clear that I would never attend chapel. I told the Dean that Sunday worship was forbidden by the Brethren, and outside of my faith. My precise words to him were: 'The seed planted by my father, watered by my mother's tears, would prove too hardy a growth to be uprooted.'

The Dean reluctantly agreed, but perhaps sensed there was a troublemaker in his charge. This was confirmed to him after my first economics lecture, when the professor spoke of the subject as being a tough one because of the lack of reliable data. The stubborn spirit of that little lad who once dived into a clump of nettles clutching his King James Bible was on show again, for I now made it very clear that I favoured the hard facts of science (as well as the rigidity of German). I simply closed my notes, rose from the body of sheepy students and walked out. I went back once, to pass, quite easily, my exams.

I always ate alone and I studied alone. However, my solitude suited me, and also Dandylyon would before long arrange for my access into a temple by King's College to socialise with other types with similar intrigues and interests to mine. These pursuits would be not of the academic kind, far more towards the extra-curricular pastimes of the Occult, but more of this soon. In short, I was never lonely. I was a liberated and happy young man, not wishing to waste any time with the superfluous niceties of my first year. I was surrounded by a more-or-less happy, healthy, prosperous set of would-be parasites.

When my brain tired of reading and writing in my study, I walked the streets of Cambridge all night many times, a *flâneur* sucking in the Will of the ages, often until dawn. I sensed the ghosts of great men who had laid foot on those same spots. I would stand and meditate in the dawn mist from the river on Garret Hostel Bridge, as it clouded the Latham Lawns by Trinity Hall or transmigrate through the centuries by Newton's Apple Tree or across from the Judge's Bedroom. Or observe the angled path of the moving rain from my window that framed the tower of St John's Chapel. Along with the well-trodden biographical paths and the newspaper lies about me, I will not repeat the obvious and waste all of our time in extoling the wonders of that bewildering city. This is never to suggest that I took her magnificence for granted. She aided me daily, hourly, in the transportation of my being to other spheres. Cambridge did not do this with a rough boot up my backside, for she is a stylish and generous lass, but rather with a helping hand up, and a comforting embrace into an unseen realm. Every person ought to see Cambridge. To live there with the latitude and licence that I had was where this god's heaven and that once fat-ankled, big-titted child's playground met. I breathed with her. I still do.

3.2 THE FRESHMAN

As I would later marionette global events, I learned the role of the puppeteer from the Master; a bearded doctor with an oddly spelled French name, who smelt of brioche and who himself seemed to be manipulated, from time to time and with his permission, by the brains and beauty over his right shoulder, that most benevolent nurse/witch, dressed perpetually in maroon and cream and a delight to inhale.

Prudence and Dandylyon kitted me out immediately with the requisite Cambridge *attire du fop*. The silk shirt was *en vogue*: drooping bow tie and the limp, broad hat were *dans le vent*. I read poetry in public while speaking to very few. I absorbed Browning, Swinburne, Fielding. I was captivated by the adventurer and scholar Sir Richard Burton and his crazed tales into Africa, the Mid- and Far-East. When Burton disguised himself in order to be the first white man into Mecca, bearded, darkened and speaking fluent Arabic, I had my first true role model, though Shelley soon allowed me to fully emulate another; a trait that had been forbidden in my hellish schooling. Recall those poor mites of 51 Bateman Street, Cambridge, a mouthful of spittle's distance from here, disallowed from scoring runs at cricket by a sodomising man of the

Scriptures. Well now, The Beast had been emancipated, greedy for flesh and knowledge. I was utterly affected by Ruskin's remark that any book worth reading was worth buying, and in consequence, like a spoiled imbecile, acquired volumes literally by the tonne. Flesh, taut or saggy, fresh or musty, eager or shy, was not far behind.

And so, the lyrical Shelley aided the flowering of my impressionable soul and urged my pained writing. One might call it the follies of youth, but, still, I squirmed for the longest time at my own nonsense . . .

> My poetic instincts, further, transformed the most sordid liaisons into romance. I found, moreover, that any sort of satisfaction acted as a powerful stimulus. Every admirer was the direct cause of my writing poetry.

This lame refrain was regurgitated in *Cambridge Magazine, Cantab* and *The Granta*. That I was being published in these venerable titles infuriated my tutor Professor Verrall, for I was also a constant absentee in his lectures, and he did not want to encourage desertion from his class. Yet when I wrote to him, explaining my epiphany regarding English literature, I was again given free rein (I do not believe any of my protectors were interfering) to explore the riches of those libraries, unimpeded by anything as crude as an instructor. There is little to tell of those early weeks and months at college, usually so fresh and exciting for young men. And this is because I was to fall in love, and so this was a period that was defined almost exclusively by that lover. The exceptions were the initiations I was to experience with Prudence and Dandylyon; rites of passage into the worlds of the Occult and politics. So, there were no frolicking gangs of fresh-faced lads on punts and by cricket fields. I remained blind to sun-flecked days so heralded by other students. I would have special and far more elite joys to relish; those of witches, spies and cock. I shall now explain and illuminate.

3.3 THE NEW REALM
It has always been thought that I spent the winter of 1896 travelling through Scandinavia and the Low Countries with a single detour to Switzerland to climb, and with the precise intent to channel the poem, 'A Descent of the Moench'. The latter was true, but the former a ruse.

14 December 1896
Prudence and Dandylyon were inside my chambers when I let myself in. It seemed they had prepared a travelling case for me. I walked over to my study desk, and saw four first-class tickets for the boat train to St Petersburg. They were for dusk the following day. I chuckled. Dandylyon approached me, touched my arm and brought his cakey beard close.

'It is time. There is much to do before we leave tomorrow. Please walk out with us, my love. Tonight, you shall finally be inducted into the Hermetic Order.'

I had read much of the Order, and had discussed it at length with them both in the past, though there had never been a precise intent expressed on their behalf that this was my destiny, as far as they were concerned. They had spoken of similar societies too, while there seemed to be always some woolly and prescribed fate they had mapped out for me. It was because of my often expressed impatience to try any or all of these organisations that they knew they need not ask my permission to take me in hand as they were now doing.

'They have observed you, and witnessed your brilliance. These are persons known and unknown to you. They have always trusted my word, but equally they rely on their own eyes, wisdom and ears. If we are the guides and advisers we strive to be, then we are sure you are ready to be elevated into the Order. We shall be proud to call you our protégé, for we know you will soon outstrip them, leave them chuntering and befuddled, and move on to become a myth, a legend, a god.'

Dandylyon looked at Prudence, who said, 'Tonight your destiny will truly start to shape itself.'

She moved close enough for me to subtly sniff her and inhale her marvellousness, as she continued.

'The puzzle falls together thus. One: you shall enter the Order. This is precisely where you will thrive as a diplomat. But this is a façade, of course. Two: this will allow for masonic knowledge in the short term. This is also a façade, though a handy one. And three: the Order is a step on the road to goddery in the long run. Each stage brings an increasing abundance of sex and power and cash. In the meantime, it will arm you with the basics of the Occult to run amok behind the lines of the true enemy of the twentieth century.'

She stopped, as if I should know the answer.

'Oh! The Russians.'

Her shoulders dropped, as I sensed disappointment and a wrong answer. Her admonishment went no further. I looked at Dandylyon who switched his gaze from me to her, smiled and nodded.

I heard her sharp intake of breath, preparing to deliver the answer.

'Good heavens, no. The fucking Germans.'

And, like a pivotal game of chess that was just hours away would end within just three of my own moves and of which I shall presently tell, *that* was *that*.

*

'First things first, my boy,' Dandylyon said. I trusted him, them both, with my life. He produced a black hood from the inside pocket of his overcoat, as Prudence drummed her fingers together in a slow and measured rhythm. 'We apologise for the melodrama, but where we are going this evening, there are certain . . . laws to obey.'

I let myself be taken into the strong current of my friends, trusting in my own belief and in them, knowing I would be washed up on a safe shore if I did not struggle. I heard her whispering a gentle incantation under her breath, the words coagulated into an undecipherable and persistent murmur.

The soft velvet and Dandylyon's touch were adequate comforts against the loss of light as the hood slipped over my skull. Dandylyon and Prudence led me across the floorboards of my chambers and towards the rear of the house and out into the gardens. They were indifferent to the chances that we might be seen, or so it appeared in our nonchalant pace and gait. Cambridge was full of boyish pranks, and so if a masked character were walking without a struggle, not a head would have been turned, I was sure. They led me to the path that ran behind St John's Street, and I was helped into a carriage, as Prudence continued to softly chunter her comforting spells. This allowed me to know if nothing else that *she*, my partisan witch was close. Yet, the sound of the horse's gentle trot set my bowels on edge, for it hinted at the power and danger of nature and things yet to be understood. It was a visceral edginess that was understandable, for soon I was out of the carriage and also out of the familiar touch of my friends and into a firmer man's grasp; two or three perhaps. I could hear their grunts, and uneven breathing. I could feel their fat and ungainly mitts on me. At least one had vicious breath that permeated the mask I wore.

My shoulder and the side of my head were used to push open what felt and sounded like a large and heavy door. Our shoes and then my knees were on stone slabs that were cold to the touch as my right palm then kept me upright. I felt a rope around my waist. It tightened as I managed to stand. I was now being pulled by it, and I held my arms out in front of me.

'Stop!'

I stopped. Still, I could hear Prudence, her tone and low volume as sturdy and welcome as previously.

'Child of Earth, arise and enter the Path of Darkness.'

It was a strange welcome, but a welcome nevertheless. There was a strong knocking on what sounded, through a definite echo, like a larger door into a more cavernous room.

A second voice spoke more slowly and with added authority.

'Very Honoured Hierophant, is it your wish that this candidate be brought into our number?'

With greater jurisdiction and solemnity still, a third voice answered from within the chamber. I thought this must be the Hierophant.

'It is! Fratres Stolistes and Dadouchos, please assist the Kerus in the admission.'

The first voice spoke again, 'Child of Earth, unpurified and unconsecrated. It is not permitted that you enter.'

A soggy finger came under my hood, and made the shape of a cross on my forehead.

'Child of Earth. You are now consecrated with water.'

There was a stink now of a rare incense, and now for the first time, Prudence was silent.

'Child of Earth. You are now consecrated with fire.'

The Hierophant then responded, 'Child of Earth. Why dost thou wish to be admitted into this Order?'

One of the large-footed types who had pushed me in, now seemed to kindly help me with my line, whispering the words in my ear.

'My soul is wandering in darkness. It seeks for the knowledge of the Occult.'

'Thou wilt kneel on both knees. Give me your right hand, and place it on the sublime and sacred symbol. Hold my left, bow thy head and repeat.'

I repeated thus.

'I, Aleister Crowley, in the presence of the Lord of the Universe and of this Hall of Neophytes of the Order of the Golden Dawn in the Outer, do of my own Free Will and accord hereby and hereon most solemnly pledge myself to keep this Order and the names of its members secret. I furthermore pledge and swear that I will divulge naught in the case of my resignation, demission or expulsion.

'I will not suffer myself to be hypnotised nor to hypnotise others or to initiate evil of any kind. This remains under the penalty of violation leading to expulsion as a wilfully perjured wretch, void of all moral worth and unfit for society.'

I now had one more line to utter.

'And in addition, under the awful penalty of voluntarily submitting myself to a deadly and hostile current of Will set in motion by the chiefs of the Order, by which I should fall slain and paralysed without visible weapon, so help me Lord of the Universe and my own higher soul.'

Again, Prudence could be heard, whispering her accompanying spell, which gave me great comfort.

The hood was roughly ripped from me, as if to remind me of the consequences of failing in my duties. Inside, I laughed. A man in a crimson cloak and hood spoke. It was the Hierophant.

'Frater Perdurabo,* you are received into the Order of the Golden Dawn.'

Now, I had yet another alias.

'Close your eyes.'

I obeyed, and I could hear the hall clearing.

Finally, I smelled apples and brioche, and opened my eyes to my two friends within my grasp and an empty sanctuary beyond.

They each held a hand, as they led me through a door on the far side of the ancient temple. We took several darkened passageways that forced us to squeeze and stoop before one door vomited us out on the quiet steps next to King's College. It was done.

The horse and carriage pulled up and we returned to St John's Street in a satisfied and glowing silence. There, they again led me inside, where the second half of the evening's entertainment would soon commence. In fact, the intermission between ceremonies lasted just a few minutes.

Once inside, we all sat.

Dandylyon opened his comically large attaché case, and brought out three small phials, containing a clear liquid. There were also metal objects in there, a purple velvet throw, small blackboards and white chalk. He took out from a side pocket

---

*   *The Golden Dawn was a magical organisation that studied the Occult, metaphysics and paranormal activities. It was masonic in nature, and highly ritualised, even to the point of the comical in the eyes of some laymen. It scared the shit out of others. Its teachings draw from Egyptian, Qaballah, Tarot, Enochian Magic and Alchemy. We drew on the spirits of Egyptian gods like Isis, Osiris and Horus. There is much dressing up and many frilly pronouncements. Fools mistake it for Black Magic. It is closer to the Wiccan and to both nature and science. It now stands forever in the shade of my then-future and glorious iteration of this sloppy, self-regarding and unctuous lot – my very own Church of Thelema.*

five fat candles of dark green, and then placed all of the other contents on the broad dining table that separated us. The meticulous and patient man then laid everything out with a measured precision that forced one to concentrate.

'We are about to enjoy a second ceremony, Aleister. With all of my surety, I know you are prepared for this too. After this evening, you are now a part of the ancient body of the Golden Dawn, and shall pass through a new stage of enlightenment. You shall be welcomed in their temple now by many who know of you already, and you might seek spiritual shelter there whenever you feel the need. Within the Golden Dawn, you shall thrive, wonder and relish each moment and stride brazenly with each new nugget of our truth. But believe me when I tell you that this is a *stage*, a necessary step, a temporary state of being; just as we all are. Understanding, recognising and nodding politely and in reverence to this fleeting transience is pivotal, and you shall know of its short-lived and momentary ecstasy when you pass into a new phase in years to come. Now drink the liquid, Frater Perdurabo.'

I hastily drank it, and they drank too. I recalled in years to come his prescient words, for he seemed to know that I would splinter from the Golden Dawn.* Of course, he did.

Dandylyon then spoke in what I knew to be Sanskrit, and it was not long before the visions and the spirits arrived, just as the door opened and a fourth person joined us. I shall write of him presently.

That night, I was awakened to the knowledge that I possessed a magical means of becoming conscious and of satisfying a part of my nature which had, up to that time, concealed itself from me. By this, I mean sodomy. It was an

---

*   *This was to be my magical motto within the sect. Frater (brother) Perdurabo (I shall endure to the end). A more apt moniker they could not have mustered.*

experience of horror and pain, combined with a certain ghostly terror, yet at the same time it was the key to the purest and holiest spiritual ecstasy that exists. This was so different to the abuse at school. It was the rough love of a large gent, aided and abetted by compelling and persuasive narcotics. Throughout it all, Prudence held my hand, and whispered encouragement, spells and sometimes filth, in my ear.

I was a pioneering young man, barely out of boyhood, who now, in the midst of passion, endured a brutally loving man's fist in my mouth and was soothed by a comforting maternal voice near my ear. Where they had previously been muffled, the words of her invocation now became clear to me. She was, indeed, my true friend.

'I am the daughter of Fortitude and was ravished every hour from my youth. For behold, I am Understanding, and science dwelleth in me, and the heavens oppress me. They covert and desire me with infinite appetite, for none that are earthly have embraced me. I am shadowed with the Circle of the Stars, and covered with the morning clouds.'

I felt her hands tighten with a loving clench on my knuckles that so richly emphasised the adoration in her verse.

'My feet are swifter than the winds, and my hands are sweeter than the morning dew. My garments are from the beginning, and my dwelling place is in myself.'

When his fist was withdrawn from my mouth, Prudence's face drew close and her cheek and nose nuzzled mine, like a friendly mare. I felt her breath on my brow, cooling the sweat that formed there before her silk skin smeared it. The words were well-used ones in witchcraft,* but I was acutely

---

* *Ever since 1592, when they were apparently first uttered from an aged manuscript by the luckless Sir Lucius Guenchen, who went quite mad the next day, and only deteriorated thereafter to a slow and ungainly end.*

aware of the subtext in her intonations that urged me to enjoy.

My blessed nurse continued.

'The Lion knoweth not where I walk, nor do the beasts of the field understand me. I am deflowered, yet a virgin; I sanctify and am not sanctified. Happy is he that embraceth me, for in the night season, I am sweet, and in the day, full of pleasure. My company is a harmony of many symbols, and my lips sweeter than health itself.'

Prudence withdrew marginally to look into my eyes. Her voice deepened markedly.

'I am a true fucking harlot, for such as ravish me, and a virgin with such as know me not. Purge your streets, O ye sons of men, and wash your houses clean; make yourselves Holy, and put on righteousness.'

I briefly wondered at that moment whether it was still she who was in control of the spell, her words and her own Will. I was very soon convinced that she was. In fact, Prudence was in absolute control of her art to the point where she toyed and played with it in the palm of her hand. Just like all those other Prudences had for centuries before her.

'Cast out your old strumpets, and burn their clothes and then I will bring forth children unto you, and they shall be the Sons of Comfort in the Age that is to come.'

Prudence continued to captivate and charm me, as the soggy and stubborn man behind me tried his best to better her brilliance. Then long into the night, she repeated that spell and the following two verses, ad infinitum but never ad nauseam,

> Black Moon, Lilith, sister darkest,
> Whose hands form the hellish mire,
> At my weakest, at my strongest,
> Moulding me as clay from fire.

> Black Moon, Lilith, Mare of Night,
> You cast your litter to the ground
> Speak the Name and take to flight
> Utter now the secret sound!

I loved her and her power so, I can barely explain even to this day.

3.4 A TROIKA OF SHERLOCK, POE ET LECOQ

The next evening, Prudence, Dandylyon and I left Cambridge for London, Waterloo Station, the boat train and Russia.

As we walked out of the door at St John's Street, Dandylyon said, 'We shall tell you of our plans when we arrive in London. These damned trains are not safe to talk about the kind of matters we need to cover.* Especially as those we might call adversaries might already know that we are booked on the 6.02 to Liverpool Street, and also, in which carriage. I shall explain all when we arrive in London.'

And so en route in a compartment of four seats (with one empty as Dandylyon had reserved all four for privacy), we discussed Cambridge, her architecture, her history and the latest instalment in *The Strand* magazine of Sherlock Holmes. It was well-disguised small talk, while in all likelihood we need not have been so concerned of eavesdroppers. As Dandylyon was carrying a volume of Conan Doyle's 'A Scandal in Bohemia', we set about comparing Holmes, Edgar Allan Poe's C. Auguste Dupin and Émile Gaboriau's Monsieur Lecoq, the trio of cerebral sleuths who vied for the affections of the broad swathes of crime readers in those days, hooked on the arcs of our heroes.

---

* *Alexander Graham Bell's Volta Laboratories had introduced the first tape-recording machine several years earlier.*

Dandylyon read several splendid passages for us, before finally declaring his conclusion.

'Holmes is my man,' he said, 'though I realise it is his Englishness that tips the balance for me. I was an acolyte from his first words in *A Study in Scarlet*.'

'Dupin for me,' I said. 'He inspired Holmes. Without Dupin, there is no Sherlock. Originality edges it for me. And Holmes's overt fondness for cats disturbs me somewhat.'

We both looked at Prudence, intrigued as to her opinion. But she stared out of the carriage window into the gloom. Dandylyon and I continued to discuss the various merits of the men.

Random lines might have been picked up by any audio tape recorder, little lad on the way to the WC or intrigued ticket collector.

'He's too nice to Watson.'

'He is too cruel to Watson.'

'He misses vital clues, he is too sympathetic.'

'Dupin is too conceited.'

'The French criminal is easier to apprehend.'

'He smokes too much opium.'

'He doesn't smoke enough.'

'Moriarty is Holmes's better, and could kill him off any time he wants.'

'Piffle.'

'Dupin didn't deserve to survive until "The Purloined Letter". I still suspect he was complicit in "The Murders in the Rue Morgue". I despise those vain enough to follow a career just to please their parents.'

'Yes, but I adore that he sticks up for the falsely accused, and does not seek payment. Only his own enjoyment.'

Still Prudence remained silent as we neared London with the smog markedly thickening outside.

When the guard blew his whistle to announce our arrival, she spoke. 'Oh boys! It is simple. I suspect that the greatest is the one who would win in a single hand of cards.'

We waited for her rationale, as the train pulled to a halt on platform four.

'Skill and judgement are nothing without luck. And in such deadly games, one cannot afford to lose the first round. We must be born lucky, and stay so. So, I say Lecoq. I have never witnessed such good fortune as The Rooster's.* Holmes has Mycroft as a mentor. Dupin has the police department's resources. Lecoq has destiny and brains and . . . solitude. Such beautiful luck is hard to improve upon. It reminds me of my own fate that landed me with you two. Definitely Lecoq. He is also the most handsome and well mannered, of course. But you forget that I am a greedy one. I would take all three of them. Three is a quite magic number. Come, a table awaits us.'

And we rose to all of our chuckles (Dandylyon's the loudest by far), and stepped from our compartment onto the grubby and well-worn stone of Liverpool Street, from where we took a hansom cab across the city to Waterloo.

Unhurried and with time on our side, we enjoyed a magnificent Beaujolais in the Royal Station Hotel, a Domain de la Romanée-Conti '45 that, I sensed, served the occasion well.

Dandylyon lit a plump cigar, and was engulfed in clouds of smoke that he refused to help shift. His voice came from within the white plumes.

'Prudence is quite right about fortune. And none are so blessed as we. I shall explain why, but it is precisely that luck that brings us allies in the right places at the right time and

---

* *Lecoq's nickname, and a literal translation.*

with the most interesting intentions. Seneca the Younger* was right when he said that luck is when opportunity meets with preparation.'

'Yes,' I said, 'but Seneca also said, "*Nusquam est qui abique est. Vitam in peregrinatione exigentibus hoc evenit, ut multa hospitia habeant, nullas amicitias.*"†

Dandylyon and Prudence looked at me, and said nothing.

It is now I look back on this, I wonder how prescient this might have been. But then again, I might just be searching for self-pity. None of us is truly immune.

'You are a marvel, lad. And with such insights, I am left in no doubt that you are right for the role, for which you have been hand-picked and groomed.'

He took a sip at his wine, put down his glass and then enjoyed another large inhalation from the cigar. He touched Prudence's hand, and she smiled.

Prudence said two words. '*Semper Occultus.*'

'Always Secret,' I said in a heartbeat and quite inadvertently.

'*Semper Occultus,*' Prudence said again.

Dandylyon repeated the words.

'*Semper Occultus.* It is the motto of another mysterious society of ours. It is not an ancient mystery like you have seen with the Golden Dawn. We shall now tell you of a modern undercover society. Some know of it as the Secret Intelligence Service. It is run from Whitehall, and is puppeteered by the highest powers within the government and the Palace. The SIS not only controls the Empire, but seeks to expand it at the expense of our enemies. We have told you before of how Orr

---

* Roman philosopher, dramatist, statesman and humourist (4 BC–AD 65).
† 'He who is everywhere is nowhere. When a person spends all of his time in foreign travel, he ends by having many acquaintances, but no friends.'

and the lads are seeking new ways to fight the wars of the future. Well, we also need to manipulate the peace, as well as stir up trouble in the homelands of our foes. It is a vast challenge, and it is the perpetual task of the SIS. Please bear with me.

'There is a young English officer, who has seen brutal action against the Boers and the Zulus. His bravery and cunning on the battlefield shocked all sides. He has been decorated more than many fusty old generals. His approach to the politics of Empire is a radical one, and one that some old guard in Whitehall have, quite remarkably, consented to test out. This officer is now a member of parliament too,* and has the staunch backing of a group of Tory MPs. His family is supremely influential, and it appears that this interesting upstart impressed at a Rothschild dinner and had viceroys, princes and ministers aghast spitting out their soup. They were all then chided and belittled by this intriguing chap, as he exhibited his cool cunning, knowledge, and political insight and demonstrated the hurtful timing and tone of his tongue.

'Orr knows him, met him one day at Sandhurst, and speaks so very highly of him. He is only a couple of years your senior, and he is recruiting a mischievous mob to cause a stir abroad. Mix it up. Bold and wicked audacity where the Japanese, Russians and Prussians least expect it. They call him a wunderkind and it seems he lives for subterfuge. He detests the old guard and is looking for some contemporaries as equals. You are one, for he has heard Orr, Prudence and me out, and he trusts our word. The other recruit we shall meet in Russia.

'These MPs he has surrounded himself with are followers of Lord Hugh Cecil. They are known privately within Westminster as the Hughligans. They are famously ill-mannered

---

* *For the filthy mill town of Oldham, near Manchester.*

around the bars and hallways of the House of Commons. Cecil has commandeered this faction of the Conservative party as his own. They are all vehemently opposed to vast and superfluous military spending, for they see a new kind of war that needs to be fought. This is a war of intelligence and counter-intelligence, espionage and danger. And so, the SIS is recruiting rebels, mischief-makers, antagonists and insurgents dressed up as fine young diplomats. This is where you come in, Aleister. You might have heard of it referred to as MI-1, and it holds an even higher priority than the eradication of dissent and insurrection at home.'

'How marvellous, I am in.'

'We knew you would be,' said Dandylyon.

'Do you have any questions?' asked Prudence.

'Whom shall we meet in Russia? And who is this intriguing English soldier, who courts me?'

'To the first part, I say, "All in good time."'

'And the second part?'

'This we can answer. It is a chap, whom we believe you will appreciate. His name is Winston Churchill.'

3.5 BEAUTIFUL BUGGERY

And so I found myself as an apprentice in the arena of international intrigue and mischief, spying for Britain. It was to be espionage and meddling on behalf of the Empire for me. As far as the rest of the world was concerned, I was to be introduced to the diplomatic staffs of the British and the Russians in St Petersburg, exchange niceties, and smile politely and modestly at all the correct pauses. In truth, however, I was en route to meet the most intriguing fellow; one who would mould my life and my philosophy, and one who would be our man on the inside of the Slavic dynasty.

Between Dover and Calais, I planned to write the much-discussed poem, 'At Stockholm'. It would speak of my new intrigue in cock.

> We could not speak, although the sudden glow
> Of passion mantling to the crimson cheek
> Of either, told our tale of love, although
> We could not speak.

But it was only an intrigue. And just as my total homosexuality was a façade and a fraudulent cover, then so were my whereabouts as far as the student body of Cambridge was concerned. No Stockholm. No Sweden. Instead, we were Russia-bound to begin to learn the profession of diplomacy. I wrote the poem in twenty minutes, and I could not have phrased my apparent enthusiasm for fucking – or getting fucked by – lads any more diplomatically. There is really no separation between buggery, drugs and the Occult. They come hand-in-hand, in-step menacingly and either to damnation or into legend.

> He who would seduce me first I could not forget.
> I hardly loved him but desired to taste
> A strong new sin. My sorrow does not fret
> That sore. But thou, whose sudden arms embraced
> My shrinking body, and who brought a blush
> Into my cheeks, and turned my veins to fire,
> Thou, who didst whelm me with the eager rush
> Of the enormous floods of my desire,
> Thine are the kisses that devour me yet,
> Thine the high heaven whose loss is death to me,
> Thine all the barbed arrows of regret,
> Thine on whose arms I yearn to be

In my deep heart thy name is writ alone,
Men shall decipher – when they split the stone.*

The name of the man who had buggered me in front of
Prudence was Herbert Charles Jerome Pollitt, and he was the
first of several generous and loving fellows as I exposed myself
with malice aforethought to experience, arming myself with
the knowledge of how I would satisfy my longings in the
future. I had not been forced or prompted to engage with this
chap. It had all been at my own instigation. The march into
degradation might be decided on the spot or overnight by
some or not considered at all by others, and I do not criticise
this. But if I were going to turn from mere beast to Great
Beast, then I would need to be knowledgeable. I was not sure
if sodomy (or to be precise, being sodomised) was for me, but
to remain ignorant of a path, well, that I considered criminal.
And I would have to be careful, of course, as these were all
still highly illegal acts that might yet threaten my liberty.

The late morning that followed my deflowering was a
dank autumnal day. He and I walked out into the drizzle. It
was thoroughly miserable to the point that only made my
excitement burn and throb more potently. He and I strolled
towards the River Cam.

Pollitt was a Cambridge man, a gentleman of leisure, tasteful collector of art, educated, stylish, funny and a fine female
impersonator. I had heard of his reputation and I knew of him
by his stage name, Diane de Rougy. He was an obvious
admirer of the great Liane de Pougy, the celebrated and notorious Parisienne courtesan, *vedette* at *Les Folies Bergère*,

---

* *When this astonishing volume was first published, some fuckers burned
down the printers and every copy of* Green Alps *and 'At Stockholm' with it.*

and a quite mucky sort. Pollitt was known to make stylish and pretty ladies quite livid with jealousy.

Pollitt was just four years my senior, but had seemed to be reasonably well versed both in the ceremony of the Occult and of a gent's delight. We replayed our tryst many times, and we were not precious or jealous. But soon I would live with him as his wife, and our desires to fuck others drizzled away.

These were erotic times in which we lived, and they had infused me with the firm belief that we were created to be pansexuals. The Romans knew it. The Greeks too. Yes, we might enjoy loyalty, and absolute fidelity might be achieved, but there is no crime in giving in to absolute sin and lust. We were empowered to choose our own path. We were not jealous children or sheep in the congregation, but rather we were mighty fucking gods in the making. And even gods were allowed to fall in love and be faithful.

As we walked, the silence dragged out, but it was not uncomfortable. He spoke first.

'I have read your poetry.'

I waited for his opinion. God, I cared for a moment.

'I sense you can do better and I can make you into a true and, even, great poet.'

Ordinarily, this slight would vex the least precious artist. However, I too knew I could do better, I was flattered by his belief in me, and even more thrilled that he might wish to be in my life long enough to blood me as that true poet.

I kept him waiting for my response, and so started our boyish games.

Eventually, I said, 'You fuck me all night and *that* is your opening gambit?'

I even peppered it with mild anger as a test.

I was thrilled that his answer then took even longer than

mine had, and that we seemed (I could have been wrong) to really understand each other.

A hansom cab came by at speed and splashed his well-chosen tweed trouser. He said naught, but I could sense the absolute disdain he felt. I too said nothing. It was his turn.

We crossed the road, and walked onto the paths by Trinity College.

'Opening gambits should always be considered and mine was. So many treat them as a standard. So much harm can be done within three moves. Most shall never understand this.'

'I agree. E4,' I said, with little thought.

'E5,' he said, with equal haste.

'Knight to f3.'

'Knight to c6.'

'D4.'

This simple minute brushed away the complications and complexities of chess and life. And although the game was played precisely as Orr and the lads had done on a May morning train to Marylebone and was only five moves in, there was an inevitability about the outcome. *Fait accompli. Les jeux sont faits.* And such is love. White had, in effect, already won. He laughed loud enough to (quite likely) vex the librarians through the stained-glass arches to our flanks.

'I knelt and stood behind you all night, perhaps, but I just let *you* fuck *me* in the name of good, clean fun. Are we even, Aleister?'

'No, let's play again. And *for real* this time.'

And play we did, as we rested our backsides on a park bench by the riverbank under a weeping willow. We fought lengthy games in our minds and without a board, mighty tussles, proverbial fists in mouths, and this time as equals, staring at ducks and posturing fools in boats on the river. As dusk settled, we walked to his rooms that were stocked with sagging shelves of decadent literature, many first editions from Aubrey Beardsley and Leonard Smithers,* framed photos of him in action as a muddied rugby half-back, tough and agile, and ink erotica of the kind that a policeman should not regard.

And this day set a pattern for the days and weeks and months that followed. I saw little of Cambridge and made few friends, because I had skipped the foreplay and found bliss. Pollitt had failed his exams, and proved that academia was no cornerstone to happiness even in this city. I was happy to follow his example of rebelling against course work and lectures, though I knew even then that I would pass *my* exams with ease. Pollitt, however, was already leaving an imprint on contemporary literature. E. F. Benson's 1896 novel, *The Babe B.A.*, was set in the city, and therefore supremely well known there. However, the popularity of the book (whose subtitle was *Being the Uneventful History of a Young Gentleman at Cambridge University*) was vast beyond our colleges and a global phenomenon within the educated strata, at least. The character of Babe himself was clearly based on my lover.

> The Babe was a cynical old gentleman of twenty years of age, who played the banjo charmingly. In his less genial moments he spoke querulously of the monotony of the services of the Church of England, and of the hopeless respectability of M. Zola. His particular forte was dinner parties for six, skirt dancing and acting, and the performances of the duties of half-back at Rugby football. His dinner parties were selected with the utmost carelessness, his usual plan being to ask the first five people he met, provided he did not know them too intimately. With a wig of fair hair, hardly any rouge, and an ingénue dress, he was the

---

* *Wilde's publisher, filthy sketch artist and pornographer.*

image of Vesta Collins, and that graceful young lady might have practised before him, as before a mirror . . .

The furniture of his rooms was as various and as diverse as his accomplishments. Several of Mr. Aubrey Beardsley's illustrations from the Yellow Book, clustering round a large photograph of Botticelli's Primavera, which the Babe had never seen, hung above one of the broken sofas, and in his bookcase several numbers of The Yellow Book, which the Babe declared bitterly had turned grey in a single night, since the former artist had ceased to draw for it, were ranged side by side with Butler's *Analogies,* Mr. Sponge's *Sporting Tour,* and Miss Marie Corelli's *Barabbas.*

He and I turned into clichés as we strolled by dusk and stumbled (from drugs and alcohol) by dawn around the city, throwing chess moves at each other in remarkably tight struggles. We walked in symbiosis, and many must have thought us idiotic, as we played games to make grandmasters perspire, not on boards but in the space above our crowns. There was, however, one fissure in our bond that, given we were just boys, grew and broadened so unnecessarily, until we had a daft fight over it. My passion for mysticism outstripped his, and this became a problem, for I became obsessed. The evening I turned down a stroll, a game of chess and a fucking in order to attend a ceremony of the Order to honour the solstice was pivotal in our affair. I slipped out of Cambridge the next day, feeling guilty, and went up to London to buy him a pair of the finest rugger boots from Lillywhite's in Piccadilly Circus. How the fuck was I supposed to know he was there in the city too, buying me a gift of the finest tuberose incense from Fortnum's. It seems that apparently we passed each other on Bond Street, each with a pal in tow. Mine declared he had seen Pollitt see me, and flick his beak in the other direction. Pollitt's chum

seemingly convinced him that I had done the same. And we
never played chess or strolled or fucked again. Never believe
anything of what you are told, and only half of what you see.
I live by this tenet now, because those two cunts, who lied to
us both, were responsible for a lifelong regret. I could not
even speak his name for decades, and only managed to type it
for my publisher when I dedicated *The Scented Garden of
Abdullah the Satirist of Shiraz* to him several years later in
1910. How unreasonably sad.

To this day I believe I still have his blasted (brand-new)
rugger boots in a locker at Liverpool Street Station.

Adieu, mon copain.

3.6 ENGLAND'S HOLY MAN

That fourth train ticket was not for Pollitt, however. It was for
Orr, who met us at Waterloo Station. The ogre had grown
again, and his vast smile, too, in an equal and truly pleasing
proportion. The journey from London to Dover took us yards
from Tonbridge School, where, years earlier, my misery had
perhaps been at its peak. The schoolboy in me would have
relished in cocking a snook in its direction, but I already knew
that was worthless and beneath me. And so as we passed, I
maintained a dignified silence in the style of a modern-day
Scarlet Pimpernel, keeping his own counsel. Perhaps the disciplined quiet I showed in that moment was the seedling of a
lifelong practice in keeping my mouth shut when the temptation was to scream the truth. As the four of us rattled along to
the east under empurpling and bruising skies, perhaps it was
in those very seconds that I turned from boy to man.

I wrote and read Russian en route, played chess, and even
once reprised the scene with Prudence from my childhood
episode of scarlet fever, as Orr and Dandylyon (I believe)
dozed. I looked at, with vast interest, a tome given to me by

the doctor called A. E. Waite's *The Book of Black Magic and of Pacts* (1898), and spoke willingly to Slavic travellers in the dining car, working on the dialects and colloquialisms as we pioneered forward. When the four of us were alone in our compartment, Dandylyon spoke.

'Let me tell you that Orr and I have been friends for a slightly longer time than perhaps you are aware. It has been since the day I walked into a South African prisoner of war camp near Smitswinkel Flats on the Cape. It was a devilish spot called Jourdan Siding where thirst and sunstroke ruled. Your fortuitous encounter with his lads between Leamington and London that day brought you into my life. I shall be ever grateful for that. When your dear papa fell ill, we were honoured to be asked to care for you from near and far. Your father so approved of our role of the adoring puppeteers. But let's be clear now that mostly we no longer see you as our charge, but as one of us. This is never to suggest that our job is done, and this is because we are but a small troupe of nosy bastards, who love to nudge and mould the continent and the Empire. You are now treading onto the boards of the most exhilarating stage of the lot. Power. You might rule the world one day, my lad.'

He touched his right cufflink, squeezed it between forefinger and thumb. He lifted his gaze to the ceiling of the carriage, and appeared to listen intently to the rattle of the locomotive. This prompted the slightest smile on the lips beneath the beard. He repeated that word with a kittenish tenderness and lingered upon it: 'Power.'

He then paused, before going on.

'First, there is an adventure to be had, and an intriguing new ally to meet. You shall enjoy Russia. They are a mauve lot. There will be perfunctory meetings and handshakes that shall take place in St Petersburg. To the outside world, you are to be a junior trainee diplomat, and you shall use your real name and confirm your status as a Cambridge student. There shall be a week-long course with introductions to the staff of the British consul and the British embassy, as well as a dinner with the ambassador. As much as I fully trust your acting skills to play the part, there is a school of thought that states the less you know, the more you shall fit in.'

He belly-laughed. We all laughed together, as if we were rehearsing for some wooden melodrama. The stakes were high, as they were throughout my life, but one should never forfeit laughter. I knew this, and thought of Stoker's *Dracula*; and specifically, Professor Abraham Van Helsing and his adorable imaginary friend, King Laugh. When one deals in the darkness of the human soul, one must tether our greatest ally: humour. For one's enemy's enemy is our true pal. And true evil fears mockery and lampoonery the most.

I still recall the precise words of Van Helsing:

Ah, we men and women are like ropes drawn tight with strain that pull us different ways. Then tears come; and, like the rain on the ropes, they brace us up, until perhaps the strain become too great, and we break. But King Laugh he come like the sunshine, and he ease off the strain again; and we bear to go on with our labour, what it may be.

I thought this so true. Even if he was cutting off a lover's head or ripping out the heart of a once-saintly friend.

And the train carriage pushed on to the chill of St Petersburg. The distance ahead was black, as the last touches of light fell behind us and we were still a full two days from our destination.

*

Upon our arrival in the city in the late afternoon when darkness had already descended, we moved into our rooms in a vast nameless mansion yards from Peter's Square. In the horse-drawn carriage, there was no talk other than over-polite and benign chit-chat. We carried ourselves as tourists would have, I as an intrigued student of the language, the country and her literature. Orr did not wear his uniform; I saw him in civilian clothing for the first time. When we arrived, I was told that on our third day we were to travel out into the countryside to execute our true mission: to meet and recruit this mysterious Russian for MI-1.

On our first full day at the British embassy, Dandylyon introduced me to many men of an illustrious stripe – social, diplomatic and military – and I was convinced this was not the exposure usually offered to a junior diplomat. On our second evening there, we attended a temple in evening suit, Prudence in magnificent maroon.* We were all given an animal mask as we entered an ancient necropolis. There were several hundred men and women there in a scene that even then, in those formative days of mischief, appeared to me as a cliché – faux heads of goats, dogs, cats, snakes. Sensing this, Orr insisted that I prevent myself from laughing at the quite juvenile drama.

The exciting part was that this was a secret gathering of clearly influential parties, but it was rather silly. This visceral feeling was confirmed to me as an accurate one, when I realised that masked individuals were waving and gesturing to others across the hall, and then stopping to chat with familiarity.

---

* *This was a Russian chapter of the Golden Dawn. The Order, despite being an ancient one, was most progressive in its acceptance of ladies. Cynics might have suggested it boosted the sexual permutations, but have they never heard of trustworthy whores, never mind beguiling witches, armed with centuries of inherited wisdom?*

Everyone knew each other despite the masks. The pretence irked me slightly. That is, until we took large quantities of cocaine. The masks would have provided an obvious problem in the sniffing of the piles, so we were treated to a small army of dwarves and midgets, who meandered around with the slow and polite shuffle of a drinks waiter. Upon the head of each small chap was a wide tray with impressive hillocks of the powder. The circular trays each had three tall silver bars topped by a round curtain rail from which there draped a crimson velvet hang. If one wished to maintain anonymity, one simply popped one's head inside the curtain, lifted the mask and ingested away. Each dwarf carried a stash of silver spoons to aid the consumption, and handed them out with broad, almost troubling grins. Although I had read of orgiastic tales that neatly described what happened next en masse, and seen it all personally on a smaller scale when our number was four that last night in Cambridge, it was still a welcome and heartening surprise to see the vigour and energy of those ladies and gentlemen for the next few hours.

Our third day was our time to rusticate, and to do what we were really there to do. The recuperative powers of the younger man would have aided a lesser being than I. The previous evening's exertions appeared to me as a frivolous opening gambit, a beguiling and alluring *amuse-bouche*; all part of a magnificent and broader frolic. We left the city at dawn. There was a train journey that took perhaps three hours, and then we took a horse and carriage to a small village of perhaps twelve dwellings. Eleven were lowly, one was underwhelming at best. Then there was the church of the Orthodox faith, infinitely more pleasant, and this is where we soon sat in the rear pew to the right. And we waited, and waited, and waited.

Eventually Dandylyon calmed me from my juvenile eagerness, and acknowledged that this delay was to be expected.

'You have not been briefed on this mission, for the simple reason that we – and by this I mean British Intelligence – would like to have your unfettered and unshackled opinion on our subject,' he told me.

This was fine with me. They trusted my opinion. I adored the word *mission*.

There were perhaps six rows of pews and a simple and clean feel to the boxy structure. The windows were of a stained glass that in those days were called *amateur*, a pernicious term today, but one that then meant produced with love; the root, a mistral one, from the Latin *amare, amore, amistad, amicable, ami*, before the nasty reference to money tarnished the term. I ought, instead, to describe them as the work of an artisan, blessed with a vision in his mind and with skill in his hands. The altar and the lectern were fine centrepieces, upon which I fixed my gaze and breathed in the style that I had taught myself in those Marylebone gardens all those years ago to abate a boyish excitement and to maintain my poise and dignity in front of those few who truly mattered to me. Such were my powers of the yoga (boosted by a hefty recent intake of narcotics) that I can only presume there was absolute silence from my cohorts, as I could block out all sensation and stimulus. That was until I saw a man in my mind, approaching me from behind, in an out-of-body experience. In my mind's eye, I viewed the scene from behind him, and I could see myself ahead of him as he neared with a lazy and intended shuffle. He was tall, seemingly young, lanky, and with limp arms. He carried a very real threat in his gait. This was a very real and disturbing sensation, and yet, I knew that it was not a peril *for me*. There was a further feeling that was even more distinct. It was the sensation of an ally, a friend and a protector.

It was the rancid smell that brought me out of my reverie.

'Aleister,' said Orr as I stirred, 'We would like you to meet someone.'

I turned with a firm measure and saw the front of the man, whom I had sensed moments before. I saw a peasant in the smock of a holy man, but immediately divined a quite absurd saintliness to him. This creature appeared to possess a dark gift, as well as a remarkable stench and troubling stare.

He spoke in a harsh dialect, and appeared to be drunk, but not in that flimsy way. His countenance was mean and robust, and portrayed an understanding of the people he was here to meet. The accent was strong, but I could just make out what he said, as he rambled at us all. He spat about the Prussians and the Irish, but changed his warring tune when he turned the subject to their females. Prudence then spoke to him in English.

'Have you been behaving, Grigori Yefimovich?'

He growled at her and then at us all, cupping his testicles through his robe.

'I misbehave in order to work for the Lord. It is my curse. But I serve Him like no other ever has,' as he turned his glare upon me.

He appeared to be marginally less stewed when he spoke of God.

'The Almighty speaks to me now. He tells me that I shall mend peasants and noblemen. I shall hold vast power. Pay me vast sums from your Queen, and let loose your frothing nurse-maid on me.'

He nodded at Prudence, then looked at, and spoke to, us all.

'And you know I shall execute this work for you. Look at her, her eyes cross in my presence. I see her exposed and ever-so-lively soul through them. Leave us in this church until daybreak. She will never know such coupling as on that altar.'

Prudence stood, walked towards him, covered the broad hands that cupped his gonads with her own, and whispered in his ear for perhaps one minute, while he gestured, nodded, glanced at the impressive scale of and the obtuse angle produced by his groin in his filthy robes, chuckled, pondered and growled between each sentence.

Then he finally roared, and tilted his neck backwards so his only view was of the ceiling of God's forsaken house. Prudence laughed. We all laughed.

Prudence turned, loosening her grip, and still did not refute his charming offer. Was she aroused, the marvellous mare? She bloody well was.

He yelled, 'You strike a bargain fit for a king, a czar, a queen and this Holy Man. I am yours, lady. Without question and forsaking ALL others for a while.'

And the four of us withdrew, marginally before, it seemed, the stinking mystic was about to make his approach to manhandle me to the ground, land on me, and stay there until he was spent. This appeared to be prevented from happening, for Prudence then spoke loudly and demanded all of our attention.

'It is agreed. The terms are as proposed. He is ours,' she said. 'We must now leave.'

As we walked out into the insipid yellowed light, produced by a mild wind and the dusty earth, and into that pivotal day when I became a spy and thus cemented a relationship between Cambridge and those Russian lands that would span the whole of the next century, *he* was still bawling from within the church.

'I, Grigori Yefimovich Rasputin am yours, my beloved. I now work for England before I work for God.'

I had still not met one of my conspirators, the one in Westminster, and still held too much of another in my nostrils, but I sensed we might run amok one day soon. Now, we were THREE. And Prudence was right, for three is, indeed, a quite magical number.

I looked at her and asked her, 'To what did you agree?'

Did she blush? I do recall that she tilted her head, slitted her green eyes and said, 'Your curiosity is a quite marvellous quality.'

3.7 MASKIROVKA

The following afternoon, as we pulled out of St Petersburg and in the comfort of our compartment, Orr spoke of military things. Now, years later, I think of the words of my firmest of all pals:[*] 'In wartime, truth is so precious that she should always be attended by a bodyguard of lies.' Christ, he had a point.

'Aleister,' Orr began, 'military history is littered with daring ruses to baffle and deceive the enemy, leading to unlikely victories. The Turks had once lined up for battle and had their front line pull their swords, each individual then beheading himself to thoroughly terrify the enemy. It was later discovered that those headless corpses were those of their own criminals who took their own life to protect their families. The impact on the opponent proved to be pivotal, such was the awe that this action provoked. There were the fake letters in the Mamluk slave siege of 1271, the dummy cannons of the Quaker gun ruse in the American War of Independence, and in ancient Japan, Tokugawa's quite ingenuous variation of the Empty Fort Strategy. This same tactic had already been recognised by the ancient Chinese; they called it simply number thirty-two of

---

[*]   *Churchill.*

the thirty-six stratagems. You see, there have been many. Yes, grubby lies, if you will, but those hideously ugly ducklings sometimes blossom at the most fortuitous moment to save our world.'

These are those bodyguards, of which Winston spoke.

Orr continued: 'The Russians have a precise word for this tactic; *Maskirovka* [Маскировка]. It is deception Russian-style, methods bespokely designed in order to prevail and vanquish. It is masked warfare, smoke and mirrors and quite hard to define; the definition as slippery as the concept itself. The nearest we find in English might be *the little masquerade*.

'The unlikely Russian victory in the Battle of Kulikovo Field in 1380, when the Golden Hords of around 150,000 Tatar Mongols was defeated by fewer than 50,000 Russians, guaranteed Prince Dmitri's place in this nation's folklore. Equally, their unexpected attack of Minsk through the swamps and from the rear was a great example of *Maskirovka*; the sheer boldness reminiscent of Lawrence of Arabia's taking of Aqaba – with its vast guns pointed out to sea, because no one was insane enough to come through the desert – from behind. The ingredients of *Maskirovka* are surprise, denial, bluff, wrong-footing, the cover of night (literal or metaphorical) and mirage. There is usually a garnish of victory, if executed correctly.'

He then looked at the doctor and his nurse.

'Do you wish to continue?'

Prudence took up the story: 'Three is indeed a marvellous number. Our mischief politician–soldier, Churchill, our ripe Holy Man and you, our Occultist double agent, shall constitute a fine force one day soon. But, of course, the number six is twice as alluring.'

'Good Lord, who are the other three, then? Which poor bastards—?'

And they all bellowed together from their solar plexus, as if, yet again, scripted and directed by that cheap melodramatist. But its effect was potent and I had my answer.

And so, after I had joined in with their guffaws for a lengthy chortle, we were now SIX.

(Our seventh samurai was still a glint in my eye. Oh! Violet, my love.)

Our aim was never to start a Bolshevik revolution. We simply wanted to have an agent provocateur, a plant, an instigator and an influence in Moscow. I guess things would one day get out of hand, for we underestimated the power of that troublesome and quite magnificent monk. We were not perfect. We never said we were, but better to be too effective than not effective at all.

'Well, we will win,' Orr said, 'because *they* do not expect Dandylyon and Prudence here to be a connoisseur and connoisseuse of their own home-grown dark art. We shall beat them at their own game and on their own turf to boot. We shall collude with our protagonists, and antagonists, to affect who governs this land. We have learned from the Crimean War, and as The Legion discussed with your father in that honeysuckled garden outside Marylebone Station, war is a different beast now. We have to evolve to win, it is Darwinist, and our survival depends on it.'

And so, Cambridge began its lengthy fuck-feud with Russia, and I was there. We soon infiltrated her royal family, her politics, prompted her revolution and so her destiny. It was not via the obvious route of their blood relatives in Buckingham Palace, but by our new friend, the Holy Man. Our Gang of Six was formed. Russia would use this same furrowed plough of dark and secret mischief back to Cambridge many decades later. Like two mauve wizards casting spells across the Highlands, the scrap had begun.

I now stir in my Himalayan paradise to turn that tide one last time. I think of and chuckle at the eleventh commandment of spying. 'Thou shalt not get caught.'

12 December 1895

And so we returned to England with a sense of achievement, as we had our man, it seemed. I still pondered at the impact that this peasant might have, but Dandylyon assured me that the Empire was a safer place, because of the monk's whispered agreement in Prudence's ear. I trusted my old friend's wisdom implicitly.

'It may take ten or twenty years,' he told me. 'But the future shall be controlled by us. In the spirit of the luscious lady who gets everything she desires, we now control our own fates. This should give you great comfort, Aleister.'

It did. And even greater excitement.

'But what exactly did you whisper to him?' I asked her.

'The only thing that could possibly make sense to him.'

'Which is what?'

She smiled.

'Tell me! Tell me!'

'You have to guess.'

'It is a long journey back to Cambridge. Let's have some real fun. Let's see how good you will be at this lark. You have twenty questions, Perdurabo. Let's see how this wunderkind performs.'

'I accept the challenge.'

'You only win if you deduce all the details,' added Dandy-lyon.

'Of course,' I said.

I sat in the compartment of four, next to the window and faced south as we travelled out of St Petersburg. The frigid temperature outside left adequate condensation on the inside of the window, and I doodled in the smallest segment by my right hand. Prudence and Dandylyon sat opposite to me and Orr to my left. I glanced at Prudence from time to time, and wondered if she already knew I was formulating not only my answer but how to deliver it to her before Waterloo.

When we were an hour from Minsk, I sat forward with a firm intent, looked at her, and then said nothing, as if I had lifted a chess piece only to regret my intended move. I said nothing, but as they all nodded off, I concluded that her agreement with the monk revolved around sex, and so I drew genitalia on the carriage window, and as we sat stationary in Minsk, I completed the doodle by incorporating it into my signature. It would be one that would last forever.

When she woke from her nap near the Polish border, I observed her to see if she was aware of my artwork. It appeared that she was not.

Of course, Rasputin wanted to fuck her. But I needed the details. As we neared Warsaw, I concluded that she had agreed. At each node on our journey thereafter, about the time when she might ordinarily have expected one of the questions, I made another firm and silent deduction in the spirit of Holmes, Dupin and Lecoq. By Berlin, I knew that the impact of the coupling would be to cause maximum impact, for the Holy Man's vanity was unquestionable. By Cologne, it was clear to me that maximum degradation was key too, so sodomy was involved, as was an insult to the church. Each conclusion was made with another image on the damp window. Now, there was a hangman's noose, a crown, a throne, a crucifix, an arse and a royal palace.

I wondered briefly whether one of the Prudences had met any of the Rasputins before in a different epoch across the ages. I considered the lofty levels of ribald, mischief and cunning their antecedents might have cast across their lands. Did they share an intertwined past in the same way as Prudence had with Dandylyon? What a treasure trove of devilry and pranks that would be. I didn't mention it.

By Brussels, I knew there also had to be maximum arousal, and by Calais, I was close to breaking my silence. But I knew there had to be a better way of simply telling my friends of my single and layered answer. And so, I executed a cheap but neat trick; one where Prudence was to find a parchment within her passport as she was questioned in our carriage by HM Customs upon entry into England. This scrap of paper bore my handwriting in an ink of her own maroon, even though I carried none upon my person, and her passport had not left her bosom. When she saw this paper, and the words *Open It, Unrivalled Witch* scribbled on it, she looked at me, and knew that I knew. She began to nod her head, as she rose and wiped the clues from the window, already proud of their judgement.

For the record, the words she was to find were as follows:

You have not just agreed to a buggering on the Czar's throne! You actually crave it. And you have demanded an audience of nuns and monks as witnesses, whose group testimony shall torture the Czar at a time of His, the Monk's, and Your choosing.

Before he read the parchment, Dandylyon had already aggressively ruffled my hair, and said, 'Good lad.' And laughed like a proud father.

And as we neared London, Prudence leaned forward and spoke softly just to me, 'Yes, you're right. Aleister. But a real

genius would have offered some conjecture that one of the
Prudences had met one of the Rasputins before in a different
century.'

I thought of *esprit de l'escalier*. That most annoying of
moments when we realise we had the perfect retort in an argu-
ment, but it is now moments too late to deliver it.

I said nothing to her of what I had considered earlier; that
I had mulled this precise possibility, but kept silent on it.

But when I removed my shirt back at St John's Street, I
found a note, in parchment form and eerily similar to the one
I had planted upon her. In fact, when I flipped it over it was
the same one. It was now *from* her. Her words read:

> Of course, a genius would have thought of a Prudence
> and a Rasputin coupling throughout the centuries, like
> soaked and rabid wolves. And I know that you did. But
> what is important is that a genius *spy* would also have
> said nothing, even when prompted by his loving witch.
> Good boy.

3.8 A PLACE TO BURY STRANGERS

Back in Cambridge, life, for the immediate future, was as it
had been for this Beast from day one with Pollitt. I maintained
a complete disregard for the curriculum, while I cultivated the
most fertile soil of my mind, my ambitions for mischief and
my groin – in any and all directions. I played the fop to perfection, fooling friends, acquaintances, current and future foes,
biographers, deans and publishers. The spirit of the Scarlet
Pimpernel had begun to fool the imbeciles and those who were
not quite a full shilling once again. I regretted less each day
that I had to keep the secrets of MI-1, Rasputin and Churchill
to myself, away from Pollitt. My poetry remained the simplest
mask, for in those days these fools were easy to deceive,

hungry as they were for insipid sentiment and putridly saccharine verse. They lapped this rubbish up.

> I contemplate the wound
> Stabbed in the flanks of my dear silver Christ.
> He hangs in anguish there; the crown of thorns
> Pierces that palest brow; the nails drip blood;
> There is the wound; no Mary by Him mourns,
> There is no John beside the cruel wood,
> I am alone to kiss the silver lips;
> I rend my clothing for the temple veil;
> My heart's black night must act the sun's eclipse;
> My groans must play the earthquake, till I quail
> At my own dark imagining; and now
> The wind is bitter; the air breeds snow;
> I put my Christ away.

I shudder at the poem, but such is the shackle of a Scarlet Pimpernel. I understand the modern-day superhero is also bound by some moribund daily employment and must fake dopery. I suppose there is wisdom in this, and, I was discovering, much fun too.

And, as further cover for my duplicity, I soon wrote an unpublished manuscript, a weepy and sappy offering called *Aceldama: A Place to Bury Strangers In.* It was dedicated to Pollitt, as my Lord and Lover, even though my bed was now occupied by a potentially useful type called Oscar Eckenstein. I could still not decide whether I had enjoyed Pollitt more in men's or women's clothing, for he made for a stunning filly when on the stage at Footlights.* That troop of lads, fellows and transvestites, continued, though I still could not *fully*

---

* *Cambridge's revered amateur dramatics and comedy stage.*

expunge the thought of woman from my mind. It was my destiny to discover both to their fullest.

Eckenstein, however, was an intriguing and odd fish. He was far older than I, by sixteen years. We were bonded by our love of mountaineering and had met in the Bernese Alps in early '97. His family was of Prussian stock, and he was thrilled to learn of my membership of the Scottish Mountaineering Club. It was a well-established myth that the English club was a rancid clique. I boasted that I despised them and that I would thrive in the meritocracy of the Scots. However, over dinner at George's, Eckenstein confirmed my suspicions of the true motive in front of a nodding Dandylyon. In reality, the English were truly fine chaps, acted like arseholes on purpose, and secretly encouraged agents provocateurs, such as I, to join the Scots, who, despite their presence on our British rock and their blue on the Union flag, still harboured rebellious tendencies that stretched back to the Tudor alliances and beyond. German spies were also well known (and covertly encouraged) to pierce the Scottish Mountaineering Club in Switzerland, usually through the joyous vices of sodomy and blackmail.

And so, I had therefore been 'placed' initially by the English (Prudence, Orr, Dandylyon, Churchill et al.) as a pioneering black pawn, then a flanking rook, and latterly an offensive queen to maraud, do my duty and cause bloody havoc within the Scottish club. It should be remembered that the air is so thin up in the Swiss peaks that the minutely affected opponent is devoured, especially when I was the disarming nitwit fop, reading (or even worse writing) poetry and practising yoga. This would be fun.

It was now 1899 and a rebellious and excited fizz could be sensed on the streets of London and of the cerebral Cambridge.

Life was a procession of Dorian Grays and naughty girls, self-pollution was never a choice. My days were also fakery, acting, espionage, opium and cocaine, invocations and ancient runes. I would soon be leaving university without a degree, having learned infinitely more than the clods and nitwits in gowns. I was following my own star within the Golden Dawn; a dark inspection of the continuum that runs between alchemy, meditation, science, love and magick, melded together by powerful intoxicants that would soon convince me and especially my followers of its own truth.

Those who thought they observed me saw a rich, young poet–scholar, full of his own bluster. Not one of them was surprised, or perhaps even cared, when I announced that my next step was to go up to London to meet Royalty. But it was true.

> The burden of bought boys. Behold, dear Lord,
> How plump their buttocks be, lift up Thine eyes,
> See how their cocks stand at an amorous word,
> How their lips suck out life until love dies,
> See, Lord, Thou knowest, how wearily one lies
> Cursing the lusts that fail, the deeds that tire;
> Shrunk is San Cresce to a sorry size.
> This is the end of every man's desire.
>
> – *White Stains*, Aleister Crowley

PART TWO

The truth is incontrovertible. Malice may attack it, ignorance may deride it, but in the end, there it is.

History will be kind to me for I intend to write it.

– Winston Churchill

Chapter 4

A Time for Youthful Mischief

When Celia cums, 'tis earthquake hour. The bed vibrates
    like kettledrums
It is a grand display of power when Celia cums.
When Celia farts, my hasty nose
Sniffs up the fragrance from her parts
Shamed are the violets and rose when Celia farts.

                                  – Aleister Crowley

A pious man* *of the church once said of black magic, quite rightly I believe, 'The lowest depths of black mysticism are well-nigh as difficult to plumb as it is arduous to scale the heights of sanctity. The Grand Masters of the witch covens are men of genius – a foul genius, crooked, distorted, disturbed, and diseased.' It has been the folly of many less wise than he to equate any study that veers from the Scriptures of Christ, to be labelled as black magic. I repeat here, it is folly.*

                             *

---

* *Augustus Montague Summers (10 April 1880–10 August 1948) – English scholar and perhaps the closest equivalent we have to Abraham Van Helsing.*

It is now almost time to go from here and expose myself to my true age in the mountain pass. I have known of others of a similar age turn to dust there. Few of them swaggered, most of them tip-toed, perhaps unwisely to their end.

And so to likely self-slaughter I shall stride. But not before an almighty brawl with Death in an unseen sphere. I shall smack him in the nose again en route. At the very least, I shall scarlet the fucker's beak.

And if I can survive the pass, there are plenty who would murder me by the time I reach Cambridge. There are those against whom I am going to rally the most unyielding and smartest of mobs. There is a new generation of those whom I have defeated, slighted and cheated in the past; governments, Nazis, agents, cuckolds.

But in 1900, I was about to enter a world where one was unsure as to who wished to fire the bullet, tie the noose, why and when. I felt untouchable, but was spry enough to know I might soon be in real and perpetual danger, and that my complacency was a function of my lordly spirit and not of reality. I would need the finest of teachers to survive and thrive. Yet again, fortune was mine.

And so now I appear as a shameless cliché. My feet are in sandals and I wear a long sack robe of ridiculous comfort. My hair has long since departed, though I do so much enjoy the deportment and stature offered by a hat of extravagant girth.

I rise and stroll from the lea through the gardens towards the perfect yards with their simple dwellings, fountains and altars that then lead to the wilder pastures. I seem to inch there as if I do not want to arrive at my destination. It is as if I know this time is precious and truly Holy. I speak to myself and am aware that I am perhaps acting eccentrically as I chuckle, I reprimand and admonish parenthetically, I nod sage agreement at irregular intervals as if I am having several conversations at once. Perhaps

I am. Throughout and despite the oddness, I maintain an appearance of an overriding sanity, for I am, after all, a remarkable, transcendent and calming giant; a Kurtzian Lord. I pass a chubby, picturesque child playing with stones, who gargles a grand joy.

'Solitude is such a glorified and authentic pastime,' I say. She smiles and nods.

Ten hours to go.

4.1 POMP AND UNSENSIBLE PATHS OF GLORY

Sir Horace Dandylyon was now personal physician to the Palace.

On my first afternoon back in London, he and I spoke predominantly of Churchill.

'You will meet Winston in good time. For now, I will remain his post boy. Spies are everywhere, and the less you two are seen together, the better,' he revealed, as we sipped flutes of champagne in his club in St James.

'Of course.'

'But there is something else we need to discuss.'

He touched my arm.

'The Queen is unwell,' Dandylyon said.

'Long live the Queen,' I dutifully replied.

'Her illness can never be known, for, as I will presently explain, it would risk her crown. The Empire would be rattled just when she needs to be strong.'

'But she will go one day soon. She is no goddess.'

'You do not fully understand what I am saying. Let us sit.'

We walked out onto one of the broad stone terraces on the second floor of the club. Other than the two of us, the spacious balcony was empty as we sat. Dandylyon elaborated on the Queen's condition.

'She has an ailment of the blood. There are wider implications for they tell of bigamy in the palaces. We should all remember what happened in France.'

I said nothing. After a brief pause, he spoke again.

'What do you know of haemophilia? And also of porphyria?'

'Sicknesses of the blood and the nervous system?'

'Precisely, and that is all you need to know. What is more important to know is that Her Majesty suffers from one and not the other. Not only is there is a robust school of thought that says Queen Victoria and Albert are both of bastard stock, for there are abundant clues now exposed to science and to me, but there has also been an abrupt cessation of paternal and hereditary syphilis in Albert's case and the introduction of the inherited haemophilia in Victoria's. Not only are they first cousins – and this alone is of little consequence to England or the realm, but they are both illegitimate. And *this* is.'

He nodded, and then stroked his beard, releasing a raft of sweet bakery air.

'Her father had a procession of young and ripe mistresses for nearly three decades that never resulted in any offspring. His sexual relations with the Queen's mother were lustless and putridly stale. This would no doubt raise the chances of a random mutation and introduction of haemophilia from perhaps fifty thousand to one to a far larger number, tending towards infinity. The Duchess of Kent,* I am afraid, had illicit proclivities too. When Wellington said that he had even witnessed 'some familiarities' between Her Majesty and Sir John Conroy, he was, as usual, quite correct.'

Dandylyon paused. He spoke with a tone that implied it would very soon have a very personal impact upon me.

---

*   *Queen Victoria's mother.*

'And not only did haemophilia appear, but porphyria suddenly disappeared. Conroy was her father. The revelation of all this would be disastrous, and inevitable were our enemies ever to find out. It would be far more damaging than their finding out that I supplied her with far more than her fair share of cocaine, heroin, brandy and laudanum. Or how I witnessed her when she'd had too much of everything; abject, growling, needy, unprincipled, magnificently soulless and absolute fun. Bless the old bird.'

This was London in 1900, the Great Binge* was at her pie-eyed peak. The unwashed were far more intrigued with Jack the Ripper and vampires than narcotics available on every corner, but a rattling of the very core of the legitimacy of the Crown and the realm could spell diplomatic disaster around the world and quite likely the swelling of an angry mob of pitchforkers on Constitution Hill. The doctors of the royal families of Europe would certainly have had all the same medical information and clues within their grasp, but would they have the nous of Dandylyon to deduce the implications. Yes, it would reflect badly upon their houses too should the bastard Queen be revealed, and of course, they had all almost crumbled together under the revolutionary skies of '48, but England would be injured the most. It was time therefore to meddle overseas and strike first.

Why? Because to attack truly is the sturdiest form of defence, and to obfuscate and deflect attention can be enough to befuddle those pitchforkers. MI-1 were keen to instigate wide-ranging and covert operations across all continents. 'The more the merrier,' Winston said.

---

* *The Great Binge describes the period in history, covering roughly 1875 to 1914, when drugs and alcohol were readily available and marketed to all, even children.*

But where and how?

In Africa, Winston planned to develop anti-Prussian alliances with the French and Belgian colonials, even the Dutch, for he suspected their path of least resistance would be to side with us when it all exploded. European policy was a microcosm of Africa's, as we jockeyed for anti-German positions with each ally; friendships that could be quite pivotal. The enemy of one's enemy shall be one's chum. In Australia and New Zealand, MI-1 would instil and promote a logical and gravitational fear of the Japanese dropping down upon them, and in doing so would cement that corner of the Empire, so geographically crucial to London, while also ensuring some brave and mighty fucking muscle in the scraps to come. In the East, we aimed to keep Tokyo, Peking and Moscow inward-looking and navel-gazing. I would find myself at the fulcrum of the coming war there.

I would find myself at a similar pivot in the United States[*], though there I would be meddling in their peace. In India, of course, we had given them cricket; the opium of the Raj, and that would keep them busy with boyhood dreams of glory with cork or willow. If only it were all so simple, and yet, of course, all of this confirmed that we lived in the most textured and magnificent world.

There would be many ways we would meddle over the decades, but, for me, it would begin with the procurement of a (perhaps) mythical aphrodisiacal drug with precipitously potent effects; ones of manly desires of the flesh and great pacifism. This narcotic had been spoken of in fairy tales by Prudences over the centuries. Had it fuelled Caligula and the Romans? Had it taught the Greeks to sodomise? Had it got

---

[*]   *I shall tell more of this almost immediately.*

Christ into trouble with whores, earning him the silent respect of the Romans in the process? Apparently, Churchill was thrilled when he heard of it. If we were able to get our hands on this, and poison the right wells and spike the relevant champagne cocktails, then vast slaughter could be prevented, and minds could be changed towards our point of view. Children were even said to be immune to it, other than it made them supremely tranquil, content and marginally less hungry. This stuff was to be found in nature in the hinterlands and jungle floors of the country we know in modern times as Sri Lanka, my darling, darling land.

And so, I was given my orders, my tickets to Ceylon and the firmest of manly hugs from Dandylyon and a kiss from Prudence. I counted my blessings in many arenas, but this man and woman had become the sturdiest cornerstone of my knowledge and my life. I was now going on my first solo mission, and there had not yet been a thrill anywhere close to matching this one. I resolved that I would do them all proud, Papa included. As if all of this excitement were not enough, I was about to meet perhaps my greatest love.

Robbie and I met, by chance, in the mountains of Ceylon at the ambassador's estate outside Maha Nuwara. Seeping with gin and tonics, we played billiards until dawn for small change under a tilting fan. It was April 1900, and I was in my *fin de siècle* pomp. We were both in our pomp. Robbie's father was there as a guest of the ambassador, they had schooled together at Eton and, both with an overactive sense of nostalgia, had remained hush-hush lovers ever since. Robbie appeared quite bored, and superbly willing to undertake an adventure, far more easily than I had ever hoped while I plotted over our memorable games that daybreak. 'Oh goody,' was Robbie's response when I suggested a stroll in the rainforests. That I used those two same words myself whenever mischief was offered seemed symbiotic and more than fitting. Robbie wrote a note to father that was left at the bar.

Accepted most thrilling adventure. Off I trot into the jungles, Papa. Too tempting to refuse. Back whenever.
   Yours, R.

And so, we discharged ourselves from the ambassador's company with nothing but a few wagered coins in our pockets, tilted hats upon our heads, and two pint glasses of icy gin, as if we were in the Crown and Anchor in Covent Garden and off into the alleyway for a slash. We walked through mile upon mile of tea fields until we came to the temple. Its approximate location had been confirmed to me by a Maharishi as my ship had throbbed and pulsed down the Suez Canal weeks before.

We spoke of our childhoods, as I glanced with consummate calm and tempered intrigue from time to time to observe the petit and angelic features of my new chum, the small button nose, verdant eyes with lashes, as long and sturdy as spider legs, hair lightened by the sun but waxed with a comforting and coconutty pomade, the leanest jaw and unblemished teeth. Robbie spoke with the authority of an older and wiser type, but the calm with which the words were delivered removed anything as gross as pomposity. This was a lesson I knew many believed I could learn, but I was, after all, acting a role, for I was a Pimpernel. Robbie spoke of a love of Sicily, Blake and warm rain.

'But do you prefer Blake to Milton?' I asked as a strong breeze, even despite the cover of jungle, started to push at our backs.

'I prefer *Paradise Regained* to *Paradise Lost.*'

'You do? Why?'

'Well, it is clearer. It is more optimistic. And I root for Jesus. Jesus wins. But it is the Jesus we imagine, not the one force-fed in England. *Regained*'s Christ is the lovely fucker, who picked his nose, refused to bathe and laughed with strumpets. I think what strikes me most though is how Milton's poetry has matured, and he does not seem to try too hard anymore. He is at peace with himself, and this happiness shows and transmits itself.'

This sounded so familiar to me.

'Are these your own thoughts? Or those of some sage who schooled you?'

Robbie remained silent, and that seemed to be its own answer and the one I wanted. The quiet was then comfortable, until broken, 'I would be happy to give you plenty of my own thoughts, if you wish, you cheeky bastard.'

And we laughed and stumbled on, aided by that friendly breeze. When it dropped and the accompanying howling abated, I asked Robbie, 'How old are you?'

Robbie did not answer. Just smiled.

Upon our arrival at the monastery, we were welcomed as liberators, as marvelled guests, as gods. There, young Robbie and I smoked opium and lost days, weeks perhaps. The monks, with hair down to their midriffs, tended to us and smiled at our conditions.

When it was time to move on, they wished us well and we departed. We left the temple not by the way we had entered. We walked on. Of course, we did.

We passed through jungle and climbed hillsides. We bathed in streams and respectfully eyed a couple of intrigued tigers.

We sometimes walked barefoot with abandon, and once a plump snake slipped from our path ahead. Our faces were creaseless and portrayed a juvenation and an intrigue that far surpassed nosiness. We spoke of what we would do if we did find our treasure. We spoke of what we would do if we invoked the Devil. We spoke of beautiful women. I spoke of my reluctant and adolescent yearning to kill, if ever required. I was but a boy. I attempted to coax my pal to speak of ill-lit wishes, but naught came.

That next day we felt a distinctive tackiness underfoot, the one precisely told to me by Prudence. We had indeed found what we were looking for, and we set up a quite basic camp with a measured mix of excitement and trepidation. I had heard it was a hallucinogen of vast potent, an incapacitating agent of precipitous disturbance, an aphrodisiac of frightening gradient (it is true, for that evening I tried to coax a lynx from a tree, and I remain grateful-ish that she remained a shy yet humbled and honoured coquette). It was a toffee-cum-resin-like substance that emitted a distinctive odour of fried onions. This was the other clue that we had indeed arrived at the right spot.

At dusk, we lit a fire, not for warmth, but to aid the absorption of the drug, it was best taken warm, apparently. An amount to cover a thumbnail was recommended for first-timers. I ensured Robbie had approximately this. Robbie saw me take this same amount, though I took much more, of course, when Robbie wasn't looking. I was thrilled to find out that Robbie had done the exact same thing. We prodded at the jungle floor with sticks and scratched armpits and arses, waiting for something to happen. I held my breath to accelerate a blood-flow. Robbie did several dozen push-ups, as I pulled myself up on branches to prompt the narcotic to take hold.

And then it happened.

We saw blurred etchings of the future that week as we melded into the trees, unsure if those rabid frothings we heard were our own or from the volcano beneath our leavened torsos and rafted souls. Each of us emitted a gentle aura of turquoise, lilac and death-white.

We sat against the trunks of trees, euphoric and immaculate. Our thirsts were sated merely by chewing on leaves, and our silence reigned magnificently.

Three young monks joined us in our revelry. It seemed that they might have followed us with intent. They found much more of the resin with ease, for they had walked this path before. They told us this in their own tongue, which we understood with clarity within the lucid and memorable high. They were neither forbidden to come here nor would be frowned upon when they returned. Their choice remained the utmost force both for them and for their peers. Their choice, their Will. Upon this matter and all others, we found a unanimous and hallowed accord. They then copulated skilfully, tenderly and yet like amorous monsters, as we chums ate more and more toffee, picking it out of our teeth as the boys, in front of us, sought impressive sacrilege, athletic profanity and astonishing desecration. They, too, shone with a turquoise, lilac and death-white aura.

It was rare, perhaps previously unknown, for me to turn down such banquets of flesh. (Oh goody! Young monks might have sufficed where my flirtatious, naughty and quite luscious jungle tree-cat had offered so much.) But out of respect for my new friend, Robbie, I would observe; a process which bubbled and boiled my loins to a transcendental spectrum of vividity; a process I encouraged and stoked and watched with a concentrated vigour equal to my stares across the verdant jungle floor at the gloried permutations of sodomy and fellatious pleasure in progress before us. We both refused to look away from the Bacchus, as rain poured upwards from the jungle floor and to the thirsty skies, and we appeared as laughing skeletons, only our hearts visible in our chests while hundreds of monks came to observe the week-long coitus. I shelved the peak of my aroused rigidity for after our farewell, as the men either elevated themselves up to vantage points of high branch or lowered themselves to the cushioned, leafy earth. They seemed to melt into the jungle as would have (and perhaps had) a thousand chameleons, and some days it was only the rich and connoisseur's detail of their fecund and ribald chatter about the exhausted and eager boys that allowed us to know that they were there at all. I had simply no idea how long we had been there. This would only be gauged by when I arrived back in civilisation.

The toffee had allowed us glimpses of the future, images that would stay with Robbie and me both, and allow us to resolve our life paths, mine at least for the next twelve or thirteen decades. We would have no choice, having seen what we had seen. We had to save England, and accomplish this in our bespoke and most well-suited manners. We were two different characters, and so our methods, while being equally audacious and effective, would follow separate, yet dovetailing paths. Robbie's were quiet, unassuming and helpful, mine were brash and public. I shall elaborate presently. Ours would be wholly brave and unsensible paths of glory, as I realised why we had been welcomed as liberators by the monks, for they too had taken the toffee and knew of the future of the world. And our pivotal place in it.

4.2 WISDOM THROUGH PACIFIC RAFTS OF BURNED WEED
In the magnificent afterglow, we scrubbed each other's backs

in the waterfalls; in solidarity against the power of and in tune with the strong drug, as well as in unison against a fearsome future, like hard, crooked Welsh miners of concrete spine at the end of fifteen hours of hard labour under the earth. My chance meeting with Robbie had indeed been a fortuitous one, for we complimented each other quite perfectly. I knew that Dandylyon and Prudence would approve of my new recruit, who had agreed to be complicit in my immediate task of finding that wondrous hallucinogenic toffee substance, as we traversed those lordly mountainsides. I had been offered the latitude by my mentors to add soldiers, conspirators, allies and *compadres* in exceptional circumstances, and these were indeed exceptional, for we searched for a drug to manage, medicate and pacify mankind. My sound judgement – as to *whom* I recruited – had been proven by my silence and our exchanged parchment on that train from Russia to Waterloo.

As we washed each other with the innocence of siblings, I suspected already that I was in love with Robbie. I knew it was more than the aphrodisiac, coursing through me still, though the drug – and our abstinence – clearly aided and abetted my sentiments. The waterfalls were loud, so I shouted in Robbie's ear, allowing more skin to touch. We were surrounded by lush and tall Indian tuberoses, wrapping us in the most delicious smells. Crazed birds sang and the skies were deep blue between the emerald leaf.

'Were you afraid?'

'I am not sure. I was fearful of something, but I was not afraid. I am not even sure if that makes sense,' Robbie shouted. I think that's what I heard.

We stepped away from the full force of the cascades, and were able to hear each other far better. I was also afforded a better look at the nude front of my friend, who continued, 'There were details, faces and cities that were and still are remarkably clear, but I am struggling to see how it fits together in any kind of order, path or trajectory. I might need to take some more. It was quite astonishing fun. Did you have the kind of epiphany you were hoping for? Were *you* afraid?'

'I barely know where or how to begin,' I said. 'I can recall the most minute detail in some moments, but these are defined for me, dated throughout the century, as if I were able to see the front page of *The Times* for decades, and each time I see a headline, I am part of the story. War, love, euphoria, misery, ignominy and glory. Precisely what I might have predicted of my existence. But I could never have foreseen the clarity and the measure of each sensation. But tell me of the small parts that you did see of *your* future?'

Robbie did not answer for a while, and then spoke, 'My life will be seen through a woman's eyes until the end of a Great War. Then my life and my world will be that of a male. My visions do not seem to have the clarity of yours. They are murky, patchy. What does this mean, Aleister?'

I sensed trepidation and fear for a few seconds before the glory of our previous days filled our beings again.

'I am not sure. I know that I must go to China. I know that this is where my next mission shall be. I know that I have succeeded in my first. I have met you, and I have found the narcotic. Will you agree to work with me? Help me? If you do, I can let you in on the most magnificent secret. And we might have the most ecstatic time of it. Please.'

I knew what the answer would be, for I had seen such complicity in my visions. I was to send Robbie west to rendezvous with Prudence in Constantinople.

I saw how green Robbie's eyes were, as we stood enveloped in jungle and waterfall and silence and mutual worship.

'Rather! Father has been encouraging a vocation anyway.

Let's make the old bastard happy. But keep him guessing first. You're on!'

How could either of us turn back now? Robbie moved forward in the shin-high pools of crystal froth, and took me in her arms, where I remained for many minutes, after which, she whispered, 'I am sixteen.'

She was a game bird; my Ms. Roberta Honeydew. Yes, Robbie was a lass. I had known this since she revealed her boyish disguise by the Ambassador's billiard table, by having grabbed my left wrist and thrust my paw onto her womanly vitals. It then became quite obvious she was a lass, and I was bewildered as to how she might ever have passed as a bloke. Her hair was cropped at the sides and back, like any young lad's, her slight frame was bosomless, her arse cheeks those of any athletic scamp I had seen at university. Her voice was magnificently hermaphroditic; if one wanted to hear male, one heard male. She certainly played billiards with the dexterity of a seasoned colonel. However, if one had felt her fine pubis, then the secret was out, and if there was one thing I was able to do to the level of godliness, well, that was to keep a secret. I was a Pimpernel *en apprentice*. Robbie too fitted the bill of being able to maintain a lie, a trait perfectly in keeping with what I had planned. Her ability to shape-shift between the sexes might also prove to be an intriguing arrow in one's espionage quiver.

And so we slipped away to the forests fuelled, for we had foreseen our immediate destinies, and then on to different ports to facilitate our departures in different directions. I was robust in my determination to suck all from these coming years, prescient of looming events and aware that the world was facing a century of bloodshed and murder, and with it a diminishing of our generation and our continent's astonishing binge. This was our heaven. This was our youth. Our time. Our now.

Dandylyon and Prudence had told me that I would likely receive clues to my next assignment in the visions from the resin. Again, latitude was mine, and all they asked for was a regular and coded message to a nearby embassy or consul. If I were stranded and needed advice, the goo would act as my spirit guide.

Robbie and I knew our fortunes were independent but intertwined. Our goals were England's. Our methods were marvellously immiscible: hers the virtuous, brave and right-eous; mine the proudly tainted, mischievous and obsidian. Both were straight-backed and audacious. Both puked at piety.

We parted and embraced with a measure that was exact and profound in its measuredness. One went north to the naval base of Kankesanthurai, a vast spit off Jaffna, whence trade to and from India passed; and one went east to the fishing port of Oluvil in Ampara, for we knew that our individual arcs were to begin here. That naughty and demanding resinous jungle-floor toffee had told me so, and yet we were both pleasurably and obediently cuffed, lectured and enslaved to the stuff.

As we left that orgiastic island, my pockets and my mouth were stuffed with the ecstatic goo. My hat held priceless ounces, and over my shoulder, a monk's liberated robes carried a hefty seam of the stuff. Just the gunk under my fingernails and between my teeth could have fuelled much revelry for a fortnight.

Robbie swanned west across mill pond and cerulean waters of bliss, while I went east only to hit a monstrous cyclone that left three crew members dead. The captain did not have to commit their bodies to the ocean floor, for they were likely already there. He might however have spoken of a cursed fat-thumbed Englishman who had shackled himself naked to the mast, halfway up to the crow's nest, and who had done so before the eye of the awesome beast hit us. He might have whispered of the madman's maintained arousal throughout the storm, for he had remained visible to the befuddled and impressed skipper. In my pidgin Sinhalese, I had explained that I would appease nature and be her first sacrifice, if required. This did not explain the three who perished during those two days and two nights of quite sensational terror.

I only became aware of the extent of the typhoon as we approached Singapore – our torn ship was still afloat by some miracle of physics – and the undulating and euphoric impact of the devilishly persistent toffee eventually began to subside. The intensity of the storm had, without a doubt, maintained and lengthened my transcendental and hallucinogenic magic carpet ride. Once untied from the mast, with a predominantly flaccidated and aching member, my launched seed washed by nature from my thighs, knees and feet, and robed in a strip of tattered sail, the sparking of a very large roll of hashish and dampish tobacco was to allow for a quite magnificent landing. The passengers were a mottled bunch of circus acrobats, British Army lads, resourceful whores and wayward spice-sellers from the Silk Road. They and the crew chatted, attempted to avoid all eye contact and bowed their submissive, deferential and possibly concerned heads as I passed them all on deck in a dense-ish cloud formation of pacific rafts of burned weed. Wisdom comes in many forms, and theirs was a visceral and disciplined one, and one that averted its gaze from this spirited being.

4.3 How to Fuck a Queen

I understand those who say that one should never mix business with pleasure. They are, however, in the wrong business.

The resin in my pockets, under my hat, in my stuffed and folded robes and even under my fingernails was not only for recreational purposes. This drug was also the cornerstone of my new career. What a lucky boy I now was.

I left England to meddle in politics, always with peace and England's illustrious fortunes and those of her allies in mind. Now I dabbled in provocation and acted as peacemaker, wherever it would benefit Whitehall. My apprenticeship would begin in the seedlings of the Boxer Rebellion. Dandylyon and I had exchanged relayed telegrams, via the British embassy in Singapore. He was thrilled to learn of the discovery and of the potency of the stuff. He wrote back.

> PERDURABO. STOP. DO AS YOUR HEART AND WILL TELL YOU. STOP. SEEK MING OF RED MIST IN QUFU, SHANDONG PROVINCE. STOP. THE BLINDFOLDED CHESSMASTER SHALL PLAY WITH HIS QUEEN.

Northern China was hostile turf. The regular notes between Robbie and me, whose delivery relied upon a well-established network of Orr's spies, tell of how I founded a mob of prac-tised pugilistic warriors, and named them 'The Righteous and Harmonious Fists'. And then later, how I convinced them that their expertise in calisthenics would make them impervious to bullets. I was the only foreigner they would suffer, for their goal was to rid China of all Western devils, as well as to over-throw the Ch'ing dynasty that had ruled for a quarter of a millennium. The international force that was soon sent to China to quell the northern rebels was a semi-honourable, semi-self-interested and thoroughly mixed one – American, Russian, British, French, Italian, Japanese, Indian – and it was through this very alliance of my own urging that war was quelled in Europe for the next fifteen years. The satisfaction of introducing several problems or obstacles (which here were mistrust between European nations, pending war and famine across China, my immediate future, progress and success as a spy) to each other and walking away with a single unfettered solution (a union of sex, drugs, love, peace, mischief, alliances and revolution) with zero by-product or waste shall please me to my final days. Well, this was one such unmessy process.

I worked the other side as a double agent too. The Empress Dowager Cixi sat on the throne of China, and was the true target of the insurgents. She was a seasoned mare, some might say elderly, but she exhibited adequately juvenile tendencies for her and this Englishman to eat toffee resin together in late 1900. Her well-brewed loins, more than five decades older than mine, were favoured upon me, as I marvelled at her while heavily influenced by the narcotic, and glad I had been so, for she was a ferocious and quite excellent lover. I can still hear her wide range of released guttural purrs and pleasured yelps. Her Majesty was such a marvellous vocal musician, while being strummed; a fine, fine trick to pull off. During these moments, she liked to shriek and yell the lyrics of 'Hoichi the Earless', an odd choice as it was a song of Japanese legend.

'Why do you sing in Japanese? You seem to venerate them so,' I asked her.

She answered in Mandarin.

我唱歌，这样没人能理解我的痛苦和我的喜悦

My understanding of the language was in its infancy, so she kindly translated for me into perfect English.

'I sing it so no one can understand my agony or my joy,' she said to me as we bathed one day, my taut skin intertwined with her loose rolls. The Oedipal overtones of sticking it to my mother one last time were not lost on me.

*

The Boxers – in Mandarin, *Yihetuan,* or the Militia United in Righteousness – trusted me throughout, but when I returned to their insurgent slopes with a broad man's fistful of her jewellery and her marginally tarnished silk underwear (both given by her as gifts, I must add), then I was heralded as a truly lordly type, and my status was legend. The females (and some of the more rebellious rebels) eyed me with an even more twisted and aroused countenance and I duly satisfied their curiosity. And so, the siege of Peking that lasted for just under eight weeks was a mock one, arranged in advance by Her Majesty and me. The city was filled with food and medicine for the duration, and the number fifty-five was decided upon by the difference in our ages, much to her amusement, and only ever shown in private.

Her Majesty would get her wish for greater support from her generals and the provinces, notoriously unruly, especially so under the reign of a female. Those who plotted against her would be exposed like cockroaches in the light, and rightfully slaughtered once the mild faux scrap was over. I got what I wanted with a European alliance that aided peace closer to home until the Great War, and I learned how to fuck a queen. It seemed to sum up what this spy lark was all about. Drugs, sex, royalty, chess-like machinations and, of course, POWER.

I smile, for I could, given I had started a mini-war just to divert it, be quite the diplomat.

I was saddened to leave China, but I knew there was a job to be done, and my departure would allow for that most beautiful of things, which is returning to China.

The spy is imbued with a Protestant work ethic, and there is always work to be done.

'Where will you go next, English boy?' she asked me.

'Africa.'

'Will you come back here to your decumbent and eager queen?'

'Even if you were to give me all the tea in China, I would not stay away, Your Majesty.'

'Good. Now go. And leave me a handful of that goo by which to remember you.'

She allowed her robes to fall, and I was unable to prevent myself from falling on her one last time.

She had eaten the toffee, could see the future, and knew I was not coming back.

Thus, the power-meddling continued as Robbie and I straddled Africa, and wrote to each other of the early clashes with Dutch farmers by the Cape, marshalling much of the gold out and away before the nonsense escalated into the Boer War.

(*Excerpt of letter sent from me to Robbie via the British ambassador in Cape Town.*)

Our navy lads are experts in the imperial exchange of precious metals, loaded to the brim in return for fools to govern them. We take Africa's treasures, and we exchange it for a conveyor belt of jauntily striding, marginally inbred Harrow types, marching off the gangplank into cushy roles of national governance. These imbeciles never quite convince their underlings whether they are befuddled or loftily gifted. Our trawls of precious metals are vast, and we shall be gone long before another and larger fight for mere land shall start.

My crew and I toast, chew and fuck, as we take angelic winds on white tops and with the speedy, racing

fins of friendly and aroused sea mammals, keen to come
along for the ride, past turquoise and teal reefs and on
to Southampton and Deptford. For Nature knows
where the good times are to be found. We are spending
days and nights with Bacchus once more.

D & P tell me that half a million very hard
Australian and New Zealand men are arriving there at
the southern tip of the great continent to fight the war
for the Empire*. Meanwhile, ours remains a magnificent
fleet, an armada of frigates, battleships, clippers and tall
ships. Anything we can commission and will hold gold,
we set to wave for Blighty. WC is thrilled.

I wanted to also let her know (but was unable for security
reasons) that the skipper of one young, lithe, lissome, slim-
hipped and girthily masted beauty, the *Wi-Wira*, was then
under instructions to head to Ceylon, and to the town the
English now call Kandy, where instructions were waiting for
him and his hand-picked and trusted deviants to walk into the
mountains to procure resin with the aid of the abetting, fornicating monks. The skipper was instructed by the Admiral of
the Fleet to keep it coming to my recently acquired mansions,
one by Dulwich Common and one by Loch Ness called Boleskine. And to keep his gob shut, for here, potentially, we had
a new weapon of love to fight a century's worth of wars.

4.4 Marriage, Peace & Count Svareff of Chancery Lane

It is a measure of the low regard in which homosexuality was
held in England that despite a fair amount of lapsed time

---

* *We had lost the first Boer War (1880–1881), but prevailed in this second
one (1899–1902).*

between those days and my last male lover, the rumours had taken root, sprouted and were flourishing. Buggery was something practised at public school, and not beyond. Every schoolboy, it seemed, knew this. The stain of such acts performed after Eton and Oxbridge was a tough one to shift, it seemed. Of course, the hypocrisy executed by the paedophilic lawmakers in Westminster was as rancid as it could be, for their craft had included also the creation and maintenance of the workhouse, the dark satanic mills and would soon turn to mass slaughter in the trenches.

And yes, I had polluted many women by now, but most of these had been overseas and beyond the eyes, ears and gossip of my British audience. Dandylyon had heard the first mutterings of my reputation back in Cambridge and London, and urged the right thing be done to quell the vicious chatter of acts that were still highly illegal. And so, on 9 February 1903, I took a wife, with whom I was not initially in love, but soon would be my first true Scarlet Woman.*

An interesting sort called Gerald Kelly was introduced to me, a friend of Dandylyon's in the Golden Dawn and an engaging and intelligent man of Irish stock whose childhood was spent in the comfortable streets around Paddington Station. His sister was the most important thing in the world to him, and he had shuddered when he learned of his parents' wish to have her wed off to society in an arranged and sham marriage. Gerald dared not face his parents' ire and risk being disinherited, but knew full well that the Golden Dawn possessed adequate power in a thousand forms to supersede his

---

* *I use this term not in any pernicious way, but throughout my life there was a stream of ladies who were more than mere affairs, they were disciples, accomplices and partisan sidekicks of the finest hue. It was my term of endearment, and the entrance requirements were, indeed, high. There were elements that could not be learned, but also some that had to be.*

own father's mauve intentions. Kelly, Dandylyon and I luncheoned at our club, and realised, then agreed that there was another one of those wasteless solutions at hand. Word of my sodomous exploits might be hushed, and Kelly's sister's utter sadness averted, for I would allow her freedom, cash and friendship were she to accept. Agreed, it was an arranged marriage, but one that would allow her the full latitudes and scopes of emotional liberty and financial comfort, and in reality thrust her forward into a realm of discovery that not only suited her, but was a remarkable catalyst for me. Yes, Rose Edith Kelly soon became the most remarkable companion, and one that allowed my spiritual enlightenment and my initial flourishing as a god and all for the sake of England's stability, but I shall tell of this presently. First, we would (quite conveniently and never reducing either my desires or fondness for Robbie) fall in love.

Diary Entry

19 February 1904

The country needs our marital union, for an artifice to cover the rumour of my unshackled pansexuality, my dabbling in the darker arts, and my work for WC supersedes all. Rose Edith and I sat today by our wintry lawns in Dulwich, preparing for our honeymoon to the near East when I received notice of pending instructions for the next conflict from D.

Rose Edith is most understanding, a quite attractive feature when coupled with her steely stare and outright willingness to be molested in seemly and unseemly fashions. I marvel at how she teaches this clumsy and chunky-thumbed Beast in the nuances of adoration, for she is a very different lass to the most elastically responsive Queen Cixi. Perhaps all that time with lads has left me comically inadequate in the care required to please a lady. Believing in the evolution of the species requires one to evolve constantly oneself too. It is only fair, after all.

24 February 1904
Our honeymoon must wait, for D & P have informed me that I must now leave immediately. Rose Edith, all cascading strawberry curls, lime-green eyes and milky skin – my very own thrice daily serving of *pico de gallo* – remains so understanding of my duties to England, while not knowing the full extent of my employ. I hope she (*yes! the cat's mother*) shall soon, but I am prepared to live with a Pimpernel's secret.

R, from her current location of Minsk, and I shall leave for Tokyo and Moscow respectively before Japan and Russia's mutual hostilities begin. I am to take the identity of one Count Vladimir Svareff of 67 and 69 Chancery Lane.

I remind you that we (MI-1) had resolved to keep Russia and Japan inward-looking, and so when war began between them, we felt some responsibility to help quell it all. No one wants to see a million innocents starve or be slaughtered.

15 March 1904
The hunger and blight in those awful days in both cities remain a stain upon humanity. A child should not have to eat the flesh of a parent to survive. There is little wonder the psyches of nations are damaged. Daily, we now urge and encourage the exoduses of thousands to citadels where food is more probable, and to the coasts for fish.

When appropriate, we do what we can in administering the low supplies of resin, for the toffee not only suppresses hunger for weeks, but is rich in nutrients for the blood, and is known to propagate deviantly long spells of rampant lust and an admirable desire for coition, but also removes any hatred towards one's fellow man or beast. If there were a cow or pig to be slaughtered, the beast would remain safe in the paths we take through those largely barren lands. It is often necessary for children to witness the lust of parents and neighbours, but we are saving lives by the hundreds of thousands. Maybe it will do them good, far better than seeing their parents beheaded, and no child is ever harmed, fondled or touched, for the narcotic is a righteous one. A pacifist movement flourishes; municipal orgies are a common sight. One glimpse at the love-strewn hillsides and those brackish generals know where we have been, and yet there are those who refuse to be caught in our treacly trap. But treacly toffee is as treacly toffee does, and, when we poison the wells with it, we ensnare dozens, scores, hundreds, thousands in our sticky web, and then conversion to love by digestion is just minutes away.

The Russo-Japanese war would last three days under nineteen months. Had it not been for our narcotic intervention behind the lines of both factions, the conservative estimate in London reckoned that the conflict would have lasted for a minimum of fifteen, perhaps fifty, years. I shall never forget the obvious admiration on a young *compadre*'s face as we watched three battalions of cut-throat warriors fellate and sodomise each other on the awed shore of the Yellow Sea, as bemused enemy spotters viewed from their vessels, bobbing on the waves in rhythm to the coastal shaftfest. And rather than wash ashore and slaughter the love-makers, the navy observed, the captains met to consult, before they gawked for three more days and then to the cheers of the sailors below and on deck, set sail for home ports, to their families and to peace, unsure whether to speak of what they had seen. The seamen told tales of how the exhausted and spent revellers on the dunes had even waved their newly erstwhile foe a fond farewell, a farewell that some had interpreted (perhaps in their own eager minds) as an invitation to reignite the quite unforgettable man-revel on the sands.

War was over. Go home, boys.

4.5 THE BOOK OF THE LAW

Maintaining a presence in two spots was a skill mastered by that first Scarlet Pimpernel, and I now mastered this art not from one side of the English Channel to the other, but straddling vast continents – China, Loch Ness, Dulwich, Moscow and next North Africa – all in the name of subterfuge. My ability and licence to spend three days in a first-class train sleeper from Moscow to Waterloo injecting the finest heroin seemed a remarkably efficient use of my time, while conveniently scratching that particular recreational itch.

In the late spring of 1904, my burgeoning darling Rose Edith, five months pregnant with our first child, and I honeymooned in Cairo where she soon revealed her astonishing gift in the shadowy arts. Dandylyon really was the finest marionettist for how on earth would he know of the latent skills of Kelly's previously and marvellously benign sister? How did he know she possessed the vision and would be the conduit to allow this Beast to become a god? Well, this happened in Egypt, as we dripped and rolled and smoked hashish and laughed and sat for yoga. And knew, deep down, a reckoning with our precipitous futures was nigh.

It all began in our impressive and sweeping hotel chambers,

fit for an army of camels to enter the kingdom of heaven, and lit with the blessed afternoon sun through the dust of the streets and desert, casting yellow, violet, teal and orange on blanched walls through thick stained glass. My aim was an avowedly frivolous attempt to impress her with an invocation, a rudimentary and basic attempt to rid ourselves of some random invisible spirit,* who was supposed to make its presence known before its harmless and trauma-free departure. However, Rose Edith saw nothing but did, quite intriguingly, fall into a definite trance. Good girl! It was then that she repeated the words clearly and several times, 'They are waiting for you. They are waiting for you. They are waiting for you.'

These were the words of Rose Edith, who possessed scant knowledge of religion or Egyptology.

A noise came from her that upon repetition appeared to be annunciating two syllables – Boo and Larg.

'Boulag? Boulag? Do you mean the Boulag Museum?'

I was pretty sure Rose Edith had no idea of this site. I immediately resolved to take her there that very dusk. I was still confounded, so I asked her to speak with the god Thoth, and for the spirit's intent to be more specific.

'Who is waiting for me? Who is sending this message?' I said.

'Horus,' she answered firmly in the manly tone of a construction worker, so at odds with her gentle and maidenish tones. 'Horus.'

I brought her out of the trance, the same way that an aroused beast might have; executed with an impressively impassioned clumsiness.

As we cooled, I spoke, 'My dear. You must show me Horus. Take me to Horus.'

---

* A spell called 'Sew to Sylphs'.

'Who is Horus?'

Rose Edith could not recall the name from her trance.

Within hours, we were walking around the museum. When we passed many of the common images one sees of Horus in Cairo, I began to prepare myself to dismiss any true clairvoyance, in its true sense from French of *seeing the light*. Perhaps after one hour, she stopped, with no prompting, in front of an ornately decorated funerary monument, the Stele of Revealing from the twenty-sixth dynasty. It showed a priest called Ankh-af-na-khonsu presenting a sacrifice to Horus. I shuddered, for not only did I see the Stele of Revealing as a clumsy nod to the Book of Revelations, but the museum had assigned to the astonishing relic the number 666, that number, my number from the Scriptures of my blissful childhood and the number assigned to me by Mother. I knew I now had to listen to Rose Edith. And so we stayed for weeks seeking out further enlightenment, a project of which Dandylyon and Prudence thoroughly approved, and were supremely keen to know of its results.

On July eighth, ninth and tenth of that year, Rose Edith dictated to me for precisely one hour each day the three parts of the verse and book I called that first great work, *The Book of the Law*. Or at least, she believed that she did. She sparked some of it, I suppose. She told me that the source of the text was a spirit called Aiwass, who was my holy guardian angel. I was taking large amounts of very strong drugs, and may have scripted far more of the text than Aiwass was (allegedly) dictating through Rose Edith. This shall always remain a fluid question as to who was more responsible for the book. Rose Edith was quite happy to be taking the credit, and at this stage in her pregnancy, she ingested no drug other than the clouds of scorched marijuana that perpetually encased her husband.

Critics and cynics may have scoffed, but there were many

disclosures in the text that could not have been forged. Rose Edith's channelling of the clues to lead us to the Stele was only the beginning for her; her solving the ridiculously complex mathematical and literal puzzles that *The Book of the Law* lays out could only have come from another. The four of us – our growing foetus, Aiwass, Rose Edith and I – we were truly immaculate and elegant in those thrumming and whirring days and airless nights in Cairo, astride the saddle of that most beguiling continent. And throughout I had the quite distinct feeling that this was all being manipulated, with personal benediction and political foresight, by my dear guardian, Dr Horace Dandylyon, and that whispering nurse-witch. But with a manuscript written and a honeymoon enjoyed to quash rumours of cock, we left.

My wife, our fruit in her womb, and I left for Scotland. On July the twenty-eighth, life exhibited her ability to startle even the likes of me when Nuit Ma Ahathoor Hecate Sappho Jezebel Lilith Crowley was born at Boleskine House, my new country estate at Inverfarigaig by Loch Ness.

I had bought Boleskine House, a sixteenth-century mansion, at Dandylyon's urging. His precise instructions were for a place to perform a quite precise ritual; a Golden Dawn ceremony known as the Sacred Magic of Abramelin the Mage, taken from a grimoire called *The Book of Abramelin*. The first essential element was a house in a more or less secluded situation. There had to be a door opening to the north from the room in which one makes one's oratory. Outside this door, I was to construct a terrace covered with fine river sand. This had to end in a 'lodge' where the spirits may congregate. The precise purpose of this ritual was to invoke one's Guardian Angel.

After a lengthy search, Boleskine was found to fit the bill quite perfectly. It required at least six months of preparation, celibacy and abstinence from alcohol (but not drugs). It also included the summoning of the Twelve Kings and Dukes of Hell, to bind them and remove their negative influences from the magician's life. Incapable of remaining celibate, I would leave before the process was complete, and some of my detractors suggest that the incomplete spell released a negativity there in the lodge, but they remain fools, who know less than bugger all, for she was a fine home with many magical memories of joyous times.

4.6 WHITE STAINS

I had grown to love Rose Edith so, and I believe she loved me. She was so much fun, but when one sups with a devil, one should do so with a long spoon. The vast highs we enjoyed over the next year masked her pain, I see this now, but they also enflamed me to write superb filth.

I was prolific. *White Stains* had been published soon after I found the resin, and now came more pornography. In these months with Rose Edith's mauled torso, perpetually bruised from my thumbprints, and rarely out of or far from my grip, I completed *Snowdrops From a Curate's Garden.* I wrote *Necrophilia* in one weekend, though it was not to be available for another fifteen years. The title seemed to offend the humourless English, for I was seen in certain strata as not only a mischief-maker of increasingly questionable repute, but a member of the ragtag Scottish Mountaineering Club. Those who needed to know the truth knew. I was the Scarlet Pimpernel and revelations thereof would mean my destruction. My life was built on lies, and any wish to have people think better of me had to be banished. This was my daily mantra, for I was well on the way to being that 'wickedest man in the world'.*

---

* *Moronic words from the clods at the* Daily Mail.

White Stains was first published in Amsterdam by Leonard Smithers, that pioneer of English pornography and contentious literature, who also worked with Wilde and whose books had filled Pollitt's shelves. I white-stained the original print-run of one hundred copies. They were a magnificent sight. When British customs took them, I denounced them as bastards. Of course, Dandylyon had sanctioned the seizure on the ship from Rotterdam. The volumes arrived at Boleskine within the week. The couriers carried each one to my library and placed them with the maximum care on my book shelves. They even called me, 'Mr Bishop, sir,' with a worthy deference, for I had used a nom de plume for *White Stains*. George Archibald Bishop was the fictional author, a neuropath of the second empire. Bishop was, of course, that cunt Uncle Tom's family name.

In the controversial book, I was of the opinion that any sexual aberrations were psychological in nature and I turned to artistic expression to make the point. I invented a character, a cloth-headed poet who went all wrong, and who began with normal innocent enthusiasms, and gradually developed various vices. He ends up being stricken with disease and madness, culminating in murder. In his poems he describes his downfall, always explaining the psychology of each act. I merely humanised the filth, and I believe to this day that is what the mucky sods that bake, preach, police, teach, drive trains, politick and farm the land really wanted. They are all secret or public monsters, flowers of Eros and Evil, no better than broiled hounds in summer with their twitching noses up another's special flesh. Magnificent perverts all, but in equal measure, fucking hypocrites.

And so with bodily joys and other worldly highs, my poetry flourished for the first time from my true self, and not from that florid posing nitwit, who flounced around Cambridge. It

felt so bloody good to tell the truth, even if I was still playing
a part, because this new identity, that of a filthy pig, now
folded in on my own to an enlightened perfection.

> Void of the ecstasies of Art
> It were in life to have lain by thee,
> And felt thy kisses rain on me,
> And the hot beating of thy heart,
> When thy warm sweat should leave me cold,
> And my worn soul find out no bliss
> In the obscenities I kiss,
> And the things shameful that I hold.
> My nostrils sniff the luxury
> Of flesh decaying, bowels torn
> Of festive worms, like Venus, born
> Of entrails foaming like the sea.
> Yea, thou art dead. Thy buttocks now
> Are swan-soft, and thou sweatest not;
> And hast a strange desire begot
> In me, to lick thy bloody brow;
> To gnaw thy hollow cheeks, and pull
> Thy lustful tongue from out its sheath;
> To wallow in the bowels of death,
> And rip thy belly, and fill full
> My hands with all putridities;
> To chew thy dainty testicles;
> To revel with the worms in Hell's
> Delight in such obscenities;
> To pour within thine heart the seed
> Mingled with poisonous discharge
> From a swollen gland, inflamed and large
> With gonorrhoea's delicious breed;
> To probe thy belly, and to drink

> The godless fluids, and the pool
> Of rank putrescence from the stool
> Thy hanged corpse gave, whose luscious stink
> Excites these songs sublime. The rod
> Gains new desire; dive, howl, cling, suck,
> Rave, shriek, and chew; excite the fuck,
> Hold me, I come! I'm dead! My God!

With Rose Edith, our physical union had seemed to transcend all that I had known before, and it now sat astride all of those experiments and forays with gents and lads. Yet I knew soon that it was merely the jungle goo and my Scarlet Woman's unfathomable attraction to magick and the spells that were driving us to an insane and unmanageable passion. It could not go on, at least not there in Scotland. We were starting to attract unwanted attention, and then visits from the local constabulary after the nosy bastards with field glasses at Urquhart Castle across the lake spotted us and reported us after some mildly illegal horseplay at dusk. Dandylyon wrote to me at that time (no coincidence, I am sure) with a mission, and I had to go to Burma.

In late 1905 when I was preparing to depart, I made a despicable and selfish decision. I could not live, I thought, without Rose Edith and Lilith, so as part of the excuse of taking them as a perfect cover for my meddling, they accompanied me on my mission. And it was there in the heat of that cursed land, that my daughter died of enteric fever the following year.

Sleep I forget. Her silky breath no longer fans my ears; I dream I float on some forgotten stream that hath a savour still of death. My angel was gone for ever.

*

Even this selfish oaf I was pretending to be, rather well I think, was permitted to display his understanding that fatherhood is a threshold infinitely more defining than any secret society or even any invocation. It stands alone in the discovery of the self; the cliché is I am afraid true, as clichés can annoyingly be. The elevation is as joyous as it is precipitous, for the loss of a child never leaves, and what appears to be the most selfless of journeys, almost by definition, is in fact a thoroughly selfish one, when one is left feeling sorry for oneself for fifty years, as one's child suffers no more and feels no pain. They were *my* days that were blighted, *my* shivers and *my* screams in the nights, *my* masking of the terror in more and more and more cocaine. Selfish, selfish. Me, me. My. I. More.

When Lilith passed, Rose Edith was already pregnant again. And so, it was a blessed time for ME when Lola Zaza Crowley was born in December 1906.

> Lola! Now look me straight in the eyes.
> Our fate is come upon us. Tell me now.
> Love still shall arbitrate our destinies
> And joy inform the swart Plutonic brow.

The bloody awful thing for me, even then, was that I named Lola after a mistress I had taken, while all I really wanted between the masking effects of my rampant aphrodisiac from the Ceylon jungle, was to bed my young Robbie, my tight, young virgin, my dream.* That solitary sentence contained three *I's*, four *my's* and a *me* from this selfish bastard.

After Lola's birth, Rose Edith wished to compensate for her quite pure lifestyle during the gestation of our second child.

---

* *That sweetest of events with Robbie would be over ten years and a world war from now.*

Here her addiction to heroin began. I fear now these excesses may have been instrumental in her demise. She should not have gone toe-to-toe with me. I possessed a large store of the jungle resin in my basement, and in my science laboratory, huge hip-high sixteenth-century Ottoman vats, plentiful with opium, morphine, cocaine, chloroform and marijuana were stocked up by a monthly delivery. The clay pots that had cost a unreasonably hefty sum at Sotheby's were all regularly blessed in dark-ish midnight ritual, more to convince those of a flimsier constitution who would ingest stacks of the stuff that they would receive an umbrella'd protection from the more perilous and thornier effects of the potent powders and liquids. This perceived defence against their destruction was just hogwash, a placebo, for the strongest (and sometimes the weakest) link in that chain is always the mind. Indeed for me, these drugs were always paths to a higher consciousness that allowed me to play God en route. I see now that they merely allowed for Rose Edith to escape from the misery I was blindly and selfishly building for her with those exact same selfish fucking drugs of mine. I also believe that had she been elsewhere, she would have been even bleaker. It was just the way she was. I weep for her regularly, my fond love.

What a horror I must have appeared, and yet I was saving millions of lives with my time of youthful mischief, as I liberated the minds of swathes of the planet, ended wars early, prevented conflicts from happening, stopped starvation, encouraged mass, frenzied, lengthy and leavened copulation. That fine fellow, Sir Percy Blakeney, be partially and politely damned in my shadow, because Pimpernelling was a new art now. And I was more Scarlet than any blighter, who had ever lived.

And in truth, still only a strutting apprentice.

Chapter 5

The Great War

– I

Falsehood is invariably the child of fear in one form or another.

– Aleister Crowley

I stop by a stone statue of a cherub holding a bird in each hand, and with lush, verdant ivy reaching ambitiously to the top of the scamp's thigh on one side, and on the other, a spinach green stem in the vanguard, tickling the lower right rib. The growth appears to have been welcomed and has brought a smile to the lad's chops.

I think of my goats in the pasture, how they will be waiting for me.

One of my early spells of low-grade tomfoolery was supposed to involve a recipe of Indian tuberose stamen, simple sea salt and young goat neck. In the spirit of the Costa Rican bullfighter who refuses to have the beast slain but instead spends a healthy two hours engaged in teasing, whispering private jokes and the odd fetlock or jowl tickle, I once used a wide and long and piped floury pasta which gave the impression to the arses in the

Golden Dawn of the animal's oesophagus and in case the Lord Hierophant wasn't fooled, I assured him that all the ingredients were genuine.

I shall miss my goats. I shall walk to them very soon. To bid them farewell.

I am now fully resolved to return to England to lead my acolytes and spark a global revolution. I am the spark they need to rally against this most inhuman Crackdown. If we do not succeed, this planet is doomed.

Nine hours to go.

5.1 THE GREAT BINGE (1875–1914)

There were wars everywhere and every day. I helped to limit and then extinguish the third and fourth Central American wars, the Romanian peasant revolt of 1907, and the Korean guerrilla insurgency against Japanese occupation (1907–10). The Melillan campaign (1909) might have lasted a decade had it not been for me. The Chinese revolution of 1911 was a little-reported storm in a teacup, though I was thrilled to be returning there. It was a shame the Empress had passed three years prior; I would have gladly revisited. The Italo–Turkish war of 1911–12 was responsible for 20,000 deaths, but had it not been for our diplomacy that might have been a quarter of a million. Two Balkan conflicts (in 1912 and 1913) foreshadowed what I had seen in my visions. This was a perilous spot to watch, full of crooked bastards, willing to torch anyone for anything and at any time.

Between these operations, I always returned to Boleskine, and to Rose Edith and Lola. The intensity of time spent together should never be undermined by periods of being apart. It was a time of constant war for this double agent. Loved ones being apart from one another is the natural state of things for any soldier in these days. *I loved and missed them so*, and these six words might be repeated between any two sentences in this memoir. When I was with them, I missed them when I blinked.

There was often a cold reception in the villages around Boleskine in those days. The Scots were a gossiping lot, though some were respectful heathens themselves. The locals believed my darling lost Lilith was buried in the graveyard by the tiny and ancient church. Of course, she was not. She was in my own ground at Boleskine. But, like my taking of women to quell rumours of sodomy, I established a façade of a Christian internment for my daughter. Every time I returned home, I visited her fake tomb in their consecrated sod, though even the early visits, while still draped in mourning black, were marred by aggressive types looking for fist fights. Monied homosexual Satanists were apparently not welcome, even holding hands with their surviving, shin-high daughter and weeping wife. And so, I dressed as Viking lords, a pissed-up rag 'n' bone man, and red-headed Highlanders in tartan just to keep up the pretence. I could have damned any of them, had them scream-ing in flight for caves, heather and hillside, with the slightest spell of fire or mischief. Yet I always told myself I had more important tasks to complete, for one great aspect of our epoch was about to come to an end, and such kaleidoscopic periods of change required my full attention.

This was the time of the Great Binge in Europe. This time of vast and widespread consumption of substances now illegal had begun around the year of my birth. It did not discriminate by age and only minimally by social class. There are modern-ish day preconceptions that the Victorians were puritanical, sober and solemn. They were quite possibly worse than the Ancient Romans. Do not be fooled into thinking that the *mirepoix* of narcotics, fornication and spicy Anglo-Saxon invective is the preserve of the late twentieth century.

First of all, the colourful curse is traceable through Geoffrey Chaucer and beyond. In the thirteenth century, he wrote in 'The Miller's Tale', 'And prively he caughte hire by the queynte.' Then *Philotus* (1603) spells the same thing a different, more familiar way, 'put doun thy hand and graip hir cunt'. Cambridge had a Gropecunt Lane before the grim sods, who believe themselves to be in charge, changed the name. The language was unsterilised, as was the food, the prevailing stink in the air from arse, crotch and breath, the fucking, the horse shit, the grime from the mill. It was, if nothing else, a time for sensations.

Secondly, the hypocrisies around Victorian sex are just staggering and absurd. I applaud their energetic coitus and sodomy, but puke at their denials thereof. The Queen was the product of illegitimacy, likely her cousin-husband Albert too. The literature of the age did not shy from discussing the duplicity and the fraud in the bedrooms; Dorian Gray, Jekyll and Dracula all told of rampantly split personalities, façades and pretence, and all alluded to sex. Those Germans, whom we shall soon encounter, sum it up the best, '*Doppelzüngigkeit*'.*

In the Victorians' defence, a fool may yell, 'Yes, but none of them copulated with a horse like the pre-eminently deviant Emperor Caligula had done.' I would have answered, 'Yes, they fucking did.' Life for some was a procession of horses, ponies, pigs, hounds and donkeys. They didn't care what they wanked off or drained to empty with their mouths.

The Devil will find work for idle hands to do, and this is never more apt than when one rules the world. Romans, Victorians, Ottomans, Greeks, you name it. Boredom in the

---

*   *Double-tongued-ness.*

bedrooms might indeed bring down an Empire. It was not that long before that Catherine the Great (1729–1796) had, we believed for the longest time,* attempted to better Caligula, for he merely fucked a horse, and this, as even any normal-minded person might suspect, is a quite different proposition to being entered, tarnished and corrupted *by* one. One would imagine. Anyway, we shall meet several doughty Russian squaws later. The point is they really were a sordid lot in the Victorian age, and this would have been truly admirable had they not lied about it.

The triumvirate of Victorian façade is complete with drugs. During that star-flecked Binge, cocaine, hashish, morphine, laudanum, heroin and chloroform were available at pharmacists across England and Europe. Absinthe, the real stuff with the potent hallucinogen of wormwood, was served universally until a French farmer, on a week-long spree, slaughtered his family, believing them to be roaches in their beds. Children as young as four or five years old around the cities, towns and villages of England were legally served beer and drank it with glee, because it was cleaner than the water. I should know, the fortune I had been left by my father was from Crowley's Alton Ales. Sherlock Holmes was shovelling white powder up his beak; Dorian polluted by opium. Victoria drank booze when she had any engagements, otherwise she was chewing cocaine lozenges, injecting, snorting and puffing whatever she fancied. Jekyll's own schizophrenia came from a concoction of chemicals, after all. Dracula stayed up all night.

And so, like any decent shindig at its peak, the Great Binge

---

*   *Even if it turned out to be conjecture and gossip, the fact that everyone, historians included, were convinced she had, still spoke volumes. And anyway, it is tough to prove a negative.*

appeared as if it would last for a while yet. But then, we failed to prevent the first great horror: Sarajevo in 1914.

MI-1 and The Legion had uncovered yet another plot to assassinate Archduke Franz Ferdinand, and we were there to help prevent it. By now, Rose Edith and our daughter were under the magnificent care of a friend of Dandylyon in what was called an asylum in private by those who ran it, but really, to the naked eye, it was a country estate in Dumfriesshire, settled in astonishing grounds and only improved upon by the warmish and snug blanket of a squadron of nurses of adoring benediction.

28 June 1914

I met Orr and a new-ish troop of his battalion of naughty rag tags and righteous scrag-ends in the city that morning. The sun shone on the River Miljacka, and the crowds, families and young scamps waving flags gathered. The soldiers appeared slovenly and bedraggled, unshaven and sloppy. From Dandylyon's immaculate brief, we aimed to have the six assassins shadowed, watched and covered. They were all clueless young boys, *café conspirateurs*, and rank amateurs. Two were wrestled away from the procession by Orr's men, two had left on their own accord, losing their nerve as large and menacing Boers stared at them. One similarly jumpy type had attempted a shot at the Archduke's car, missed by a long way if the crack in the upstairs window was to be believed, and then necked weak and ineffective cyanide, before jumping in the river for a glorious martyr's end, only to be fished out, puking and weeping in agony, in the least heroic manner possible. The final one lobbed his grenade too soon, clearly unnerved by Orr himself. Orr lifted him under his arm and marched off with him, as if he were carrying a fresh baguette. However, the bloodshed that we all know ensued that day was absolutely contrary to our plans, as we wished to curtail the clairvoyant horror-vision I had seen on the Ceylon jungle floor. That European alliance I had forged in the Boxer Rebellion frayed and then dissipated into the heat of that fulcrum of a day.

I meandered away from the parade route, looking for troublesome types, and was intrigued by nothing other than several caricatured sorts. They seemed to be plentiful. It was as I was observing one such fellow, a large Englishman chatting to two small boys playing chess in a park, that I heard one, two, three shots ring out. There was an odd silence, and it would not be for several weeks, months and then years that one would truly begin to grasp the pivotal nature for the century, for the planet, of those seconds. The lead Serb assassin had given up for the day. We believed we had prevented murder, but chance had him walk out of Schiller's café still masticating his food, revolver in his pocket, when he encountered a stalled car carrying royalty in his precise path. And that was that. How can anyone legislate for such awful fortune?

It would signal the end of the Binge, for now boys and men were not to be focused on fornicating or entering an inebriated, frazzled, harmonious or tranquil state. They were going to war and to slaughter. We had failed, but we would be back. We would always be back. It was the way we were all built.

5.2 THE MURDEROUS CARICATURES OF SARAJEVO

And we did not hang around in getting to work. It was later that day in Sarajevo, when Orr showed to me the fellow whose dangerous acolytes would provide my mischievous focus for a large chunk of that century. He entered into the lobby of the Hotel President in the late afternoon. He was an amorphous gargantuan, who walked in with a rolling and waddling motion, and stood beneath the tilting and grinding ceiling fans, as they struggled in the battle with the afternoon heat. Behind him was a small trail of sycophants, who perpetually mopped his neck, helped him to fix his monocle onto his pudgy cheek, and lit his broad turd of a cigar. I was struck immediately by what appeared to be feet the size of a ten-year-old girl. The elephantine was dressed in a suit of the vilest mustard shade, and sported an unsightly and patchy ginger beard. His jacket did not hide the patches of sweat around his soggy armpits that had already soaked a dress shirt beneath, the pleat of his damp arse was equally as guilty, it appeared.

They spoke German loudly and with a Bavarian twang.

'*Getraenke! Jetzt. Komm' schnell.*'*

He reclined his head to expose his circular pink and pulpy face to the fan. In doing so, his broad hat fell, a minion swift to catch it before it hit the polished tiles. Such was my friendly ogre's height, Orr's elbow nudge struck me in the shoulder, but I had already seen the clod, of course. The German scowled, producing unhealthily deep trenches in his beaming half-moon of a forehead. The effect was one of anger and discomfort, though whether the anger was the cause of the discomfort or the discomfort was prompting the anger was more difficult to determine. Both may have been true, and the agony on his most unpleasant mug was only extinguished temporarily by the first of many loud swigs of the schnapps awaiting the troupe at a table. The other three were all in morning suits. They said not a word unless it was in utter deference. They laughed at or nodded along with everything the fat man squawked.

It was not just this little scene that appeared to have come from some cheap melodrama. The chaos of the day's events seemed to have seeped its way into the exaggerated movements of the befuddled burghers of Sarajevo, as they tripped, juddered, head-rolled, wept or stood silent and still. We all

---

*   '*Drinks! Now! Come quickly!*'

appeared to have been forced into some caricatured and inflated state, seemingly prescient of the looming horror. A handsome uniformed young man with a large head sat at the bar and seemed to be more agitated and frayed than the rest of us. He scribbled on paper, whimpering and sobbing, as we approached and ordered drinks. He drank vodka and was quite prolific with it. I was impressed by his intake, but felt for the poor soul in the midst of his despair. We sat by the bar, where a young Prussian was serving, concerned for his customer who also appeared to be his friend. After he had filled the wastepaper basket with screwed up leaves of paper, littered with scribbles of tear-blotted purple ink, he finished the bottle of vodka, stood and as he stumbled past me, grabbed my lapel and announced in a precise Queen's English: 'It is a microcosm of the apocalypse. It is a microcosm of the apocalypse. Tell them all I am sorry.'

And he left, apparently without having paid his bill.

Orr shrugged, for he was more concerned with observing the raucous and lardy Fritz. However, I was intrigued, and watched the youth leave the front of the Hotel President and narrowly avoid a passing carriage. A car's horn sounded and men yelled. And he was gone, off into the distance. I would recognise his face the next day from a grainy photograph on the front of the newspaper, seated behind a steering wheel and a yard from a dead princess, clasping the bump in her belly, and a dying Archduke. His anguished and afflicted expression seemed to broadcast a torture to last a lifetime. I shan't forget it. Perhaps my foreknowledge of the wider impact of that day's slaying magnified the horror of the snapshot of the boy's face. I knew a Great War was coming. Orr spoke to me as he looked at the dripping colossus glugging the schnapps. The unforgiving and unfortunate proportions of the monstrosity's toad-ish neck resembled those of my own troubled youth.

'His name is Hühnerbein. I know him from Africa.'

'Stupid bloody name,[*] that is,' I said.

'Yes, it is rumoured he is part-English, but hates them so.'

Orr closed his eyes and I soon knew that he was calculating the precise importance of this chance encounter. For several minutes, Orr remained silent, opening his eyes from time to time, saying naught and not even looking at me to request my silence. This was, of course, a given, for I worshipped this great lug and the ground in which he left the deepest of defined footprints.

'Let him drink some more. I shall introduce you shortly.'

I knew that Orr had not taken this length of time to deduce an obvious and immediate tactic. I knew shortly thereafter exactly what he had computed, and it was a beautiful and precise thing, an explicit and defined stratagem that would never make up for the misfortune of that lunchtime, but would aim to limit the slaughter. It had been a pitiful moment in history; a chance showdown between a diseased wretch with a gun and my confused, bawling pal from the bar, who was trying to find the reverse gear on the government car, with which he had been charged for the day.

War was coming. I'm so sorry, lads. We fucked up.

From Orr's planning we would get The Legion back in the game, not just for the pending scrap with the Hun, but for the next thirty-one years until the second one. I still shudder at its

---

[*] *In German, it translates as Chickenleg, but also Drumstick, for this chap's spirit, since childhood, had marched to a military beat.*

astonishing accuracy. I now knew that chess with blindfolds was how all of those lads kept that muscle in the brain, that one for protracted and patient strategy, suitably taut.

Orr had computed the precise impact of all of the pacts, treaties and alliances. He told me the plan was to infiltrate the Prussians and Bavarians, this is where our enemies now presided. Our meddling in Moscow would now be replicated in Berlin and Munich; Russia was now our pal, Germany our foe. We had known this shift would happen one day, and it was largely always a case of recognising the moment and seizing it. And here in the Hotel President, he calmly informed me, it was the soggy monster in front of us, the one who waddled and yelled and sweated, who was their Achilles' heel. Orr's prescience was a thing of beauty.

I walked over to the bar where the Germans were. I listened to Hühnerbein for several minutes. All four of them were now on their second bottle of schnapps. My German was excellent, but a combination of their southern dialect and their inebriation did not help my translation of their ratcheting nonsense. It was ridiculous that grown-ups behaved so inelegantly. I wish I were able to report that they were funny, but they were not; they were the Marx brothers without the guile, timing or wit.

'I was in the cab. I had no idea where we were,' said Hühnerbein. 'I was a little bit sloshed from lunch. I then spotted that old church we always see at the beginning of the motion pictures at the Mutoskope around the back of the Karl Hedwig III monument.'

One of his bootlickers fawned, 'Ah, I so miss the Mutoskope in this backwater.'

Another brown nose chimed in, 'Oh I do too.'

'Shut up, you fools. So I said out loud, "Ah, we are here." I did not mean we were at our destination. I only meant to express that I knew where we were.'

'At the Mutoskope?'

'I think you mean the Kinetoskope.'

'Of course, at the Mutoskope. But I was going to the Regierung Strasse.'

'But the Mutoskope is not near the Regierung Strasse, Herr Hühnerbein.'

'I know, but the driver let me down there.'

'You know it is run by Communists, don't you?'

'And perverts.'

'No! That is the Kinetoskope. I was fondled there in broad daylight while waiting for a strudel.'

'And you got out?'

'But why?'

'I was potted.'

'And a long way from the Regierung Strasse.'

'I do miss the Mutoskope. I saw *Der Weisse Geist Von Meiner Grossmutter** there. What a masterpiece.'

'It is owned by Communists.'

'And perverts.'

'So how *did* you get to Regierung Strasse?'

'Enough, you damned fools. Take me to piss. Get the trolley, my poor put-upon legs hurt.'

One backslapper jumped up from his seat and motioned to the bellboy, who promptly delivered a wheelchair to their table at the bar. Several chairs, tables and customers had to be shoved and displaced in order for Hühnerbein's carriage to be adjacent to his table. The three subordinates grunted as they lifted the fat man into the broad seat, which was still rather snug for the backside of the humongous oaf. Two of them

---

*   *My Grandmother's White Ghost.*

then took a handle each, tilted the vast load slightly backwards, taking huge care not to pass his centre of gravity, and
rolled him off to urinate. The third toad slumped behind them
all. I could only imagine the poor soul was to help with the act
itself.

Orr walked over to where I stood.

'What sort of state are they in?' he said.

'They are pie-eyed.'

'All of them?'

'Yes, I think they are.'

'Excellent.'

Orr waited there at the bar with me until the troop
returned, almost spilling their load en route. The concierge
and several other guests frowned their stunned disapproval.

When they were almost back at their spot, Orr turned to
face the elephantine, and greeted him in a phlegmy Dutch
German.

'Hühnerbein! You old scoundrel. What a delight!'

'Oh dear God. It is *you*!'

The three fawners lifted Hühnerbein back into his seat,
unable to avoid the large puddles in his crooks, which were
now accompanied by a new one on the front of his trouser.
Just as the stooges had deposited the rotundity in his chair, he
leapt up and moved reasonably nimbly, given his unfortunate
and possibly perilous combination of fleshy girth and tiny feet.

His harsh Bavarian softened marginally in the presence of
the foreigner, but also from appearing to sober up by a sliver.

'Good God. It has been so long. What a surprise!'

'I would like to introduce you to a dear friend of mine,
Hühnerbein. Please come and meet Aleister Crowley.'

I moved in, reluctantly shook the insipid mitt, though
this was masked by my enthusiastic grip, and said, 'How do
you do?'

We then continued in Bavarian. They do so appreciate that, it all points to an inferiority complex, the same fuel that sparks their faux superiority and pretentions to conquer.

Greek mythology tells us of Achilles' mother, that sea-nymph, dunking him into the river to bless him with the gift of immortality. The legend speaks of how she held him by his heel, and so this spot remained vulnerable and therefore mortal. Well, the German spirit has one such weak spot. It is their belief in their own pre-eminence that is the nearest thing humanity has to the spirits, the gods. This factor was at the heart of Orr's foresight. This is where The Occult and its bidder, Aleister Crowley, the acclaimed protégé, precipitously rising star in the Hermetic Order of the Golden Dawn, with its own sturdy connections in Berlin and Munich, became crucial. For here in this arena that dazzled them all, I was a noted devotee, erstwhile wunderkind, burgeoning Dark Lord, practitioner of the metaphysical and paranormal activities, a Rosicrucian* hell-bent on spiritual development, drugs and genitals of all kinds. How could they not be cowed by, intimidated by and, hence, enamoured of me?

'Crowley? Crowley? I know of you, young man. Yours is a fearsome repute.'

'Thank you, Herr Hühnerbein. Most gracious.'

'You must join us.' In hindsight, his terminology might have been purposefully ambiguous.

So we joined them, exchanging small talk and hot air about the assassination, until Orr took Hühnerbein's appalling frame

---

* Rosicrucian (def): The mysterious seventeenth-century doctrine of the order is allegedly founded upon esoteric truths, which 'concealed from the average man, provide insight into nature, the physical universe and the spiritual realm'. Their manifestos do not elaborate extensively on the matter, but clearly combine references to the Kabbalah, Hermeticism and Christianity.

off to one side. The German's high spirits had subsided and the three lackeys, following the example of their leader, had now lost much of their drunken bluster.

When the vast Orr and the roly-poly Hühnerbein returned, he was very precise and quite business-like in his approach to me.

'I hear you are a member of the Scottish Mountaineering Club. This is of the greatest interest to me, Herr Crowley.'

'I am indeed. It is a fine honour for this Englishman.'

I knew precisely his intent.

'And why are you not a member of the English Mountaineering Club?'

'Because I despise them. They are a moribund lot. A quite despicable clique, who are eternally jealous of my abilities. Had they any wit or decency about them, they would welcome me in and increase their own standing but, as is the English way, they are far too concerned with themselves, the fucking rules of the game, and playing it straight. This is not my way, sir. The Scots are a feistier lot, and would attack a mountain any way they saw fit, just to sit upon her. And they recognise unshackled talent when they see it. This makes it a pleasure.'

'How very intriguing. We have so much to discuss. And tell me what you really think of what happened here today, and what brought you to Sarajevo, for this is quite a coincidence that we all meet here today of all days.'

'I knew what was to happen today. I wanted to witness history. But it is more than that, sir, for I also wish to define history.'

'You and our friend-in-common,' he nodded at Orr, 'must come to visit me at my castle near the Wetterhorn. The Scottish Mountaineering Club have the chalets down the road, I am sure you know.'

'I do.'

Orr and I exchanged glances and minuscule nods to encourage the great lump.

'Do we find you here at the Hotel President?'

'You do, and that is most kind. I am sure we shall be delighted to accept.'

'Marvellous. It has been a true pleasure.'

'That pleasure, believe me Herr Hühnerbein, has been all mine.'

'One of my men shall be in touch in the morning.'

We moved our heads marginally closer together, and we clasped hands to say 'Farewell' for the evening. This tiny gesture became a magnified detail of our intent.

As my dear and mischievous friend and I walked out into the thick and hot Sarajevan evening, Orr looked straight ahead with a military precision and said to me, 'That fool has murdered hundreds with his own hands. He has ordered the slaughter of thousands. We must be careful.'

And it would be this fat fool who would allow my proximity to, truly, the most evil man of the twentieth century; not I, for heaven's sake, though Fleet Street would have you believe otherwise. I write of that grubby and resentful little Austrian. I tell of that viciously peeved reject from the Austrian Army, at that precise moment struggling to paint like a grown-up, up the road in Munich. But my acquaintance with that over-mothered and under-fathered vulgarian is still two decades ahead.

Meanwhile, I would think of how Rasputin had hypnotised a German (the Czar's wife) with sex, drugs and the Occult, and how I now planned to do the same.

5.3 DAMAGE LIMITATION
We were now unable to prevent the inevitable march to war. We might have controlled many things, influenced even more,

but we were still just human beings. We were neither unstintingly prescient nor ever-judicious, and mistakes happened. Sometimes we were only reactive, but we still acted for Good and punched bastards in the neck with a righteous glove whenever we could. We had already prevented and shortened conflicts while spreading lust and love from that generous and weeping pustule on the spicy mountains of Ceylon. I would have spoon-fed it to the whole fucking world, but Winston and MI-1 were my masters. I would not defer for ever.

We would have to do what we could to curtail the bloody mess in Europe. This was hampered when within months of hostilities beginning that summer of 1914, the transport of the treasured resin from the East was stopped, as boat after boat was sunk in the Atlantic and the channel. Many ships carrying the raw goo from Ceylon were torpedoed by U-boat. This was the first war on drugs, I suppose. But Robbie, now dressed almost exclusively as a chap, and I still managed a modicum of rebellious chaos with our meagre rations.

We were there at the Marne in September '14, but we carried no narcotic. I sat in tight on the German lines with special dispensation from Hühnerbein. I gave rallying speeches to the lads and to the officers on the power of the Teutonic spirit. We played Wagner and drank. The poor boys did not seem too enthused, and I knew from Robbie's letters, neither were our boys. It was heartbreaking to know that the youth, to whom I was preaching, were the poor buggers who were next over the top and into the flying flak. Desperate souls shat their pants and spoke, in varying tones of sanity and clarity, of Mama, as they were ordered to oblivion over excellent cognac and pulverised snuff by the church-going monsters in London and Berlin.

*

My sturdy accomplice and I both slalomed across front lines all the way to the North Sea from 1914 onwards, conversant in invective-stuffed lower Prussian, snot-raking Flemish and swaggering Italian. We sent daily messages to each other by pigeon, and bellowed laughter until the poor bastards around us joined in, such was its infection and their lack of hope. They believed we knew something they did not, the intuitive and exhausted and hollow beauties. As fifth columnists, we sat in trenches with boys from Stuttgart and Mainz, and rather than send them to their deaths, when possible, we urged them to desert, and ensured their safety from their own firing squads. We shovelled away hundreds, thousands, pouring more than the authorities would ever admit onto vessels in Genoa and Dubrovnik and Hamburg bound for anonymity in Peru, the South Pacific and of course, Ceylon. From our side, the weary Tommy found passage to Marseille and Lisbon. The giddy and deranged generals had no idea for months, such was the indiscriminate piles of bones perpetually ahead of them. The cunts just frothed orders and banqueted in vast chateaux. Meanwhile, our elaborate route would have thrilled that Pimpernel Sir Percy Blakeney, for it was also his turf from a hundred years previous. *Plus ça change, plus c'est la même chose* – well, apart from the fact that he had shovelled aristocrats over the channel, while, with us, it was the elevated classes who were being fooled and robbed of their human fuel for the fire that raged.

Imagine only stopping the carnage on both sides for a few hours, only so the corpses out of the trenches could be shovelled away. On the German side, I saw them discard the bodies, and we all knew they were going to the glue factories. It was called the *Kadaververwertungsanstalt*.[*] The British

---

[*] *Carcass-Utilisation Factory.*

naval blockade had cut off the supply of fats, so now corpses of boys were rendered down for lipids, which were then used to produce nitroglycerin for explosives, candles by which to write one's last letter to mother, the missus or the kids, and dubbin for the boots that would carry the next sorry lot to their ends.

The most profound misery we witnessed when we saw those teenage boys and fathers and brothers climb to their annihilation, unable to divert them away for we were under the glare of a gutless officer, was matched by the absolute rapture, the euphoria and the enchantment of when we were able to veer these blessed boys, with cowering mothers, across a stretch of water, or hollow and frantic fathers out to the East, to a new land, where mornings might be greeted with delirium and elation, a beatitude to persist all day and for a lifetime. And yet, the reality would be that many of those we saved would be scorched not by shell or mortar, but by the guilt and stigma of not being taken by explosion, bullet, gangrenous trench-foot or gas attack. Dandylyon was a middle-aged man now, but spent his days sweeping through the oases and the enclaves around the world that we had established for these fellows, nursing and counselling those blighted by what they had seen in and in-between the trenches. Prudence was always at his side, of course. They were a formidable team.

5.4 Hey Tommy! *Heilige Nacht*

Then one day, the toffee arrived. A minuscule amount came to me just inside the Belgian border. I split it with a foot-long section of wire from no man's land. I requisitioned one of the company's malleable and brave carrier pigeons that I had recruited for mischief, and sent her to Robbie, whom I knew was within a mile on the other side, that late December day.

We only had enough resin to make the weakest of brews, and to spike the shots of grog that had been sent to the front by the King as a Christmas gift. Robbie and I not only synchronised across no man's land in front of us, but then zipped with gusto along the frontline towards the sea, leaving sabotage and monkey business in our determined slipstream.

When our droplets were empty and once again with the collusion of a pigeon, Robbie and I marched from opposing trenches, and shook hands in front of the startled thousands in Flanders Field, sparking a moment in Mankind which is still to receive its full and proper recognition, for its disclosure undermines the evil bastards who kill hundreds of thousands of boys for profit and represent to them far, far less than a stolen pawn on the queen's rook flank. The Germans then allowed this moment's hope to spread. They all began to sing Christmas carols, the echo funnelling down the trenches in the eeriest way, undulating and reverberating for miles and from miles in the oddest manner. It was quite impossible to know if the effects of the resin were totally responsible for this trick of the ear or whether mother science herself was sticking her oar in through the radio transmitters and stirring up the rebellion. Music, music, music. The British sang along with them, and their own bizarre echo of tens of miles of trenches spilled over the top and danced over the wires, shells, the potholes, the mud, and the bones and the bodies. The blessed Germans even sang in English.

Silent Night, Holy Night

The Hun then began to light cigarettes while standing in full sight of the enemy. There was no sniper fire to take off the head of the smoker.

The British stood up and did the same.

'*Oi Fritz!*'

'*Hey Tommy, Merry Christmas.*'

That Christmas Day in 1914, we played football on the mined land between armies, and we almost ended the whole war by the twenty-eighth, such was its mass stretching from southern Belgium to the umbra of Montparnasse. Lads from Bristol and Leeds and the Lakes lit cigarettes for men from Heidelberg, Halle and the Schwarzwald. Candles were burnt and carried in small pine trees. The candles may well have been made from the processed fats of someone's son, splattered across still tough and patchy green earth in the first days of the war.

The men compared weaponry, armour, and helmets and gave minute stores of rations wrapped in muslin to each other as Christmas gifts.

I saw a German trimming the hair and the beard of an Englishman, for he had recognised his barber from Jermyn Street in '09.

Those small moments might have torched a crooked and sparkling line of turquoise, lilac and death-white, visible from space. My pal and I kicked that first ball, and shouted, '*Heute und Morgen. Kein Krieg.*'[*]

Our rebellion seemed strong, as it extended beyond the points where we had administered the droplets. The stone-cold sober joined in from both sides. Some officers relented with them, others were simply ignored. Several were gagged and bound to bunk beds, left to be sniffed and nibbled on by rats. I stood on a hillock of mud, and for hours preached to a revolving crowd of a hundred or more, imploring them to spread the word to demand a campaign to unionise and to raise the

---

[*] *Today and tomorrow. No war.*

pay of soldiers that would make war too expensive. They seemed so responsive.

Christmas Day passed and rifles remained down, Germans and British explored each other's trenches for diaries and letters, for they had once been their own. The songs abated and then piped up again, filling the line with a renewed vigour for peace. The immediate future of the planet was in the hands of these belligerent boys and hard men, just as it had been decided upon an unfortunate street corner in Sarajevo, a scorching day just months previously. I had read much about the Will of a people, the German hierarchy revelled in it, but, by God, *this* was so very different. This was a visceral desire to live, to survive, and to see one's children and one's home again. They were, after all, just over that twenty-one-mile stretch of sea. So close from decency. Yet it felt like they were a lifetime away, but perhaps if we were all to spit together, we could drown the bastards who'd sent these fine and worthy runts here. It was no longer a scrap of nations for me, for those German lads were a magnificent lot. It was political and unashamedly revolutionary. Of course, I despised the monsters that sanctioned this murder. How fucking dare they?

I spent months crossing from one side to another, in the vein of the little boy with no friends who plays chess against himself or the tennis player who sprints and leaps from one side of the net to the other to return his own lofty lobs. This was achieved with the help of the Imperial German Flying Corps and the Royal Flying Corps. I was dropped by biplane well behind lines, each time with the best wishes of a pilot who was convinced I was on his side. Only the British lads were correct, of course. I knew Manfred von Richthofen, the Red Baron, met him several times and he even dropped me into Belgium at midnight after a hefty schnapps session. He was an entertaining and large-hearted bloke with incredible skin, a mad gaze and lips like figs.

High above the Western Front, he asked me at full volume and in a comically Germanic accent over his shoulder, spittle jisming over his goggles and flying cap, 'So, Crowley, you are a double agent in more ways than one. How is it when you are taken by a large man?'

I put my finger to my lips, smiled and yelled, 'Please watch where you are going!' as we entered a thick cloud. 'And do you really wish to know the enemy's secrets?'

He laughed so hard, until we entered a tailspin. He coughed, and I was unsure whether it was from laughter or whether he had inhaled toxins from below. We dug ourselves out of the dive with inches to spare, flicking a poor, startled and skinny horse's arse with the tip of the wing as we did so well behind the lines. These Germans really do have the most remarkable and misunderstood sense of humour. I suspect they might be so evolved in this regard that the English simply do not hear the pitch of their nuanced dog whistle.

But maybe not.

Just as there are the perks of double agency, mainly being believed by both sides, then there is always the equal and opposite disadvantage. That is, one might be disbelieved by both (or even one) side. I might well have been shot were I not to be withdrawn from my mischief on the front, for who knew if Winston could protect me here in the theatre of war. The generals crushed the Christmas Truce rebellion, and in doing so, I was given new orders. I was removed from the front, and was told I was to be shipped to the United States. I was given a new mission, to collude with the German political meddlers in New York, but I would be back to liberate more of those lads. I swore it as I arrived back in England. And I knew Robbie would continue in my absence. Robbie, dressed as either lass or lad, did not so much answer to Whitehall, as she did to me. She was my own personal insurgent.

January, 1915

From London, I sent letters to Robbie thrice weekly. And soon our mischief was an interlocking charm, as her movements stitched a neat thread over the wound of the trenches of the Western Front, and I prepared first with Winston's pals in SW1 and then alone in Manhattan to engage the military and political chiefs of a new Germany in the Occult. I frolicked in a Blackness that they simply cannot resist. This was a singular and a lonely pursuit, and one into which only I wished to delve. I feared naught. Perhaps I should have for I was a) amid the enemy during wartime and b) I was prodding the darker edges of the human mind, and this is perilous ground too.

The arcane and demonic tendencies of the Nazis twenty years later were not a new whim. They were deeply rooted. There was an old German sect called the Ahnenerbe,* who researched the cultural and archaeological history of the Aryan race. National obsessions like this don't just crop up. They are cultivated with malintent.

The Germans' expeditions – geographical and spiritual – into magic were camp and melodramatic farce. Their research was largely shoddy, boyishly cart before the horse, and always in the vast shadow cast by the keenness to find a proof for their theory of their own superiority. Usually so adept in technology, this was reverse engineering of the worst kind. Such is hubris. I encouraged this, for they saw me as the very essence of knowledge, reason and wickedness. (No one is totally

---

* *Inherited from Forefathers.*

stupid, after all.) But let us not pretend that they were not dangerous, for viciousness straddles the undulating borders of intelligence with a light and eager thigh.

MI-1's plan was for me to become a triple agent, for our threesome was now inclusive of Satan; or so those juvenile and gullible Prussians were concerned. There is no fucking Satan, of course. If one speaks for Him, or, more pertinently, if the Germans *believe* that one speaks for Him, one does not even need to speak sense to have them do as one wishes. Any instruction marginally north of gibberish would be executed by enthusiastic jackboots within the hour.

And so, it would all be such a lark with them. Or it would have been had I been able to forget about the horrors at the front. I could at least leave with the knowledge that the reasonably roomy channels we had set up to allow for desertion from the trenches, would work for the next three and a half years when no one was watching. It was scant comfort, as I prepared to leave for New York in early 1915 when I completed two important missions. I secretly arranged the air-dropping of anti-war propaganda and opium across the front line in France and Belgium. I also went to Moscow to see an old friend, and as I walked out of my front door in my beloved Cambridge, my heart broke upon receipt of a letter from a Sussex hospital. I had lost another daughter, this time to consumption, and then as a direct result within ten days, my certified wife followed into the ground, her cause of death, a broken heart and lunacy. This Pimpernel wanted to die with them.

> Be extremely subtle even to the point of formlessness. Be extremely mysterious even to the point of soundlessness. Thereby you can be the director of the opponent's fate.
>
> – Sun Tzu

Chapter 6

My Nemesis & My Doppelgänger –
A Poet & a Holy Man – London & Moscow

> The first discipline of education must therefore be to
> refuse resolutely to feed the mind with canned chatter.
> – Aleister Crowley

*There are faces I recognise from a smile and hello, many
more I know as friends. Time allows this to happen, as
does a thoroughly humane spirit and mind. Time has forged a
unity of pleasantness here. Shangri-La is not conducive to
malice, and would not welcome it, though it is rarely tested. If
we think it seems too good to be true, perhaps that says more
about us than it does of this place where a gentle and non-
invasive Buddhism seems to handle most eventualities. The
deep breaths required up here should be mandatory down there
for there is indeed a magic right under our nose.*

*The locals are encouraged to either stay here or to find their
way in the modern world. It is their own True Will. There is
adequate room here were everyone keen to stay, but there is an
infused way in these people not to slacken in their industry. For
them, this means exporting their unique product. This means
they willingly seek to spread the word of peace in the barren*

terrains down the mountain and into the cities and overseas. To do otherwise would to be like the farmer who keeps his harvest in the field, while the children in the city go hungry.

I have been supremely happy here. Perhaps they might welcome me back one day, though I might have to make use of a sedan-chair and several Sherpas to bear both it and me on the trip up next time.

Eight hours to go.

6.1 MAGICK & THE GOLDEN DAWN

I was now to go to New York City for MI-1. There were two missions to complete en route. The second one was with a holy man in Moscow. The first was with the Hermetic Order of the Golden Dawn in London.

Magic is a vastly misunderstood term. When I spoke of it, it confused those misinformed types and those who believed the boyish tittle-tattle and the fairy stories about me. When I wrote of it (and spelled it out), it became clear to my audience that I referred to something quite different. *Magick*.

This is not the hocus-pocus of clods and clowns. This is not sleight of hand. This is the science and the art of changing how one lives one's life, and fulfils one's true destiny. It is how we become the best we can be, and achieve those lofty ambitions we set ourselves in our dreamiest moments. It is a selfish *and* a thoroughly selfless process, for in fighting for our own self-actualisation, we add to the well-being of this heavenly body called Earth, creating a symbiosis with Her and with Our fellow man. The power of the unlocked, unshackled and truly liberated mind of one individual is a potent force. The unification of tens of millions of such free and determined thought shall in turn unshackle the world. We are capable of this change, and simply put, magick allows us to access that.

The Golden Dawn refused to acknowledge its elements, preferring instead to revel in juvenile back-slapping, melodramatic role-playing and masonic self-preservation.

Magick is achieved through banishing negativity, and through invocation and evocation, Eucharistic ritual, consecration and purification, astral travel, yoga and divination. Some do it through the group ritual; some possess the might to achieve this through their own meditation. Some are liberated through the severity and intensity of the pleasure orgy. Some have their minds changed and set free from constraint by powerful drugs and a forceful but amicable, welcoming and benevolent leader, such as me.

The end is the same: an evolved human being whose own free Will combines with his or her destiny in a unified and simultaneous crescendo. What a marvel.

And so as magic and magick are not to be confused, then neither should be the vital term, Will, for this is not some whim upon which to act. The Will is the fulfilment of life itself, and I achieved mine on many mountainsides with torrents of youthful flesh. This I called sex magick.

Yes, there was trickery and there were hoaxes in the midst of narcotic highs, but these were merely aids, just as the blacksmith bends the horseshoe while it is white hot. Nature allows this, and one must use everything at one's disposal. The horse is certainly thrilled at this assistance.

I knew I was evolving and outgrowing the Golden Dawn. My time at the front, and my years of mischief with MI-1 had only highlighted how pathetic their charades were. The realistic visions of war scorched into my memory made them and their flouncing appear absurd. I was reaching out for greatness, while they pranced around like arses. This was confirmed to me by the most trusted of sources within hours of arriving back in London.

'Their usefulness as an ally has ebbed,' said Dandylyon, who appeared to have aged not a day. We had met over a bottle of magnificent Beaujolais in the hotel bar at Waterloo Station.

'They are not worthy of you, Aleister,' Prudence told me. That fragrant nurse-witch was as astonishing as ever.

'Their usefulness as an adversary might, however, be on the rise,' Dandylyon added.

'Now, *that* sounds interesting,' I replied.

'You see, when it comes to the darker arts, they now exhibit many of the flimsy characteristics of the Germans. They show no desire to really improve themselves,' Prudence said. 'They want the trinkets and the trophies and the perks without yearning to grow.'

'This is what happens to human beings who have all the worldly goods and riches they could desire from an Empire's trawl and expansion,' Dandylyon observed. 'There is a rotten ego that comes with undeserved power. Bored to tears, they scratch their arses in their weeks, months and years of leisure. They, quite erroneously, believe themselves ready to move onto a higher spiritual plane.'

'*You* are ready to do that. *They* are not,' Prudence said.

I knew they were right, of course. The Golden Dawn were banal and dull freemasons, bloated on themselves, as they gambolled, frisked and minced around in masks in lordly temples, invoking nothing other than my disdain.

Bolstered by the cockiness of one who had recently strutted behind enemy lines in the filthiest war yet, I now believed the Golden Dawn to be malleable, and while I was still aided by some senior members therein and had remained somewhat grateful to them, it all now felt like a necessary discomfort in the rump.

'Whom do you most dislike among them, Aleister?' Dandy-lyon asked, a smile brewing behind his beard.

I sat back, took a large swig of wine, and thought of which of them I would most like to spike with jungle goo.

'Yeats,' I said, as I stuck my chin out and straightened the fat-knot of my scarlet tie. 'Yes, that fucker, Yeats. Why do you ask?'

'Now let it work. Mischief, thou art afoot. Take thou what course thou wilt,'* said Prudence.

We all looked at each other, and that same melodramatic burst of laughter, which we had now perfected, made the other patrons of the palatial room stop and look over to us, and quite likely wonder what the joke was all about. If only they knew.

I thought William Butler Yeats to be the quite perfect manifest-ation of the buffoonery of the Golden Dawn. The Irish poet had joined the Order some nine years before I did, and attempted to belittle me as soon as I was inducted. Dandylyon knew of his politicking to have me first refused and then black-balled. It was well known that I knew the scriptures, teachings and literature of the Order better than anyone and, so, I suspect he saw me and my knowledge as a threat but perhaps also because of my burgeoning reputation as a poet. I have always believed that language and the pen are for a nation to share, not for small circles of the elites to stick a limp flag in and call their own. How dare they?

Yeats would not even look me in the eye. He was quite

---

*   Julius Caesar, *William Shakespeare*.

happy however to shriek about me when my back was turned. If he wanted a fight, I was his man.

In hindsight, and with the mellowing of age and the serenity of Shangri-La in my very being, perhaps I might admit that my hatred for him was grounded in an envy of the reputation he had garnered for himself as a poet. Perhaps, I was jealous of this, but I remain steadfast in the belief that he was still a loathsome stiff-neck.

Meanwhile, I had rapidly advanced to elevated levels like no young man ever had, and a lot had been made of that. But, again, it was really just an old ladies' knitting circle, well trained in flouncing and posturing around, and designed to stroke egos and cockshafts. The experience was useful in making some friends, but enemies were always so much more fun. The reading of hundreds of turgid volumes of nonsensical prattle would be worth it just to punch that fucker Yeats on the beak. And this is where Prudence and Dandylyon's plan came in.

The Battle of Blythe Road, we decided, would happen on Epiphany,* 1915.

'Attempt a *coup d'etat*. The joy of this plan is that it does not matter whether you succeed or fail. Either way, we get what we want,' said Prudence.

'Which is?'

'Notoriety.'

'Yes, I know that. But specifically.'

'Because in Manhattan, where you are heading, it is far easier to have the natives chatter about a new and troubling God if He is feared and despised.'

'I see.'

---

* *January the sixth – the official end of Christ's birthday.*

'Oh! and Winston sends his regards. You will meet one day very soon, he tells me. And you have impressed him.'

Tick tock. Tick tock.

6 January 1915

36 Blythe Road, W14, was the headquarters of the Golden Dawn in Britain. It was a broad Edwardian mansion town-house behind wrought-iron gates and set back on a vast drive-way of gravel, bordered with cedars and a couple of oaks.

The temples of central London were used for regular worship, those rituals that included the broader swathes of riff-raff. When the higher echelons wanted a more intimate and elite spot, they headed to Blythe Road, W14. Epiphany brought out all of the main characters, as a faux mocking of Christ. They headed to their secret temple of worship beneath this mansion in London's Olympia, tucked between Holland Park, Hammersmith and Shepherd's Bush.

Prudence and Dandylyon had offered no other advice than to cause a stir.

I was beyond requiring minders at this point, so headed there alone, very aware of the fact that the more lonesome the mischief-maker, the scarier he shall appear. Had I started throwing punches with Orr at my side, the impact would be trivial. There are some things a chap must do alone. In this case, the task began with polishing off large piles of cocaine, a fingernail of goo and many large Scotches in a snug bar of The Prince of Wales public house off Kensington High Street.

'Are you all right, fella?' the sweaty landlord was kind enough to ask of me. I excused my appearance with a High-land shield, pentagrams etched on my face and a scabbard on my belt as a fancy dress stunt for a chum's stag evening. He might have been enquiring more about my health.

I entered the ritual on Blythe Road easily enough, for at that early hour I was still a member of the Order, and still knew the passwords. Several hours later, however, I was dispatched towards the kerb by two chaps of Orr's dimensions, with the inky pentagrams on my cheek trickling with blood from the left tear duct, shoulder limp and dislocated from the socket, the silver point of a large and spiky Egyptian amulet lodged deep in my skull above the right ear. I steadied myself on the caked ice underfoot, but still yelled provocative and confused invocations. Yeats gestured like a ponce behind the oafs. Such solitary shows of strength as mine that night, against great odds, can put fear into one's opponent, especially in those times when they walk the streets alone or sit in solitude late at night in front of their fading hearth fire in their girthy, creaking houses. They all knew I had large and dangerous friends, but still decided to instigate violence on my own. Yeats was, by all accounts, now petrified of me. And now I was the *bête noire* of all of them. And their equally limp affiliates across the ocean in Manhattan.

I had always treated the Order as an apprenticeship, to see how not to do things, pretty much as the Christianity of my boyhood had equipped me with the knowledge to undermine the cretins of the church. Always know one's enemy. When I started my own religion (and the time was now almost here for that), then that would be something to behold. And I still had plenty of tricks left for Yeats and the Irish, for I would slide comfortably into the scrunched anus of that particular Trojan horse in New York City later in that Great War. And many, many years later in 1937 as I returned from a brief-ish mountaineering expedition from Germany to the Himalayas and then China, Rangoon and India, the greatest pleasure of returning to the modern world was a pilgrimage to Drumcliffe in County Sligo, where I dropped my trouser and fouled that fucker's tomb every midnight for a fortnight. I digress.

If one truly wishes to speak of that cheap stunt called magic, then I am also able to elaborate on that, for the greatest trick was that large one played on the world by Winston, Dandylyon, Orr, Prudence, Robbie and me. This was the chicanery and fraudulent flimflam that told of me, the supposed wicked-est man in the world, a murderer, a paedophile, a Satanist, while I was, in truth, saving thousands of boys from France and preparing for the bigger fight against the Evil ahead. This was the fast shuffle, the bait and switch, one that the true Pimpernel not only bears for the greater good, but truly relishes when he guffaws at the nitwits who know less than bugger all and yet posture like egg-heads and savants. I had now grown out of the temptation to set them right. Time would look after all of this, as would some schoolboy meddling and shadowy giggles from the greatest spy in the world.

And thanks to what I had seen on the lines in France and Belgium, this was no longer a simple case of fidelity to one's country. My spymasters did not need to know that there was a further nuance to my double-agent status. I would now set up a third front and fight forever for *them,* those poor boys and their weeping mothers of all sides. It was now a three-dimensional game of chess, a doddle for me even blindfolded in the style of my heroes at The Legion, as I left London on that old boat train, and then a steamer to St Petersburg, where I would overland to Moscow to see that ripe and aroused holy man, Grigori Yefimovich. My pal and ally, Rasputin.

6.2 Twins

For nearly twenty years, we had connived and compared notes, inspired and colluded with each other. We were mischievous twins. We wrote to each other and of each other. He appears in several of my works under different names and guises. Intrigued by the Golden Dawn, he came to Cambridge in 1903, and caused untold melodrama until he was escorted to the city limits by the police. There were then tales of his deeds out into the fenlands, legend and myth of bothered ladies and farm girls, furious husbands and livid fathers. Orr finally pulled him out of a ditch near King's Lynn and had him taken to London, where he was administered strong opiates and put on the boat train with several members of The Legion.

The shelves are full of the charlatan *stanniki*,* his story is well documented, and often laboriously so for one of such sparkle and life.

He had always been of particular interest to me because of the power he was able to exert through the Will, through his physical threat, through alcohol and drugs, through sex, and bundle them all together under the excuse of religion. This was a marvel, so closely were our philosophies aligned. When I saw him again in 1915, though, I have to admit we were separated by one despicable act if one believed the newspapers. He had just been accused of raping a nun. However, he had *not*. Grigori claimed the sister had thrown herself at him, and finally, even the Mother Superior capitulated and agreed with him after the lightest of questioning. I knew Grigori was not beyond casting his persuasive powers and his grotesque shadow across those elder nuns too. Had he hypnotised the Mother Superior? Had he even pleasured her? Both of these, to me, remain more likely than his being guilty of this crime. I know that he possessed a moral compass, albeit oft misplaced in a dark drawer.

---

* A *holy wanderer, pilgrim.*

It is remarkable how we left almost identical furrows with our mischievous, enlightened and wilful ploughs. We were contemporaries, born just six years apart. Like me, he was no Holy fool, but a true Prophet.

As with me, there were so many lies about him.

The list of our similarities goes on.

He, like me, was a vehement pacifist, despite a voracious proclivity to a brawl.

He, like me, thoroughly appreciated the company of the paid lady, despite an eminently potent ability to hypnotise the most frowned brow and the most dotty lass, for sex by commerce was a thrill.

He, like me, took acute financial advantage from those God-seekers and sorrowful Bible-thumpers, who could afford it. In the shallowest and most mean-spirited of times, those morons, searching for mysticism where there was little were easy to part from their silver and gold.

He, like me, was a rabid advocate for narcotics to either discover the true nature of the Occult or fake its flimsier elements.

He, like me, held the power of personality with panache, vaulting daily over the banalities of religion and into drunken orgies, casting spells and sowing social scandal.

And we would both make do with an arse in an emergency.

He also owned the most dangerous eyes I ever saw. His power was a calming one to horses, dogs, wolves, the insane, the perilous and to small children. He was all gypsy sex, second sight and drugs. That fine pre-eminent devil.

6.3 Moscow

They say that Russia's history is scribed in pencil, so that it is more easily erased. But then only a fool shall attempt to remove Rasputin's indelible markings from the psyche of that land. They are emblazoned upon her in blood.

When I arrived in late March of 1915, that fiend, that great hound, was convalescing, having survived a fourteen-inch cut to the gut with a carving knife that had spilled his intestines. The woman who had shanked him was convinced he was the Antichrist.

I sat by his bedside as he slept. I had been there perhaps five minutes, holding his left hand, my eyes resting, when I was forced into a shudder. He was now staring at me with that consuming and fervent glare, the one that I worshipped. He was my equal in many regards, but I silently sensed a vast and largely untapped power within him. He seemed to possess the ability to fight gods and spirits, as well as large numbers of humans, and much of this came both from his silence when he chose it and, conversely, the turbulence for which he was famed. It was a frightening and inspiring combination in a man. He spoke to me in his peasant dialect, one that I had now studied, conversed in fluently with bemused and honoured gypsies,* and practised with intensity for this very occasion, for over a decade.

'Ah! Beast. It is marvellous to see you.'

'You too, Grigori. I did not know you were on your deathbed, or I would have come sooner. And anyway, I thought you would last for ever, for only the good die young.'

He laughed violently, which caused the minutest of twitches in his right eye, but a patch of vermillion soaked into the bandage around his midriff. He noticed it as it grew, and carried on speaking.

We had corresponded to a degree whereby pleasantries

---

* *Dandylyon had the remarkable blighters shipped to Cambridge, Dulwich and Boleskine to school me. They were supremely shifty and great fun.*

were unnecessary, not that either of us suffered from small talk. We had sent the letters to false names and addresses, and we were careful to use banal code for the more secretive detail.

'To hell with you. I thought at least I could count on you over and above this country of potato-pickers drowning in puddles of vodka and crowned inbreds. Russia is a country on its knees, Beast.'

'Oh really. Do tell.'

'Christ, what would you like to know? I can tell you about the plight of these damned peasants who surround me. Russians used to be such an imaginative lot, although I have to say, the female of our species continues to show an insight and an artistry that borders on the visionary. Just when I think originality is finished, one of them exhibits true inventiveness. Just look at this mess! They are now attempting murder of the Enlightened in broad daylight,' he said, and he glanced at his centre.

And he bellowed again, which nudged the edges of the scarlet map on his torso an inch in all directions, this time without as much as a facial tic.

Since 1905,[*] I had only twice seen him – in Cambridge and then London. This was around the time that Winston and Dandylyon – through a chain of MI-1 chaps in Moscow – had introduced him to the Czar and his physicians[†].

The Czar's son, His Imperial Highness Alexei Nikolaevich, Sovereign Heir Czarevich, Grand Duke of Russia was already

___

[*] *Russia had suffered defeat against the Japanese and the first Revolution had happened. The Royal Family remained in power, but concessions had been made, and a parliament, the Duma, had been established. This quelled the rebellion, but that was a matter of time, according to that ever-prescient marionette, Dandylyon.*

[†] *Winston and Dandylyon's London connection, George V, and Czar Nicholas II were first cousins.*

suffering from haemophiliac bleeding. This sent his mother into pitiful nadirs. Her towering adoration of her infant son appeared vaster than a Russian war memorial, and she jack-knifed at his smallest and most innocent tumble. Our plan soon worked like a treat. Our spies in the royal household encouraged the Czarina to doubt her closest physicians, encouraging her to listen to the Holy Man with a burgeoning reputation for magic and healing. Dandylyon had armed Grigori with a small array of medicines, both natural and manufactured. She relented, and was soon impressed both with Rasputin and the effects on her child.

The boy adored Grigori and could be soothed just by his lordly presence. Grigori equipped young Alexei with an ability to tap into the power of his mind. He encouraged him to breathe deeply, to meditate, and even when absent was able to control the boy's moods by specific words and sentences, ones that reminded the young prince of his potent wizard of a friend. One might say he had been brainwashed, conditioned, but only to force positivity upon the boy when near and far from Grigori. When he heard the words spoken by the monk, he recalled happy times in meadows and in front of hearths, slowing the heart, mellowing the spirit and allowing his impaired and frail blood to simmer. The youth was encouraged to practise a yoga that removed all adrenaline. This was the monk's magic, and it was apparently enough to purchase the initial adoration and loyalty of the Queen.

When I arrived in the city in the early blooming and supremely mild spring of 1915, the boy was now ten years older, and Grigori a national figure. Adored and hated in equally impressive measure, the *stanniki* aroused rampant passions in all. Of course he did. Even the nurses, who right now were running around the luxurious regal ward, pampering him and squealing like well-fucked mice at the burst stitches in his gut, were impassioned. Even in his relatively sterilised and cleansed form with a combed beard and washed hair,[*] sober and ponderous, he spiked these little squaws into an intuitive frenzy around their warm and highly conductive centres. The larger matron, well sketched by cliché, seemed to be all the more at the Master's Will, perhaps his power and influence was a function of surface area.

6.4 EPIPHANY

He spoke.

'Beast, listen to me. There is an exciting path ahead for you and me. I have been practising this of late, and with the most remarkable success. I wanted to write to you of it, but I am so glad to reveal this to you, sitting here. You are one of the few people, perhaps even the only one, who will fully appreciate what I am going to tell you.'

He shoo'd one of the girls away with a wolf's growl, as she attempted to approach his wound. She retreated while her gaze remained fixed on his face. She bowed as she moved backwards, as if away from a grumpy and capricious king or a she-vampire from the sated and spent Dracule, limp and white virgin on his lap.

'This epiphany I had is to be found at the pivot of happiness and reaching God. It came to me, as I knelt at the altar at midnight by the Ivan the Great Bell Tower, while devouring a doubting whore with my mouth. She found the spirits there, as I led her to Enlightenment. Then it occurred to me. I had, indeed, found a new Truth.'

He paused. His apparent and intense sobriety lent further weight to his pending revelation.

---

[*]   *He still stank.*

'Beast, I propose to you that sin is purged from the soul by giving in to more of it. Sin to drive out sin.'

It was so simple, I was fleetingly furious that I had not thought of it myself. He went on. 'How do we rid ourselves of the roasted beast's flesh on our platters in our banqueting halls? How do we empty the beer in our jugs? How do we sate the lust in our loins? We indulge in it, and we never ignore it as the foolish puritans would wish. This is the only way it is subdued. In short, bestiality, buggery and lust are the swiftest ways to The Almighty. Endless fornication will bring the souls of the prude masses to the Lord.'

'I can only assume your flock approves.'

'Astonishingly so. These are strange times, Beast. The world is about to burn. The Book of Revelations told us. This is the End of Days. We must enjoy them, for the Lord gave both man and woman instruments of vast pleasure and we must use this pastime to cleanse our souls in preparation to meet Him. We must always fornicate.'

He chuckled, for he was sane enough to recognise the near-lunacy and absolute clarity of his approach.

'We do not express malice. We do not propose evil for the sake of evil. We are not even sorcerers. We are the instruments of our own desire, an exponential, spiritual and tangible, pursuit of joy. This is simply the furtherance of purity, ecstasy and rebellion, with the euphoric goat-headed gods waving us on. Even Jesus would howl with delight at us all.'

6.5 We Practise as We Preach

Moscow can be brutal in March, but she was treating me to a sliver of her summer. The sticky evening was moving in and the majestic windows of the palatial villa that had his ward at its womb let in stunning pre-nocturnal pockets of released gardenia, rafts of lilac and teasing breaths of honeysuckle. A lush crocus tree moved by the window, captivating with its yellow and green, permitting the scents to pass intermittently, with her own slight gestures and sashays in the breeze. The tiles underfoot released the slight musk from a gentle and delicious coconut wax, while the sinks supplied a whiff of soapy sterility. It would have been very easy to convalesce in here. The curtains fluttered and blew in like intrigued butterflies, rhythmically and politely pushing their boundaries. They too had heard tales of the monster on that bed, it seemed. There was a large supply of chloroform, morphine and cocaine lozenges next to his bed on a chunky turquoise table. Apart from this piece, the scarlet patch of blood and a black wrought-iron bed frame with matching vast beard and eyes, the room was universally white.

And so, there lay supine the rousing body of a miry and soiled god, fondling his manhood of mythical length* with his scarred peasant mitts beneath the finest Egyptian cotton.

He lay on his vast plinth slab like a medieval king in stone on his tomb grasping his battle sword. The bed was large enough to fit six chaps the size of Orr. He saw my perfunctory glance at his medicines.

'Go ahead, my friend.'

We then indulged liberally in all three, and as overtly as taking fruit from the bowl. There was the sense that my extravagance was minutely more hurried than his. That was the way of things, for he had had a head start. Admittedly, I had whiled away the boat journey in my cabins in my own doped fog.

---

* Thirteen inches according to legend. A group of nobles were said to have removed it on his deathbed, and his daughter Maria to have kept it in a pickling jar. I know this latter part to be false, I shall explain momentarily. Its supposed length would certainly explain much of his popularity and powers of persuasion.

We continued to speak on the same plane as each other; it was just a slightly different one to previously. It was possibly best described as a mellow enthusiasm, given the contrasting but powerful trajectories of the drugs. It was a transcendent and ebullient comfort, made so much more pleasant by the fragrances of nature drifting in from the orchards that stroked the sensations from the liquids and lozenges. We were leavened further by the servitude of the nurses, who clearly fizzed at the raw power in these two physical forms and the supernatural penumbra that we cast. There was a definite feeling that the clips, trots and occasional canters on the tiles outside in the corridors were all tuned and paced to please us.

He closed his eyes, as he spoke of his epiphany again. His lids were lowered not from fatigue; he seemed to be channelling an attempt to move. His fire was silver-hot. To him, these were wasted seconds and minutes that he ought to be spending blemishing a factory girl or a lady-in-waiting, though this was not to undermine the tenderness and the cleverness of the Colossus. Flesh remained as enticing to this ogre as to a frisky self-polluting and virginal schoolboy. His cravings were perpetual and self-fuelling raptures in the spirit of the lucky chap who trims lawns all day and is never far from the sensual bliss of cut grass. And the more he had, the more he wanted. We were so alike in many ways. It is hard to tell of him, without reverting to that hackneyed style; that same one I have promised to avoid in the telling of my secret life. I mean it is difficult to avoid cliché around him. It might always be so with giants. So, I merely tell you what I saw and the words he spoke. And the impact he had on me.

The tap of the girls' shoes outside intensified. They seemed to react to the stirrings of the Master, as would Renfield and the vampire bitches when the Dracule neared.

'Listen to them, the children of the night. What music they make.'

'They tried to put a man in charge here, but Alexandra is a dutiful schoolgirl in my presence. The girls soon returned.'

'Is she not jealous?' I asked.

'Oh, good God, no. She knows not to be so flimsy. I shall go and take her with a brutish passion in the palace tonight. You must join us.'

I now add to our list of shared traits – *We both fucked queens.*

Was he being serious with his hypothesis of this lustful ladder to God? Did it matter if he was or was not? I thought it brilliant anyway, and if he was teasing then I would gladly take the philosophy as my own when I left Russia. Of course, I would credit him as and when it was wise, advantageous or permitted. It was all academic, however, as he was, indeed, thoroughly serious.

'They just all want any excuse to be tarnished. What better one than the Lord Jesus Christ to grant them entrance to the Kingdom of Heaven? They will say, "But it must be true. The Holy Man told me so."'

It worked for everyone. It was delicious in its neatness, but then all the truly great plans are. I suspect that this was the very reason Dandylyon had insisted I visit Rasputin at this time. He would have known his life was in danger, and there was no real need for me to see him in person to further execute our political plans. It was also the safest way to get to the United States.

I knew as Grigori began to stir to go and cause mischief in the Moscow evening that I was simply being exposed to the Holy Man's philosophy for never had two such grotesque and wicked souls marched in such a righteous and symbiotic beat.

*

As I witnessed the fight between his physical tang and that loveliness from nature around him, I was reminded of that time as a boy when I realised for the first time there was a God and Satan. But I did not know which was which. I was puzzled as to why I thought of this now. I was disturbed from this thought, when there was a definite and collective trot to be heard, as the monk began to rise from his repose.

'Pocket all of that stuff there,' as he raised his unruly eyebrows, with a flick, at the stash of drugs. 'There's more down in the cupboard too.'

There I found powdered cocaine, two bottles of vodka and four opium pipes.

'There is so much kindness in the world today, Beast. If you know where to look.'

By some defiance of logic and kinetics, the broad, pink elephantine matron was the first at the door of his ward. The pleasant *cassoulette* that emanated from her neck and forearms drifted ahead of her and her blushed countenance. She closed the door when she saw her patient stirring. I expected some school-ma'am-ish admonishment, coupled with sensible medical advice. It was the joyous and giddy sprightliness with which she marched to Grigori's bed, slumped herself face down as if being roughed up by a malevolent poltergeist, hoisted her starched skirts and offered her rump, that I recall being the most impressive and life-affirming of acts. Her guttural urging to be blessed and brought close to the Lord for one last time was the prompting of an animal in its pomp, though the magnificence of her jack-knifed centre and the revealed womanliness had two immediate acolytes. Hers was then a Gregorian rhythm and chant, as we both treated her as soulmate and sailor.

Several times, he howled some words I did not recognise.

'*Ai lins bilele unui înger.*'

A small, well-formed gang of frisky nun-nurses gathered at the open windows to ogle the sexual union, like youths stretching to witness the cricket from a large oak. Their giggles and whimpers accompanied the released honeysuckle into that summer evening, and the sighs of the grateful lady, now at one in an intoxicated trance with her twisted god. It was over.

The sated demon just growled and looked for his smock. It hung in a sturdy armoire with his rope belt, and beneath were his wide sandals. The nurses had attempted to scrub the robe, but it still carried his zesty scent. He dropped it over his head in a single move, and reached for the rope. He then tied this around his bandaged waist with a powerful tug that ignored his injury. He slipped on the sandals, soaked a towel in chloroform, took a huge inhalation, crossed his eyes momentarily and declared, 'We are late for royalty.'

The panting matron remained still and euphoric in her breathing, as he ruffled her hair as one would a long-lost school chum, who was face down with a hangover. He repeated the same words as earlier.

'*Ai lins bilele unui înger.*'

Within minutes of passing through the pungent blossoms and lush plants, I became aware of his unique aroma yet again. It truly thrived and flourished outside of the confines of the sterile ward. It too seemed intent on achieving its own Will with an admirable stubbornness. The *mirepoix* of the stench was precisely the same concoction that had stirred me from my meditation in that Orthodox Church in the Urals almost a decade and half previously, when we first met.

We walked in the Moscow night, and the drugs allowed us both to drift along in comfortable silence, minds wandering. He led us towards his queen, striding with an oddly inelegant swagger as if perhaps his soul had finally just drizzled out of his anus, or maybe a deviant cowboy, who had proudly shat himself. The gait suggested both confidence and unhealthily swollen gonads.

As my mind meandered quite blissfully, he spoke.

'I think of how vicious rumour has engulfed you. It should make you proud. Let them say what they want about alleged sexual unions with beasts and children. This vicious rumour fires all we do, and hides all we do.'

He was right, and I knew, of course, I had to endure this utmost horror to maintain my Pimpernel's cloak.

'You know, if the truth be told, I admit to once having ended the life of a frog. This is the worst I have done. Its spine was needed for a spell by the banks of Loch Ness with an impressionable crowd of London fools and intrigued German members of the Scottish Mountaineering Club.'

He laughed.

I continued, 'And the reason I never took another life was because of something that happened the very next day. It was the following noon, when a lass appeared at my door asking for work at the house as a maid. The girl was most remarkable for the intensity of her stare. This might have been enough for me to offer her a position anyway, as I was, after all, in need of help. But I was most persuaded by her uncanny resemblance to the frog I had killed the previous evening.'

We both stopped walking to lean on each other and laugh.

'We had all taken many drugs, and I seem to recall believing that this was a visitation from the transmigrated soul of the departed amphibian.'

Grigori planted a joyful, manly, protracted and stinky kiss on my lips. When he let me go, I said, 'She got the job. I called her Frog, and I never killed again.'

We continued to walk, and soon, I spoke once more.

'Yes, there was a rumour that I sliced a goat's throat as it reached climax on the back of my lover in a ceremony. This was reported back in London in a newspaper, relayed to the editor by a scandalous and libellous trollop, of whom I asked just one question. "What makes you an expert in the precise pitch of a jisming billy goat?"'*

He threw his arm around me and we walked into the sunset, a pair of loveable silhouettes to trouble a rank world.

It was always honour among thieves between him and me. He too had enjoyed a shaft, and impaled a youth's arse, for sure. But who hadn't? I was said to prefer to receive buggery, but this was true only in the pursuit of pain and magick. Intensity and sensation are musts. Yet we both could not be without the charms of a lady.

And here we were, approaching the Czarina, Alexandra. She was an unquenchable type, and I suspect she always knew that the monk would bring down her monarchy and ignite *the* revolution of the twentieth century. It was difficult not to ponder at how these palaces would change after the collapse of their worlds. It occurred to me, as Grigori wrapped a cloth of chloroform around the mouth of the willing prostrate Queen, and began his molestations as she wept with joy, that I now knew precisely why I was here. This was a personal tutelage in how to corrupt and use power for Britain's rule of the world to continue. I was in the presence of the Master.

---

* The billy goat has a sexual appetite that peaks with the seasons and with a doe's heat. They refuse to eat and exhibit an obsessive interest in the female. A buck in rut will curl his lip like a frazzled stallion to spread its own pheromones and urinate on his own front legs and face to attract his amour. Potent sebaceous glands add to his odour. It finally dawned upon me as to why I thought of these animals as I strolled with the monk. He smelled like a randy fucking goat. I loved him even more.

So what if he grabbed a lady's breasts in public in order to weigh her spirituality? Or started to undo her bodice before even uttering a word to her? And who cares if he nibbled their necks, sniffed their groins or bit their hair, while still exhibiting a percentage of his most previous meal in his beard? For this was also the very same beard that was pulled at by eager sorts pre-, mid- and post-coitus, so that they may then have their relic, which was soon sewn into their underwear, often famously alongside his trimmed fingernails? Let it be noted that this level of worship takes some achieving.

So what if he hypnotised the myopic and mean Czar, 'saved' his son many times over ten years with a median indifference, often from thousands of miles away, and fucked the king's wife far more regularly and with far greater gusto?

It was a fine night when the monk turned a steely Queen of the Realm into a shuddering and twitching imbecile with his firm and plump amorousness. However, he continued to emit from his extensive groin, a certain over-musked tang, which I found quite pungent and vile, but she wailed to have him take her. It was a relief in the end for Her Majesty, and for me too, when he wedged that monster into her, if only to remove the immediacy of the clogged stench, the rank and putrid hum of an unwashed, unsheathed and highly active bull, and therefore prevent the almost absolute certainty of my own imminent puke. I was full of respect for them both. These gods.

It was Rasputin, our Great Filthy Prophet, who finally eroded the people's confidence in the Royal Family, and so began the rebellion. And so yes, we caused the Russian Revolution, but as an inadvertent by-product of an earlier experiment. We had wanted to disrupt and sow havoc there. But now we knew that we might have to get those Americans involved in any conflict with Germany, if the Russians withdrew from the Eastern Front.

When the Czar, Alexandra and those five children were murdered by firing squad in a dingy basement in the Urals, Grigori's portrait was found scrolled in the crucifixes around the necks of all seven. I could weep. Imagine the horror for those little ones. They could not be blamed for their parents' greed. Those sweet innocents. Helpless, confused and weeping. Pissing their pants, and then dead.

And so began my journey eastwards, where I would push on over the Pacific and into the United States. This route was by far the safest to avoid the Atlantic U-boats. I would spend two years in America, doing what I did best. Mischief for England.

Legend says that when the flames touched his corpse, Rasputin sat upright on the pyre. What nonsense.

On 30 December 1916, Grigori Rasputin was poisoned with cyanide, shot several times in the head and torso, and then allegedly drowned in the icy River Neva. Some said he survived. These particular legends, myths and tittle-tattle are, however, all true.

How do I know this for sure?

Because he was here, as ripe as ever, in Shangri-La in 1938, and still spreading his Gospels and yelling, 'Ai lins bilele unui înger.'*

A young Romanian priest heard him say this once in my company, and later, on a shadowed path en route to my pasture full of goats, he stopped me and then blushed as he translated for me something that he thought I needed to know.

---

*   *'Blessed are those, who lick the balls of an Angel.'*

Chapter 7

New York City
1915–1917: WANTED

Free women cast a lustful eye
On my gigantic charms, and seek
By word and touch with me to lie,
And vainly proffer cunt and cheek;
Then, angry, they miscall me weak,
Till one, divining me aright,
Points to her buttocks, whispers, 'Greek!'
A strong man's love is my delight!
    – 'A Ballad of Passive Pederasty', Aleister Crowley

I remain on the steps of the statue, a brooding master. I glance up at the boy's midriff.

A cockroach appears from the mouth of the cherub statue, peers around, and seems to like what he sees. I clap my hands and fresh water is brought to me almost immediately. Before I drink, I offer some to the young girl who has brought it. She declines initially but accepts after I have taken several gulps. It revives us both, for she takes the remainder of the water with the grateful and honoured gusto of a runt wolf bitch lapping up the remains of the scabrous carcass. She stretches with subdued joy in her fragrant buttercup-lemon-yellow smock, smiles at me, turns and runs off with the empty jug and cup. I laugh like a friend into the space she has left behind her.

I suspect I may now appear like an old man, low on sanity and reason. This makes me smile, which of course only adds to the illusion.

I think of illuminated yesterdays, and this shall all have its supreme relevance if one is to truly understand and therefore approach the evil facing our times, and the reason I must return to England.

Seven hours to go.

7.1 AMERICA I
Winter, early 1915

Since that Battle of Blythe Road, when I tried to storm the place like some inebriated thug with no resort to nuance and quite purposefully so, my name was despised by those lousy clods of the Golden Dawn. They had been active in New York for some time. I thought I would provoke them before and upon my arrival. They would soon learn that I so very recently had founded the British Rosicrucian brotherhood of the *Ordo Templi Orientis*,* the ancient Heidelberg-based esoteric order.

I had decided to do this on the day I left Moscow after my time with Grigori. He had inflated my soul, and I knew that I had already outgrown any requirement for membership with desperate and needy morons. I would mould the O.T.O. into my own religion of Thelema – with a simple message at its heart.

DO WHAT THOU WILT. LOVE IS THE LAW.
I aimed to take the structure of the old Order, its writings

---

* *O.T.O. These were a more evolved strain of Germans, led by a pair of enlightened marvels called Carl Kellner and Theodor Reuss.*

and scriptures and texts, and thrust them into the twentieth century. We would strive for a global ideal of sexual freedom and self-providence.

The foundations of the O.T.O. were thoroughly sound. They were also refreshingly progressive and honest, for they preached personal freedoms. The Golden Dawn had always relied upon the shadiness of self-interested freemasonry and mutual commercial masturbation under the guise of ceremonial and lawless mumbojumbo. They were really just utterly dull and reactionary, ultimately grey and Presbyterian.

Instead, I would forge a resplendent, ecstatic and liberated religion based on the love of mankind, our innate desires to copulate, expand one's mind and succeed, and a deep and profound adoration of our planet through science, drugs and nature.

Hesse was partly right when he wrote, 'For me, trees have always been the most penetrating preachers.' He had clearly forgotten to mention ripe Russian Holy Men.

Indeed, Rasputin imbued me with much of this new spirit, and gave me the scope and courage to start on the long journey to becoming a god, by creating my very own church. In the days heading east from Moscow, I bristled with the excitement of a boy and the exactitude of a Prophet at this prospect, and in feeling this silent and measured thrill, knew this was my true path. I could also have burst with joy for those who would ally themselves with this wisdom.

Just as thrilling was the news in a telegram from MI-1 brought to my rattling train compartment that Herr Hühnerbein, now keen to encourage my role as a double agent, was also going to be in New York City. Two days later, I heard the same news from the gargantuan himself, also by telegram. All correspondence from either side would soon be neatly coded in the classified section of the *New York Times*. I would not be able to afford anything as amateur as a telegram coming to where I slept, for the city would be crawling with cut-throats for hire, menacing spies and ugly provocateurs. New York had a perilous repute that excited me so. I would be there soon.

Despite my concerns, guilt and protestations to Prudence and Dandylyon, Churchill apparently remained convinced that I would be far more use to the Empire there than I would be in the trenches. I comforted myself that I had already stepped on more no man's land than those putrid generals, and I would return for a full year in the front line, executing my own brand of warfare. Apparently, they needed my mischief there across the Atlantic, and not to start a soldiers' revolt. For now, my mission was a far more subtle, but still potent, one; one that would impact the globe. For London, I had to counter German propaganda that encouraged the States to stay out of the war, or even join it in support of Berlin.

This was not as fanciful a proposition as it appears today.

I would execute this plan for London, while allowing Berlin to believe I was doing precisely the opposite. For their double agent would spend his days spouting anti-English bile for the Irish and Germans. I shall explain presently, but it was all a question of nuance and measure. Therefore because of these subtleties, agile London would always prevail over these large-footed blockheads from the East. And furthermore, I had hatched a plan to sink a large boat, blame the Germans, and start to win the war, while Winston had a precise and personal motive for me to be there as well. Both will become clear very, very shortly.

7.2 A New Dawn While Soiling Delicious Twins

I sparked juvenile gossip between my graceless former accomplices in the Golden Dawn, when, while in a cloud of heroin passing through Mongolia, I announced, via a costly but worthwhile telegram, my intentions to found an English chapter of the O.T.O. and my very own Thelema with a full-page advertisement in the *New York Times*.

> I hereby announce the formation of my own Religion. I revoke all who are not ready for this Utopia. You limp spirits know who you are. And little else.
>
> Do What Thou Wilt; because men that are free, well-born, well-bred, and conversant in honest companies, have naturally an instinct and spur that prompteth them unto virtuous actions, and withdraws them from vice, which is called honour. Those same men, when by base subjection and constraint they are brought under and kept down, turn aside from that noble disposition by which they formerly were inclined to virtue, to shake off and break that bond of servitude wherein they are so tyrannously enslaved; for it is agreeable with the nature of man to long after things forbidden and to desire what is denied us.
>
> A new day of Thelema is here.
>
> Aleister Crowley

The Golden Dawn would hate the challenge of this upstart. I was told that the English Mountaineering Club squawked loud disapproval over quality gin or port in The Mall, Temple and Conduit Street, but silently and staunchly they were cheering on their man, urging him to new heights. I was now readying to cross the Pacific Ocean from the port of Tokyo on a passenger ship called *The Betsy*. The journey would be a fair excuse to relax on board with some fine poppy taken from a Yokigama hustler after several games of one-sided and then blindfolded chess. I smoked days away, but only after I had joyously soiled a pair of large-toothed, middle-aged twins (a wealthy divorcee and her sister) from Thermopolis, Wyoming.

I then meditated through hours of yoga on board, burned

marijuana on deck with new pals and again tied myself to the railings in a storm. Just for old times' sake. I reminded myself that being despised back at home really ought to prompt me to travel more. It was, after all, most liberating, for sailors, skippers and travelling twins could be so very hospitable.

7.3 'Best of Seven, You Cheating Fucker!'

Upon my arrival in the States, my meddling began almost immediately. I mailed the society card of my pseudonym, Count Vladimir Svareff of 67 and 69 Chancery Lane, to several known members of the Golden Dawn in New York City, who might or might not have known of the arrival of some demonic royalty from the East (though really arriving from the West). The response I received would act as a fair barometer of support and would indicate who had and who had not been tipped off by Dandylyon that Svareff was descending upon Manhattan from the north-west route. I billeted myself at a hotel of no luxury and in an unseemly south-eastern part of the city to avoid any gossip that was likely to arise from my checking-in to a finer establishment near the park.

I immediately enjoyed moving around the streets and neighbourhoods of this remarkable city. It is so vital to feel grounded and get some perspective in a new town.

I read this, and chuckled to myself, in the social letters to the *New York Times* within four days, as I sat in a walled garden café to the west of the park on 60th Street.

> Two days ago I received the enclosed card anonymously, and just glancing at it briefly, thinking it an advertisement of some sort, I placed it on the mantelpiece.
>
> Within a few minutes, disasters of a minor kind began to happen in my little home. First one of my most valuable vases

fell to the ground and was smashed to pieces. My little clock stopped – the clock was near the card – and then I discovered to my amazement that my dear little canary lay dead at the bottom of its cage.

The card had come from this boor, Count Vladimir Svareff. I urge anyone receiving such a card, to dispatch it from the nearest window or preferably not allow it to pass the threshold of one's property.

Who shall help me find this cad and avenge my darling bird?

Of course, I had written this, as I would write several others. The rumours truly began when other imaginary recipients of similar cards had unfortunate incidents happen to them, and they then shared these in the same letter pages of the newspaper. It appeared that odd things were happening across the tearooms, parlours and town houses of the city: mud ran from taps, ceilings leaked, roaring coal fires froze over, rabid dogs bore teeth at their puzzled owners, fires engulfed washrooms, the mayor's horses contracted botulism and developed abscesses in the groin, an infestation of pubic lice struck decent society, and the son of the French ambassador grew breasts. Each victim had, of late, been introduced to this Svareff chap, it seemed. Or so the crazed grapevine would have it. The hunt was on for this evil stranger.

The director of Central Park Zoo wrote an Op-Ed, and offered a full description of a giantsome European count, who had strolled the paths, clicking and chirping at the cages, before several animals experienced a fevered heat out of season, some just rolled in defecate, masturbated or squawked in frenzied laughter. Of course, I had written this on his oblivious behalf. Several ladies, who had all been to the same evening performance of Puccini's *Tosca* where a shadowy figure was seen, all complained of uncomfortable insomnia and gut cramps as if aligned with a thousand and one full moons.

Those gossamer and society-minded nincompoops frothed themselves into a higher state of flimsiness, until I, Aleister Crowley, finally stood forward from the shadows to challenge this tormenter and flat-track bully, Svareff.

Several friends of The Legion and MI-1 were recipients of Svareff's card, and knew full well that it was I who was writing multiple letters each day to the paper from different parts of the metropolis in different handwriting and ink.* Not even the simpleton in charge of the zoo had written in to refute the tales of mischievous and aroused beasts.

The next note in the *New York Times* came from me (Crowley), threatening my other self (Svareff) in public. It was published on April the ninth, 1915.

Dear Count Svareff,

I note your harassment and vexation of the natives. You are a bully. Your childish conjuring and juvenile sorcery shall not be endured while I am a guest of these great villages. I demand satisfaction and hereby slap your boyish cheek.

Pistols? Witchcraftery? Ingestion of powder, smoke or grog? Or chess. I will even play you blindfolded.

Name it and be careful, Svareff. Even a small child or an infant rat knows not to stare at the sun.

Yours, most bounden and devoted until I expose you,

Aleister Crowley Esq.

The following day, I was trumpeted and heralded as some kind of Nazarene saviour had been on a Palm Sunday long

---

* *I have to admit however that I was* not *responsible for the letters about the pubic lice.*

ago. Many rubbished the nastier rumours from London that had surrounded me, while all were thoroughly intrigued to read Svareff's response in the *New York Times*. I continued to threaten myself in public, once again in the spirit of that bored yet resourceful lad playing chess or tennis against himself.

Crowley,

I know well of you, you Satanic shamster and limp fraud. I presume all of England cannot be wrong when their views of you are voiced. You are out of your confused depth, sir.

I shall take you by all means, but considering that I cannot thump you at chess when you are in the ground and drained of your diseased and poxed blood, let us make a real adventure of this and start with, as you shall be well versed with the term, the lowest common denominator.

Chess.

Your Regal and Imperial Menace for Lifetimes to Come, Friend to None of Yours,

Count Vladimir Svareff XXIII

I had considered the implications of each of the challenges. The idea of pistols was an interesting one, for it would have provoked much romantic nonsense and adorable melodrama. It would have been easily faked too, for I already had found an actor who would aid and abet. Randle Dibdin, thirty-three, was trustworthy and compliant, for his wife would not wish to discover how he had impaled his buttocks around my old boy by the stage door behind the Van Gaal Theater. As for a battle over alcohol, I was supremely confident in my constitution to be victorious in any kind of inebriation. However, blindfolded chess seemed to impress far more in this walled-off faction of salons and butlers in Presbyterian New York.

Dibdin was the first of two fine Manhattan *collaborateurs*. He was to play the part of this newcomer Svareff for the night. He had very few lines to memorise, only his precise chess moves would be a challenge.

The fortunate dimensions of this orcneas, six feet ten inches in his darned socks, would help to propel the myth of my courage beyond the boroughs first, and then the decades.

To keep up the charade, and to everyone's gain, I would pay him adequately not to appear in any stage performance for the duration of my stay in New York City, which Dandylyon had estimated would be about a year. As part of this payment, I thought I would extract as near to a pound of flesh as possible, and Dibdin also became my bodyguard, drug-dealer and very occasional driver.

One night soon after, he brought a friend with him to my scrubby room. She was a Spanish gypsy dancer called La Gitana, who within days would blossom into the role of my next poetic, magnificent and broiling Scarlet Woman. She was tall and as thin as a lily, and just as beautiful. She spoke with the same lilt and rhythmic ferocity as her flamenco swagger. Her ability to make strangers think of sex was a marvel, it seemed. She even brought out the moonliness in otherwise reserved ladies, ordinarily well versed in keeping nature's amorous beastliness to themselves.

That night, on our first encounter, she brazenly exited my stinky third-floor room to climb the wrought-iron ladders to the roof, in order to near herself to a passing storm (and – if our seasoned ears did not deceive us – to masturbate). This prompted Dibdin to tell me how he had met her.

'For three years, I worked as an ambulance man in Atlantic City, and witnessed the destruction of the town from the 1909 hurricane. A Spanish and Trinidadian clipper could not get into port and was left to be battered out at sea. After she was towed into the marina after the storm, there were tales of a single survivor, who had survived the ravages of nature by having been tied to the ship's mast for reasons of arousal that overrode those that increased her chances of survival. The rest of the crew were washed overboard and drowned. The beauty then convalesced in a city hospital, mumbling tales of the helpless men, incapable of resisting her lustful and begging charms, who had lost their lives, lured from their cabins and captain's deck, by the Amazon, grinding in the rhythmic spray of tons of salt water, seeming to fill her mouth, eyes, ears and lungs. She recalled at least fifteen lovers lost from her muscly grip as the oceans took control and swept the grinning and pumping sailors to their end. It seemed to her that each had calculated the risk and the joy at hand, and willingly gave all.'

That she insisted on smoking rafts of spicy cannabis weed to bring her down from her maritime high, well then I knew, of course, she was for me.

I should explain that when I saw her first, I knew that I had a very precise intention for our union. I knew that I would fall in love and that it would mean my heart would break when I inevitably lost her. She was untameable and unownable. It was also wartime, and this only added to the feeling we might soon be copulating like hyenas on a high wire. I *wanted* my heart to break for I wished to write the greatest poetry of my life. I knew that only absolute desperation would spark this creativity, and so with absolute malice aforethought, I gave myself to La Gitana.

She immediately meant far more to me than her mere attraction, animal conductivity and physical pre-eminence; she was an Ava Gardner type, imbued with fire, poison and turquoise. From the outset, I (quite correctly) suspected her to be capricious, flighty and in obeisance of the moon. Our passion would thrill, and our fall be from a height, and destined to be doomed. It would, however, last far longer than I had ever hoped it would, when I first saw her that jewel-flecked night in New York City.

Within the first hour, I had scrawled a note, sparked by her presence.

Kindlier than the moon, her body glowed with more
than harvest gold. Fierier than a portent of a double
Venus, her green eyes shot forth utmost flames. From
the golden chalice of love arose a perfume terrible and
beautiful, a perfume strong and deadly to overcome the
subtler fragrance of her whole being with its dominant,
unashamed appeal.

I entered into a new world where the pain of our love might end my life from the undulating joy and misery, and the (presumed) guaranteed tragic end. I did so with a trot and then a canter. She bit when she kissed, she hissed as she drew blood, and that was before exhibiting her vast appetite for hillocks of well-powdered and strong cocaine, ingested up her nostrils, when she then liked to slap my worryingly exposed scrotum sack until I wept from joy and pain.

Dibdin and I rehearsed and rehearsed the classic chess encounter from the banks of Lake Geneva between Frederick Rhine and François-André Philidor (1795). Our game was to take place in the lobby of the Waldorf Astoria Hotel at 10 p.m. prompt on April the twenty-seventh, 1915. It was unseasonably warm, the hottest night I could recall since those demented Cairo nights.

On the evening of the challenge, I arrived in Highlander's tartan and a crusader's cross on a chainmail breast plate. As I entered in front of the packed lounge, I made the sign of an inverted pentagram, slurring like a drunk, yelling insults and threats at my opponent as he sat waiting at the board. When he unravelled his long frame to welcome me to the table, I gestured at him to fight if he wished. Some gentleman stammered a nervous laugh, fearing for my health I presumed. Ladies gasped. I invoked some words from a new central text I had written for the O.T.O. and my Thelema.

'Let him sink (when no longer can he strive, though his tongue be bitten through with the effort and the blood gush from his nostrils) into the blackness of unconsciousness; and then, on coming to himself, let him write down soberly', and as my volume increased to a yell, 'and accurately a record of all that hath occurred, yea a record of all that hath occurred.'

Then I screamed some Sanskrit, Latin, Bavarian, Romanian and gibberish for good measure.

A purple velvet sash was brought by La Gitana and tied around my eyes. To lessen the importance of any accidental vision and any accusation of cheating, my back was turned to the board. I chose black, of course I did, and away we went. I could have beaten him blindfolded anyway, but the drama would only come from a truly classic encounter. It was one we had plucked from the history books, and one Dibdin would have won by complete accident had that most mercurial of acting talents forgotten to exchange rooks at d3, which it seemed like he might for an eternity.

I believed at this time that he had presumed throughout (and who wouldn't?) that the blindfolded stunt was only for high theatrics and drama. I did not tell him that I really could perform this trick. When we had been rehearsing the moves, I had believed that he thought it had been for both of our benefits, when it had been really just for him. But it was *I* who had been fooled.

The end game was as masterful as the rest of it had been tight, attritional and cautious. Dibdin had a most mauve sense of humour, something I adored about him. When I purred my checkmate to a collective murmur of wonder, as if the Bearded Ladies of the Maximus de Paris Rouge circus had been revealed by the swish of a curtain, only to find them all in circular cunnilingus, Dibdin bellowed, 'Best of seven, you cheating fucker.'

He told me later that he knew that I could play blindfolded, and therefore the best-of-seven-challenge would not expose me, merely surprise me and make me chuckle. When I pressed him on how he would know such a thing, he said he had chatted with a (clearly disguised) chap in a wheelchair outside the Van Gaal Theater, who said he knew me. He would not give his name, but his beard smelled of brioche and he had a quite magnificent nurse with him, dressed in cream and violet, a hint of green spring apples in her *cassoulette*.

'He even told me to use these words[*] as my challenge after the first game,' Dibdin admitted. 'He said you would find it amusing.' That I indeed did.

So we played some more, though the following games were a disappointment in comparison, for they were so one-sided in my favour. After the fourth game, when my victory was complete, Dibdin/Svareff stood to withdraw through the crowd, just as the invisible ink we had scribed on his forehead before the game began to empurple. Within seconds, an indigo pentagram appeared on his forehead, an inverted crucifix on either cheekbone. He might have overacted in declaring the heat that he claimed was created, but only marginally and within the bounds of exasperation from the gathered higher strata of

---

[*]   *'Best of seven, you cheating fucker.'*

Manhattan. He ran out into the sticky and soggy night with a fine sense of theatre.

As the crowds thinned, several audacious types challenged me in similar fashion, and not one came close, until a stinky German, under whom the chair creaked, sat behind me at the board. Still blindfolded, I knew it was he. I could sniff his pits, schnapps and masticated wiener. The grunts were those of an oaf, and also, I knew he would not be able to resist.

'Hühnerbein! You old dog,' I whispered, before I took him in twelve moves.

And so, just like in the old spy movies, the wickedest chap in the world had now made contact with his man. And that coward, Yeats, whom I knew was in New York City, had not even shown up.

I now courted the attentions of the unctuous Germans in Manhattan. I reported back to London over the wires, as well as to Washington D.C.. Both were heavily coded, of course. The Prussians trusted me to write essays in their pamphlets, though these were loftily pitched dog whistles to the reasonably well-informed that the Kaiser's men in New York were out of their depth, both politically and spiritually. I brainwashed them during spells and invocations. I spiked them with powerful hallucinogens, and sculpted their thought patterns. There was no challenge, but that did not mean they were still not very perilous adversaries.

I, Aleister Crowley, had arrived in the New World, and my mystique ratcheted even higher that Sunday when rumours spread of Svareff leaping off the Brooklyn Bridge, begging me to liberate him from my spell. Dibdin was a marvellous swimmer and we luncheoned shortly afterwards in the privacy of his family home in Queens with his wife and seven children. The neighbours must have thought us all insane, as we roared and howled until sunset.

Count Svareff was barely heard of again (in this town, and for now at least) other than in bogeyman stories at bedtime and an apology printed in the *New York Times*. I once again wrote and mailed anonymous letters to the editor of the newspaper to tell of several mailed cheques to cover the loss of possessions (teapots, clocks, canaries) and a rather generous donation from Svareff to the welfare of all animals at the Central Park Zoo, even though they had always been just fine, if a little cramped. The Count, giving in to his English vanquisher, was quite clear in his demands that the zoo's beasts should be granted much more room, something the donation made possible by the purchase of three extra acres from the municipal authority and the release of all caged butterflies into the grime of the air of the finest city on Earth.

7.4 THE ALCHEMY AND THE LURE OF A NAZARENE ANTICHRIST

The word of the alleged Antichrist who saved Manhattan from Count Svareff was the fashionable new gospel in opium dens, six-star hotels and *The Age of Innocence* parlours, while high-standing families of the original Dutch aristos were torn apart over the issue.

'Crowley* may be the Devil, according to the English. But he also saved us.'

According to several witnesses, the Romanian canary-killer, defeated at chess, unmasked and left in ignominy, had leapt from the Brooklyn Bridge. The avian population was now safe, and the park's butterflies had been liberated. Perhaps the pentagram and the inverted crucifix were to be trusted after all. The English could quite feasibly be wrong about this

---

* *These Manhattanites, quite bizarrely, seemed perpetually capable of pronouncing my name correctly.*

Crowley chap. And, when one thought about it, either he held inordinate sway over police chiefs in London and New York or he had not committed the crimes that were whispered, and that made society ladies shuffle and their servants blush.

In late April of 1915, I advertised in the society pages the announcement of several upcoming ceremonies of the O.T.O. The dates were withheld to cause a frisson around the city. I published short essays and the tenets of Thelema, announcing the forthcoming pamphlets and books by the same author. *Thelemic Principles, Alchemy and the Lure of a Nazarene Antichrist* was available, with a gold binding, for purchase through a postal-box service. I placed a ridiculously high price on them ($15 per copy) and then almost immediately announced in the same column the following day that they were all sold out. A shipment might or might not have been expected from Wilde's erstwhile publisher in London. It might or might not have been seized by Customs. It might or might not be at the bottom of the sea. It might or might not even exist. The clamour for information about me was quite a marvel. Manhattan now purred my name.

And throughout these months, I believed that Yeats may have been trying to avoid me. However, I did manage to sit opposite from his father at a dinner party one evening. My welcome and treatment by him provided, in microcosm, a fair barometer of how differently London and Manhattan viewed me. I recall most of the meeting with the father and that I performed that evening one of my several famed party tricks. This was the one where I guessed, to gasps and cheers, with a frightening accuracy the birthday, hour and rising sign of each person present.

With Winston's urging, I had yelled some of my early and rehearsed lines about Irish independence from London, and this seemed to go down well. Yeats Senior wrote with a fair, but still typically cock-eyed Gaelic bent, 'Of course, being an Englishman, he was throughout the hero of his own tales', but he obviously found it impossible not to like me. Partially aware of my differences with his puny spawn, he still wrote to his boy of me thus,

> Do you know a man named Crowley? A strange man and witty. Miss Coates and I met him at Quinn's at dinner, his conversation not witty, but that of a witty man. Have you noticed that any man possessing the gift of expression but absolutely without sympathy is inevitably a wit and a man of humour? A complete detachment from the people about him – this complete and perfectly natural estrangement puts him in easy possession of all that makes for humour and wit. It also makes him seem *formidable*. The combination is that of a *formidable stranger*, so that you pay attention to every word he lets fall from his lips. And if he makes you laugh, you hear him with a sense of relief and are almost grateful, this effect enhanced in this case by his bullet head and strong clumsy figure – his fingers thick but tapering. Have you noticed that one is always inclined to like a formidable man? It is our way of getting our courage back.

The father was clearly a more astute lad than his flailing and hatched offspring, who could only muster this answer, while cowering in private, scared shitless in some outer borough, likely with false beard, eye patch and awfully executed mid-West twang.

*

Crowley is not a man I appreciate. I am amused to find
that he now praises Mrs. MacGreogr (sic), he slandered
her in a very cruel way in one of his books but I
suppose that is the way of things. I am sorry our friends
have now taken up with Crowley.

In fact, I think he is quite mad. He has written about
six lines, amid much bad rhetoric, of real poetry. I
asked about him at Cambridge, and a man described
him as being dragged out of the dining hall by a porter,
thrown out while struggling, because of the indecency
of his conversation. He is an English and French type.
You, in New York, have nothing like him, I believe. He
used to be a handsome fellow, but now cares more
about cheap prostitutes, redheads and masturbation.

Yeats Senior responded with a dismissive:

Well son. If one sups with the Devil, one must have a long
spoon.*

This admonishment – in my defence – apparently justified the
postage across the Atlantic, for the letter contained nothing else.

Do not be confused by my jests about the Irish. Their boys
at the front were among the most game lads I had ever seen.
And any halfwit or blockhead who has ever entered the snug
bar of a tavern on a Sunday knows the truth. Robbie and I
once shovelled three battalions of green-eyed, cream-skinned,
red-headed scrappers from County Wicklow out from the
front line and onto a steamer set for Singapore and then

---

* *Yeats Senior had at this point returned to London (yes, the capital of that
country the Irish despise so), showing a courage to cross an ocean in wartime
that was not inherited by his poisoned spume, his gnarled mutant of a son.*

Ceylon to live out their days in a small village near that marvelled monastery. These days, it is still possible to meet dark-skinned Sri Lankans with emerald eyes and carrot hair, fluent in Sinhalese, but with Grandpa's highly detailed knowledge of Gaelic football, horse racing and whiskey. These lads and lasses remain a demographic with a high propensity to brawl and warble romantically. It is good to have such friends.

Their antithesis, that ponce Yeats, was now perpetually livid at my aura. I know he was, because he had already called me a 'rough beast slouching towards Bethlehem' in his pathetic 'Second Coming'. Was this the best the awful cunt had? He could not forget the Battle of Blythe Road, still scarred at my audacity to breach two giants to punch him, and how I had now started my own religion and had made all of New York fawn far more than he ever did or could. I swore that I would one day rupture the gossamer membrane of the Golden Dawn's HQ – *That Temple of the Faux* – at 36 Blythe Road, London, W14, and that day was now approaching.

7.5 THE RETURN OF AN OLD FRIEND / A NEW LOVE
On the first day of May 1915, the weekly seances and rituals of ceremonial magick began to a grand hurrah. Three of Mrs Astor's closest family were there, but all requested anonymity. I only maintain their secret now, for the drooling trio, a horrid scapegrace, a cross-eyed poltroon and a chinless and inbred rapscallion are not worthy of their mention in my company. Edith Wharton was there and as giddy as a teased schoolgirl, and she was quite a game lass, that one. Charles Van Dusen thought his twelfth-generation Dutch aristocratic standing permitted him to be there, but the upper case V exposed him as a nouveau know-nothing. He would be begging with the best of them by dawn, this I knew. Three Van Burens, who

went by the absurd names of Freelove, Wealthy and Increase, pitched up and were allowed to gatecrash. Three Roosevelts would not be immune from my power that gloried evening. The British and French ambassadors (and their *madames*) were there to promote a quite pioneering kind of *entente cordiale*.

I am not sure that many or any of these new acolytes had any idea of what they were supporting and championing. They were like obedient lambs, their incessant bleats almost identical, desperate for hope and leadership and enlightenment. This was perfect for my needs.

The Masonic Temples of the Lucifer Lodge of Manhattan on East 23rd Street was the setting. The demonic name should not indicate the presence of black magic. The Lucifer in the name simply referred to an eighteenth-century theatre that had once existed on the site, famed for innocent ghost stories of turquoise, teal, scarlet, mahogany and stone. It was a handy obfuscation that I was glad to exploit.

I had waited this long for the first ritual in order to build expectation to a crescendo but I had also been waiting on a small consignment of Ceylon jungle resin toffee. MI-1 allowed this, for it would cement my legend, Dandylyon had argued. By Christ, he was right. It arrived wrapped in a box from Fortnum's, expertly repackaged by Prudence and those dextrous mitts. Bless her.

On the early evening of the ceremony, the toffee was caramelised and then boiled in an Ottoman crucible, and served as chilled tea to the hundred or so paying guests. They had no idea what they were taking, as many seemed to presume it a palate-cleansing *amuse-bouche*, while waiting impatiently for the main course of more devilish powders and more renowned liquids.

I then strolled around the nooks and crannies of the halls and cloisters, admiring the stonework and sniffing in the history. I thought of the degenerates who had wandered there, and the pious who would puke at this evening's schedule. The venue, finished in 1799, was ancient by New York standards. It was unlikely anyone present had ever been inside this building before, and its grandeur and menace seemed adequate to put most of the natives' bowels on edge. Fully aware of this, I ordered the toilet facilities be closed off twenty minutes after the tea had been passed around. I did this to inflict the most discomfort on the nervous and tender of spirit, for a combination of nerves, cocaine and goo tea would loosen both bowel and inhibition until almost everyone had crapped themselves. This would separate the truly keen disciple from the flimsy onlooker.

The shame and the ecstasy they would discover in the following hours would only add to my power, leverage and mystique across that burgeoning town. And the more I was vaunted by society, the more I could control Hühnerbein and the enemy. Nothing speaks of utter control over someone more than having them fornicate to the rhythm of their own laughter, while they drip in the shit of a hundred new chums. Footmen and hansom cab drivers gossiped and chuntered for many a year about the depravity and stink that next noon delivered to them on the sidewalks of East 23rd Street, employers and lords chattering nonsense, faces contorted and in a strange fizz of arousal.

Earlier that night, New York had spewed forth my magical Spanish gypsy once again. She had circled me from the moments she entered the old stone dungeony halls. I smelt the slightest tang of tuberose that I knew to be hers.

Your hair was full of roses in the dewfall as we danced,
The sorceress enchanting and the paladin entranced,
In the starlight as we wove us in a web of silk and steel

Immemorial as the marble in the halls of Boabdil,
In the pleasaunce of the roses with the fountains and the
yews
Where the snowy Sierra soothed us with the breezes and
the dews!

'La Gitana', Aleister Crowley

That sizzling bitch, La Gitana would soon define New York
for me, as the metropolis's initial façade fell away and the
throb and the thrum that would become its astonishing hall-
mark were revealed. The bedroom was never far from our
thoughts and there were those repeated frenzied and eager
dashes into August storms up flights of wrought iron that
often saw my humping her like an ill-trained coyote in the
hallways of the hotel. But just as thrilling was that we were
flâneur and *flâneuse*, for she too loved to stroll the city, day or
night, to dunk herself in the gush of sensation that New York
so generously set forth. There were not many paving stones
south of Harlem that had not been touched by either her sandals or her naked flamenco feet. She suffered so from a
chronic back condition* from years of training, and we eased
her pain with hours of steady strolling, heavy opiates and our
own mischievous exertions.

After our regular six-hour lap of the southern half of the
city, she would flood forth with a concerto for her piano or a
new dance for her loyal troupe; one that they would perform
to perfection after a single rehearsal in that spicy Little Madrid
Café that her blistering and incandescent spirit filled on West
22nd Street.

La Gitana constituted far more than a mad love affair to

---

* *Often the curse of the perilously under-fucked, but not in this instance.*

me, for she also shared with me the secret of who I really was, and what I was doing in New York. And it felt good to share this with a lover.*

She used to tease me, and control my days.

'*¿Eres inglés, irlandés o alemán hoy, Aleister, querido?*'†

'I have yet to decide, Señora Escarlata.'‡

'*¿Que tengo a mi espalda?*'§

And thus whatever it was she held in her palm behind her back would determine how we spent our day. If the *shamana* believed I needed to cause international mischief, she would hold one of three objects that represented Ireland, England or Germany. A potato, an umbrella or a sausage. Other weeks, my options were a Catholic cross, a teabag or a bullet. Depending on what she held, I would further the cause of that nation on that day. She even overrode the word of Winston Churchill, England and Germany.

On days when she firmly believed that I (or she) needed recreation and love, she held a phial of delicious cocaine or heroin. Upon her reveal, away we went to our hallowed bed or to the roof and the heavens.

'*Mi querida. Mi querida escarlata. Siempre te adoraré.*'¶

So, she knew well that my mouthings in favour of Irish inde-pendence were a sham to impress my anti-English credentials upon the Manhattan Germans, who, sanctioned by Hühner-bein, now commissioned me to write weekly pieces for *The*

---

*   *Sir Percy Blakeney was not able to do so for the longest time.*

†   *'Are you English, Irish or German today, Aleister darling?'*

‡   *Scarlet lady.*

§   *'What do I have behind my back?'*

¶   *'My darling. My scarlet darling. I shall always worship you.'*

Fatherland,* as well as generously publishing my own ponderings on The Battle of Blythe Road.

I did not need the money, but the platform was perfect and, to the clumsy eye, the stipend gave the illusion of a bond. My introductory column began thus:

> It seems to me that Germany stands for everything worth keeping – science, foresight, order, and so on. I am intensely sorry for France; I regard her as having being dragged into it all by her rotten statesmen. To put it in a word, I hate England, I love France, I admire Germany, I fear Russia. My hate for England is now being replaced by contempt. But I have always taken care to write as an English Isaiah.

I then had columns published entitled, 'Cocaine', 'Perhaps Germany Should Take Poland?', 'The Darlings of the Gods' and 'An Orgy of Cant'. My piece, 'The New Parsifal' declared Kaiser Wilhelm a Knight, in a quest for the Holy Grail. This excerpt had them all reduced to fawning knaves.

> I am going to hear Larking tonight. Of course, as a man, I am an Irish rebel of the most virulent type, and I want to see every Englishman killed before my eyes. I would ship all the English women to Germany, but I fear this may after several weeks be a major disservice to the Fatherland. But, of course, speaking as a man of the world, I am a reactionary Tory of the most bigoted type. This confounds the English so much, they are so easily confused. They have no idea when they are being toyed with.

*

---

* *A pro-German rag. I also had my* Vanity Fair *column, but that never crossed over into politics.*

It appeared to me that the Prussians had been willing to welcome me in merely because of the Irish roots of my fore-name and my surname. All the fuss and propaganda I man-aged on top and my deep knowledge of the supernatural had not hurt, of course.

'Are you sure you should write that Kaiser Wilhelm is a new Jesus Christ? Is this not too much?' La Gitana asked.

'Ha ha ha! I know what you are saying, my love. But the hubris and arrogance of the Germans seems to know no bounds, for they believe this dog shit with a verve and a gusto. They also shan't see the comic farce of my declaration of Irish independence in front of the Statue of Liberty with you hooked onto my arm, as your worst flamenco guitarist strums and plucks and pulls odd faces of badly measured melodrama.'

'Is this not also hubris?' she asked.

'No! This is humour, *mi querida*. Such a distinction is vital. They shall even believe us when we tell them yours is a gesture of support from the Spanish. Our intention is to make the German lobby appear ridiculous to the American public while exciting our "allies" in Berlin. The event will even be reported with a perfect pitch by a "friend" at the *New York Times*. It is quite feasible that the land that gave us Wagner and Beethoven really could be tone deaf.'

'Come here,' she interrupted. And towards her, I went. And again, we were gone to ecstasy.

I wished I could have been of more help in Europe itself as the slaughter continued. However, I was about to pull the stunt to end the war with our victory. While I was at it, I would try again to allow a steady supply of my toffee into the country, but Dandylyon quite wisely advised that it might upset the balance of my relationship with the Germans, for I should not appear to be a pacifist. The stuff had served its purpose in cementing my spiritual ownership of, not just the socialites of the town, but those of the whole country as my legend spread to all four corners of the United States. I was now mythical in the New World.

I had still not met Winston, who was now, quite handily, the First Lord of the Admiralty. My old accomplice was in charge of the most potent navy in the world, and MI-1 agreed with my joyous promptings that the Americans were our trump card.

I had been urging the Germans in New York to sink a boat like the *Lusitania* for a while, convincing them that the Americans were sending food, medical and military supplies as well as any individuals requiring safe passage. She was a British ship, owned by the Cunards. Her callous sinking would send a powerful message as to who the likely victors in this war would be, I told them.

I convinced Hühnerbein to place this advertisement in fifty American newspapers, as well as in German language publications.

NOTICE!

TRAVELLERS intending to embark on the Atlantic voyage are reminded that a state of war exists between Germany and her allies and Great Britain and her allies; that the zone of war includes the waters adjacent to the British Isles; that, in accordance with formal notice given by the Imperial German Government, vessels flying the flag of Great Britain, or any of her allies, are liable to destruction in those waters and that travellers sailing in the war zone on the ships of Great Britain or her allies do so at their own risk.

IMPERIAL GERMAN EMBASSY
Washington, DC

*

When they finally torpedoed the *Lusitania* on May the seventh, 1915, not only did they believe she was carrying Churchill and 137 American citizens, but they had absolutely no idea that she was completely empty. They were quite fooled by several decently dressed scarecrows with Homburgs and beards and fat, bedraggled mannequin lasses in cheap ball gowns on the upper decks. It seemed that they had quite a low opinion of the American and English lady. The British Navy had emptied her of a skeleton crew fifty miles out into international waters off New York harbour, and set her on a straight line to Land's End.

That giant, Randle Dibdin was paid handsomely again, this time to recruit a tight band of his loyal friends, along with all the Thelemites in Manhattan. This was a decent number, and crossed social strata, a façade aided by Dibdin's access to the costumes (evening suit, coal miner, steel worker and maquillaged whore) at the Van Gaal Theater. All this lot had to do was to turn up at the docks and outside the German embassy after the sinking, weeping and wailing and, encouraged by me, throwing bricks through the ambassadorial windows and attempts at arson, especially after I had heard of the slaughter at the Little Madrid Café. Some were seen coming ashore from British Navy ships in Deptford and Southampton and Liverpool, allegedly having been picked up near the Irish coast, but had really been supping Ovaltine and playing cards in between lending a sturdy and courageous hand out at sea with whatever the skipper asked of them.

The *Lusitania* went down and down and down. The insurance company had no idea about the truth, for it was owned, managed and staffed by mean-spirited arses who would sell their youngest daughters' hymen for a nickel. We could not afford any hint of a dispute over payment and therefore responsibility and guilt. If one kills a cockroach, they say a thousand of the bastards turn up for the funeral. Well, the Germans would one day feel like they had used a shoe injudiciously, for the Atlantic would in the future be traversed by 4 million eager young American *doughboys*, heading to war. The Cunard Line took the cheque and, with Winston Churchill on their executive board, never breathed a word.

The *Lusitania*'s sinking did not bring an immediate response from President Wilson, but it did end all chatter of an American alliance with Berlin. There were now only two options for Washington. It was either a neutrality that masked overt assistance to London and Paris or aligning with the allies. This fat-thumbed, bullet-headed Samson, still fully charged from the debasing of his Delilah, was shoving at the sturdy stone pillar of American public opinion. But it would take a couple more pushes before we collapsed the bastard temple and the pain of war would end. This delay in the Americans entrance to the war only provided marvellous cover for me, because my advice was good and there was no clear and material retaliation from the Yankees. This meant that Hühnerbein was easily convinced.

'The Americans and the world respect Berlin like never before. The Atlantic is now ours,' I told him. 'This was a brave and audacious move, my friend. It was a righteous show of strength that shall starve Britain of food and weapons, and shall win us the war. You are a genius.'

But one day, this Samson would be back to make a nonsense of all that. And I would finally help to bring this fucking war to an end.

7.6 AMERICA II
On the advice of Prudence and Dandylyon, La Gitana and I left New York for several weeks. It would help to re-establish an element of mystique. Away from the sturdiness of the

Jewish, Italian and Irish diasporas, much commerce of the city is built upon the transient nature of those passing through to the Americas. This is seen in how a chic restaurant remains *en vogue* for a fleeting moment. Manhattan has always been flighty like this. And so we left the party fashionably early. We departed to show them precisely what they would be missing.

I felt real guilt to be sightseeing around the United States while boys were dying in trenches. Dandylyon and Prudence calmed me by nigh-daily letter, assuring me that I was playing a truly vital role and that my days here were coming to an end. We all knew the Americans would soon be joining the war. This would not only bring the conflict to an end, but it would mean victory for us. Dandylyon's precise tone was hard to ignore, for everything he had so far predicted had occurred to the letter. In the spirit of my father and me traipsing from town to town in the English countryside with our Bibles, I was now to spread the good news of the O.T.O. and my very own gospels of elevation through sin and nature – my Thelema – around the country, and this would mean, of course, that the Germans remained malleable, for they were thrilled that my/our message would now go nationwide.

La Gitana and I invoked pleasant spirits, took drugs and instructed sex magick, first across that highly tuned and spiritual land to the Pacific Ocean and then down the western seaboard from Vancouver to Tijuana (aaaah, Mexico, *mi amor*).

In California, I discovered the real magic of the movie business, and realised that this was the finest form of new propaganda. I found a welcoming fleapit cinema on 12th Street, where La Gitana and I spent glorious afternoons re-watching Victor Sjöström's masterpiece, *The Phantom Carriage*. We also inadvertently looked at D. W. Griffith's *The Birth of a Nation*. We only went in originally to avoid the heat of the day, but returned many times, because La Gitana thoroughly enjoyed pondering the permutations of our joint-tarnishing of Lillian Gish, whispering them in my ear, as other cinema-goers kept one eye on us and one on the moving picture. I recall that the place also showed *The Battle of Chemulpo Bay*, that famed maritime scrap from the Russo–Japanese war. If the cameras had been revolved, one might have seen the frenzied coitus on the shoreline caused by young Robbie and a fat-thumbed bullet-head called Crowley, back in those clear and immaculate days when Ceylon jungle goo first ruled.

I now knew I had to establish a solid chapter of Thelema here, for this magnificent medium could well become a new front for righteousness and my rebellion through allegorical tales of ancient Egypt, murder in the Californian heat, cowboy rebellions, ghost stories and that strumpet, Salome. I had pretensions to write my own horror films, a genre that stirred me not so much from the ghouls and goblins but I saw how these stories were truly righteous, democratic, rebellious and revolutionary, for the poor, disenfranchised and hideous monster often gets to torture and slaughter the entitled. Oh goody.

And so, I sent for Dibdin, the best actor I knew. I trusted him to become my man here. It was the time before the talking movies, and he was also supremely gifted at keeping silent. After my departure, he sent weekly updates to me from there, with paragraphs from fake and supposedly secret reports from our friends and allies within the police force, who, for the benefit of Hühnerbein's confusion and in the eyes of the public at large, had to remain our enemy.

(January 24th, 1916)
It seems likely that Crowley's order has obtained a significant foothold in this colony, and certainty is lent to this theory by the frequent occurrence of alleged drug orgies among the movie

stars. Some drug-crazed maniac or jealous woman of the O.T.O.
may have been our mysterious turncoat. We have seized nearly
900 copies of *The Equinox* (Crowley's hideously pornographic
poetry, picture and ritualistic publication). Thousands are still
unaccounted for in Britain and there is every reason to believe
that many of these reached the Pacific coast.

(LAPD)

(March 2nd, 1916)
Months after his return to Europe, we repeatedly raided poor
half-crazed R____'s house, a small chateau in West Hollywood,
in search of some evidence of *The Devil Worshipper's Guide to
Love-Making and the Mystic Love Cult*.

Crowley wrote in *The Equinox* –
'. . . and, of course, the police found nothing from which they
concluded not my innocence, but that my pact with the devil
contained a clause guaranteeing me against the discovery of my
crimes. If any of those obstinate arses had possessed sufficient
intelligence to study a single page of my writings, he would
have seen at once what ridiculous rubbish the accusations made
against me were. And by foul-minded and illiterate cheats whom
I had never so much as met.'

Despite this madman's ranting, we shall continue unceasingly
with our brief. To keep California safe from this abnormality
called Crowley.

(LAPD)

These leaks from my lads in uniform were perfectly measured, I believed, and ideal fodder for Hühnerbein to believe
that his recruitment skills and judgement of character were
unmatched. Meanwhile, Randle Dibdin and his vast family

settled in very quickly to the Californian lifestyle. He could be seen surfing most mornings, trailed by his missus and thrilled offspring, in famed surf swells from La Jolla to Malibu. They were an astonishing sight, encapsulating familial joy, perhaps because of, rather than despite, Daddy's infrequent and easily sated desire for a rigid cock. Such monthly sodomous mischief, it seemed, could truly be the cement to keep a family together. Hühnerbein's recruitment skills and judgement of character were nothing compared to mine. *Fuck him!*

As we travelled on and back east, the glow of war on the horizon stuck perpetually in my guilty mind. I tried to forget, and Louisiana helped distract me. New Orleans was hard to leave, for there the true misfits and the marvellously loose of faculty gather from swamp to dungeon, they don't care, to act weirdly with remarkable skill and deft precision. When we did depart, we found a stretch of heaven on a magical retreat on the Hudson River in a wilderness called Esopus Island. I set to work on the translation of the *Tao Te Ching*, while I painted humongous Thelemic slogans on the cliffs along the river, creating artwork of vast awe for those fortunate sailors and holiday makers who floated by. They must have wondered what sort of nutcase was waking each morning, and saying to himself, 'Today I shall paint Satan with the precision one might have on a four foot canvas, but onto a sheer rock face a thousand feet high.'

And on the adjoining rock face, I daubed in full view of all the tourist steamers,

DO WHAT THOU WILT SHALL BE THE
WHOLE OF THE LAW.
EVERY MAN AND EVERY WOMAN IS A STAR.

*

Well, that nutcase was I. And quite proud of it.

There on those mountain passes at night under the heavens, La Gitana and I shared in dreams the past life experiences of Pope Alexander VI, Alessandro Cagliostro and Eliphas Lévi. We shared a sliver of toffee each night. There we were immaculate. There we thought we had reached our zenith, as I declared myself the Eighth Magus of the World. Perhaps we had peaked, though gods are both resilient beasts and wicked recidivists.

There under a winter lunar eclipse in late 1916 and with Mars on the wane, she spoke to me. 'I want to introduce you to a friend of mine,' she said as we sat on that high rock over the river one dawn.

'I would be honoured, my dear.'

'He is a former lover. I know you will adore him.'

'His taste is clearly impeccable, though I would have to question why he would ever let you go.'

'Well, you will do precisely that one day, my Beast.'

'Never! Never, I tell you!'

And we laughed and I rolled onto her.

And so, we then agreed I would meet him in Manhattan on Christmas Day 1916, two years to the day since Robbie and I had almost provoked a rebellion across that wretched nadir and muddy fissure of mankind that straddled France and Belgium.

Our rustication around the country was over, and it was time to return to New York City. He and I met by appointment in the middle of the park around 64th Street. We neared each other across deep snow, La Gitana by his side. She leaned slightly on his sturdy forearm in that delightful way that she did, and it thrilled me to be meeting someone of such standing in her eyes. Any Christmas strollers would have stopped to witness the calmness and the pending union across the vast stretch of virgin snow, for it was like a cinematic production.

We were both disguised, though this was more to protect him. He came as a travelling salesman, I as a Hasidic, scratching like a lunatic at his beard. My clothing was less important than his as I was friends to both sides, of course. As he stood twenty yards away, he opened his macintosh in the style of a massive pervert, exposing his worth.

Beneath, I recognised first the uniform of the top brass of the British Navy, then a boyish face I suspected I knew, the hair receding from it. His skin was pinkish, fresh and only slightly chubby.

La Gitana presented him with great pride, and yelled, '*Mis dos amantes favoritos en todo el mundo. Sé que cosas especiales vendrán de esto. No puedo predecir si serán buenos o malos, pero ambos saben lo mucho que adoro el mal.*'*

We shook hands firmly, eyes narrowing to focus our mutual intention to respect her wishes.

'Aleister, my holiest of terrors, please meet the very naughty First Lord of the Admiralty. Winston Churchill.'

Ah! At last!

7.7 LITTLE ITALY & THE ATLANTIC

He came towards me in my own dressing gown, on the roof of that roach motel on the Lower East Side. He carried a plate of imported cream crackers from Fortnum's and Italian *accasciato*, a fatty sheep and cow's milk cheese from Tuscany. He carried it with him perpetually, it seemed. A small shop on the corner of Lafayette and Grand was now a favourite of the boys and girls of MI-1, who ran the errands to keep him afloat in the stuff. Quite feasibly, a sneak attack at any time of the

---

*   '*My two favourite lovers in the whole world. I know that special things will come from this. I cannot predict whether they will be good or bad, but you both know how much I adore utter mischief.*'

week by Hühnerbein et al. on the dairy counter there would have been a bitter blow to Blighty's resources in the city. However, such an attack on the heart (and spirit) of Manhattan's Italian neighbourhood would have been unwise. Those particular natives should not be stirred, not even by a world power seeking global dominance. If we ever wanted to wipe out the Germans in the city, faking a Prussian attack on a pasta restaurant or a *forno* bakery would have been a smart way to do it. Even the New York Police Department would have turned their backs and concentrated on the shifty-eyed perverts and pickpockets until the fuss over three dozen Germanic corpses (one in particular elephantine, piss-stained, sweaty and stinky) on the embassy steps had died down.

'I want us to sink another boat. One of ours. It will win the war this time.'

'Talk on, my friend,' said Winston, picking his teeth and then swilling the more stubborn cheese and crackers with a very pleasant *Château Margaux* 1868, its quality quite at odds with the surroundings.

'Again, no one dies. We empty a ship, any ship really, sink it, blame it on the Germans. The American cavalry rides in. I can frame the Hun with ease.'

'Elaborate!' Churchill said. 'And why is this different to the *Lusitania*?'

'Well, this time I have an accompanying plan. I have a friend in the Mexican embassy . . .' and I thought of myself again as Samson, shoving at those unforgiving pillars of stone, veins bulging, as his Delilah shuffled on the spot.

And then as she walked past us, she kissed him on the head, me on the lips and whispered in my ear, '*Me alegro de que trabajes para Inglaterra hoy*.'*

---

*   '*I'm glad you work for England today.*'

She offered us both a toffee, took one herself, and without a rehearsal, we copied precisely that same choreographed and melodramatic laugh that Dandylyon, Prudence and I had perfected over the years.

I shall miss her. I shall fight like fuck to see her again.

Churchill loved my plan with the Mexicans.

'Mexico! Yes! That is fucking genius, old boy.'

More of this in a moment.

And the following day, a new Epiphany, January 6th, 1917, I left New York on the Cunard Line's *Duchess of Cumbria*. She would be safe from both sides.

The Germans had been instructed by me and by Hühnerbein to give her an untroubled passage across the waters. The decks were quiet and dinner almost deserted, as nervous passengers stayed in their cabins, closest to the lifeboats. The low numbers on board, however, would have guaranteed a spot in a raft for all.

For the crossing, Dibdin's pals back in Manhattan had provided a healthy stash of fine golden heroin to pump into my arm and piles of weed to burn. He even came to New York to see me off. Dibdin waved and wept, and started a whole new wave of tittle-tattle and gossip around New York before retiring full-time to Hollywood. Mad rumours began once again and apparently Count Svareff had not drowned in the East River after all, as apocryphal tales of stopped clocks and dead budgerigars returned. I had trained the mischievous lad, my chum, well.

I was now well versed in pacing my journey with yoga, drugs and arse. There was again the obligatory storm, and the captain had been warned ahead of time of my perverse penchant for being strapped to the bow if the highest point of a steamship was inaccessible. This weather lasted a day and a half and given I had taken far too much of an industrial strength amphetamine,

I yelled and bellowed at the storm and the waters far too much in an attempt to get my point across, thus swallowing enough salt water to make me puke for another day. I noted this new verse to La Gitana in my head in the eye of the tornado.

> Sleep, with a last long kiss,
> Smiles tenderly and vanishes.
> Mine eyelids open to the gold
> Hilarion's hair in ripples rolled.
> (O gilded morning clouds of Greece!)
> Like the sun's self amid the fleece,
> Her face glows. All the dreams of youth,
> Lighted by love and thrilled by truth,
> Flicker upon the wide calm brow,
> Now playmates of the eyelids, now
> Dancing coquettes the mouth that move
> In all overtures to love.
> The Atlantic twinkles in the sun–
> Awake, awake Hilarion!

Sensations are so important, I find.

I heard mutters as I passed a rare couple on deck that MI-1 would be following me around England; I yelled back at them, 'Then at least, I shan't be burgled by peasants like you.'

The ghost of Sir Percy Blakeney roared, for if the police were to be on the dockside, then it would be to shake my hand, thank me for my services to King and Country, and then take me for a fish supper and an ale in a dock tavern.

I believed that I was in the odd position, as a supreme double agent, of being the only chap on board who knew we were entirely safe from harm, a microcosm of how I approached the whole of that century, and just another secret for this Scarlet

Pimpernel to keep. In fact, many of those who did travel on the *Duchess of Cumbria* had done so in the private knowledge that that Crowley fellow was on board and that his own powers (as either German sympathiser or friend of the Devil) would protect the voyage. They were correct, of course, but not for the reason they believed.

Two days into my journey, the ship's captain (a pal of Winston's) told me of a wire he had received of a mass murder in a New York flamenco bar. I feared for my love. The headline of the paper had told of *Slaughter at Little Madrid Café.* Three Spanish gypsy dancers and their guitarist all had their throat slits in a late night attack that appeared to be coordinated, even according to the unreliable and pie-eyed sources who frequented such a place at such a time. The killers, there were four of them, drank schnapps. Three were skinny sycophants in sharp black suits, while their ginger-bearded boss was a rotund and sweaty creature in a soggy suit, and all spoke a harsh Bavarian. They had all appeared quite sloshed, until the word was given, and they acted with a shuddering synchronicity. On the door to the male WC, a medium-sized paintbrush had been used to leave some simple graffiti in one of the victim's passionate blood.

WC NOW READ **W** INSTON **C** HURCHILL.

But if the nasty bastards were after La Gitana for her association with him, the nitwits had missed their target. And this warning was enough for her to disappear from view. I would see her again in the strangest of circumstances, but much was to change for us both in the intervening years.

Ordinary morality is only for ordinary people.
            – Aleister Crowley, *New York Herald*, 1916

Chapter 8

The Great War II & A Second Coming
1917–1920

The supreme satisfaction is to be able to despise one's neighbour and this fact goes far to account for religious intolerance. It is evidently consoling to reflect that the people next door are headed for hell.

– Aleister Crowley

The modern-day craving for things is caused by an internal misery. Their use reveals the slavery of the soul. If one is really free, one can take cocaine as simply as saltwater taffy. There is no better rough test of a soul than its attitude to drugs. If a man is simple, fearless, eager, he is all right; he will not become a slave. If he is afraid, he is already a slave. Let the whole world take opium, hashish and the rest; those who are liable to abuse them were better dead.

For it is in the power of all so-called intoxicating drugs to reveal a man to himself. If this revelation declares a Star, then it shines more brightly ever after. If it declares a Christian – a thing not man nor beast, but a muddle of mind – he craves the drug, no more for its analytical but for its numbing effect. Lytton has a great story of this in Zanoni. *Glyndon, an uninitiate, takes an Elixir, and beholds not Adonai the glorious, but the Dweller on the Threshold; cast out from the Sanctuary, he becomes a vulgar drunkard.*

I rise and soon greet my goats. I spend many glorious minutes in their proximity and continue on to the meadow on the slope, flecked with midges and flower.

My chums are quite likely to follow me, when I leave the gate on the far side of their pasture open.

As I tickle the animals, I think back to a time at our abbey on Sicily, and ponder the rumours of the night with the goat. Herodotus once told of an Egyptian priestess copulating with one during a ceremony. Many cultures celebrate the union of man and beast, and the Egyptians are no different. The Greeks too had their Minotaur; Leda and the swan also. My darling Scarlet Woman of the time was Leah, whom we shall soon meet, and she lustily agreed to play the priestess. I recall how she knelt on all fours, only to find the goat a possessor of lofty standards, impervious and indifferent to her quite charmed offering. This was the nearest we ever got to bestiality. The beast resisted ALL coaxing, so for the sake of damage limitation, I took his place and atoned for the youngster at considerable length. I do so detest waste. I admit I was rampant; a fully unfurled and stoned pervert, innocently hell-bent on radical satiation of the groin, the execution of which provided the perpetual fuel for the next plunge into erratic bliss. The chomping kid I chat to now seems to eye me, as if he knows not only the rumoured tale of Leah and the billy goat, but also the truth. His is a begrudging respect. I chuckle, which only seems to please him more. We were all young once. He is my friend. I his.

I am healthy, though aged. I am blissfully cheered by each moment, each hour. I have an existence that almost all men

*should crave. But I am no ordinary man. I expect within hours
that I shall be dead. As Hamlet himself sat on that high rock
and pondered suicide, there is also here talk of a distant
England, a girl, rumours of murder, insinuations of insanity,
and yet with a textured calm, there is at the root of it all, a cold
and targeted sanity. It is a sanity that aims to save the world
from a dystopian horror, already in the late planning stages.
They call it The Crackdown. And I have its abysmal fucking
architects clearly in my crosshairs.*

Six hours to go.

8.1 CHOKMAH DAYS
6 January, 1917

As the ship sailed from the harbour in New York, I consulted
my tarot and read from it that my Thelemic calendar was
entering a new phase. This time was known in the Kabbalah
as the *Chokmah*. It speaks of a time of questioning wisdom
and offers guidance in how to act in a crisis. My crisis had
been formed on the front, enough to send any man hunting
for a razor to slit his own neck.

On this January dawn, on an ocean steely and drab enough
to camouflage a battleship, I pulled the required series of
thirty-one cards, culminating with that of the Devil. The Devil*
is not a literal translation.

Just as our dreams are not faithful and accurate, but are
simply symbolic, then so it is with The Devil card. It speaks of
the seduction of the material world, immediate gratification
and of physical pleasures. The card is a warning to revert to
the beauty of magick and the Will; to joy and to freedom. The
Devil card warns of an overabundance of luxury. This seemed
appropriate as I left the security and thrum of New York City

---

* *How could it be? The fucker doesn't exist.*

and headed for a Europe still at war, and one where Hühner-bein had recently arrived. He had been convinced by me that our work there in the United States was done, for Russia was crumbling and the States neutral. Germany's victory, I told him, was nigh and inevitable.

I never fully relied on such devices as the *Chokmah,* but if I found myself in a mild crisis, Dandylyon and Prudence had convinced me that these methods might provide the minutest of flicks on the barometer to offer the correction for which I was searching. This period, I was assured by the cards, would last for three years. And the cycle would begin with a series of innocuous fires on the same day.

It was February 12th, 1917 and I had not been back in London long. I remember it well. An enemy of mine within the Golden Dawn announced to the Order in Blythe Road that I was to be the subject of continued attacks from him until I relented in my vocal dissent, fled the country or died in flames. I received note of this in the post from one of my spies. I immediately requested a cab to take me from my home in Chancery Lane to visit two allies of mine, a Mrs Simpson and a Dr Berridge in Kentish Town and Camden. I also intended to tell of my plans for an insurrection that would unfurl as had the First* Battle of Blythe Road, that notorious scrap with Yeats's large-footed monsters.

On the way to Berridge's, the paraffin lights on the cab caught fire, and I had to change into a different carriage by Euston. As we passed Regent's Park, the horses bolted as a result of a bonfire by the side of the road. When I finally arrived in Kentish Town, Mrs Simpson was struggling to light

---

* *Yes, more are to come.*

her hearth fire, something she swore she had never had an issue with ever before. As she did this, the rubber raincoat I had left in her hallway spontaneously combusted and the gaslights in her street exploded, six of them in ten-second intervals. These tales were ten-a-penny, I had just happened to witness these coincidences with my own eyes. I found this wholly unworrying, for in order to believe in such ill-lit viciousness from Satan, it stood that one would have to believe in the goodness of God. And I knew that to be an outright and despicable fucking lie. I can easily take or leave this magical flimflam, it is mild entertainment.

Really, I just wanted power, drugs and naked flesh.

Despite much hot air of this cartoonish magic, my ship had landed in a Europe of the starkest realism, and I had one immediate goal, regardless of the several factions who believed I worked for them. I would harness all of my powers and every inch of political, sexual and magickal leverage to end this war.

We knew long before the actual date of the revolution, in October 1917, that the Bolsheviks would take Moscow in a *coup d'état*. MI-1's intrusive politicking from years before (and without intention, of course) had ensured the Russians would soon be withdrawing from the Eastern Front. That would just leave their allies the Romanians to handle the Ottomans, the Austro-Hungarians and the Germans. The vast redistribution of the armies of the Central Allies onto the Western Front in France and Belgium would mean an early defeat for the British and French. This fat-thumbed, bullet-headed and very English Samson, now without his Scarlet Delilah and his locks of hair, would now have to shove that stone pillar, as he had promised. We needed the Americans in the war or we would face certain defeat as the Russians withdrew. Churchill had thoroughly approved of my idea to sink another boat (in a precisely similar manner to the *Lusitania*) and to use Mexico, of all places, to ensure victory in France and Belgium. He had immediately conferred with Downing Street. All was agreed. And Samson's plan was set in motion. The old lads in the English Mountaineering Club purred into their gins. I shall explain.

I had been dropped from a Sopwith Camel and by the Royal Flying Corps behind the German lines outside the French village of Sin-le-Noble near the ancient commune of Douai. The precise spot for our meeting had released an emerald-green flare at five-minute intervals after the striking of noon. I had arrived an hour early at eleven, and sat scratching my arse and reading a copy of *Faust I* on a deserted mud hill. It was the only thing on the English side that would fit in my pocket, and reading German was always good to get into the language and character.

I inadvertently commandeered a stray horse to get the final two miles to our rendez vous. It seemed in need of company and gladly meandered to me, nuzzling my shoulder. It was a chunky beast, and therefore, I deduced, a recent arrival. He seemed to be as confused as the rest of the poor bastards on two legs around those parts.

The first flare went up and off, just as Faust was on a stroll with Wagner and being befriended by that large poodle.

The stallion even moved down into a large-ish crater in order to allow me to mount him. I then nudged his ribs with my boots, and we moved off in the direction of the green rocket.

Soon after I got there, Hühnerbein arrived in a staff car, spread wide across the rear seats like a strumpet's thighs.

He needed help to exit the vehicle. When he did, he moved

the minimal distance to a bed frame with a mattress on it. There was a risk of landmines, even back here and, for a coward such as he, it was a minor miracle that he even left the car. It seemed his laziness and his desire to be horizontal won out over the danger of walking and the discomfort and filth of the frozen bed. It was January, and fucking vile out.

The bed was not the only household piece out there by the road and in the fields. For hundreds of yards, there was furniture, beds, kitchen tables, dog beds, budgie cages, gas lamps, commodes, potties, quite attractive folding screens and room dividers, armoires, mirrors, garden tables. These were signs of normality from the deserted village that no longer had any use in the perilous and collapsed houses and farms.

'The poor bastards were taking them to the trenches to be reminded of home, when there was a gas attack. Look closely enough and you'll see the bones,' he chuckled.

I looked more closely, walking around the site, distracting myself so as not to dive on the fat bastard and throttle him. There were children's clothes, the single unstrapped shoe of a five-year-old. He picked up a teddy bear from next to his bed, and lobbed it in the air repeatedly, as one would a cricket ball.

My toe nudged a violin case open. It was empty. I thought of a slip of a girl in long socks practising. A chessboard peeled and scorched at the rooks' corners. A small boy's dreams.

I flipped open a school desk to see a ruler, a fountain pen with a lilac nib and a copy of Maupassant's short stories. I recalled the bliss of 'Mouche' and the horror of 'Le Horla' from my childhood. I opened the book at the start of 'Idylle'. It is the one where a lactating woman rides on a train. A man cannot stop staring at her breasts. Unless they are drained thrice daily, the woman suffers great pain. They pass through a tunnel, and the man obliges, helping the lady and also satiating his hunger. I flicked through the six pages of the tale and noticed some of the English translations in the margin in the same lilac ink.

> The young man, confused, stammered: 'But ... Madame ... I could relieve you.'
>
> She replied in a broken voice: 'Yes, if you want. You will do me good service. I cannot hold out, I cannot.'
>
> He knelt in front of her, and she leaned toward him, carrying to his mouth in the gesture of a nurse, the dark tip of her breast. In the movement she made by taking her two hands to bring it towards this man, a drop of milk appeared at the top. He began to drink it eagerly, seizing that heavy breast in his mouth like a fruit. And he began to suckle in a greedy and regular way.

It was a girl's handwriting, florid and round with the tails and spines of the letters, extravagant and passionate. It all hinted at intelligence, and the skill level of the translation verified this.

> He had passed both his arms around the waist of the woman that he was holding to approach her, and he drank with slow sips with a movement of the neck, as a child would.
>
> Suddenly she said: 'That's enough for this one, take the other one now.'
>
> And he took the other with docility.
>
> She had placed her hands on the back of the young man, and she was breathing forcefully now, happily, enjoying the breath of flowers mixed with blasts of air movement being thrown into the cars.

What the fuck was I doing here? I dropped the desk lid down and now saw lilac-inked graffiti, where I had previously seen none.

Victor Hugo est un hérétique.

Victor Hugo is a heretic.

Cette chaleur estivale me rend folle, tenez moi à l'ecart
    des hommes.

Save me from men in the heat of summer, or I shall go mad
with passion.

Je veux que Gilbert me branle.

I want Gilbert to finger me.

The corpulent arsehole brought me out of my reverie.

'What shall we discuss today, my fine friend?' he said.

'I would not want to get ahead ourselves, but this war will
be won within months. The Russians will be going home, trust
me on this. The British will surrender within days of their
retreat to Moscow. We must consider how best to take advantage of our victory.'

'What are they saying in London?' He scratched his balls.

'They are hoping for an armistice that will be kind to them.
The King will impress this upon the Kaiser. We must think of
our own personal gain, my friend. We can carve out our own
notability and legend. It is there for the taking. For you and
me. God knows we have deserved it,' I said.

'Go on.'

'I have a friend in Mexico. A good friend. They are willing to
form an alliance with Berlin. If the Americans join with the British, they will, under the terms of our armistice, be forced to
hand back all the lands she has taken in the last seventy years
from Mexico. Think of our riches. This means California,
Texas, New Mexico and Arizona will all be given back to them.
Another possibility is that if the Mexicans go one step further
and declare war on America *with us*, there is no way we can
lose in Europe, for there will be no American troops sent across
the Atlantic if they are at war on their southern border.'

'This is most intriguing. Continue, please.'

'It is a done deal, if you wish it. All Berlin needs to do is send a cable to Mexico to confirm this. I will facilitate everything.'

'I will speak to them about it. This is remarkable work, Aleister. And we split all profit from this down the line.'

'As always, my friend.'

I pocketed the Maupassant book, and the lilac fountain pen. I would give both a better home. My horse pal was looking at me, seemingly with an adult acceptance that we would soon part and also with a pride and an understanding of my having just fooled this over-fed moron.

Two weeks later, the British Navy intercepted the following cable in code.

We intend to begin on the first of February unrestricted submarine warfare. We shall endeavour in spite of this to keep the United States of America neutral. In the event of this not succeeding, we make Mexico a proposal of alliance on the following basis: make war together, make peace together, generous financial support and an understanding on our part that Mexico is to reconquer the lost territory in California, Texas, New Mexico, and Arizona. The settlement in detail is left to you. You will inform the President of the above most secretly as soon as the outbreak of war with the United States of America is certain and add the suggestion that he should, on his own initiative, invite Japan to immediate adherence and at the same time mediate between Japan and ourselves. Please call the President's attention to the fact that the ruthless employment of our submarines now offers the prospect of compelling England in a few months to make peace.

Signed, ZIMMERMANN

They did not need to crack any code, for I had already told them the precise contents and the timing, the origination and the destination of the message. They instead reverse-engineered the message, to reveal the intent of a thousand other missives they were holding and which had confounded them for a year. It was sent by a high-level clerk called Arthur Zimmermann in the German embassy in New York to their ambassador, Heinrich von Eckardt, in Mexico City. The British heralded the cracking of the cypher, and *this* appeared in many British and American newspapers, so that the Prussians would never suspect me. Even then, the Germans might have got away with it all in the eyes of the public had Zimmermann not simply confessed to an American journalist. 'I cannot deny it. It is all true.' He backed this up with a similar admission in the Reichstag of all places.

Samson was shoving and shoving. Wilson was close to declaring war, I knew this much from MI-1. The final straw appeared close when we repeated the illusion of the *Lusitania* with the sinking of the *Housatonic* on January 31st, 1917. But still Wilson prevaricated to Samson's dismay and near exhaustion.

In late March, four more cargo ships were emptied and sent to the depths. The sailors aboard were all redirected to Ceylon, Costa Rica or West Africa to join thousands of other lads we had saved from the trenches while the officers and generals scratched their groins or crossed their eyes towards the bottom of a brandy tumbler. On April the sixth, 1917, Wilson finally relented under huge pressure from coast to coast, from left wing and right, and we finally had ourselves the greatest ally of them all. The United States of America. And Samson could rest.

Hühnerbein was furious (but not at me), and I truly believe that that was largely because I expressed my anger and absolute disappointment at him. His fury was apparently unspeakable when he saw Churchill shaking hands with President Carranza of Mexico in a copy of *The Times*. Winston was claiming that victory was now close. Christ, how Hühnerbein despised my pal, and as much as he now adored me, thus making for a supremely malleable contact. The Prussians never even figured that the preponderance of ghost ships in those years were early attempts at bait for them to sink. They were certainly tied in knots by Winston and me, befuddled and thoroughly compliant and supple, and magnified by the blind spot created by Hühnerbein's vicious hatred of the future prime minister of the United Kingdom of Great Britain and Northern Ireland.

8.2 There is No Glory in a Clod's Approval

'But *exactly what* did Winston do to deserve such anger from Hühnerbein?' I asked Dandylyon, as we strolled in Hyde Park on a cloudless mid-May day in 1917 to the sound of songbird and an odd whistle I could not place as precisely as I would have wished.

Dandylyon squawked with laughter, covering the flutey whine I was hearing and allowing me to re-focus upon my chum.

'Sit down, old boy. You will enjoy this one.'

And we slumped onto a soft gradient of billiard baize.

'Well, some might point to their run-ins in South Africa, the North-West Frontier, India and Cuba, and they would have been warm. You see Hühnerbein's mischief was generally concentrated over the years in the same spot as was of prime importance to England. They met like touring golf champions or moneyed ladies on their trots of perpetual summer from Nice to Florence.'

He shouted for Prudence to join us from the path by the

Serpentine, as she smiled and waved at rowboats. She was blowing kisses in the direction of two young children who watched their young mother paddle, bumping into other boats and scattering swans, seemingly unable to take her gaze from her giggling little ones. Prudence swivelled, saw us and began to stroll over. She was there within three minutes.

'I am just explaining about Winston and Hühnerbein.'

She chuckled as she sat gracefully upon my suit jacket, and then admired the perfection of the azure blue above.

Dandylyon continued, 'Well, each time their paths crossed, Churchill stole the Prussian's glory. Even more annoyingly for Hühnerbein was the crediting of Churchill for some act of his own heroism or decency, for I don't know if you have noticed it, but they might have once borne an uncanny resemblance to each other. This likeness has, I admit, waned over the years as Hühnerbein has widened and now wears a filthy beard on his face. But if one looks hard enough, one might notice a kernel of similarity that several years ago would have them mistaken for each other.'

He paused. I considered it. It was true. He pulled out two photographs from the school years of the two young lads. I did not know which was Prussian and which one was English. An aroused swan piped down from its shrieking to reveal again that odd whistle that had now upped its pitch by a whisker.

'In Plettenberg Bay, Hühnerbein saved a four-year-old on a beach from an errant wave. Society proclaimed Winston a hero. At a Madras garden party, a twelve-foot python had cornered three ladies, when Hühnerbein played a *pungi* with great skill to distract the snake, hypnotised it until the lasses were safe. Later that same afternoon, an escaped and famished white tiger blocked the route of his *tuk-tuk* by a crowded market and did so with menace, until the Prussian pulled out a catapult and hit the beast in the left eye with a pebble. It slunk away in ignominy, and bothered no one else that day or there-after it seemed.

'On both occasions, it was Churchill who was heralded as the gallant saviour, and while these events were happening, he was, first, copulating with two twin sisters in the billiard room and, secondly, sitting on the roof at the party, meditating and smoking hashish with the governor and his missus. This was all more easily explained by the facts that Hühnerbein could almost seamlessly drift into Harrow English and, similarly, Churchill was able to bark quite excellent German.

'The more Hühnerbein tried to correct these tales and these apparent injustices, the less people believed him, and lauded, extolled and revered Churchill. He was able to stomach them, until the day at the King's Cup at the Oriental Park racetrack in Havana when Winston's future wife, Clementine, mistook them, and, after having gone there with the German, left with the grinning other. By this time, Churchill was quite aware of his good fortune and had Hühnerbein followed, and his bets noted by large-eared gents with stubby pencils and folded newspapers. Yes, he empurpled at losing the beauty with the legs and the bosom, seeing her get in a car with the English-man, but when his winnings had already been collected by a grinning doppelgänger, he now vowed revenge. This was sim-ply too much.'

I chuckled. 'Yes, Clementine is a bit of a sort! I'll give him that.'

'Wait, there is more,' said Prudence.

'You tell him,' said Dandylyon.

I saw many people had stopped and were staring towards the sky. There was no panic, mild intrigue at most. I then looked up, because the sun was blocked for a brief moment, odd for a tranquil day with no cloud.

And then it came towards us from the direction of Park Lane, zeroing in on the rowing boats.

The Zeppelin was called the Baby Killer for a reason. That bastard Hühnerbein would pay for this. I would focus the filth of my anger on him, as I told myself that he should ponder how fucking dangerous *I* can be.

His countrymen were the first to suffer the ignominy of defeat. MI-1 estimated that ten thousand American troops arrived every third day from the spring of 1917 for the rest of the year.

In early 1918, the Germans were now being crippled by vast losses, instigated from their own ill-considered Spring Offensive, a last gambit perhaps. Three decisive American victories in rapid succession at Cantigny, Château-Thierry and Belleau Wood turned the tide inexorably in the other direction as the Hundred Days Offensive of the Allies buckled Berlin's resources, and the end was almost near. By the early winter, the horror was over, but only after I told them that the Americans had 6 million more troops ready to embark. Whitehall's conditions of the armistice that I laid out to Hühnerbein were now a summation to surrender, and they dutifully surrendered. I wept with him, but I was instead crying for my Spanish friends at the Little Madrid Café and that decimated boat on the Serpentine that left severed legs floating and the prettiest of pigtails soaked, wiry and choking the ducks that survived fleetingly. And many millions of others.

London, Berlin and Paris had privately conceded the stalemated horror would go on until 1925 at least. 'Thank you, Aleister,' I may have even heard late one night in Duke Street. But then again, I might not have. My glory was in the act, not in some clod's approval and fawning.

Again, boys could go home, but the nervously delivered news of my greatest sadness and my ultimate loss was just hours away.

8.3 Always Remember Me

They found my letters in the breast pocket. The corpse was cold. It could have been any one of thousands, but some marvellously romantic crackpot* had had the notion to honour the war dead with one honest Tommy whose identity would remain shrouded and hidden. A symbol, they called it. A shrine to all the blessed lads. They took three cadavers from Flanders that day; unsure which would be interred in Westminster. It was only upon arrival back in England that a colonel randomly touched the tilted boot of the soldier on the left in the back of the odorous ambulance that the choice was made.

I was summoned to Whitehall. What did I know? Could I identify the body?

I wept, as I saw the marbly purple of Robbie's face.

I read the final letter written to me. It carries dark maroon fingerprints and Whitechapelian splatters. They suggest an urgency that hollows me to this day. The event to which Roberta refers took place in March 1918. Winston had insisted that she and I spend four days of luxury in Paris. We were dropped, in battle clobber, by a pair of Sopwith Camels in the Bois de Boulogne. We landed near each other and then marched with malice aforethought the five miles to the centre of the city. We walked into the Hotel Royal Monceau by the Arc de Triomphe, where they were expecting us. They saw us once pass through the lobby, when we went to stroll through the Parc Monceau at

---

* *David Railton's well-measured concept in 1916 of The Unknown Warrior.*

midnight. We left by Sopwith Camel and from the Bois de Boulogne. I would have no idea of the consequences of our sojourn. How could I have?

Cambrai, Hauts-de-France
France
November 9th, 1918

My darling Aleister,

You must know that I have always loved you, and wanted you as my own.

It might have been a forbidden love. It would have been a scary one.

We were too close, I felt. Perhaps our destinies to save England and run from no one clouded what we always knew, I sense. And I must pay homage to your kindliness for being gentle and understanding with a novice such as I. The one time we were intimate shall remain the summit of my life; but I must also tell you the baby you planted inside me is a troublesome one, as I lay here on a scarlet-soaked bunk in a trench, German-built, it seems. We must have gained a few yards, my love. There is just one chaplain here, a gypsy fellow of great skill he assures me, but I sense he shall not be able to help us.

I might have let you all down in the hour of all of our greatest needs. You, our child, England. And myself. I saw more in seconds with you than most women and men shall see in a lifetime, my whirring, thrumming Master. And that part within me that the romantic foolishly might call the soul shall very soon walk into the wilderness. But with each step, there will be just one Great Man, of whom this stirred mare shall think. Without the Gentle and Great Beast, I am naught; but I hope He shall be forever boosted by my thoughts, wishes and rampant Love.

Always remember me.

Your adoring Roberta, forever in True Worship xxx

8.4 FAREWELL

Robbie, with her flat arse cheeks, raspy voice and moundless sternum, had shape-shifted quite astonishingly and most effectively from soldier to nurse, woman to male youth; all most pleasing for this Pimpernel for her to fake such disguise, while staying both safe(ish) and meddlesome. The second war was rich in tales of girls' courage and boldness, but that just made Robbie's pioneering in the first scrap all the more impressive and audacious. This remained so, despite the relative ease of convincing clods (Generals drunk twenty miles behind the lines) or brave and scared soldiers clinging on to life itself and minute-by-minute, with her gift for seamless androgyny. Robbie showed her talent for applying stage make-up to fake a day's stubble and a sleepless milkman's fertile vocabulary, while growling intermittently her/his desires for cunt of any kind and news of the cricket. There was also the latitude and cover offered by the British Army's gently twisted and pleasingly perverse tradition of the hard-bastards-in-a-frock variety shows and cabarets of six-foot-six Welsh miners rouged like desperate, unfucked aunts in panto. Just how the baggy bloomers and snug bras would make it to Japanese POW camps, one could only marvel.

Robbie had been a day away from returning to a care home near Worthing when the fatal shell hit the earth where her final inter-trench mischief was being executed. She was busy switching messages, and therefore cancelling plans for wave after wave of German offensives. They had been pointless for four years, this was beyond the absurd. The foetus was just twenty-five weeks; Robbie barely showed a bump, they say. She had planned, I now suspect, that when she did show signs of motherhood, she would have retreated to the role of a nurse to continue her own Pimpernelling. We were less than two days from the armistice that I, in particular, knew was coming. The first, second and third vicious wounds had been made by flying metal, as she was exposed outside of the bunker, exchanging nodes of a radio transmitter in order to broadcast those four final communiqués to prevent thousands more casualties. She wrote on a piece of paper, as she bled. On another scrap, a name and address in Dulwich Common, London SE and one by Loch Ness. Our child was taken from her womb by an army chaplain of Romany extraction called only Zealand, doing his befuddled and frowning best.

The sliver of a minuscule youth was lobbed onto a bunk that held diseased rags that were masquerading as bandages, and with the presumptuous prioritising that saw the mother's survival chances infinitely greater than the determined little sod, barely able to breathe, never mind scream. Zealand felt the minutest of pulses and heard the softest of yells. Within thirty minutes, Robbie had lost consciousness and within the hour, she had passed. Paperwork and bureaucracy had been abandoned four and a quarter years previous, and there were no procedures there for a man, let alone a woman, never mind a pregnant one and her foetus-cum-child.

The famished rats and the Prussians appeared to move in at a similar rate, one polite-ish rodent of a liberal mind sniffed, nibbled and then tucked in to the placenta, as the first boots landed in the mud, and they were seen by the chaplain at the tiny passageway to the bunks.

The godly man was now sitting next to the cold corpse of Roberta, as the young boys from the 2. *Landwehr* came in. He did not know whether their silence and dismay was at the presence of a still foetus or a naked woman, for it was clear to him that they had seen neither before. They then all slumped like dominoes onto the earth, unable to speak from what appeared to be a combination of exhaustion and relief to have made it across the battlefield. After a pause of barely more than a minute, one addressed the chaplain.

'*Darf ich Dir helfen, mein Freund?*'*

8.5 GLORIED DUST
11 November 1918

It was all over. It was time to traipse home.

Zealand was the kind to follow the path of least resistance. It was in his gypsy blood to wander. There was a route to the east; he took it. This was not the second war when a nation was toxic. It is so easily forgotten that in 1918 (as in 1914), Germany was pretty similar to England, to Britain. There were no Nazis, no concentration camps, no sterilisations, no Final Solutions. But innocent civilians had died at sea bringing food to friends. And yes, gas had been used in the trenches, but by both sides and away from the populace. Bombing of cities was limited. This was a daft brawl between lands with Asia and Africa in mind, fuelled by gourmands with infinite wealth and a hunger for puissance. They were countries lorded over by inbred cousins. For sure, Hitler needed a thumping, but, for the first one, the Kaiser and the King were of the same family. And so, it was no big deal for Zealand to join the young boys, with whom he had become pals when the sirens were sounded on the 11th, and to go with them to their home town of Halle, where their mothers would, they were sure, welcome him.

It seemed to be a slow and endless journey on viciously

---

*   '*May I help you, my friend?*'

retarded rolling stock, but by Christ, it felt remarkable to be above ground.

Zealand read an English–German dictionary. And spoke the odd word from time to time.

The boys smiled, and slumped across the floors and seats, seemed to be speaking of German cuisine, interspersed with the name of a school sweetheart. Their joy was in abrupt contrast to the stern countenances and unrelenting miens of the officers down the carriage, castrated of their honour and elitist pride.

Zealand carried only his small medical bag and chaplain's Bible with him. They all reacted as one and with a fatherly silence, when after an hour of talking of Mutti's Apfelstrudel and girls with names like Katrina Goetz, Beatte von Schorlemer and Heidi Schaller, there came a small pulsating purr from the satchel. It was the weak cry of a small boy, whom the gypsy chaplain and the boys had named Edward at the dying Roberta's request. This orphan, while never knowing his mother, might at least have a small brigade of fathers, and an impassioned squadron of doting and relieved grandmothers. Some wallowing cretins would see misfortune from day one, but not this lad. He would grow to know of rich gratitude for his own miracle, despite the youthful curse of fat ankles, a toad's neck and by the age of nine a burgeoning pertness to his chest.

8.6 CREATIVITY

I had lost Papa, Rose Edith, Robbie, two daughters, several pals from The Legion, and possibly La Gitana, but there were very few left unscorched by the horror. I knew I would never pity myself either, what a vile state. As much as I told the world I hated the English, I held the stiff upper lip, as any god should. I was still a triple agent of crimson subterfuge, and I had to maintain the confidence of my acquaintances: Hühnerbein, above all. I would destroy him in good time, and when he was no longer of any use to me.

The war had also ended the liberalism of the Great Binge, and we all felt the hangover, and with such withdrawals, I nursed the guilt and pondered how to channel the arousal. The answer was with more drugs, more rituals, more scandal, more mischief, more yoga, more female arse and more Pimpernelling. However, I feared a period of pending creative and spiritual block. I wrote in my diary:

> I am tempted, for example, to crucify a toad or copulate with a duck or sheep or goat or to set a house on fire or murder someone with the idea – a perfectly good magical idea to some, of course – that some supreme violation of all the laws of my being would break my Karma or dissolve the spell which seems to bind me. These actions were abominable to me, and I would never have done them. It just seemed that I would need such extreme behaviour to spark me from an inertia that filled me with dread like no ghost or policeman or German or venereal affliction ever could.

In February 1919, I retreated to Loch Ness, to Boleskine House. There I would walk the mountains and sniff the lake, I planned to find inspiration amid the elegant cliché of nature and from liberating rustication.

The Frog maid, who I had imagined quite unaware of my arrival, greeted me with a vast pot of mushroom soup, a peck on my cheek and a punctuality, as if I were arriving back from the office on the usual rush-hour train from Waterloo. I still chuckled at how she had arrived the day after I had, to my eternal shame, sacrificed the frog, and, given her prescience with the soup and my otherwise unexpected arrival, now firmly suspected even more her connection with some spirit or other. This further confirmed to my fried brain that some strange force or other approved of my withdrawal to the countryside.

The more I watched Frog eat, burp, curse like a steelworker, fart and shit, the more attractive I found her. This is usually the domain of the true beauty, but Frog was not that. She was quite the bewitching marvel, in fact. Minute tics that might send another man to anger, despair and distraction only cemented my worship of her. Whether she was picking her teeth with a chewed-off finger- or toenail, or whether she was plucking black hairs that resembled fat spider legs from her nostrils, I only wanted to stare at her more. She wore my socks without asking, cooked only what she wanted to eat and her arse was as wide as a barrel, but, like her behaviour, it would not have been right in any other proportion. I do miss her.

When Frog walked me to my desk and a new typewriter with a stack of fine vellum sheets, with a view from the bay windows that looked out onto the waters, I knew that she and some perverse force was goading me to write. I was intrigued enough by the oddness of it all. So we smoked vast piles of marijuana and snorted molehills of white powder. The sole condition was that after taking on board an ounce of both between us, we had to maintain an absolute silence, and then to write and write and write. We were disallowed from talking or fondling or fucking. We were allowed to look at each other, to smile, to nod, to smoke and then tap away at the keys. This channelled grand energies and thought patterns and revelations into two hundred pages of *The Gospel According to St Bernard Shaw*. I knew the Scriptures of course, and had just read Shaw's disposition on Jesus, Androcles and the Lion. I had to tell the world that Shaw knew less than bugger all about Christ, the East and mysticism. This thesis of mine, despite its excited spelling errors, established the outline of an entirely final theory on the construction of Christianity. Well, it did to me.

The fine and tasteful British novelist, Francis King CBE reviewed it thus:

> A treasury of Crowley's wit, wisdom and criticism which, even if it was the only book its author had written, would suffice to rebut the slander that Crowley was a pleasure-seeking fraud whose occultism was no more than 'making a religion out of his weakness'.

The next time Frog and I did this neat experiment together, we were only allowed to paint and this is when I created *Four Red Monks Carrying a Black Goat across the Snows to Nowhere*.

I can thoroughly recommend this highly disciplined (and ill-disciplined) method to anyone wishing to re-spark their creative Will, as this piece uncovered my ability to daub oils with aplomb. Frog was so adorable as we began the second sitting. I recall her desire to taste the powder again and to experience once more the animal froth that she contributed quite beautifully to our times of pleasure, but before we began, her last words were the innocent and concerned enquiry, 'Is there a good doctor nearby, Beast?'

'I do not know about a doctor, but there is a first-class undertaker in the village.'

She laughed for a full five minutes, before we both shut up for four days of ritual drug-taking, silence and artistic intensity on several dozen canvasses, each the size of the main wall in the vast hall. Her crowning glory was a quite magnificent self-portrait that was part-human and part-amphibian, and which she signed Frog, and scrawled a line from Blake beneath her signature.

'If a fool were to persist with his follies, he would become wise.'

I was back.

8.7 The Second Battle of Blythe Road

I returned to London. Orr met me at King's Cross, and took me to see Dandylyon and another old pal from Whitehall. Spiritual and creative vigour were renewed (and a damned good sleep had) and when such positivity is sourced, fine things happen. And in this case it was Winston Churchill.

We met at Winston's Hyde Park Corner mansion. It was a place full of secrets that seemed to echo from evenings of fun. It was darkened hallways, stunningly lit at dusk through the stained glass of the door arches, as dust danced in preparation for a large dinner and a night of mirth, plot and laughter. The exterior style was Italianate and clad in Royal Doulton Carrara and green, blue and turquoise Burmantofts bricks. The lavish and extravagant inside was of the Arts and Crafts school, glazed surfaces, teal domes, marble and hardened tiles to lessen quite purposefully the effects, even internally, of city pollution. The trellis wallpaper in the Japanese *mingei* style was a spectacular addition by his regardful missus, Clementine. Winston described the house as 'an alderman dressed as a discerning street strumpet'. They were both most proud of her.

Orr and I were let in by Rex, the butler. We were led into the library, where I soon gravitated towards an abundant corner dedicated to the dark arts. The scarlet drapes were almost closed and let in minimal light. More light came in from the hallway. Orr played with the large globe that stood by the mahogany desk central in the room. Next to it, Dandylyon reclined in the large armchair. We may have whistled or hummed tunes; no one spoke, I remember that. After a minute or two, Winston stood forward from the shadows, wearing the gingerest beard and made his eyes bulge. He waddled viciously, barking harsh Bavarian invective and looking uncomfortably energetic. It was a scarily brilliant impersonation, but I knew we had not been brought here for a cheap dramatic stunt.

When our chuckles had subsided, Winston opened the curtains. He paused before turning on his heel, to look at us all one by one, 'Gentlemen. Peacetime calls for a very different kind of naughtiness.'

I knew what he wanted, as he continued, 'It is time to really mess around with Hühnerbein.'

'Oh! Let's have a newspaper scandal with scarlet strumpets in a cheap hotel. Or boys. Or animals,' Dandylyon said.

'I have a better idea,' I whispered.

Dandylyon was adept at allowing me to believe things were my idea. I spoke.

'Gentlemen! The fear and hollow horror that one's enemies feel when they realise that one will never let an issue rest is a real and persistent one. If they are convinced that the dull and sickening thud of revenge is to come a year or five years or ten years later, they must then believe that the threat will be there until one of you dies. If *I* were your enemy, then you should make arrangements for a perpetual and infinite menace beyond the day you are boxed up in a coffin and dropped into the soil. And this shall be the precise intention of the Second Battle of Blythe Road. We can scare Hühnerbein but impress him at the same time. And by attacking Yeats, we can make him fearful for the rest of his pitiful days and beyond. The goal of piercing the Golden Dawn's temple and headquarters shall not be to steal relics or ancient manuscripts. It shall be an old-fashioned roguishness and a bullying waggery. I want to defecate, literally and therefore fiercely symbolically, on their altar. And quite crucially, I have a perfect plan . . .'

Winston was to wear his ginger beard and we would dine in the *Schwarzwald*, a *Stammtisch*, next to the German embassy in South Kensington and within easy reach of 36 Blythe Road. We would take a quiet and ill-lit corner, I would do all the ordering, the unhealthiest fatty wurst for him with schnapps, of course. Our presence would be noted, and that would be all that was required, for Hühnerbein was egotistical enough to take great joy in a mere rumour of being seen out with me, even if, in this case, the rumour would be founded in more than idle tittle-tattle.

Winston was already widening around the girth, but still was infinitely thinner than the German. We started taking vast breakfasts, lunches and dinners at his house. Chef was ordered to use extra butter, lard and cream in all of Winston's dishes. We had both developed a taste for hot curry in India, so the kitchen stuffed him with the highest-caloric fare, while I took it hotter than anyone could handle. To truly slow his metabolism, Winston did not walk anywhere, and had a hansom cab on a twenty-four-hour station. Every other day, we were driven down to a fleapit cinema called the Gaumont Rialto in the cut-throat backstreets of Waterloo. Next door we ate the greasiest fish and chips, and then rammed our gobs with milk chocolate as we watched afternoon matinées of *Rebecca of Sunnybrook Farm* with Mary Pickford, Chaplin's double bill of *The Immigrant* and *Easy Street*, Fatty Arbuckle and Buster Keaton in *Coney Island*, John Ford's *Straight Shooting* and my favourite, *El Apóstol*. We chuckled and were often told to be quiet by old ladies. Given his diet, Winston was just as likely to pass wind and nod off, leaving me awake to deal with the ire and disgust of the horn-rimmed aunts in our immediate vicinity. Not one of them looked like their emissions would have been any less sickening than Mr Churchill's.

He expanded at a marvellous rate and soon was, with red beard in place, a doppelgänger for his nemesis. Having one's greatest foe resemble one's greatest ally is an intriguing combination that offers thrilling prospects for wickedness.

Our first mission of mischief one night in June 1919 was an unprovoked and unsuspected attack on those arses at the Golden Dawn. We chose the evening of the summer solstice, for, like the Epiphany, it brought them all out to Blythe Road like cockroaches.

Both Winston and I were sturdy types, who could hold our ale. We had consumed enough at the restaurant to add to the myth. '*Ja*, Herr Chef. They were both here that night and sank two large *Flasches* of peach schnapps.'

We smoked spicy marijuana at the table and snorted spoonfuls of cocaine. I made sure our waiter took his gratuity in pounds sterling and in face-numbing powder. It was the only kind, polite and decent thing to do, but also anything that added to the mystique, allure and standing of Hühnerbein would please him. The *Dummkopf*!

'Why does he hate you so much? I heard some of the reasons,' I said.

'Ha ha ha! I shall tell you one day, chum. I promise.'

It was just after 7 p.m. when we walked out into the drizzle and to our waiting vehicle. We got into character and costume on the short ride to W14. It was an easy process that really just involved swinging our metaphorical scrotums in the style of an inebriated ogre, convinced that Satan and Lucifer were over our

shoulders, egging on their chums and ready to come windmilling into our scrap. This would be our role once inside, but
first we had to slump on the seats of the vehicle and wait for
our driver to oblige with his rather simple task, which was to
pierce the guard of the two gargantuan trolls on the front door
of the Edwardian mansion. He pulled the brand-new Packard
onto the gravelled driveway, with the slow steady intent of the
consummate chauffeur he was. He stepped out of the car, nodded at the large-footed fellows and casually engaged with them.

'I am here for Lord Albury.'

'Very well.'

There was no Lord Albury, of course.

He smoked a cigarette, and then pulled out a small bag of
toffees, which he offered to the guards.

'Fank you 'squire. Don't mind if I do.'

'Fank you very mach, gav'nah.'

And that was that. Who, after all, doesn't like a damned
good toffee?

A forty-five-minute wait was a fair estimate, and my anticipation seemed to be matched by Winston's. We approached
the elephantine thugs once we were sure the effects were close.
We wanted them to remember us. In fact, I was convinced one
of them had been there at the previous raid. Joy! I wanted
them to remember too, who had done this to them. I sensed
that Winston was quite shocked by the ferocity of the passion
sparked by the jungle goo, as the bearded Cockney monsters
shuffled into an understood embrace that did not even fake an
interest outside of the intense clinch. Their giant cocks
twitched against each other, we could both see this much.
Winston and I walked straight past them smoking a very large
reefer, as they chomped noisily at each other like famished
peasants presented with a warm meal.

*

We both wore horned helmets, our faces bore the tattooed ink of the pentagram and inverted crucifixes that the crowd at the Waldorf Hotel had once seen me produce on dear Randle Dibdin's face. We had steel breastplates, adorned with five-sided insignia and rams. We carried a large tankard that resembled a holy-ish grail. It contained human blood from the Shepherd's Bush mortuary. We both wore Japanese warrior *Oni* masks, but Winston's fake beard stuck out below his. I yelled spells as we burst in through the double doors on the raised ground floor. There were perhaps forty of them in there, in crimson gowns and facing an altar. They too wore masks. I recognised the limp and awful gait of Yeats at the chantry. I drew a pistol on him and ordered him, and everyone else, to remain still and silent.

'We only wish to join your ritual. Do precisely as I say.'

I poured the blood from the grail all over myself from my helmet down, and screamed, 'Man, unable to solve the Riddle of Existence, takes counsel of Saturn, extreme old age. Such answers as he can get is the one word "Despair".

'Is there more hope in the dignity and wisdom of Jupiter? No; for the noble senior lacks the vigour of Mars the warrior. Counsel is in vain without determination to carry it out.

'Mars, thus invoked, is indeed capable of victory: but he has already lost the controlled wisdom of age; in a moment of conquest he wastes the fruits of it, in the arms of luxury.

'It is through this weakness that the perfected man, the Sun, is of dual nature, and his evil twin slays him in his glory, and who shall mourn him but his Mother Nature, Venus, the lady of love and sorrow?

'But even Venus owes all her charm to the swift messenger of the gods, Mercury, the joyous and ambiguous boy, whose tricks first scandalise, and then delight, Olympus.

'But Mercury, too, is found wanting. Now in him alone is the secret cure for all the woe of the human race. Swift as ever, he passes, and gives place to the youngest of the gods, to the Virginal Moon.'

Several seemed to recognise my voice and shape, Yeats for sure.

For the more finely tuned noses, there might well have been a stench of pheromone and adrenalin from the arousal and the fear.

'I wish only to take ritual with my beloved brethren one last time. This has haunted me for years.'

I moved to the altar with my pistol cocked, and the crowd stepped back from me. Winston drew a sword, and waved it with B-movie theatrics. I almost laughed. It was a mob of cowards who offered zero menace. I ordered them to take sacrament from my partner, as I stood on the altar and screamed some more hyperbole that they all seemed to think impressive.

> O virgin in armour
> Thine arrows unsling
> In the brilliant resilient
> First rays of the spring!
> No Godhead could charm her,
> But manhood awoke—
> O fiery Valkyrie,
> I invoke, I invoke!

They stepped forward as obedient toddlers, and sipped from Winston's cup a concentrated version of the jungle resin brew that took effect within five minutes. For that period, I forced them to sit on their arses and meditate, while telling them all silently, with a thudding and concentrated whisper of the power of the mind, and the vast potent of yoga. The last part of my diatribe informed them that their leader was an Irish fraud and an enemy of decency. When this festivity was over, they would note him as a pederast and a liar. Aleister Crowley and the murderous Bavarian, Hühnerbein, in spite of their dreadful costumes and histrionics, would be the True Masters.

I yelled vile Lower Danish invective that even made a drunken Winston blush, he told me later. The toffee was back. We gave them a huge dose and watched them get filthy in their own mess. Yeats's treat was an altogether different ignominy. The smug poet was made to flick two fingers for several hours in the style of the English soldier, something that would hurt the Irishman until the day he perished.

Meanwhile, our driver, a friend of Orr's with similar dimensions, went to the boozer on the corner where a crew of cameramen and lighting technicians, pals of Dibdin, waited. They soon lumped into 36 Blythe Road heavy cameras and audio recording equipment, courtesy of a pal of the great oaf in the Lumière Pictures offices in London.

We barricaded the doors and filmed until Monday morning. Masks were removed to reveal lords, ladies, royalty, members of parliament, surgeons, actors and brigadiers. The well-known duchess present outperformed all others in vileness and earned everyone's respect, but that can be seen around the fifteen-hour mark on the fifty-seventh reel. It was a monochrome masterpiece with the subtlest hint of the toffee's trademark aura of turquoise, lilac and death-white, as I now added accomplished and menacing film-maker to my curriculum vitae.

Several copies were made, and Hühnerbein was installed as the Chief Hermetic of the Order of the Golden Dawn. It was the least I could do. I told him I had made him a god in London society, and he, dizzied by it all, went along with it like a dutiful little wretch. I was in his finest graces, which was helpful given that I would need one vast favour from him before too long.

The film of that glorious summer solstice was called *The Word of Sin*; my debut, if you will. The title came from a suitable passage of mine in *The Book of the Law*.

> The word of sin is Restriction. O man! refuse not thy
>   wife, if she will! O lover, if thou wilt, depart!
> There is no bond that can unite the divided but love: all
>   else is a curse.
> Accursed! Accursed be it to the aeons! Hell.

The First Lord of the Admiralty was as aghast as he was thoroughly impressed. We left and discussed my travel to Italy. He would arrange suitable passage. I would miss him, for he was a fine companion in mischief. Our alliance, however, had barely begun. But together, we had won The Second Battle of Blythe Road.

The *Chokmah* cycle was over. The creative block I had temporarily beaten by Loch Ness with Frog was now considered by me to be a blip in the larger picture of the equinox of my spirit. According to my Thelemic calendar and more importantly MI-1, my *Chokmah* days now required the commencement of a new cycle and a new challenge, and the obligatory storm would soon hit us in the Atlantic shortly after having left for Italy.

England was now a changed and marginally more emetic land. She was about to pass the Dangerous Drug Act.* What scandal. For heaven's sake.

_____

* *of 1920*

It was a new decade, and the Italian Fascist Party had been formed by some friend of Hühnerbein, a horrid cretin called Mussolini. It was time for mischief, sabotage and monkey business in the sun. Sicily was calling. Sicily.

Excerpt of a *letter to Dibdin, 1920*

> I am just off to D___ to give those lectures – Labour, Religion, and Death – and thence by the Beard of the Prophet to a Free Country, I am trying to find an Abbey of Thelema for free men, a love cult with high ideals. I shall reorganise freemasonry and religion to replace the pomposities and banalities of their ragbag of rituals by a simple, lucid and coherent system.

Chapter 9

Mussolini, Sicily & the Abbey

You've got enemies? Good, that means you have stood
up for something sometime in your life.
  – Sir Winston Leonard Spencer-Churchill KG OM CH
                                    TD DL FRS RA

I *burn and smoke a lot of hashish.*
  This is my hypothesis: 'Perhaps hashish is the drug that
loosens the girders of the soul, but is in itself neither good nor
bad. Perhaps, as Baudelaire thinks, it merely exaggerates and
distorts the natural man and his mood of the moment.'

  I am no Black Magician. I am a sweet and dangerous soul
who shall save this world; this beautiful place, in which we get
to live for free.

The goats, seemingly understanding each nuance, and I, quite
euphoric, stroll like best mates would have strolled in long-gone
summers across the South Downs or on the approach to
Canterbury: short-trousered scamps with grubby and tanned
knees; scorched, happy pilgrims to a new dawn. Yet we are
several goats and a gnarled-yet-vibrant old man in his fifteenth
decade.

And I think of how I shall read tonight, my final evening, supine on my bed, by a dandelion-yellow lamp in my sparse but magnificent stone chambers until the night takes me to sleep. I shall fight it though, for why waste these moments, as I shall be gone for a long, long time.

I tell the goats again that 666 is merely the number of the sun.

I tell them, 'The crass Fleet Street editors should have therefore named me Sunshine.'

If I ever evoked evil spirits, it was only to bind and control them for a good purpose, as we might if we use the dangerous elements of fire and electricity for heating and lighting. I say it again: Black Magic is dangerous and practised by the morally bankrupt. And never by me. My sheet anchor is decency, common sense and love. And I know the value of ambition and dreams, for they provide fuel for the soul. I know the worth also of recognising true genius when one sees it – or just good old-fashioned determination (for this, stubbornness can be a partial substitute).

I say one must not cut one's coat in accordance with the cloth, for even the meanest tailor knows that one must cut one's cloth in accordance with the size of the man.

And that fellow should suggest to one's foes (with the aid of drugs, superstition and chums if required) that they cower, hushed, shrivelled and with belittled hardihoods.

Am I shouting?

I know, forgive me, I am very, very high.

Five hours to go.

9.1 LEAH SUBLIME

Why my sexual preferences should be of any interest to others baffles me. Or does it? I know most gossip-mongers are lonely sorts, who would benefit greatly from an hour undressed and prone with me. (I'm not fussy.) I try to recall the first two lines of *Gatsby* in such situations.

> In my younger and more vulnerable years my father gave me some advice that I've been turning over in my mind ever since.
>
> 'Whenever you feel like criticizing anyone,' he told me, 'just remember that all the people in this world haven't had the advantages that you've had.'

It is only after reading that masterpiece that one realises the narrator is not referring to the advantages of money, but to those of love, true friendship and decency. And so I shall go against my instincts to dismiss the intrusive types, and instead, I shall feel gratitude.

And if you want to know the truth of my predilections, for me, red-headed ladies were, by far, the sauciest. My Scarlet Women. And Leah Horsig was the next one.

We met in Paris as the brutal and punishing terms of the Treaty of Versailles were being decided in June 1919. I was en route to Italy. The Germans feigned gross indignation, but from Hühnerbein to the Kaiser, they were thrilled with how punitive it was to the Prussian spirit. That spongy lard-arse had a proclivity for figurative and literal flagellation and sado-masochism. He revelled in the role of the victim and never more so would he, along with the whole entitled officer class, enjoy being force-fed browned globules of turd by the British and Americans. In the spirit of that fine erstwhile Manhattan-ite, Randle Dibdin, after a blindfolded spanking at chess, the Prussians yelled quite privately for now, 'Best of three, you cheating fuckers,' to the Allies.

The thing is, as with that shit-eating masochist the

Marquis* in the Bastille down the road, they generally revel in coming back for more, the mucky sods.

The Treaty was signed on June the twenty-eighth, 1919, precisely five years after the assassination in Sarajevo and also on Saint Vitus' Day, a supremely important time in the calendar of the cock-eyed and troubled Serb nationalists. This was guaranteed to irk Belgrade, and therefore Moscow, while the terms would be so vicious on the Germans (scuppered Navy fleet, lands handed to Poland and France, and appallingly steep reparations to be paid in American dollars) that the putrid little inbred Austrian painter was already screaming (to himself in all likelihood, but certainly with no friends) for a re-match. I have a tale to tell of that talentless little arsehole to come, when he tried to glory and elevate himself in my sparkling midst.

I was there in Versailles as it all happened, and then saw the high brass celebrating their guaranteed future employment and toasting their shares in the munitions factories. I spoke to Hühnerbein and the generals one night at Le Chat Blanc, our regular spot on Rue d'Odessa in Montparnasse in the filthy industrial layers of Paris, past the graveyards and the rancid slums that one invariably finds on the eastern fringes of any European city, for the poor bastards there are forced to choke on the shitty air blown from the hub and the elegant west. Forget the frowns, the hand-wringing, the froth and the self-piteous posturing at the terms of the Treaty. These Krauts were all, at their very core,† privately thrilled and I recall them laughing about it and proposing a toast, as out of their midst

---

* *The Marquis de Sade was moved out of the Bastille the day before it was stormed on July the fourteenth, 1789 leaving just seven symbolic clods in there, but wars have been fought over less.*

† *I avoid purposefully the term, 'soul'.*

that night, walked Leah Hirsig. Her sister was one of Hühner-bein's broad-minded scrubbers.

The ecstatic shit-eating antics of the Germans were a precise duplicate of my putrid desires for *her* that very evening. I considered the exact tang and bitterness of our pending and lengthy analingus. I began to compose a verse to both foxy siblings. The little sister Leah reminded me of Solomon's friend,* for she had no breasts. She radiated an indefinable sweetness. Without wasting time on words, I began to kiss her. It was sheer instinct. She shared this emotion, and equalled my ardour. We continued with occasional interruptions, such as politeness required, or to answer the mindless intrusions of her sister in the rare intervals when Leah needed to catch her womanly breath. A monumental poem was forming in my mind, as we embraced in front of the intrigued crowd.

I saw Leah as the fortuitous culmination of much searching. She was another astonishing redhead, more pre-Raphaelite tangles to tumble on my cheeks and verdant pupils on the whitest of canvasses. As Frog was known to me as Frog, and I was generally regarded as The Beast, and other chums and lovers had names such as Horse, Rabbit, Eagle, Pony and Shrew, then I would know Leah as Frankenstein's Monster. Just as the other nicknames were in no way derogatory, then Leah's moniker was, in fact, the most complimentary of them all. I had by this point landed upon and thrust into several thousand mouths, bums and cunts, and so when I called Leah by this name, she knew that she was the very best bits taken from my vast legions of previous amours. It was as if each detail had been removed from another almost-faultless cadaver with adoration and then stitched by the lightest and

---

* *Solomon 8.8 – We have a little sister. And she hath no breasts. What shall we do for our sister in the day when she shall be spoken for?*

deftest of hands to create the completeness of Her. I should not embarrass her or those with the original body part (or element of personality or characteristic), but suffice to say, this new Scarlet Woman of mine was, in the eye of this beholder, rampant fucking perfection. This chiselled and bespoke formula would not have worked as well for everyone, for not all would appreciate her lunacy or her peppery and marginally oversized feet to sniff or her tendency to claw at my eyes, but such is life. She also liked to slap my exposed and dangling sack until my heavy tears of excruciating ecstasy fell like June rain, and with even more gusto than even darling La Gitana had managed to inspire. Our understanding was telepathic from within that first week. This is indeed rare, and ought to be treasured with vigour and steep gladliness.

Leah was the daughter of a mercenary Swiss gold-panner and her Peruvian lapsed man of God. They robbed around three dozen banks from Lima to Cartagena while both dressed as pregnant nuns, one with a giveaway five o' clock shadow, a penchant for anything female and massive hands that seemed to have sprouted patches of the wiriest pubic hair below the knuckles. Leah was born in Martinique, after her parents had been stranded on a Dutch clipper in a vicious and unseasonable tropical storm while fleeing the continent of their crimes. Leah lived there on the island for eighteen years, charmed by the Frenchness of it, according to their façade of a story, but far closer to the truth was that they were comforted by a gargantuan stash of American, Peruvian, Venezuelan and Colombian currency and gold, and the absolute lack of any extradition treaty. On her eighteenth birthday, Leah was gifted from Papa the almost untouched take from the Central Bank of Caracas, and she was on the first available ship to Marseille, determined to transmigrate the spirit of her renegade parents to the Old World. She spoke Martinique French quite perfectly, and English and Italian too. Given her parents' stylish evasion of the law and their maximum joy from crime and wrongdoing, Leah wished to continue this mischief on a stage for more worthy of her than little old Martinique, as delicious and spicy and comfortable as her almost-perfect youth had been. Like those morons at the Golden Dawn, when everything in life had come so easily to them, the natural response is to get ballsy and strive for contact with godliness and with a god. This is where I was so very charmed to oblige her. By Christ, I would oblige her.

The following morning, as she slept, tempting me with her arse, I resisted her exposed charms and instead wrote of her in the form of that nagging poem that had started to form in my mind the previous evening. I had real fun penning it, but tried, with real concentration, not to think instead of that Treaty, those scraps of paper in Versailles that would soon sculpt the century and all of our futures. I had seen this in my visions with Robbie in the Ceylon jungle, it was now making so much more sense.

From my diary:

Against all beastly instincts to wake her roughly and in worship, I sit here in the heat, writing a poem to Leah.

One long poem – an occasional publishable line thrown in when I weakened.

7.00 a.m.: I think I'll collect all my filth in one poem and mark it Leah in plain figures.

10.00 a.m.: I think I did it.

It contained 666 words, just for my darling mother.

Leah Sublime,
Goddess above me!
Snake of the slime
Alostrael, love me!
Our master, the devil
Prospers the revel.
Tread with your foot
My heart 'til it hurt!
Tread on it, put
The smear of your dirt
On my love, on my shame
Scribble your name!
Straddle your Beast
My Masterful Bitch
With the thighs of you greased
With the Sweat of your Itch!
Spit on me, scarlet
Mouth of my harlot!
Now from your wide
Raw cunt, the abyss,
Spend spouting the tide
Of your sizzling piss
In my mouth; oh my Whore
Let it pour, let it pour!

That clear and distinct Paris morning, I wrote of Satan's number, but I thought of Christ at this time. I hold the poor fellow totally innocent of the religion that was foisted upon him posthumously. We have much in common, that great man and I, facing trials against the morose of mind and void of spirit, up against the twisted intentions of the self-interested and the vicious. Jesus' penchant for warm and lustful flesh, his intriguing proximity to men and whores alike remind me of a younger me. Oh ye! Sufferer of trials and holder of victories, all warped in world view by the desperate and the imbecile. We would have been fine pals, he and I. How we would have bellowed across the centuries, bellowed at the stupidity of Man for believing in the slops of faecal mess, for which they hold the Truly Enlightened responsible. We both spread a simple and unfettered message of True Love, and one must question those hollow fuckers who find that distasteful, subversive or dangerous.

True Love. True Love.

During these days and nights in Le Chat Blanc, Hühnerbein spoke to me excitedly of burgeoning fascist movements in Spain, Portugal and Italy. In Rome, a melodramatic and prancing cut-throat called Benito Mussolini was the new pioneer of the right. In 1920, he was still eighteen months away from seizing power, but his star was certainly on the rise, convincing the wobbly-minded and desperate of spirit. The silly arsehole called himself Il Duce. (Oh! please. For heaven's sake. I preferred to call him Fat Head.) I was briefed on him by some visiting chaps from Whitehall, and given reams of research on the clod. I adsorbed the lot, spouted the bully's own rhetoric back to Hühnerbein and used this vast knowledge to impress him to the point of giggles.

If Germany were to have her revenge for defeat and the spiteful terms of the Treaty, then Hühnerbein's chums and he would experiment in fertile Mediterranean soils and unforgiving national psyches first. While he was both daydreaming and pontificating to me, Prudence and Dandylyon provided some balancing soulful and nutritional ideas. They spoke instead of my destiny and how I must now finally found my own religion of Thelema. We took its inspiration and concept from François Rabelais' *Gargantua and Pantagruel*. Rabelais was a sixteenth-century French scholar, essayist, humanist, scholar and monk. In this text, he described the ideal of Thelema's abbey as an anti-monastery, where the people were 'spent not in laws, statutes, or rules, but according to their own free Will and pleasure'.

'Just the ticket,' I thought. And I pondered Rabelais' own words: 'If the skies fall, one may hope to catch the larks.'

The final consideration – a wholly selfish and personal one – was that I was now quite smitten with Leah, and needed to be with her and by her side. She knew Italy and Sicily well, and was ecstatic to learn of my intentions to take her with me as my Scarlet Woman. MI-1 thought it ideal that I observe the Italian situation up close while still laying the groundwork for my future infiltration into Germany. They knew already, of course, that a second war was inevitable.

In the summer of 1920, I told the Bavarian that it was time to define my own religion, by giving her a bona fide home. I would leave immediately for Sicily where I planned to find and found the Abbey of Thelema. Here I might be near enough to Rome to aid in his plans for a right-wing insurgency. Hühnerbein was thrilled by this, as his proximity to and friendship with the founder of a religion, a living and collaborating god, would only boost his standing in Berlin.

Leah and I both needed the countryside. After all of the horror of war and then the excesses of Paris, it was certainly once again time for me to rusticate. Prudence and Leah (with MI-1's help) gathered a small mob of willing adherents and their eager children, all eager to breathe fresh Mediterranean air. They were all a carefree, barefoot and bohemian lot, quite unsuited to the England or France of the time.

We needed an unadulterated spot where I could tell the urchins in the morning that, 'Up there is the sun. When it gets over *there*, you may return.' I could send them off to play and know they would come back with grubby knees, smudged foreheads and a reddy-pink tone to their chops. They would then soon eagerly divulge their tales of mischief, stealing fruit from trees, handkerchiefs from washing lines and swimming in forbidden streams. I had a very precise picture of what was required for my Abbey. And most thrilling, I knew Leah would perpetually be offered on my altar there. And I on hers.

> You stale like a mare
> And fart as you stale;
> Through straggled wet hair
> You spout like a whale.
> Splash the manure
> And piss from the sewer.
> Down to me quick
> With your tooth on my lip
> And your hand on my prick
> With feverish grip
> My life as it drinks—
> How your breath stinks!
> Your hand, oh unclean
> Your hand that has wasted
> Your love, in obscene
> Black masses, that tasted
> Your soul, it's your hand!
> Feel my prick stand!
> Your life times from lewd
> Little girl, to mature
> Worn whore that has chewed
> Your own pile of manure.
> Your hand was the key to—
> And now you frig me, too!

I had always fancied Italy. Byron and Shelley adored her, and like me, had her love forced upon them by exile, though mine was pretend, of course. In London, that rancid rag, *John Bull* was in the midst of one of its lunatic public attacks upon my character. It sold copies for them, but I benefitted more for it also gave my name the highest currency across the continent in Berlin. The last headline I saw in a copy that had made its way to Paris was

ANOTHER TRAITOR TROUNCED
Career and Condemnation of the Notorious Aleister Crowley
We await an assurance from the Home Office or the Foreign Office that steps are being taken to arrest the renegade or prevent his infamous feet from ever again polluting our shores.

You get the idea. People continued to believe this nonsense, even without an arrest or a charge. Any sane, reasonable or analytical person would surely wonder why, and come to only one conclusion, as fantastical as it may have appeared. And that was that I was not who they claimed, but then again, I was not who I claimed to be either. So little imagination is such a let-down, but as I tipped my cap and winked boyishly to the spirit of Percy Blakeney, I left the Pimpernel's Paris for my Sicilian years.

9.2 SICILY

Drunkenness is a curse and a hindrance only to slaves. Shelley's couriers were 'drunk on the wind of their own speed.

Anyone who is doing his true Will is drunk with the delight of Life.

– Aleister Crowley

4 May 1921

We landed in Rome and, by train, dropped south. Of course.

I found the abbey after having consulted my I Ching* each day while in Italy.

Perhaps fifty of us – at this point I was not even aware of many of the names of the willing mob assembled by my friends, and this added to my Kurtzian elevation – sailed south from Naples to the northern coastline of Sicily on a fishing boat provided by the First Lord of the Admiralty. It was odd that I only missed Winston when I sat opposite him and looked into his eyes. I then cherished each second, and privately wished I could enjoy this deep-shag carpet luxury every day. I guess this is the measure of a perfect friendship and the greatest of friends.

The crossing was smooth and blissful, as the adults burned weed and the children dipped their hands in the cerulean waters. Leah laid her head on my thigh and whistled, sang, whistled. The wind enveloped us, and bade us a good morning. Those who imagine the spirits of Italy reluctant to accept these bad seeds should think again. The porpoise squeaked a welcome. I knew them to be easily aroused critters, and we exchanged a glance. Upon departure from the mainland when the rope was lobbed onto the bow, Pompeii puffed out a smoke ring to wish us safe passage. Then as we neared Sicily, Mount Etna exhaled an almost identical chuff of dust to welcome us all.

We landed on the beach at Cefalù (pronounced *Chay-fah-loo*), a tiny fishing town with only a handful of dwellings and soft sand underfoot. We carried no baggage, no belongings.

---

* *An ancient divination text that offers advice and direction through the choice of random numbers.*

We were pioneers, adventurers in a vanguard that was beautiful and obscene.

When we climbed out of the boat, Leah stayed right by my side (I could sniff her), and we splashed the gentle breakers. Our skin dried from the knee down in the heat as our shins emerged from the Mediterranean. Leah, my emotional alchemist, seemed to turn the fishy brine on my hands into an aphrodisiac, as we inhaled the scent from our palms. She wanted me to take her there. Rasputin was indeed correct, God wanted us to fornicate. Even the Lord's Prayer corroborated it, 'Our Father who art in Heaven. Hallowed be Thy Name. Thy Kingdom come. Thy WILL be done.' Thy WILL. Thy WILL.

> Rub all the much
> Of your cunt on me, Leah
> Cunt, let me suck
> All your glued gonorrhoea!
> Cunt without end!
> Amen! 'til you spend!
> Cunt! you have harboured
> All dirt and disease
> In your slimy unbarbered
> Loose hole, with its cheese
> And its monthlies, and pox
> You chewer of cocks!
> Cunt, you have sucked
> Up pricks, you squirted
> Out foetuses, fucked
> Till bastards you blurted
> Out into space—
> Spend on my face!
> Rub all your gleet away!
> Envenom the arrow.

> May your pox eat away
> Me to the marrow.
> Cunt you have got me;
> I love you to rot me!

This unruly mob bade farewell to our skipper. He gave a very English salute, then bellowed across the small expanse of foam, 'I am sorry, sir. But this is from the First Lord of the Admiralty.'

He raised two fingers at me, his middle and forefinger with his palm facing towards his face.

'He said you would understand.'

It was the invective of the English army, that curse* and abuse reserved from the Anglo fighter to all of his enemies abroad.

I bellowed back across the waters, 'Tell your boss that I am eyeing his wife. And she knows, and writhes at the prospect of being tarnished by a bullet-headed and fat-fingered god.'

'Yes, sir!'

'Repeat my message!'

He repeated the message, word-, intonation- and spirit-perfect.

'Good lad!'

'Thank you, sir.'

He grinned, saluted again, and set to sea with a business-like and happy swagger.

The children led the way, for the marvels appeared to be attuned to the quest of my Great Work of founding the Abbey and my religion. But first they took us to an ice-cream parlour,

---

* *The apocryphal word has the archers of King Henry flicking the Vs to the French at Agincourt to show they still had their crosshairs. The dispute to its origins lingers. It might be more simply a version of the cuckold sign. Quite simply, it means 'Fuck off'.*

where we all sat and were brought icy water. I had some coins in my pocket, adequate for us all until the Bank of Palermo opened, though this, it soon became clear, was an irregular and unpredictable occurrence. The locals were, however, as welcoming as the porpoise, and allowed us to run an account, once they discovered that we were intending to stay. They knew of the generosity of those English poets who had gone before, and many a struggling business had flourished through the patronage of those strange foreign types, all heavy eyelids and slow melodramatic gestures of well-intended pomposity from too much opium.

MI-1 knew of three empty and rentable properties along that coastline. The children played games with the maps, as if searching for buried treasure. I guess, in a funny sort of way, that was *precisely* what we were all doing.

That afternoon, we all walked inland to the middle one. We did not need to look any further when we found her some three hours later. The moods of the tired children crescendo'd and thrummed as we neared the plot. This was a fair barometer, for both Leah and I knew we had found our paradise. We approached from the north, up the hill, that began to carry a tang of an orange and peach orchard, until the aroma was heavy and dense, forcing a mad delight upon us all. The wildflowers that framed the broad stone pathway were of intense whites, yellows and crimsons, all in a peak of bloom and pristine, as if the King of England were expected on that mountainside. And yes, the angle was steep enough to be considered as a perfect gradient for sex magick. The stone walls at the boundary of the property were overgrown with moss and high grass, capeweed and lanky dandelions. Golden midges danced in the sun and rested in tulip trees. They seemed as eager as giddy sons and daughters to show off the charms of the property that they had found first, inviting us generously into their secret. We walked over the threshold of the boundary, and the children already knew that we were home.

Immediately, I noticed two wells, and both were plentiful. The water was fresh, clean and chilled. The house itself was a large old place, perhaps three hundred years old, and imposing enough to take the name Abbey. It seemed to correlate perfectly with Rabelais' vision of where one might found such a movement. She radiated this liberal desire, with her robust horticulture, her generous water and her well-lit rooms for lengthy consideration of sciences and arts, leavened yoga and intense meditation. We had vistas from weedy scrublands to the east and west to track the sun from morning to evening, where the orchard on both sides offered a dappling of her glare onto white walls and happy faces. It was almost impossible to feel melancholy on either flank at dusks and dawns, thrusting the artist into a frenzied creation that I had not experienced since Frog and I had snorted an ounce of powder by Loch Ness and then shut up.

> Spend again, lash me!
> Leah, one spasm
> Scream to splash me.
> Slime of the chasm
> Choke me with spilth
> Of your sow-belly's filth.
> Stab your demonic
> Smile to my brain!
> Soak me in cognac
> Cunt and cocaine;
> Sprawl on me! Sit
> On my mouth, Leah, shit!
> Shit on me, slut!
> Creamy the curds

That drip from your gut!
Greasy the turds!
Dribble your dung
On the tip of my tongue!
Churn on me, Leah!
Twist on your thighs!
Smear diarrhoea
Into my eyes!
Splutter out shit
From the bottomless pit.

In the midst of my manly desire for Leah, I was very aware that this affair, this adoration was a fuel to achieve my True Will. If the love affair with La Gitana had forced me into accepting the likelihood of heartbreak and poetry, then I knew this romance was also not just lust and filth for its own end. Leah might even help us all expunge the drugs and the reliance on them from our lives, and propel us into greatness. Was it even perhaps a time to grow up? These thoughts would soon lead me to write my first and largely semi-autobiographical novel, *The Diary of a Drug Fiend*, there on Sicily. In twenty-seven days, twelve hours and forty-five minutes, I dictated the whole of the 121,000-word manuscript of this to Leah. I even added *this* in the notes to Part II of the text, and by crikey, I was serious.

The Abbey of Thelema at 'Telepylus' is a real place. It and its customs and members, with the surrounding scenery, are accurately described. The training there given is suited to all conditions of spiritual distress, and for the discovery and development of the 'True Will' of any person willing to seek a higher fulfilment. Those interested are invited to a) communicate with the author of this book through the publisher and b) visit with him upon request. He awaits you ecstatically.

It sold well, and kept us comfortable as Father's wealth eventually started to erode. This was never a worry to me for I could always rely on the gullible to fill my coffers, and this of course, meant old ladies, the infirm and the Germans. The lads at MI-1 were perpetually generous with pounds sterling and the boundless resources afforded to an Empire: accommodation, transport, restaurant tabs for nourishment and booze, drug-dealers, doctors, lawyers, publishers. Unless I was travelling, I rarely carried any money. Everyone knew me, and either wanted me as a friend or wanted to avoid me as an enemy. I used this state of notoriety, but preferred not to exploit it. It was a fine line. I believe I judged it to perfection, even when in the nebulous midst of a week-long jag or the cloudy trough or pristine peak of a regular bender.

After *Drug Fiend* was finished and shipped off to my publisher, Mandrake Press, in London, I then wrote *Moonchild* in a six-week period. It was a time for real work. Next I attempted the notoriously tricky format of short stories.

'The Testament of Magdalen Blair' brought this review from some half-baked rotter. I was most proud.

'One of the most horrible stories ever written' (*Penguin Encyclopaedia of Horror & the Supernatural*)

The lad at the marginally more informed *Manchester Guardian* managed to grasp at least some of 'His Secret Sins'.

'Menacingly beyond the margins of sanity, and too troubling to even consider it as good or bad. Read it.' (the *Manchester Guardian*)

And perhaps the best of the lot was a precise critique of 'Stratagem', a tale that had been accepted and published immediately by the *English Review*. I had long admired Conrad.

> 'A subtle exposure of English stupidity. Without a doubt, the greatest short story I have read in three decades.' (Joseph Conrad)

And so, a love like Leah's allowed for a true roaming of the creative spirit. It was so efficient to have perpetual perfection in one's presence. There was always a depressing stupidity in having had to waste uncounted and priceless hours in chasing what ought to have been brought to the back door every evening with the milk. I wrote my novels, we had sex magick, and, despite our best intentions on some days, we continued to take drugs, while the rules of the house allowed for and encouraged climbing, swimming and long walks. We were introduced to Palermo's premier dealer in heroin, cocaine and peyote. His name was Amatore, and he was introduced to everyone at the Abbey. We shall meet him momentarily. Everyone had access to a limitless supply, but this was not to sanction vast use, but to provoke the opposite response of removing all temptation. I hoped that by doing this, the lesser beings in the commune would therefore not embarrass us when the Germans and the Italian fascists visited, for this time was coming and central to my plan and the goal of MI-1.

> Turn to me, chew it
> With me, Leah, whore!
> Vomit it, spew it
> And lick it once more.
> We can make lust
> Drunk on Disgust.
> Splay out your gut,

Your ass hole, my lover!
You buggering slut,
I know where to shove her!
There she goes, plumb
Up the foul Bitch's bum!
Sackful of skin
And bone, as I speak
I'll bugger your grin
Into a shriek.
Bugger you, slut
Bugger your gut!
Wriggle, you hog!
Wrench at the pin!
Wrench at it, drag
It half out, suck it in!
Scream, you hog dirt, you!
I want it to hurt you!

9.3 BENITO THE FAT HEAD

I was now known to all as *The Beast*. This was a term of endearment, a moniker of love and, to me, a celebration of earth and nature. Well now, this *Bête et Belle* had pranks and devilry in mind. Our target was the Fat Head.

Leah shouted to me, as she held the fat rope and lowered the bucket containing a grinning and playful urchin into the chill of the well on a stuffy and airless June day. I do not even know if it was male or female, I just recall that the innocence of its androgyny ruled. That elegant and towering summer was in her early pomp, urging us on, nudging us to a euphoria that made us wonder if this was all real.

'*Daaaah-ling* Beast?'

'Yes, Monster?'

She always expelled a small gasp of (almost animal) delight

when I called her that. This was especially amusing in the company of those who did not understand the depth of the compliment and adulation behind the name.

'I have been thinking about Benito,' she said.

'Yes, so have I, my love. He might be a tough nut to crack. What were your thoughts? What are your conclusions?'

The child in the bucket touched the surface of the crystal water down the stone hole. There was a shriek of ecstasy that brought a visible joy to Leah's face. Utter happiness lived between our gazes in those seconds, compounded and multiplied by the unbridled innocence of the gaiety and mirth in the well below us. Perhaps this is when we were at our best. Stop the world. Yes, I knew that evil was beginning to bubble across the blue water, but I already knew, deep down, that we would beat it.

'Our victory over Benito must be a lasting one, and be a stain in his mind that he cannot scrub. We must leave here both as victors, but also with an ability to remind him of this at will in the future. We have to be able to trouble him and make him shudder whenever we wish and from a distance,' she went on.

'I agree. But what of the Germans?'

'Well, it is key that they trust you over Benito, hold you in greater esteem. Their alliance with him is one of convenience. Their reliance on you comes in the form of speaking to their gods.'

'Go on. I like it a lot.'

'Men like Mussolini are used to getting their own way. And this feeds their power. It is self-perpetuating. He needs to experience misery and fear. His type is not used to it.'

She was good, this Scarlet Lass. She was *very* good. She was also most attentive to the splashing child and its safety, as she plotted the destruction of a dictator. She put her head below the rim of the stone well, at her hip height and yelled down to create her own echo, 'I love you . . . love you . . . ve you . . . you . . . you . . .'

She stood erect again and continued speaking to me.

'I love you, Leah,' came out of the well with the deftest of pitches.

'He is a coward, and this is where we attack. I have thought of several nasty tacks to take. He might be exposed as a pederast, but so what? His supporters wouldn't believe it or would simply ignore it. Others would die for speaking of it. We could cripple him or assassinate him, but we would not want to be exposed and it is quite likely such martyrdom might increase his popularity.'

'Exactly. We need to hollow out his mind, and let him know it is we who have done it. And this needs to also be our protection from him. We need him to know that our deaths will bring his own demise,' I said. 'And we must remember that it is the Germans who remain the true enemy. Benito is a means not an end,' I added. 'Subtlety makes these things so much more fun. These European types are quite blind to it, you know.'

'I heard everything that you were saying,' a voice came from behind us. It was Amatore, that strange fish of a drug-dealer, that marvellous outlaw with righteous wickedness within the grasp of his slim and manicured digits.

'You need to be quiet. This talk is . . . how you say . . . *seditious*.'

Amatore really was a quiet and studied sort, who knew, of course, all kinds of weirdoes from his trade. I heard that he handled the wide spectrum of types with lofty but endearing even-handedness, and from what I saw, offered each of them that even-toothed grin set in a handsome, olive cheekboned frame that seemed so alluring; almost perfect both to Leah and to me. And *that* was the evening he had brought ether to us as a treat. He interrupted our shameless and overt plotting.

'*È un gran cagasotto. Dorme ogni notte con la luce accesa. Potresti spaventarlo a morte.*'*

'Really! Continue!' I said.

'Oh goody,' squeaked Leah.

If he were really afraid of ghosts and ghouls to such a degree, one of a whimpering brat, perhaps it really was time to dabble in all that Black Magic stuff I was consistently accused of man-handling.

Leah said, 'Take your own advice, Beast. If you're going to get blamed for something, say, "Balls to it." And do it regardless.'

She was right, now it was truly time to have some measured[†] fun with it all.

'I love you, Amatore,' I said.

'No problem, boss. Tell me when you want more ether. I must go into Palermo. Those jazz lads are fiends and need feeding.' Leah's Italian was as proficient as his English, the impressive and stylish brute.

'What *else* do you know about him?'

When Amatore spoke his own dialect, he always spoke in Milanese.

'*È un prudente. Petrificato del sesso. Avresti spaventato a morte per una seconda volta. Anche parlare di un'orgia lo spingerà alla distrazione.*'[‡]

---

* '*He is a big pussy cat. He sleeps with the light on. You could scare him to death.*'

† *Measured is key, for my pre-eminent knowledge of the Occult allowed me to walk the most precipitous of lines with bold confidence.*

‡ '*He is a prude. Petrified of sex. You would scare him to death for a second time. Even talk of an orgy would send him to distraction.*'

'Anything *else* we need to know?'

'Sì. Se sa che sei cazzo con lui, lui ti farà morire tutti.'*

And Amatore left, leaving us with vital new clues as to Benito's destiny and a vast stash of ether and other goodies.

> Beast-Lioness, squirt
> From your Cocksucker's hole!
> Belch out the dirt
> From your Syphilis soul.
> Splutter foul words
> Through your supper of turds!
> May the Devil our lord, your
> Soul scribble over
> With sayings of ordure!
> Call me your lover!
> Slave of the gut
> Of the arse of a slut,
> Call me your sewer
> Of spilth and snot
> Your fart-sniffer, chewer
> Of the shit in your slot.
> Call me that as you rave
> In the rape of your slave.
> Fuck! Shit! Let me come
> Alostrael—Fuck!
> I've spent in your bum.
> Shit! Give me the muck
> From my whore's arse, slick
> Dirt of my prick!

---

*   'Yes. If he knows you are fucking with him, he will slaughter you all.'

9.4 *He is Back*

Rumours of my constant orgies had swirled around London. Apparently and according to the *Daily Mail* and *John Bull*, I had forced many men into anal sex, the children had been given drugs, and one loud-mouth called Raoul Loveday claimed that I had made him drink cat's blood and urine. Does no one ever know how to simply say, 'No'? Am I so powerful to have everyone simply do what I say, even when they find it so abhorrent? For this is precisely what the clods appear to be suggesting. Grown-ups might make up their own minds.

Rotters and imbeciles had published lies. Nincompoops had bought and read those ghastly tabloids and relished the gossip, while neither Sir Percy Blakeney nor I had given a jot. We had declined legal offers to sue for slander, preferring to claim we were destitute in Italy and unable to fund such extravagances. The truth had been that we simply had to keep our innocence quiet, for behind the lines of mischief, one might run amok. To be precise, we were planning our move on the head of the Fascist Party and I now wanted to wield his fear of Black Magic as an ancient and troubling sword. My Benito, that Fat Head who was now running Italy.

I had been accused of being a black magician. No more foolish statement had ever been made about me. I despised the thing to such an extent that I could hardly believe in the existence of people so debased and idiotic as to practice it. I could not have celebrated The Black Mass, if I had wanted to, for I was not a consecrated priest of the Christian Church. The only black things about me were the resin I smoked, the occasional splendid Negress I joyously polluted in Cairo, and the night skies above Cefalù that we, as the oddest family in the land, so adored.

*

From down in the well, the playful child yelled to be brought up, and Leah pulled in the rope. I helped her, but only so that I could rub her from behind through the thin yellow cotton she wore. My dubious and loving intentions could not be masked, for I too wore only thin cotton around my centre. The child climbed out, exhausted, spent and ecstatic. It fell to the weedy floor, gasping out laughter. We both stared at the vision at our feet. I knew Leah to be maternal, but suspected her to be barren. Leah never let this cloud ruin her day.

Leah then looked at me, and spoke.

'I wish we were able to control his dreams. Instead, we might have him seduced by three vampirical beauties, cursed with a venereal disease or with persistent lice.'

'Yes, but the madness from syphilis would only make him more unpredictable and therefore dangerous,' I said. 'I too have considered cheap stunts, traditional tricks and ghost stories, but these are always too flimsy and not sturdy enough to last over time, for, as even that child knows, there are no such things as ghosts. Never mind ones that we can control. The weakness and the belligerence of his mind are our key points of attack. Spiritual fear and sex are his weak points.'

'Beast, let us sit and meditate. The malice we seek shall come to us.'

And so three hours later, after a lengthy meditation on the eastern slopes, I yelled, 'Leah, my love, I have it.'

It was that remarkable morning in the rosy June of 1922 when that strange aroma passed my nose. It made me gag for a second, it was wholly out of place in the orchards. My tantra was interrupted, but so blissful was it that my landing was cushioned. I smiled and heard a child giggling through the trees, the birdsong competing for the air waves. The wind brought the vile tang again, a sliver of a stench that fondled a memory from decades earlier, and, in my mind, I heard the sturdiest of words. And the inspiration that we sought came from the recollection and the spirit of a filthy Russian holy man.

'*Ai lins bilele unui înger.*'*

I heard it again in my mind, even more loudly. Rasputin, you magnificent fucker.

I now yelled out those same words.

'Beast? What is it?'

'Can you smell it? Can you smell the shit?'

And there, from a frothing sewer pipe that simmered in the early June heat, I had my answer as to how we would goad a dictator.

I smiled at Leah, confident in the coalescing plan around my magnificent Russian cornerstone. 'Our salvation, my darling, is Grigori Yefimovich Rasputin.'

I resolved to use the teachings of a mad monk to haunt this pioneering fascist. My Russian brother, my friend and my hero would lead the spiritual cavalry charge and come to our rescue, blaspheming, copulating, neck veins prominent, and worryingly ripe.

'I shall explain, Monster.' *(Gasp!)* 'Come sit between my knees, while we stare at this day.'

Leah moved to me. She dropped to the ground, settling down with her back to me and between my knees, holding my ankles with those slender fingers.

'First, my love, I shall dine with Benito in Rome, both arranged and attended by Hühnerbein. Towards the end of our dinner, invisible ink shall turn deep lilac on my forehead and cheeks in the form of a pentagram and two inverted crucifixes. I shall chant mumbo jumbo and Sanskrit as if under a spell, a troubling invocation. I shall laugh it all off, as I then

---

* '*Blessed are those who lick the balls of an angel.*'

calm and order a fine brandy, sending the coward scarpering for his staff car. Several playful fires shall then start around him in synchronicity in the coming hours and then again throughout the following days. This will make him afraid of *me* and know the rumours of my devilish connections are true. Hühnerbein will not know that this will petrify the duke, and he will be looking instead for an impressed Benito. This will make Benito will feel even more isolated. Bear with me.'

Her head dropped back onto my thigh.

'Secondly, I shall then write an essay to be published in London, Moscow, Paris and across Italy, each in the local language. This piece shall declare the New Tenets of Thelema based on the teachings of the New Obsidian Lord, the Holy Man Rasputin. In it, I will be heralded as a god. It shall be called something,' and I waved my left hand skyward, 'like *How Perpetual Fornication Can Deliver the Vilest Sinner to God the Quickest*. This will make him afraid of *Rasputin*, whom he believes to be dead.'

She laughed. Then she laughed again and more loudly this time, as the idea seemed to seep in.

'The final part of the plan is thus. Now always remember that the Italians are suckers for visions. They see the face of the weeping Madonna in browning apples, drying paint, and bruised thighs. And so, I shall employ a whole squadron of mischievous sorts. They shall be tall Legion-types, and then some lanky agents of England, and then some actor friends of my pal, Randle Dibdin, currently not employed at the Cinecittà Studios in Rome. These lads will all be avowed enemies of Il Duce.'

'And what will they do, Masterful Beast?'

She, of course, already knew the answer.

'Ha ha ha! They shall dress in stinky robes and appear yelling Slavic filth outside churches across the country. They might or might not be joined by an actor, playing a chubby-thumbed, bullet-headed Englishman with demonic symbols on his face. They might or might not be joined by an actor of unimportant dimensions, for all he or she needed to do was to wear a goat's head.'

She shuffled in excitement.

'These apparitions and visions of Rasputin (with troubling chums) shall be coordinated and synchronised across his country, as well as the islands of Corsica, Sardinia and Sicily to cause absolute confusion and fear-mongering. To further weigh on the prancing Duke's mind, exact replicas shall also be reported from several locations in Italian East Africa and around the Horn. They are an even more superstitious lot there, and so these myths shall soon be magnified and exaggerated; all the better to make Mussolini shudder and lay awake at night, sweating like a well-worn whore in church.'

'And if he knows you are cavorting with the ghost of Rasputin, he dare not touch you in this life – or the next – for fear of reprisals by your spirits and by the spirits of your pals and followers.'

'Precisely, my darling!'

'There is only one thing he would fear more than the man who brought down the Romanovs.'

Leah finished my thought.

'And that is a dead Russian holy man, an English demon-invoker and a representative of slaughtered nature all coming to ignite Italy into a frenzy of fucking for God.'

'Yes.'

And then we sat and smiled, as I thought of how we could even desecrate a few altars here and there, and perhaps pay a few ladies to claim they had been soiled by the spirit of the Russian monk with embellishments of animal ferocity, near-death climaxes afore the Godhead and shuddering man-widths. And how He growled and drooled and slobbered in what appeared to be a rural Romanian twang.

Meanwhile, in front of us in the long grass, the androgynous one, with its yellow curls and lilac aura, gurgled a rare and guttural joy. And made daisy chains, as I thanked the stench of shit in that generous June breeze for helping me to hollow out the mind of one of the biggest cunts that ever lived.

Checkmate! Best of three, perhaps?

I knew that this would plant a fearful and horrific Pavlovian seed within Benito, one that I might then trigger at will in the future with the appearance of a bearded giant and his pals at Faustian crossroads and by deserted churches around that marvelled land.

The Italians are famously rigorous within the constraints of the church, but just imagine if that faux passion could be harnessed through their equally eager groins and become instead a thoroughly righteous fuel to sexual union. What I mean to say is, what if God Himself were to sanction free love in Italy, it would be a magnificent and self-fuelling chaos. *This* was my way in.

Grigori would have been so proud. I imagined that that fair lad, Christ himself, would also have smirked at the humour of it all. Dandylyon, Orr, Prudence and Winston were ecstatic at the news of the prank. They scoured *John Bull* on my behalf at a luncheon at the club (Prudence was permitted as a nurse) and found no mention of a fascist dictator, petrified to leave his palace. The editor did, however, cover at length Rasputin's printed essay on free love from beyond the grave. MI-1 types all chuckled across the breadth of a continent at the thought of the Fleet Street fury in their little boy paws and bubbling piety as they typed of my genius and my filth.

Eat it, you sow!
I'm your dog, fuck, shit!
Swallow it now!
Rest for a bit!
Satan, you gave
A crown to a slave.
I am your fate, on
Your belly, above you.
I swear it by Satan
Leah, I love you.
I'm going insane
Do it again!

The propagandists, the purposefully misinformed historians and the gossipers will tell you that I was ignominiously thrown off Sicily by Il Duce's strongmen. Of course, this was nonsense. The truth was, in 1923, after three years on the island, my work was largely done. I could make Mussolini cower and shrink from a thousand miles. I had written like I never had, I had performed rituals that would take my infamy to new levels, I had even hosted Hühnerbein and his Bavarian and Prussian clowns with a regularity and proximity that made us all feel like brothers. Winston considered all of this as mission accomplished, especially as the Germans who had passed through the Abbey had names that history would note: Hess, von Ribbentrop, Goebbels and Speer. I wrote thus to Dandylyon:

In the absence of the magical jungle resin goo, I charm the nasty bastards with bawdry poetry in English and German, anti-London chat, and even a few mirthful songs that describe the shortcomings of the Anglos in sexual union and cuisine. Many times at supper with them, I lash out at Benito, for I know that if I am to be seen as a truly audacious and brave menace, then slandering Il Duce on his own turf in front of his allies shall certainly achieve this. I see them glance at each other with impressed nods. I know that if I were in a fist fight with Benito, they would cheer me on. Remember too, they think I have Satan on my side. What an ace to hold that is!

Sicily has inflated my spirit and my cause. The intensity of the sex magick has thrilled the grown-ups, while leaving us leavened, youthful and delirious. Our drug intake has peaked and then subsided as I feel more in control than I ever thought I would. My filthy poetry has reflected my true self for the first time, I feel. We frolic with children, and I have gained a window into what a true childhood with other small friends might be like. It makes me think of my father a lot, and always fondly. And quite crucially and a source of great pride to me, I have founded a religion of my own. I thank you, Mr Churchill, for this.

MI-1, Winston, Leah, Dandylyon, Orr, Prudence and I all knew it was time for me to return, but it was far more important to allow Hühnerbein to believe that he had hatched a plan to have me spy for Germany in London. It was 1923 and *they* were now on the rise. They wanted their best man in London. Again, I was thrilled to oblige.

We all walked down to the port of Cefalù in a similarly ecstatic and thrilled manner as to how we had all arrived, the children played, the flowers bloomed, and the family at the ice-cream parlour fed us all into sated raptures. The same small boat and mariner welcomed us with a very English salute.

We waded out to the boat, void of belongings, just as we had arrived.

I turned to bid farewell to Sicily's nature and smiled at her king, Etna. He exhaled a smoke ring to acknowledge our departure with a fondness. Sicily would miss me, for she appreciates the mischievous and sly imp. I blew her a kiss, and promised to come back one day. And I always preferred to keep my promises, and I still do.

> Have not I spoken, even I, Benito,
> The big, the brave, the mighty Mussolini,
> The ultra-modern Caesar. With my 'Veni
> Vidi, Vici'? – let all the world agree, too!
> Does a mere mountain think that it is free to
> Stir up sedition? Shall such teeny-weeny
> Volcanoes venture to display their spleeny
> And socialist cant? – Subside, mosquito!
>
> – 'A Song for Italy,' 1923, Aleister Crowley

Chapter 10

Stately Euphoria in Tunis & Scotland

The joy of life consists in the exercise of one's energies,
continual growth, constant change, the enjoyment of
every new experience.
To stop means simply to die.
The eternal mistake of mankind is to set up an attainable
ideal.

— Aleister Crowley

There are moments in every man's life when he glimpses
the eternal.

— High Lama, *Lost Horizon*

I ponder this concept of absolute happiness. Despite my gourmand Himalayan attempts, I know that true perfection in life cannot be maintained at length. But by God, she can be achieved for a few breaths. The real key is to recognise and acknowledge her in our midst, grin and wink at her, breathe her in, sniff, molest and fondle her by all means, but not to ponder her absence morosely like a filly's blouse and with a dewy, sugary eye when it is too bloody late. Remember that many have never ever had the good fortune to know bliss and experience contentment.

Yet perversely, it is partly my boredom of such bliss that has pushed me to the edge of today's nonsensical but wholly necessary hara-kiri. The meadow is now full. Of shaved heads, robes, acolytes and young friends. There are many who dress as I do. They are here to wave me on my way.

I smoke a lot more hashish and drift back to London and the time of the court case of the Golden Dawn upon my return from Italy. I had been charged over the Second Battle of Blythe Road. (Did they not remember I had filmed them all? You might be asking.) In truth, it was all MI-1's doing for larks and the public diet of nonsense around me. It was all a show. I enjoyed it thoroughly.

After years of having listened to obscene charges about me, I was now supposed to remain silent and considered in court, calm and serene, disciplined and well measured. I was able to do this, confident of my own responses, but there are points when the most saintly among us are tested, not by the exposure and revelation of one's malfeasance and selfish joy, but by the fools one is asked to suffer with gladliness. This weakness caused my only real outburst during that infamous and notorious trial at the High Court that took up much of that year, as I defended myself against my high-jinxed intrusion into 36 Blythe Road. I was not aware that my whispered 'Oh, eff awff' had carried to the distant and rippled reaches of the Old Bailey. Such is the echo, I guess, for I even heard it myself seconds later, perhaps even more loudly than when it had passed my disdainful and curled lips. The stenographer allowed herself a coughed giggle, the judge frowned in horror while seeming to allow his juvenile spirit to beam and several of my acolytes rocked forwards and backwards in their seats and in a fluid unison, sensing the Beast was stirring.

Before the jury's decision, I was allowed to speak, albeit as high as a kite, and only told the judge, 'Age is not a question of years, but is instead a function of the arteries, as well as knowledge and passion, of course.' I think he approved of this.

Of course, I was found innocent, but sought no damages, for that would be unseemly and we preferred to cause confusion. There was a new god in town, and I was still not finished with 36 Blythe Road.

I then retreated to Loch Ness for lengthy orgies and mischievous rituals, where I hosted Germans by the score. It was in that late summer when a new daughter of mine was planted in fertile and womanly flesh.

And so, I would like to begin to tell you of my vibrant, whirring and hyperbolically thrumming baby girl. I say begin for she shall follow me to my real end. I will tell of how she and I – through a marvellous childhood grudge of hers and our own clairvoyance of a quite remarkable pitch – helped to save England from certain defeat in the second war. And almost certainly the end of civilisation as we knew it.

Let us go back a short while to those years in London, Cambridge, Scotland and Tunis between those days in Sicily and Germany. And I shall soon begin the tale of my luscious third daughter and my galleon of sailed treasures. Violet Ambrosia Fagg.

Four hours to go.

10.1 'OH GOODY! VITRIOL! YOU *SHALL* LOSE!'

We arrived back on the Italian mainland a blissful legion of misfits and renegades. I knew that there would be cheap talk in the press back in England. That chap Loveday had fallen ill at the abbey, but it was bugger all to do with me. The same liars who claimed animal sacrifices and goat sex said that

Loveday had died from drinking cat's blood. They perhaps should have noted the doctor's reports, one of malaria and persistent diarrhoea and one that put down the loss of an eye two months earlier to gonorrhoea. And since none of us had suffered that particular uncomfortable blight in the trouser – nor anyone that I knew of had coupled with the ugly arsehole – then it is a mystery quite easily solved. He was independently poorly.

The papers were still brutal, and a flimsier man than I would certainly have buckled. My own publisher was quoted as saying the 'vilification was unparalleled in the history of journalism'.

On February the 24th, 1923, the *Sunday Express* had led on the front page with

NEW SINISTER REVELATIONS OF
ALEISTER CROWLEY
VARSITY LAD'S DEATH
ENTICED TO 'ABBEY'
DREADFUL ORDEAL OF A YOUNG WIFE
CROWLEY'S PLANS

And they followed it week after week, chasing their crippled and lame dragon, like prancing pillocks. Cakes of goat's blood and honey, I ask you.[*]

When I finally threatened to sue (just to rattle their cages, of course), they printed this on the front page too.

The *Sunday Express* promises Crowley that it intends to pursue its investigations with the utmost ruthlessness, and that next Sunday it will endeavour to supply him with considerable

---

[*] *I love my goats.*

further material on which to base any action which he may care
to bring.

Oh goody! Vitriol! You *shall* lose!

With the national press wading in on their side for once,
the cretins at *John Bull* felt unleashed and vindicated, and
swaggered like a bitch in heat, presuming that at last she had
attracted the attention of those more respected types who
found her regular state unworthy and unpleasant.

The headlines that they ran in that spring were dedicated to
the man who was really their master.

A WIZARD IN WICKEDNESS (17 March)
THE WICKEDEST MAN IN THE WORLD (24 March)
KING OF DEPRAVITY ARRIVES (11 April)
A MAN WE'D LIKE TO HANG (19 May)

John Bull sank to new desperate depths when they claimed
that I had, many years previously, chopped up two young coolies in the Himalayas when provisions were low. Their precise
words were,

'One of the most shameless degenerates who ever boasted
of his British birth.'

Even the American newspapers from the *New York Times*
down picked up on the scandal around this time. Of course,
the *Times* story was carefully worded by MI-1.

I sat in my club, lit a girthy cigar and congratulated myself.
This was high praise indeed. It would be nice to see their faces,
if I were ever to pose on the steps of MI-1 with Churchill and
the King, but for now, my pleasure and contentment had to
remain an almost personal one, with my eye on the central

prize of the twentieth century. One never checks a soufflé until one knows it is ready to be served.

It was even revealed in a half-sensible newspaper (the *Manchester Guardian*) that there had been a plot, hatched by a chap by the name of Raymond Greene to have come to Cefalù to assassinate me. He was a friend of that unpleasant clap-riddled Raoul Loveday fellow, school pals by all accounts. The article was one of the few decent pieces of independent journalism not crafted by our own chaps in those days.

Greene, however, backed out of the plan to murder me when he received *this* in the post.

> Dear sir,
>
> Do what thou wilt shall be the whole of the Law.
>
> Forgive me if I suggest, from a little experience that I have in such matters, that when one is establishing a spy system it is rather important to prevent one's principal plan coming directly into the fat hands and broad dangerous thumbs of the person whom you want watched and/or slaughtered.
>
> Love is the law, love under Will.
>
> Yours truly,
>> Aleister Crowley
>> Knight Guardian of the Sangraal

I recalled how I had then invited him to visit, and he, to my slight dismay and my utmost respect, had actually obliged. I remember that we'd sat out in the Abbey's orchard to discuss sex, drugs, witchcraft and libel.

I had asked him, 'Did Shelley bring libel actions?'

Before he had been able to answer, I'd said, 'No, he came to

Italy. Did Byron bring libel actions? No. He came to Italy. Did I bring libel actions?'

Greene had fully understood my point.

I remembered how we had chatted for hours over the coming days, and an hour before his return to England, Greene had said to me that he would correspond with Loveday's parents. He had intended to write that I had been a reasonable and genuine man, that those happy children of Thelema had larked with more of a rapture and ecstasy and persistence than he had ever witnessed, and that his full Sicilian experience had brought to him a true and indescribable joy.

'I am flattered to the point of silence, but I must ask you never to spread any of this to the newspapers, however,' I had said.

He had seemed truly puzzled, but, after a dozen seconds, smiled and I had known in that moment the respect he had for me had ratcheted exponentially. I know he had not suspected the full extent of my global shadiness, but I knew that he had been both shocked by and utterly admired my wish to keep my own counsel despite the murderous onslaught at home. He'd then sat alone in the dappled light for a few hours and had appeared to rest his consciousness on the rafts of my own meditations out there in that acre of bliss.

I'd found him inside in the great hall, just before he left, holding a note from one of the children.

Dear Beast,
    My first tooth came out. I want you to have it. It is L___ who is writing this.
    Beast, I love you.
    L____

Greene had been clearly moved, as I had been when he passed it to me with a firm and manly look, full of honour.

He'd left a different man, enlightened and admonished by his own proclivity to judge. This always gave me true satisfaction.

Throughout this period of newspaper inspection and intrusion, Hühnerbein was easily convinced that everything I did in those days and months would somehow benefit Germany and her friends. There were even old-style duplicitous missions abroad, as there had been before the Great War. There was the Holy Man's Rebellion in Siam, the Saudi Conquest of Hejaz, the Nicaraguan Civil War and in Bulgaria, not only the Incident at Petrich (also known as the War of the Stray Dog), but also the September Uprising. Here I sat and advised Germans, mauled their strumpets, ate and drank with them, and took their payment that I insisted be in gold or sterling.

And when I was not playing the role of the visible agent, I moved between Boleskine House, Cambridge, London and Tunis. Passage on the seas was so pleasurable* and simple thanks to Winston and those obliging sailors. The stories of our evenings in port could sag a shelf.

As I passed through London, I would see Dandylyon, Orr, Prudence and Winston. When I sat on the deck to or from Africa or in the portside cafés of Tunis, I dictated to Leah. We were working on *Hag*,† a work I predicted would be in the region of 600,000 words.‡

I wrote in the notes:

---

* *I often caused harmless mischief en route, like the time, ridiculously high on cocaine and chloroform, I faked my own death in the caves of Boca do Inferno – The Mouth of Hell – by Cascais in Portugal, and then, days later attempted to invade Spain, with some crazy toothless Castillians I had met in a tavern on the coast, and who saw me as both mercenary and Dark Lord for hire. They wanted to restore the Jacobites to the throne for some inexplicable reason, and I went along with them until the drugs wore off.*

† *Short for Autohagiography – the autobiography of a saint.*

‡ *Over 2,000 dense pages.*

The manuscript though lively is censor proof. It can be represented artfully in prospectuses as the Confessions of Aleister Crowley. A great fuss can be made about mailing copies to subscribers in a plain wrapping and otherwise ensuring their delivery. There should be no difficulty in selling outright 2,000 copies at $10 a copy. During the issuing of these prospectuses, the Author will undertake some feat which will bring him great extra publicity.

But what would this stunt be?

I consulted my I Ching. I was advised that all I needed was patience, and not much of it.

Within five days, I received a letter at the Tunis house, a sturdy old spot whose vast single key was lent to me by Winston. The place was a marvel, a vast and cavernous affair, laced with incense and spice, in that old African style whose central torso was an astonishing five-levelled library, with the finest collection of naval tomes, pornographic literature, and fruit-growing almanacs. He had dedicated the bulbous hall to his knock-out missus, Clementine, that feisty and majestic rock of his.*

The letter I received had been re-addressed from Cambridge, so it was marginally dated. The information therein was, however, still most relevant. It was a cutting from *Variety* magazine. My old pal from Le Chat Blanc in Paris, W. Somerset Maugham, had sold the motion picture rights to his recent work, *The Magician*, whose lead character, Oliver Haddo had, quite complimentarily, been based on me. My words had been used, my manipulative character and even my physical

---

* *Hitler should one day be thankful it was Mr – and not Mrs – Churchill, with whom he was going toe-to-toe.*

description. I was flattered and thrilled by Maugham,* a far superior talent to the Yeatses of this world. Now, the chaps at Metro-Goldwyn-Mayer were the owners of the property, and had vast plans for the project. And so it seemed to me that this might be the very feat I needed to bring me the very headlines I required to shift those prospectuses for *Hag.*

And so, I wrote to Maugham on the Cap D'Antibes and to Mr Mayer at MGM in Hollywood to find out what my recompense for this would be, as well as offering my time and energy in helping to promote the picture.†

Maugham was clearly embarrassed and allowed the lawyers to answer first from the States. It soon became apparent that I was to receive no monetary compensation. On the wire, I threatened to file an injunction against the release of the film in Los Angeles, New York City and London. Without these centres, the film would flop, I squawked. A telegram arrived the following day, with an offer for a fairly adequate sum, but by then I had also become quite excited at the prospect of being closely attached to the film, and wished to tie the exposure to my own autohagiography, as well as having become childishly giddy about a contract to make a series of documentary films on magick.

I wrote back, with a purposeful and abrupt tone, but one I hoped a busy (and humorous) man might appreciate.

---

* *He also later admitted that I was the kernel for* The Razor's Edge, *the story of a thoroughly principled young man (Tyrone Power in the picture, I shall accept that too) who, having witnessed the horrors of the Great War, puts all temptation of wealth and façades of happiness to one side to seek out the larger truths and the higher path of consciousness. In doing so, he passes up several decades of fucking Gene Tierney. I am not sure I am that principled.*

† *I do so wish they would reignite the custom of saying, 'looking at a picture' instead of the quite vulgar 'watching a movie'. I find that it is generally the small and almost imperceptible effort that most boosts style and panache.*

The lawsuit is a pretext for a grubby-ish business deal. I am now holding out for publicity and power.

Maugham then chimed in,

My Dear Friend,

This now is all out of my hands, Beast. I truly suspect they will claim that your name is already so blackened in those three cities that zero harm can ever be done to your repute.

They will say that it must have been your own True Will to be the Beast, and, of course, a white-washed Beast is a useless commercial vehicle.

You should have collected the cheque, and sodded off, though I know this has never been your motive.

You are portrayed by the most unalluring chap, however. I know you will chuckle. Enclosed is a publicity shot of the lead – keep your pervert's drooling to yourself – and the obligatorily dull publicity poster.

Yours, bounded in the kindest and lengthiest friendship,
WSM

He was right. The value of the publicised froth around the film had superseded any bona fide connection that I had been fishing for. My name was now in the papers for slightly less soiled reasons, and this made *John Bull* livid, as they began a campaign to ban the film. This helped me shift my prospectuses, as Leah and I completed the dictation sitting on the ramparts of that medieval house in North Africa, watching the sun set in the West, where Dibdin was already considering my next foray into the motion picture industry, for this, it was abundantly clear, was the propaganda of the future.

10.2 Young Ali Abu Hasan Saves the World

On my fiftieth birthday in October of 1925, I was visited in Tunis by a still lively and enthused Dandylyon, with Prudence as close to his side as ever. He must have now been near his seventieth birthday, while she remained youthful and radiant. Orr and Winston came too. By crikey, Prudence was magnificent. My fulfilled boyhood fantasy of her had not only never wavered, but had thrived and blossomed, as she had. Leah and I had supper prepared on the terrace of the house, a flat roof overlooking the port that was three quarters ramshackle and a quarter lordly, a similar ratio to the city itself.

Up there on that serene deck, we enjoyed a broad space that could easily have housed a crowd of two hundred fatties. It was flanked by tall candles laced with marijuana so we all slowly but immaculately got stoned as we ate *cous cous* royale (no meat for me), drank several bottles of *Château Lafite Rothschild* '97 and watched the sun set and then rise, without the aid of any powder. We gossiped, plotted and philosophised.

Winston told stories of Africa and India, I recounted the daring on mountainsides in the Alps and the Himalayas, Prudence revealed herself as the best card trickster I had ever witnessed, all sleight of hand executed, while keeping us all up to date with such schoolboyish tittle-tattle of a list of the quietest perverts, surprising bestial-types and most behaved homosexuals in the worlds of politics, society, literature and stage. She spoke of their private mischief and described it with the most marvellous euphemisms that I had ever heard.

She threw a deck of cards at the ceiling, with the card I had secretly chosen sticking to it as the other fifty-one fell. This was quite a stunt, and as we nodded our approval, she said, 'You know that L___ M_____ molested his poodle and contracted some unshiftable itch on his vitals?'

For someone who was just about to demonstrate her ability to imitate the deep growls of our Russian monk friend, her normal tones were supremely luscious and feminine.

'And you might be surprised to learn that the Home Secretary is "quite fond of his mother",' she said, as our squawks died down.

Winston nodded with a wisdom, for it seemed he had first-hand experience of this.

'Oh do go on,' we all urged.

'Well, the playwright, S___ S_____ has "very smooth elbows". And Lord P_____, despite the vast beauty of Lady P_____, is a "gentleman of the piers", who "tidies before the maid's day".'

'Fluttersome', 'in the way of uncles' and 'rides the carousel' were apportioned to the actor, D__ B_____, the newspaper proprietor, H___ H_____ and General O_____ respectively, as Prudence appeared to be only just beginning and also becoming quite joyously high.

Her *pièce de résistance* now neared, as she began to crank out incredible impersonations of Dandylyon, Orr, Me, Leah, Winston and an astonishing likeness to Rasputin, as she rammed a church candle from our dining table down her dress to resemble an erection, and belched and burped Transylvanian invective in an attempt to mount the future prime minister of the United Kingdom, and then her boss of fifty years, then a seven-foot-tall mercenary menace, and finally pushing the wickedest man in the world, who was now unreasonably high on the candle fumes. Prudence pretended to hump me from behind and then force her fat candle into my face, while imitating to perfection the priest's favoured Romanian line about the licking of an angel's balls, even achieving the manliness of the tone and inflection, so that if were one to close one's eyes and nip one's nose, one would think the over-ripe Holy Man were indeed present.

Dandylyon bellowed, jack-knifed and also crumpled to the deck. His aroused nurse ignored this, while Winston, now His Majesty's Chancellor of the Exchequer of Great Britain, was moved to crippling glee and merriment, as well as to perhaps less than a tenth of a yard from the sheer drop and falling four floors onto a Tunis chestnut roaster on the street. He was only stopped by a truly concerned waiter, only on the roof at that moment to bring him a chilled cigar from the freezer downstairs with a single malt and a cocaine lozenge, merely for digestive purposes. When the roll call of the Second World War is spoken across Westminster Abbey and Parliament, we should all remember the name of Ali Abu Hasan, for who knows how we should have fared had that oaf of a true chum moved through a portion of the pentagram, a further seventy-two degrees of his wide torso and belly-flopped onto the hot coals a hundred feet below.

Ali Abu Hasan then had several of his colleagues stationed along the edges of the roof terrace for the rest of those ghostly and bewitched hours, though the fog was strong enough for them to be forced to rotate every thirty minutes or so, or they too would have toppled, quite likely to their end. The clouds were potent but aphrodisiacal, and I knew that all of the young Arabs wanted to desecrate Prudence. Ali Abu Hasan had seen her with her candle *in situ*, and they were not used to such sights. For them, cock had been a youthful and mischievous intrigue, then meanly magnified by the almost norm of pederasty and buggery in Tunis. Well-shafted weapons casting the curved shadow of a scimitar on a white-washed wall were simply their Pavlovian *amuse-bouche* in life, bless the

mucky little blighters. Of course, Prudence was well aware of
the projected lust towards her, and she might even have lingered in the ladies' room marginally too long on three or four
occasions as she might just have helped to relieve, one at a
time, the intense heat these poor lads felt in an almost identical way to how she had once relieved a suffering wretch,
under the spell of scarlet fever, decades before in Redhill, Surrey. I did love her so, she always thought of others.

On one such occasion as she returned to the table, Orr was
comforting me.

'The brutish press will soon be thanking you for decades of
service to the cause, Aleister.'

'You've got enemies? Good, it means you have stood up for
something some time in your life,' Winston said back in his
comfortable seat, before he fell into further mirth. He continued, words laughed between plumes of cigar smoke, 'I hope that
I am the one to break it to you that such a revelation might
actually force you to resign from the Scottish Mountaineering
Club, and have to accept a lifelong, and quite public membership, even an honourable chairmanship of the English version.'

'Thank you, Winston. I am now fifty years old, and all of
my instincts, as well as your most pristine intelligence from
Whitehall, suggest to me that we are timing our late runs for
greatness and glory to perfection, gentlemen.'

Not that it mattered to me in the slightest, but I could, in
theory and at any time, expose those *John Bulls* for their obvious arsery, and grab that comforting victory for me and more
importantly my loved ones. The British, especially the English
public, do so appreciate a happy ending, the recognition of
redemption and, of course, silent strength. And the newspapers, when not bullying, shall fawn to their ultimate power
and opinion.

'You know that it does not have to be this way. There is

another way,' said Dandylyon, stroking his beard, then falling into silence.

'Stop teasing him,' Prudence implored.

Dandylyon looked around, and instructed all the waiters to leave us for fifteen minutes.

When they had all gone, it was Winston who spoke of that special place first. The other four knew of it, only Orr had been there.

This was the first time I had ever considered that Shangri-La was actually a real place. The answer had been there all along. I felt ashamed that all my claims to the Godhead had been made while I was quite unaware of the most preposterous, yet entirely feasible direction. Living for ever. There, with the greatest friends of my adulthood and watching the sun rise in the east, stoned and deliriously contented with the power that existed around that table, we hatched a plan.

We few.

It sounded like a perfect plan for one day in the future. There was a flaw, however, and one that I knew immediately I should accept like a man.

'I want to go there soon. Very soon, for I think I am dying,' said Leah in my ear, as the others continued to speak.

She smiled like she had not grinned in weeks.

'What is wrong, Leah darling?'

'I have King's Evil.* I am convinced of it. Orr has assured me that I shall live for years up there in the mountains. Down here, I shall be gone before the daffodils come. I shall meet you there one day soon, my Beast.'

And like *that*, within three days, she was gone.

'I shall miss you, Beast. Be happy, my Pimpernelling love.'

---

* *Tuberculosis.*

10.3 STRUGGLES, 1926–1929

If I had become adept in the split personality of the double agent, then I now began to attempt to master my own internal quadrophrenia of international actor for Berlin and MI-1, drug addict, artist and lonely host of Scottish orgies. I withdrew to Boleskine for lengthy periods, often for many months, but could be roused from heroin's slumber and the selfish fizz of cocaine to do my duty. I sailed with Hühnerbein to witness the Kongo-Wara Rebellion (1928), in '29, the Women's War, and then to the Central Plains Mutiny. I went with him to instruct him in the Occult, to lecture him en route and guide him in still the most basic of rituals on the decks of ships at midnight and in large desert tents at dawn. He was an utterly clumsy and cack-handed type, struggled with concentration, and continued to labour with even the more basic concepts of the ceremonies and magickal texts that I both laid out to and wrote for him. His enthusiasm was not in question though, and he would perpetually introduce me as his mentor and guru, and quite giddily so.

In the first half of 1929, he and I instigated the Chittagong Armoury Raid, plotted the Nghe-Tinh Revolt and helped the nationalist League of Blood organise their (purposefully) disastrous *coup d'état*, known as the May the Fifteenth Incident, against the tipped-off Empire of Japan.

And I really believed Winston when he assured me that these missions were more about Hühnerbein's schoolboy crush on me than they were about any global politicking. But my life was to change towards the end of that year. It was nearly time for light and love and the squawks of children to reign again. My supreme Violet was almost here.

10.4 A FETID BAD SEED IS STEWED

My daughter was conceived on September the twenty-second, 1929.

Mars was rising above Luna and rather threatening, but there were no close bad aspects either to the Sun or to the Moon, so probably there was not much to worry about. There was no big complex to make the child distinguished. She was likely to develop into a fairly ordinary little whore.*

She was the product of a harvest moon orgy at Boleskine. She was one of those rare creatures: a bastard child who knew her father but did not know her mother. Yes, I had been liberal with my passions as any good host should be. Violet had then stewed and mashed in her mother's womb to full term and beyond. There is a sound school of thought that suggests this can lead to ridiculously high levels of intelligence, sex drive and/or malice. And greed, I would say, for my daughter was abundant and lush in all three. Genghis Khan had allegedly been *in situ* for a year. The Dalai Lama, Charles Darwin, Rasputin, Christ and Mother Teresa are also reputed to have gestated for almost a year. Were one to gather such a mob for a dinner party, I suspect it would be Violet sitting in the head chair, recommending that Khan had his steak *au point* and that the Messiah chose the wine. '*And do it well and promptly, you scruffy little cunt!*'

The young Violet Ambrosia Fagg was an Amadeusian protégée who would evolve past mere bickering by the age of four. Her first name (I hesitate in using the term Christian) had its genesis in the empurpled velvet in which she was swaddled as a newborn. The choice of her middle name was rooted in the fragrant rafts and the spicy tang in that thrumming late summer Scottish evening so long ago. Her recently Violet-free mother had then rejoined with haughty obedience a small squadron of willing sex slaves to this Kurtzian Lord in the

---

*   To the Thelemite who venerates the Whore of Babylon (Full name – Mother of Prostitutes and Abominations of the Earth), this is considered a compliment.

tower, who, for days, meandered the battlements and ramparts in the August dusk, pondering how to excel in death and love, and a controversial ancient incantation of real and vibrant nutritional value to welcome in my child. I would be far more careful with this one, I promised myself.

Violet's mother's first request after labour and the swift execution of twelve neat-ish stitches in her juvenile perineum had been for a full-strength Capstan cigarette to be rammed into her tiny blood-stained paw and lit. Mauled syllables delivered, in a broad Cockney twang, a rank and shocking sailor's invective wrapped around each verb, adverb, impersonal pronoun, subject, object, article both definite and indefinite, and noun. As she puffed on the potent tobacco, a surname was thus revealed, and the naming process of her well-brewed, lengthily steeped daughter was complete. *Violet Ambrosia Fagg.* For those of a bent to interest themselves in the debate of nurture and nature, one might trace a line from her mother's turd-lined potty mouth to Violet's seemingly inherited Tourette's. Biology can possess such a mischievous sense of humour. There *was* indeed a Loch Ness Monster back then, and it was not I, for most of the time I was the kindly type, someone whom one might invite to the Test match. No, it was the bubbling vitriolic young wench, product of a gloried fuckfest, a fetid bad seed born that bejewelled and sapping night, August the twenty-first, 1930. My new and quite precious daughter.

10.5 'UP YOURS!'

As her cursing paedophobic mother slipped back into the highly fecund and adolescently firm throng of boyishly buttocked and jasmine-necked tartlets, a facsimile of events was occurring over the suggestive and redolent heather and the saucily wild flowers, petals flapping akimbo, to the south-east towards the North Sea coast near Dundee.

Glamis Castle, ancestral home to Windsorian royalty, was where the malformed but really quite pleasant, King Malcolm* had been slain in the eleventh century, and where things had remained equally dreary and moribund since.

The newborn at Glamis was a girl too, named Margaret and fourth in line to the throne of the United Kingdom. The memories that I now offer to you of a balmy and pungent night at Boleskine, the sticky air made more uncomfortable by the preponderance of midges, larking summer flies, pollen-fleck bees and frolicking hornets, was a stark contrast to the reports of an evening so chilled towards the sea at Glamis that the boiled water prepared for the Princess's imminent arrival froze within minutes. '*Oh father!*' Violet would later chortle at my amateur and reasonably easily executed mischief.

Glamis remains an odd spot for such a wealthy and important family, and it too is reputed to possess its own ghoul: the Monster of Glamis.†

It is an austere yet impressive structure. I was always impressed by its murderous history, as well as the anecdotes of hauntings, telekinesis, apparitions and researchers' chunky file notes on the poor buggers who'd gone insane there. Tales of princes, princesses and whole branches of families being bricked in to starve to death are well known and perhaps overtold. The internal structure is a confusing one, and still befuddles the more thick-skinned staff that has remained for decades. They often find themselves lost within the corridors and mazed hallways. An attempt to map the house – and to transpose the perceived layout from within which never seemed

---

* *This murder allegedly offered a blueprint for Macbeth.*

† *Vi would have her own thoughts on its identity.*

to correlate with that from the outside – led a small mob of inquisitive souls to hang sheets from all the windows in the rooms that they might access from the inside. When they trooped outside to check upon their work, there were several windows that bore no sheet. The instincts which some had possessed of the existence of darkened vortices within Glamis were not mocked as they had been before. Glamis possesses a black and vicious quality.

10.6 A LUNACY OF TURQUOISE AND FIRE

As a child of eighteen months, my daughter Violet, the burgeoning filly of disrepute, spent hours staring at and pointing at the moon. She was a maelstrom of turquoise and fire, even then. All the signs were of a hyperbolic romantic, however this arcane sage would hesitate, rearrange himself and perhaps foresee that the lass was preternaturally rammed from the wispy curls of her milky crown to her ten little piggies with concrete realism, for she was already planning her brazen and audacious escape from this planetary, spiritual and mortal realm. But first she would hold her father's hand and walk him to Greatness.

Chapter 11

Sein Kampf

If you're going through hell, keep going.
  – Sir Winston Leonard Spencer-Churchill KG OM CH
                                                TD DL FRS RA

F or me Ceremonial Magic, as a means to attainment, has in common with all other methods, Western or Eastern, one supreme object in view; and that is an identification with the Godhead; and it matters not if the Aspirant be Theist or Atheist, Pantheist or Autotheist, Christian or Jew, or whether he name the goal of his attainment God, Zeus, Christ, Matter, Nature, Spirit, Heaven, Reason, Nirvana, Asgard, No-Thing or No-God, so long as he has a goal in view, and a goal he is striving to attain. Without a goal, he is but a human ship without port or destination; and, without striving, work, or WILL to attain, he is but a human derelict, rudderless and mastless, tossed hither and thither by the billows of lunacy, eventually to sink beneath the black waters of madness and death.

I stand by a fence that leads into a field. There are perhaps a dozen goats with me. I tickle the neck of a young beast, before she yields to her friends.

Three more hours to go.

I have tried to see the world beyond fear, to revel and welcome darkness and to approach the world with love. But right now it's high time that I scarletted my knuckles afresh in the mountain pass.

I sit and meditate one last time, knowing I must leave this place to muster my troops against a coming darkness for Humanity. I have to go to finish my life's work and accept my crown as the true rebel of our age. The Orwellian Crackdown is nigh. Washington and London have not factored in the return of a god to stir the people to victory.

I shall return for the spirit of Cambridge in the twenties. I shall return to save the world. I shall return for revenge. For revolution. Glory or Bust.

I stand.

Two hours to go.

11.1 THERE'S A NEW DEGENERATE IN TOWN

The horror in the East was now truly fermenting. We had all heard and even seen how viciousness had taken hold in those testing grounds of Spain, Portugal and Italy. It was even taking root in England.

My Whitehall chums and I acknowledged that we all bore a sliver of responsibility for having unleashed the virus, what with Rasputin, the Revolution and that damned Treaty of Versailles, but we would all now struggle to orchestrate its end.

By the time I left Boleskine after Violet's birth in 1930 for the major mission of my life, the perversely named German

Workers' Party had become the NSDAP* and *he* had been in charge for several years. Winston advised us all that soon he could be running the country. It was time to make my move and fulfil my destiny; well, perhaps not the destiny of my wild and ambitious dreams, but certainly that of my day job of double agent.

January 2nd, 1931

(I shall be back soon to dote on you, Violet, my love. I promise. Frog will be more than good to you. And I shall keep this world and myself safe. For you.)

I left Loch Ness. I travelled by train to King's Cross, then onto the boat train and through to my final stop of Munich. I carried with me some volumes that I knew would impress Hühnerbein, and allow for a comfortable welcome in Bavaria. The books, which were all originals and had been given to me by MI-1 to tease and tempt them all, were on the Runes, *Völkisch* Magic and the Occult Reich. One was the priceless *Codex Sangallensis* that dated to the ninth century, written by the abbots of the Reichenau Abbey. This would make not only Hühnerbein drool, but would certainly prick up the ears of the Führer. After all, it was these very runes that had established the importance of the Germanic languages over Hebrew. This should do the trick.

I kept the tome in my possession when I first arrived, showed it to Hühnerbein at a suitable first convenience, and then kept it in a safe place well away from my luxury rooms at the Elmendorff Hotel. A covert colleague in MI-1 then

---

* *National Socialists, Nazis.*

stored it outside of the city, and I knew full well that my hotel accommodation had been scoured several times. I do not think even Hühnerbein would have been so daft as to take it while our relationship was sturdy, but he was adequately astute to want to know of its location, for in our business, alliances can shift so rapidly.

I honed my language further, improving upon the precise Bavarian I had modelled on Hühnerbein's. I was often taken as a local of central Munich. I knew too that I would benefit from a harmless vocation for the sunlight hours, something to balance out the obsidian naughtiness of hooded midnight sex and drug ceremonies with clichéd pentagrams and theatrical squawking. It should be something that would allow for minimal mischief, but mischief all the same. (Why not? What was the effing point otherwise?) And I would soon identify that perfect German pastime for my daylight nosiness.

First, I had considered mountaineering, but it was so limiting to steep slopes and a tiny fraction of the population. Yoga was too liberal, poetry too rebellious and chess too Jewish.

Next I pondered painting, and studied the art of the Nazi party. But it was not just fucking appalling, but also truly banal and unreasonably mundane. I had hoped to stumble upon magnificent pieces, distorted, odd and abstract. However, the works of the gems of modern art, Otto Dix, Ernst Barlach, Franz Marc, Karl Schmidt-Rottluff or Oskar Schlemmer were all first discouraged and then, when soon after in 1933 the Nazis came to power, all banned. The truly distinguished, exciting and vital pieces were seen as degenerate, swiftly removed and destroyed. Degenerate. The bastards loved this word. Well, they had seen nothing yet. I was now in town.

What was puked up on canvasses instead was comically awful and perhaps purposefully so, for anything approaching decent would have exposed the Führer's own laughable, gruesome and squalid efforts with a brush, for what they were. Such is the narcissist.

In the autumn of 1934, I found myself visiting Heidelberg for weeks at a time. It reminded me so much of Cambridge. Munich was important to me, so that I might witness the street brawls between Communist and Fascist. These were not polite Queensberry Rules scraps. These were the smashings of skulls, and leaving hungry and desperate fathers to die on concrete. These fuckers meant business. Heidelberg, however, was sedate and allowed for reading, yoga, hashish, meditation, ritual and ceremonies. And it was in the ancient libraries there with their haunting shafts of afternoon light and the burly and persistent stink of naphthalene from the mothballs that I found to be an aphrodisiac, that I stumbled on shelves that would reveal to me my almost-bespoke form of expression. It was a dying art of that time, but one I knew I could resurrect with great joy.

Freikörperkultur literally means 'free body culture', but what it really meant was removing all clothing and walking in a state of nudity in public, usually surrounded by my other most basic and most stimulating accomplice, nature. I championed that the Aryan body was nothing of which to be ashamed, but instead celebrated. For centuries, I explained, there had been no sexual connotation for most Germans in this practice. Hitler was confused by the liberal nature of the pastime on one hand, but celebrated the inherent implications of superiority of a lithe young lad or firm strutting lass in the altogether. I wrote dissertations on the recreation, how it intertwined with the Aryan, the *Ahnenerbe** and the *Völkisch* (or German People's) Magic.

I also wrote to Whitehall.

> The self-absorbed lout will before long listen to me at length, drool forming, for I know more on the topic than anyone else on the planet. I swear, Winston, old bean. I shall soon be his High Chief of Ritual, the Supernatural and the Metaphysical. When it comes to Lucifer, Adolf shall do precisely what I tell him to do.

If nakedness and nature were vital, then the final element of my *mirepoix* was youth. Naked rambling was not exclusively the preserve of the young, but it is more easily explained by its utter attractiveness. Yes, a more mature lady or gent was not overtly discouraged from participation, but their photographs would certainly not be regularly published for a wider audience. And yes, there were some frankly ghastly sights, but

---

* *A sect, an established body that promoted the concept of the Aryan, and spoke of the proximity of nature and German purity and beauty to those Wagnerian spirits. The Aryan myth represented Germans as humanity's gateway to the heavens, but it was based on the gibberish of an old friend of mine, the pivotal mystic, Madame Helena Blavatsky, as well as those perverse early Nazi fantasists at the Thule Society, who mentally and possibly physically masturbated over Wagner's* Die Nibelungen, *and how it dramatised myths and propelled them into the warped consciousness of a willing mob. In truth, the Germans had no physical or architectural or literary signs of their ancient greatness. They were not the Greeks, Egyptians, Persians or Romans. They were all in mud huts. There were no remnants of their greatness, other than some obscure reference in Tacitus, when he wrote of the blue eyes and blond hair of a race lost to the seas with Atlantis. A desperate Hitler took this and clung to it, vaunting it much as the precise evidence of a Germanic superman, and thus justifying his own land grabs. It was the last refuge of the frantic, madcap and rash. As Darwin once put it quite marvellously, 'Ignorance more frequently begets confidence than does knowledge: it is those who know little, and not those who know much, who so positively assert that this or that problem will never be solved by science.'*

these types were really to be admired to the full in the eyes of this ever-grateful pervert.

And so, as I worked by night preaching and teaching the Occult, my portfolio grew during office hours with a clean and righteous bent. *Freikörperkultur* tapped into the German spirit and was a perfect pursuit for me. As I ogled their arse-cheeks, I knew of the potency of this next generation of lads and lasses for they would likely be the soldiers and wives in any second war.

I trumpeted and heralded the true joy of the body, while allowing for the golden and toned muscles and lithe torsos of young blond nymphs and future warriors to be revealed as a truly Aryan wonder. I was, of course, just goading the fine young things into the liberating purity of youthful coitus, the precise antithesis of the vulgarians in power.

While in private I pondered, and in well-coded missives to Dandylyon and Prudence, I wrote down my intentions.

Dearest of all Friends,
   I might have cracked it.
   My hope is to stir a few rebellious minds at least.
Just a few will be worthwhile. Hundreds would be a
victory, and thousands, a miracle. It is a near-impossible
challenge in proportion with that blessed trench
rebellion on Christmas Day 1914, but worth it if only
for a single life to be corrected. Let the children walk,
unencumbered by clothing.
   Remember, my friends. I am, after all, a *flâneur*. My
happiest times were once with Father in the Cotswolds
and my best work as a writer has come from the
exertions of a ten-hour stroll around London, Sicily or
New York.
   As you know, I was myself cursed with fleshy ankles,

a toadish neck and a quite spectacular bosom, and will
be delighted to announce this, with pride and in
encouragement, to young boys and girls all over the
land. This is not the message I am supposed to be
spreading to the misshapen and flabby *Unterjugend*,*
but I shall continue to urge young Germans of all
shapes and sizes. I even intend to point to the waddling
and fleshy vastness of the gargantuan and elephantine
Hermann Göring as an example. Such fair and seditious
talk is taking other poor souls to their death and
rapidly so. I am therefore being very clear to define my
latitude to speak with such frankness. I may not have
the official sanction of the Führer† right now, but I
certainly do have the support of perhaps an even more
fearful ally in Satan, and this trumps all here. They are
all so bloody gullible. It is a foolishness matched only
by their bloodlust, hubris and ego.

Remain mischievous in my absence. I shall chat and
chortle with you both in my dreams.

Yours, Beast

June 15th, 1935, Heidelberg
I became president of the F.K.K., and the editor of the association's newsletter. In it, I openly lectured how I had suffered
phlebitis and bodily ugliness as a child and this gave me even
greater authority (than even that granted by Hitler) to encourage the youth to strip off their clothes for the good of Germany.
The tone even carried echoes of Rasputin's call-to-arms to fornicate for godliness, he would have applauded this so heartily.

---

* *The less than perfect youth.*
† *Years later, when I told him to, he allowed me to chair the first naturist Olympic Games in Thielle, Switzerland in August 1939.*

The subliminal message of the F.K.K. was one of individual courage, but, by 1935, it was being deafened by the noise and the nastiness of the Nazi Youth movement. That month, I began to write for Occult magazines and the Naked Ramblers pamphlets. I received fan letters, some that even fawningly referenced my mad ramblings and essays in *The Fatherland* in New York two decades previously. More than anything, I was trusted and now seen as a German and, increasingly and quite conveniently, as a Nazi.

The library of ancient manuscripts I had brought were equally as pivotal as my reputation in piercing the most durable and robust protective circle. The books were the physical embodiment of the intrigue and mystique I brought. We inched closer and closer.

It was now time to cosy up to Adolf. He knew of my reputation within the Occult, and on June the twenty-eighth, 1935, I received an invitation to a small art gallery with a quite astounding temple beneath it, to consult on his and others' I Ching, *Chokmah* and Tarot.

Adolf had invited Mussolini. I scared him senseless in private, once again with the invisible ink trick, more wild invocations and overdetailed talk of devil orgies with Rasputin. I then pulled cards for Hitler, and made faces of concern for his future. He twitched, and instead instructed us to speak in private.

'Tell me of the *Codex*,' was his first enquiry.

'Ah yes, the *Codex*. She is a beauty.'

And these were the first words I spoke to Adolf Hitler as his friend. The next were, 'But she is enjoyed even more with burned cannabis or a soaked gag of chloroform.'

He eyed me with suspicion, knowing that anything other than a future pal's forthrightness and honesty would have ended in my death.

'I mean it, Adolf. I enjoy the lot. I love laudanum, heroin and amphetamines. I adore morphine, analgesics, Benzedrine, opium, peyote, absinthe and mescal.' As soon as I uttered his name, he knew I could not be so stupid as to be underhand or devious. A hefty chuckle and a manly hand around his untouched shoulder sealed our union. This fucker was already mine.

He paused and was about to answer, when we were interrupted. By *her*.

11.2 Eva & The Spaniard That Blighted My Life

The Führer was too myopic, too self-centred to see that Eva Braun was widely attracted to me. In a clash of the Titans, his selfishness trumped his paranoia. She was a truly odd fish. I saw her put up with the most abysmal torment from the brute, agony that only magnified and cemented her feelings for him. He rarely touched her, I never saw him affectionate once.

She loved to nude sunbathe at every opportunity, and I, as the head of the F.K.K., could only encourage such behaviour in my proximity. She so wanted to find passion, I remember her saying to me that she yearned to be a sexy corpse. I thought it an odd thing for a young girl to say, but that was between her two very genuine suicide attempts in 1932 (she shot herself in the neck, but missed her jugular) and in 1935 with sleeping pills. The second time was after Hitler had made her stand away from the dining table as he ate, as was usual, and he said loudly to Albert Speer across the table, 'A highly intelligent man should always take a primitive and stupid woman.' Eva was neither of those things. He just was exhibiting all the hallmarks of a quite silly boy.

I would one day become melancholic when I thought of her leaving those orgies in the bunker as the Russians neared, and young boys, in short and shat pants, hung from the power lines outside, as women and children pulled flesh from lame and live horses as shells exploded, just so she could see that marvel called daylight one more time.

If I could see her one last time, it would be to relive the twinkling nights when she filled her veins with cocaine, boot-polished her face and gave the most marvellous (and quite remarkably well-measured and perfectly timed, given her racing veins) renditions of Al Jolson's 'Toot, Toot, Tootsie' and 'The Spaniard That Blighted My Life'.

She was always most happy at Der Berghof when he was away, though, oddly, his absence hurt her so. We spent many afternoons by the Königssee at the bottom of the mountain. At the chalet, she could at least be with those Alsatian dogs of his. Her master's hounds truly adored Eva and seemed supremely transfixed by her bouquet. I must admit that I sensed a previous (sexual) frisson, so fawning were they, and so mismatched were his and her libidos. There also was no chance of her canine lovers telling, though their attention to her every move did offer a clue to the keen-eyed.

Eva always maintained to him that she found me intimidating, though we always laughed as true friends, and she always denied to him that she and I were even that close.[*]

I admit, with manliness, that the day that monster stopped breathing, I sat and thought of her at length. That poor and bullied child. I think she deserved far better.

11.3 'I WAVED AT HIM! I FUCKING WAVED AT HIM, ALEISTER!'

I studied well T. E. Lawrence, and noted his Twenty-Seven Articles in dealing with the Arabs. They seemed particularly relevant here in Germany, especially his final insight.

---

[*] *Nope, I fucked her. Even with the boot polish on that covered almost all of her.*

27. The beginning and ending of the secret of handling Arabs is unremitting study of them. Keep always on your guard; never say an unnecessary thing: watch yourself and your companions all the time: hear all that passes, search out what is going on beneath the surface, read their characters, discover their tastes and their weaknesses and keep everything you find out to yourself. Bury yourself in Arab circles, have no interests and no ideas except the work in hand, so that your brain is saturated with one thing only, and you realise your part deeply enough to avoid the little slips that would counteract the painful work of weeks. Your success will be proportioned to the amount of mental effort you devote to it.

This advice seemed to serve me well.

Again, as with Winston and Rasputin, I simply shall not regurgitate old tales of that monster, but I shall note just one sliver of his personality and then one tale about him and me.

And I shall mention them both as I do not believe they have been revealed. I know the latter has not.

After a lengthy Tarot session at the Berghof, he spoke to me on the terrace as we sipped lemonade and sat in quite uncomfortable chairs. I recall that mine had at least one wobbly leg that might be tested by my broadening waistline, a bit of a bay window by now. It was the summer solstice of 1937, almost a year after his Olympics in Berlin. When (somewhat) relaxed (for his twitching from too much speed and from Parkinson's was now almost persistent), he spoke in the broad Austrian of his youth for some odd reason, and he sounded like a halfwit farmer, excited by some rural oddity or another.

'You know, Aleister, what upsets me more than anything is

being blamed for something that I have not done. I do not care about that for which I am responsible.'

I knew this latter part to be thoroughly true. The psychotic sociopath is able to justify most things. He was, however, not of my school of thought that said if one is going to get blamed for something, then one may as well do it.

'I see that you are different,' he said. 'I have seen you shrug your shoulders and chuckle along while they speak ill of you. This would send me into a rage.'

He certainly would not have been able to execute a life-long exercise of absolute restraint such as that of a Scarlet Pimpernel.

'Do you remember last year at the Games? They say I snubbed the American Negro. But I did no such thing. I waved at him. I fucking waved at him, Aleister.'

At this moment, Adolf began to cry; slowly and softly at first, but then he soon crescendo'd into a shrill pitch of self-pity.

What was remarkable was that I later discovered this to be absolutely and utterly true. Even Owens later acknowledged that Hitler had gestured, quite politely, in fact. There was even the hint of a smile, though, as I shall soon reveal, this smile was often misunderstood and had quite unintended consequences. Owens revealed how this had happened after the heats on the first day.

But then Adolf had missed days two, three and four after an amphetamine bender.

It took him a good two minutes to complete the next three sentences, so distraught was he.

'Lewald* asked me if I would shake hands with all the winners or no one at all. Uniformity was only polite, he said. I

---

* *The head of the organising committee.*

told him for the sake of ease, I would shake the hands of none of them.'

When he finally stopped wailing, Adolf sniffed, wiped snot from his moustache, and then blubbered some more. 'It is the damned hypocrisy of those pious Americans. That fine athlete won four gold medals, and the only head of state to publicly blank him was Roosevelt.'

This was true.

'And do you know what else, Aleister? The bastards never even invited him to the White House with the other winners. They made him enter the Waldorf Astoria hotel for the winners' banquets through the service elevator. *God Bless America*. But I had waved at him. I had smiled at him! I had even fucking smiled at him, Aleister! This is so unfair!'

I said nothing. What could I say?

And *that* was that. I would laugh later in my chambers.

11.4 THE BET

Perhaps this final tale is of more interest and intrigue to the broader audience accustomed to tittle-tattle, especially one familiar with that marvellous concept so beautifully encapsulated by that skilled sister of ours, the German language. That concept is *Schadenfreude*.

After a banquet in Heidelberg in the summer of '39, we strolled on the lawns of the university and smoked reefers.

'Adolf. I think it would be a marvellous idea for you to have the seat of the Reich in Oxford.'

'Oh, yes. I was there in '12. After my time in Liverpool, you know.'

He was politely obsessed with the English. I told him to never have his air force bomb her. It was not so much Oxford I cared for, but Winston was supremely concerned about the munitions, plane and tank factories in the neighbouring town of Cowley. The city of Oxford would one day escape all air barrages and there would be no loose shot on a spire or a library or a lawn. My reputation, his yearning for the Occult and his Anglo obsession fired his interest in me. As we walked back into the lordly hall, we saw that most English of things, a billiard table.

Snooker, of course, enthralled him. So I challenged him to a game and our duelling was underway. Not only was he chronically colour-blind, but he was packed with his own military's MDMA, which they were generously developing as a truth serum. We agreed upon a wager. I won so very easily.

The details of his forfeit to me were mine to deliver to him within the week. He suspected quite rightly that I was a gentleman and would be fair, not too demanding or spiteful. And fair, I was. For I also asked him what my forfeit to him would have been had I lost the game, and when he said to me, 'It would have been a day spent together at the zoo with me.'

I pondered and then said to him, 'Let's do it anyway.'

11.5 A WET DAY AT THE ZOO

And so, I woke and I bathed. I shaved and I parted my hair in preparation for a day at the *Münchner Tiergarten** with the Führer of the Third Reich. It was July the eighteenth, just six weeks before the invasion of Poland, and angular rain was persistently falling in the Bavarian heat.

I had a very simple goal: to find his weakness, and to inform him quite subtly that I had found his weakness. As with that Italian Fat Head, I aimed to plant a seed that would lead to his ultimate destruction over time, and the moment when it all began would be our choice.

---

* *Munich Zoo.*

In the rooms where he would soon arrive, I took a breakfast of three soft-boiled eggs with buttered toast and Rangoon
satsuma marmalade, strong Himalayan tea and injudiciously
sugared grapefruit. I left adequate signs of my very English
ways, for these still charmed Johnny Foreigner and reminded
them all too subtly just who was the boss around there. Especially the Führer. He made no secret of his admiration for us.
He knew that we, all once his kind of Teutonic tribes, the
Angles and Saxons, were the Germanic spirit made good.
Adolf, for that was what I now always called him in private,
knew this. In public, I refrained from using any moniker, for it
then left him room to appear to remain superior to his lackeys, while offering a sense of mystique to this strange Wiccan
of an English man; unholy, potent and in *his* ear. And if I had
done away with the boiled eggs, the suspicious, the narrow-
eyed and the twitchy might have seen someone trying too hard.

He appeared at the door of my grandiose and noble chambers early, a bit giddy in his shuffling and manner. Something
seemed different about him; several things in fact. He wore an
English tweed trouser that resembled my own preferred cloth,
and beneath the hem, his shoes showed all the signs of having
been fitted with lifts to the precise point where our eyes were
level. His moustache had been subtly cut back, as if it was in
the early stages of a full-on retreat, and his hair was parted
like mine. Did I smell my own bespoke *cassoulette* of lemony
cologne and Bohemian Dewberry soap on him? He now even
carried a pipe with the precise curvature of my own, and his
matches were Swan Vestas, the ubiquitous match of my homeland. He studied my movements, I knew this. He used some of
my English lexicon, even though we spoke predominantly in
German. When I showed him a copy of *The Times*, with his
face on the front page, I heard him whisper (my own favoured
refrain), 'Oh goody,' as he moved with stealth and purpose on

the darkened walnut floorboards, as if over-rehearsing a Brechtian play. He walked to the lengthy, heavy scarlet curtains to check if the rain was relenting through the imposing arched windows that looked out with a gentle arrogance over Munich. He was deep in thought, fallible with a proclivity to boyish self-pity. 'Oh goody,' he tried again, this time even more softly. I found it hard to believe that he acted like this with anyone else.

'Adolf,' I said.

He turned and looked at me, in the eye, but he seemed to use the opportunity to assess and regard, once again, his man, the angle of my posture, the tilt of my head, how I looked marginally down my nose and fractionally from the left, and the slight breath I left between using his name and my measured, deliberate and authorial speech patterns.

'The rain is expected until mid-morning. Superior sorts as we always meet in a downpour. It shall always remain our secret. I say we use this opportunity to get soaked, as the plebs cower from nature. They would benefit from a good drenching, remove the stench and all that.'

Adolf was so revered and dreaded, he had forgotten what it was like to be spoken to as an equal. From time to time, there were even several reminders of my being his better, though I was smart enough to keep this unspoken as is required. Satan was a fine and generous ally against him, and even better when he (Satan) didn't exist, and therefore needed not be feared by me. The Old Lad offered such leverage like that, like stories of the bogeyman to witless children at dusk. And this was how I saw Adolf. But children still needed to be feared. As both a rampant paedophobe and the greatest champion of youth, I was well aware of their potential and their perils, for they valued life so little, while finding instant and total forgiveness so simple. I continued.

'I do love the zoo so. Do you know that I could spend all summer in the butterfly house, but I would just find myself plotting how to free them all,' I said, 'They should be liberated. Just like my boys and girls in the F.K.K.'

He seemed initially truly baffled by my love of butterflies, but soon nodded and bellowed, throwing his head back, 'Yes!'

'I am glad you agree. One's love of butterflies is always such a fair barometer of character, I find,' I said.

'We have much to learn from them. You are right, Aleister. We all need our living space, yes. But this is too obvious. What I admire most of them is they only mate with their own colour. Red and red, white and white, yellow and yellow. They are most discerning, most tasteful.'

I chuckled to myself, for I knew him better than he believed. I knew he was also obsessed with the precise and perfect symmetry offered by a butterfly, which according to his physician, Theodor Morell – a long-time plant from MI-1 – was rooted in the inferiority complex that any quarter shilling of a psychiatrist was able to trace back to the asymmetry and the lonesome testicle rattling around in his own misshapen and under-functioning scrotum.

'Not as discerning as I, Herr Führer,' a term which I used almost mockingly as I pulled out a large personally rolled cigarette, stuffed with quality cannabis. I smiled, and he smiled back at me, though this was a rare occurrence, for he knew that his face contorted with apparently painful discomfort as he grinned. He was quite conscious of the consummate horror he produced. It was such an unnerving countenance when it lent itself to pleasure, that I would rather have witnessed his unfurled and pre-eminent rage, so perturbing and soul-sapping his joy appeared to be. He had that most rare ability to bring more misery to a chat with his smile than with his anger and disdain. I thought long and hard, but was unable to recall any other soul I had ever met with this deformed and unholy gift. I considered how this might have affected him. Had this led him to his path of death, murder and destruction? The angle and menace of his ecstasy became only more disturbing as we smoked and became quite high. Also, I did not need to spike him with any of the high-grade sodium pentothal I carried perpetually, for his hubris and elevated state urged him to spill all, other than the obvious forbidden sexual confessions, to me.

'I should tell you that my chemists are working on some remarkable drugs that you and I should try. I intend to have my soldiers use them, they will be unstoppable.'

Many years before, I had passed through that juvenile stage whereby all conversations were viewed through the prism and frame of a narcotic. It was documented in *The Diary of a Drug Fiend*. I was now a gentleman of stature, but entered into this boyish excitement for I knew full well that this was my route to, if not manipulating and controlling, then at least nudging and misdirecting Adolf.

'I would love to try them. What are they?'

'We have one, it is a form of amphetamine.* Soldiers can fight like supermen for a week on it without sleep.'

'Oooh! I should love to try it. That sounds quite delicious.

---

* *Pervitin – crystal methamphetamine, later sold widely across the Reich – was soon to be pivotal in the blitzkrieg, for it would keep panzer tank crews awake and itching for violence for perhaps six days at a time. This would also be used in North Africa under Rommel, audacious military manoeuvres executed by soldiers who simply did not care if they lived or died. The British would respond with their own use of Benzedrine, and finally, when on a level playing field, would crush the Germans at El Alamein in 1942. We would then be victorious in Africa and able to control the flow of oil from the Middle East through the stronghold of Suez. Pervitin would prove to be so potent that there would be thousands upon thousands of tales of German soldiers advancing on the Russian front, unaware of their own frostbite until the moment that a foot fell off.*

When might I have some? This stuff might be most useful in a ritual I have planned for the spring. The spirits can be so domineering, so to be fearless is the true path to tethering them to our Will,' I told him. He believed it all.

I was already pondering the possibilities for sex magick, though I knew any overt mention of this would only rile him, for such was his weak spot. I was more oblique in its reference, just to remind him of my might over him.

'This might be useful for so much of my work,' I said with a raised eyebrow and as if as an inadvertent afterthought. In truth, it was just a prompting from my own beastly groin.

'They have also developed something I know you will find of interest, Aleister. We call it D-IX (D9), it will win us Europe one day. Maybe the world.'

'Oh goody, do tell.'

'It is the same methamphetamine, but mixed with morphine.* The results are miraculous. I can send a determined man to sea in a tin can, no larger than your bed there. He will power on for days on its potency while the morphine calms him precisely enough to not be concerned of his claustrophobia or his suicide mission. He will ram a hole in the side of a ship and find certain and immediate death.'

I had to hand it to him. For someone who was now ridiculously high on the most potent cannabis in this land of starving junkies, zombies and speed freaks, Adolf was remarkably

---

* This was D-IX or D9 – a morphine-based analgesic and performance enhancer. The aim was to use D-IX to redefine the limits of human endurance. Pharmacologist Gerhard Orzechowski and a group of other researchers had been commissioned in Kiel to develop this drug, and develop a formula which contained in each pill, 5 mg of Eukodal (oxycodone), 5 mg of cocaine and 3 mg of Pervitin. German researchers would soon find that equipment-laden test subjects, such as inmates from Sachsenhausen concentration camp, could march in a circle for up to ninety kilometres per day without rest while carrying a twenty-kilogram backpack.

single-minded in his desire to discuss mass destruction and new ways to fill his creaking and aching veins with more vigorous and persuasive stimulants. Meanwhile, this lordly bullet-headed and fat-thumbed English pervert was simply thrilled beyond words at the prospect of the leverage these new stashes would allow him to bugger, sodomise and perform frenzied analingus upon thousands of twitching lovers. But Adolf here wanted to send a man out in a sardine can to the Atlantic to die. I was disturbed by this, yes, but far more, I was comforted by my own highly evolved state with its proclivity to raw lust and tender-to-rough mass coupling. I knew my way held the moral high ground, though the bar with Adolf was clearly very fucking low.

We exchanged the lit reefer with its delicious tang and kick. 'You are a genius and an inspiration,' I said.

He was boyish as he tried not to blush at my compliment, though he was unaware that he only inspired me to be utterly different to him in all ways. The words allowed me to say this without a hint of guilt or mendacity. I held his eye, as I told him. He checked from pupil to pupil to gauge me. He was emboldened by the firmness of my stare. He dropped his gaze first, and gulped.[*]

I said to him, 'We should wander around the zoo, while the rain keeps the morons at bay.'

We stood, smoked some more and then turned to leave. He watched how I rose, inhaled and comported myself, while his observations of me were made all the more obvious by his puddled state. I would have slaughtered him, but Dandylyon,

---

[*] *The British would soon try to poison Hitler, but the only way to bypass the food tasters, who would have died from arsenic or strychnine, was instead to use the female sex hormone, oestrogen. It was colourless and tasteless, and their hope had been to turn him into a benign housewife. It was a noble effort, but no amount of femininity would have tempered this sore-headed grouch.*

the sly puss, was of the opinion that if I had, then a more dangerous and more calculated politician would have taken over. I was at least able to witness and modify and redirect and stupefy this fucker's idiocy. Another man would not have thrown out the nuclear scientists for being Jewish. Then we would all have been in trouble.

And so, an un-slaughtered Führer and I, we rusticated into the persistence of the Munich morning drizzle. Of course, he had no idea of the games, courtesy of an unruly mob of lads and lasses *en accomplices*, I had laid on to fiddle with his mind on that day. While maintaining the show of my being a good friend of his, I intended for him to finish this day slightly more hollow than how he began it through plumes of spicy weed smoke in my vast hotel chambers overlooking that ceremonious and courtly metropolis. It was a minor segment in my role to undermine the balance and cohesion of this perilous muttonhead of demi-genius Will.

He wore a raincoat with an almost comically erect and tall collar that, along with the oversized hat much the fashion in those days, managed to disguise his identity. The lifts in his shoes aided this too, as did his silence for now. No one, other than his driver and I, knew the Führer was there at the gates of the zoo. The place appeared deserted, other than caged nature and an elderly lady in the cash booth, with a supremely unfrowned brow, the voice of a sergeant major and an eye-patch lifted to her forehead. I eyed her with admiration as she asked for sixty pfennigs, and momentarily pondered her story, but now was not the time to engage unnecessarily.

He was a hypocrite. A huge fucking hypocrite.

As Adolf and I picnicked under a vast awning by the elephants, I thought to myself that this man wanted the Fatherland to believe he was an animal-loving, non-smoking, vegetarian teetotaller. And yet I got to see him chug on reefers, devour lamb sausages raw and inject himself with a ferocity and regularity that I had never seen in another human being. Even his much-vaunted German shepherd dogs up there in his mountain Berghof disliked and mistrusted him.

He intermittently voiced his anger at Goring's morphine addiction, yet I now believed this may only have been out of envy and his own perverse and persistent wish to be different, yet accepted. Drug addiction, he thought, was *his* terrain. I had, of course, chatted with his Dr Morell, and it was quite likely that he had never been sober for a full day in five years.

We sat and then reposed for an hour, relaxed on our elbows, as we shared a love of the elements and the sensations on that day, one that I had meticulously and mischievously prepared for in several ways. First, I had had a lad spike many of the beasts throughout the paddocks, cages and houses with aphrodisiacs and Spanish fly.* Adolf's dislike of anything sexual had a parallel in Benito's fear of coitus. What was it with these people?

We rose from our blanket and our lunch of foie gras (proving that he was really selfish and approved of animal cruelty), champagne (suggesting that he was a hopeless addict), and boiled cauliflower (confirming that he possessed no taste). We started to stroll, as pals. As we arrived, the monkeys' rate of intimacy and self-pollution now bordered on preternatural. I thought of Ancient Rome, and already I sensed his discomfort. I wondered if he eyed with envy (as I did) the impressive shade (almost angry in its arousal) of the monkey's deeply marooned

---

* *A green beetle called the* Lytta vesicatoria, *the digestion of which offers vast sexual energy.*

appendage. I was less enamoured by its unbecoming spikiness, possibly capable of taking out an eye.

As we meandered along the route, it seemed that even the geese and the ponies in the zoo were unimpressed with Adolf's ungenuine advances for company and friendship. His aura bristled with a vile and flaming burgundy outline. The Shetland preferred to sniff the root of his friend's leathery undercarriage. The geese huddled. One chimp seemed to be choking on his own vomit as he, perhaps, sensed Adolf's contempt for life. Another seemed to weep for him, and that monkey was a tenderer mammal than I. I would have killed the horrid fucker, this uncouth sourpuss, right there and then if I had thought it would have helped. He sashayed like a cunt towards the macabre qualities of the demi-monde, while revealing to the trained eye that some part of him had perhaps once desperately reached out to the light and to decency, but that doomed attempt for redemption had been quite viciously squashed.*

As the animals conspired with The Beast and ignored and shunned Adolf, I asked him if he wished to see a motion picture, knowing that the path of least resistance would have meant an exit from the zoo and its lustful air of passion. And away from the perceptive animals, he might have once again enjoyed the anonymity that his disguise and the rain may have afforded him elsewhere.

'Yes, let us do that. We should leave now,' he said, as a small but determined pony attempted to climb aboard a leggy lady horse, the apes formed a circle of vast and shameless enjoyment, while birds fluttered for their obligatory three-second stint and then retired, thin-eyed and seemingly under

---

* *Imagine the guilt of the poor and well-meaning art teacher who, quite rightly, failed Adolf and unleashed the Austrian's ire upon the world.*

some smallish cloud of guilt and self-reproach. The poor lonesome male tiger lurched around his enclosure unable to deflate himself with a partner, and yet, sadly, he remained without the manual dexterity of the fevered and industrious chimp. Nature could be so cruel.

We strolled along the streets of the city, as the rain ceased and warm sunshine was felt intermittently.

There were whistles and wolf calls from ladies and lads in my direction. I heard cries of 'das Biest'* from well-placed allies and from many impromptu ones too, such was the fun to be found in chirpy and friendly strangers. This both impressed and miffed Adolf, I could sense it. He was the supposed leader of this land. In my company, he was solid in not allowing his anger to be shown, though his fury was towards them. As far as I was concerned, this made him admire me even more.

We arrived at the *TheaterKino* just off the Bavariaplatz. We again managed anonymity, as I paid a tall African gent. I wondered how this lad had survived in this land to this point. He laughed a formidable welcome to me, and I sensed it was the power he possessed in his infectious roar and shrieking mirth, as well as that in the hands of a giant that had shone fortune upon him to that day. I did not engage as I ordinarily would have, for in those very seconds, this angel required maximum protection through minimum fuss.

Once inside, my chiselling of Adolf's spirit continued, as we silently observed the mischief of the projectionist – one of our lads – who quite wickedly played a series of pornographic trailers of girthy boys, and then added similar interstitials of proudly hung chaps and scrotums with *two large* balls, in the

---

* *The Beast.*

main feature of *Vom Winde Verweht*.* I knew Adolf was lustful and eyeing Gable, so this really was now bordering on bullying. I pondered on how Prudence might have described him with one of her fine euphemisms. 'A man with specific mannerisms', 'he was born with the caul' or perhaps, 'a son of the moon', who 'rides the carousel'.

I still had my two main courses of psychological warfare to come as we rose at the end of the picture. My penultimate treat as we walked back to the hotel required my conspiring pals once more. The act we were to enjoy would soon spread around the land, just as unholy visions of Rasputin, a goat-headed man and me had once tortured Il Duce in Italy, the islands and North-East Africa.

The first weapon that I employed was a pastime that was, at that time, unfortunately missing from our culture, and one that I suspected would cut further at his spirit. *Der Exhibitionist*† – if done in the right way, unthreatening, fun, gallant, celebratory and heroic – represented the true rebel and flighty boldness of the human spirit, and was the antithesis of his thin-lipped meanness.

The stroll from the *TheaterKino* to the Hotel Elmendorff was approximately two miles, and followed a marvellous route for a late summer afternoon. The rain had gone, but my companion kept his collar high and his hat low, as we swept past outdoor cafés and restaurants, redolent gardens that were pungent and balmy, precise hedges and imposing military statues on broad Bavarian boulevards.

We turned the corner by the park, when from the seclusion

---

* Gone with the Wind.

† *The flasher, clichéd raincoat and an unashamed sharing of the beauty of the human form, very much in the vein of the* Freikörperkultur. *I was about to introduce a new twist on this classic art form.*

of the seven-foot sunflowers, stepped forward a gentleman. He was deliberate as he pulled the cord of his macintosh and allowed the tied garment to fall open, revealing total nakedness beneath. He looked down at the impressive sight, and then lifted his head to illuminate a broad beam from his handsome Mediterranean face. His stomach was flat, youthful, lean, while he had removed the majority of the length of his lower lawn to exaggerate the longevity of his shaft. He purred the first verse of 'Deutschland über alles', while framing his tool with his fractionally small hands and atop his slight and slim thighs. He then raised his left hand to his temple, and gestured a farewell, withdrawing, with an intrepid and bantam step, into the lanky stems of the flowerbeds. I did not turn to look at Adolf. I did not need to. I had cut to his core.

Over that summer, *Der Exhibitionist* was witnessed around Munich, Berlin, Hamburg and Vienna, and then in small villages, university campuses and market towns. I arranged for a series of flashers (friends of Dibdin's through his network at UFA Films in Berlin), until it seemed to catch on and any old jack was doing it. I was sturdy in not discriminating, for a number of actresses and lady friends of mine also obliged me and a grateful and intrigued populace.

Der Exhibitionist was soon reputed to gesture in to his victims with a friendly welcome, and to invite them to smoke on a special spicy and tangy cigarette of delicious hashish or (on stiller days) to inhale swiftly a lengthy fingernail-full of face-paralysing white powder, as his raincoat remained open, thus allowing all to get a better view of his much-debated controversy close up.

Through my old friends at the Maximus de Paris Rouge, I soon sourced a troupe of rebellious circus and travelling theatre types in the Shakespearean Players' vein. For me, they appeared in parks and *biergartens* performing *Die Geschichte des Goldenen Exhibitionists.*＊

It wasn't clear now whether life was imitating art or vice versa. Theirs became a popular and perpetually sold-out stage story of an unloved king who was driven to suicide by a popular flasher who appeared to ladies, gents, military types, surgeons and a well-known editor, whose thrice weekly updates revealed the grubby secrets of the unloved royal. This heavily maquillage'd cast exposed the impolite sexual procliv-ities, the meanness to animals, the financial misdoings, the overtaxing of the poor, the incest, the plotting, the drug habit, the impotence and the abundant inadequacies of the monarch.

Before that summer was over, *Der Exhibitionist* would be handing out gold coins, as then our fine ladies (*Die Exhib-itionistinen*) began to show their vitals to lonely and shy types, spreading joy across the land, even sometimes with swift sex-ual favour to those never in receipt of that kind of fortune, as the raincoat became the fashion item of the day. I bought shares in them and made a killing.

I even took to the raincoat myself some nights, for, as I shall always maintain, it remained one of The *Great* Pastimes.

We stood still for thirty seconds or so, long after the gent had disappeared into the bushes. Adolf was fucking livid, I knew. He was unable to speak. Perhaps it was the fury of not being able to lift his mask of anonymity. Was it that he wished to slaughter this man for having shown his mighty weapon to the Führer, believing it to be a stranger? (Adolf would have been even more furious were he to have known that it had been a targeted and deliberate attack upon *him*.) Was it that such horrors were happening in his Germany?

＊ *The Tale of the Golden Flasher.*

But I brought him out of his haze.

'So, let us discuss the forfeit from our wager?'

'Go ahead, Aleister. I am intrigued.' These six words took perhaps a minute and a half to exit his mouth. He was close to tears, and his fury would not subside even with the distraction of my question. His proclivity to anger was otherworldly.

'This is my price and your own forfeit for having risked playing snooker with an Englishman.' I attempted to make light. 'We shall take four decks of unmolested playing cards. Your uninterrupted company for five days is required. We shall remain on the top floor of the Hotel Elmendorff, with narcotics adequate to blind with permanence the most seasoned and thick-thighed players.'

I did not reveal that there would also be a painted whore of pleasing and hermaphroditic proportions, and a bouquet of further forfeits to be won. Or lost.

He nodded. Adolf had no choice.

And so our day at the zoo as hidden strangers twisted and turned into an evening, and then several days, nights, dusks and dawns of debauchery and muckiness, and my final twist of the knife into his inevitable fate.

And so I gave Hitler the first taste of his own new strain of amphetamines, upon which he later would become viciously dependent. Sage historians now concur that this addiction was at the root of most of his appalling military decisions. Like the inflamed youth who flails and chases the chess game, thus making his cause all the more improbable, his now rash instructions to his chiefs of staff would instigate the accelerated crumbling of the Third Reich.

We played cards, and with each hand the loser ingested piles of powder and puffed on strong hashish. The winner, usually I, joined in voluntarily.

Of course, with the minimal knowledge of a Magic Circle beginner and someone who had observed Prudence for decades with her seamless bait-and-switch trickery, I seemed to win each hand. When he could take no more powder, he was obliged to remove an article of clothing. I lost the odd round just to keep him interested and enthused. When he was given potentially winning cards, I still produced a royal flush, and I tipped him to the edge.

He was now as naked as when his cursed mother had pushed him out.

He now had a royal flush, but I turned over four aces. Blind.

This made him seethe, of course, but his elevated anger was now hugely and comically magnified by the quite remarkable belittling effects of that wondrous drug on the gent's vitals. The consequences were always quite unfair, and enough to turn any saint to frowns of viciousness and gruesome acts of misjudged plunder.

Another vast shaft of well-chopped white powder sent the remnants of his already-meagre lad receding into his wild pubis.* That this retreat was happening within a yard's radius of my own smug old chap of an adequately manly dimension played on his seized mind. Power is an aphrodisiac, but I was the Master and he had cultivated this pathetic crush on me, allowing this game and his shame to flourish.

When the strong cannabis and the mescal beans began to hit us, we both giggled, albeit he to a vastly girlier shrill. He seemed not to care, as, his legs akimbo'd, he slumped into his high-backed chair. His minuscule pink undercarriage, now resembling the genitals of a slightly bulbous lady, went missing in the messy growth, and bade a final farewell.

---

* *Adolf suffered from a rare condition called penile hypospadias in which the urethra opened on the underside of the penis. He also had a micro-penis.*

His high-pitched girl-squawk was all quite comically at odds with his five days of manly facial growth that had forced his doormat of a moustache* to expose flecks of a rusty ginger and to droop, curl and turn under like Nosferatu's toenails. His loud, but quite hollow assertions that he would soon be the ruler of the world seemed utterly absurd. And it was still only the first night of five.

After this most private of benders, I informed MI-1 that I would now, at their direction and discretion, accelerate the seedling growths of his insanity, prod his paranoia and pre-cipitate the abysmal decisions that will change the direction of the war. With a note from me, he would soon abort Operation Sea Lion (1940) – the planned invasion of Britain – then he would expel those sub-standard Jewish nuclear scientists in the same year, and would then give the go-ahead to trigger Operation Barbarossa, the disastrous attack on Stalin and Russia in 1941.

And so after this lengthy jag and long after my departure from his unattractive shores, Adolf would never be the same again. One might have also reasonably synchronised each call of his infamous and disastrous governance thereafter to the arrival at his mountain chalet or in his Berlin HQ of a regular photograph from me and of him with the hermaphrodite whore. What a true and game starlet he/she had been. Each time this happened, we, in SW1, would spark and prod what had, up until that moment, been, for him, a lost memory of a five-day binge with the real moulder of the twentieth century; This Great and Pimpernelling Beast.

*

---

* Rotzbremse *or snot brake. What a fine language German is; misunderstood, slandered and libelled like me. She, similarly, is robust and cares not.*

The rest (or some of it) you may know for it is reasonably well documented.

It was well-worth noting that I first conned and then delivered to a field south of Glasgow, Hitler's henchman Rudolf Hess on May the tenth, 1941. Winston saw this as my gift to him, quite rightly so. He urged and begged me to leave. It was now far too dangerous, he implored. Any night I might have been slaughtered in my bed, or in any of my waking minutes, dragged off to have my throat slit, be shot or shipped to a camp.

I stayed for six more weeks until the day he turned on Stalin at my prompting. This was June the twenty-second, and, if the Battle of Britain ensured the war would not be lost, then this was the day that made sure the war would be *won* by the Allies.

I then relented, for I now knew it was time to eff awff.

One of our lads, embedded there at an airstrip near Heidelberg for this very eventuality, got me into a Messerschmitt. And home we flew, with the lads and lasses at station command cheering us in, as once again the English Mountaineering Club purred their appreciation, and walked around all evening in those fizzing and ecstatic St James clubs, just smiling, saying naught, to others of a similar stripe. They knew their top boy was safe and about to land, as the Messerschmitt was guided and waved in, and onto an undulating, but so very welcome, Scottish cow pasture, with my daughter there to run to the aircraft and bellow with laughter. I wept. And I wept. I was home.

I had used magick on both sides of the North Sea, but now retrenched to help Winston, like a marauding white queen that had nabbed two rooks, a bishop, and three pawns, sweeping nonchalantly back to her own back ranks.

The final victory and VE Day were still four years away, but my days in Germany were over.

For the record, Winston's famous V-for-Victory sign was all *my* work. It is all there in black and white in my book *Thumbs Up! A Pentagram – A Pentacle to Win the War* (Mandrake Press).

I saw the now-famous gesture as a reworking, a magical antidote to the swastika. I considered the use of the letter V in Hebrew – *vav* is phallic, literally meaning nail, though I considered this more one for Hitler's coffin than a metaphor for a penis. It has been interpreted both ways, and if the cap fits . . .

The V-sign was easily gestured by every soul on that stubborn island, boys with pudding-bowl cuts to the grubby-thumbed defiant ones, sifting through the rubble of bomb sites, pilots flying home and relieved lads pulling into port from icy seas. It was also the precise reverse of Winston's relayed message to me from that English seaman who had delivered us to the base of a puffing Mount Etna on Sicily in 1920. He would see the symmetry. Let's face it. We were *all* just telling Adolf to fuck off.

Mission accomplished.

> I do not want to father a flock, to be the fetish of fools and fanatics or the founder of a faith whose followers are content to echo my opinions. I want each man to cut his own way through the jungle.
>
> – Aleister Crowley

Chapter 12

Mowgli, Death & Torture (1945–1948)

> Modern morality and manners suppress all natural
> instincts, keep people ignorant of the facts of nature,
> and make them fighting-drunk on bogey tales.
>
> – Aleister Crowley

*B*reathe, Aleister. Breathe.
  One more hour to go.

War was over, and I was at retirement age. Blessed Violet was
at school in Cambridge, while thriving in mischief and major-
ing in thumping. My magnificently dubious lass would soon
take a central and pivotal part in my life. My best pal, Winston, lost his election in early July of that year to a landslide,
and so I decided to eff awff too before I was pushed.

I intended to sit down and write the second part of *Hag*.
Mandrake Press had published the first two volumes under the
title of *The Spirit of Solitude* an age ago in 1929.

I had received an invigorating reminder of my true artistic
calling, over and above espionage and nudging righteousness
to victory in wars, in the *Occult Review* that very week. A

man of the church, Reverend Frederick Henry Amphlett Mick-
lewright, had written a six-page feature on me called *Aleister
Crowley, Poet and Occultist.*

> It is not always the case that the poems of occultists are essential
> to an understanding of their work. But Aleister Crowley is
> fundamentally an artist. He is a creative personality, expressing
> his individuality in terms of rhythm. His sense of the rhythmic,
> which ultimately implies the sense of a fundamental beauty, is
> aptly expressed whether in prose or in verse; his art is a necessary
> entrance to an understanding of his occultism.

I had decided as a very young man that I would extract fuel
from my wise admirers, as I would in equal measure from the
seethings of my detractors. I would take great pleasure in having confounded the buffoon, as well as having annoyed the
grim of spirit. Joy might be found in all of these reactions. It
always so happened that those whom I pleased were precisely
those I would have wanted to appreciate my work. And similarly, those who disliked my output were exactly, and to a
man, the ones whom I had wanted to displease. Perhaps this is
one of my greatest achievements, to divide so accurately while
creating one superior mob that mankind should strive to save,
while in that other field, a squadron of arses to engulf in flames.

My plan had been to have six volumes in total, but Mandrake went bust shortly after the Crash. Winston wanted me
to go to his own publisher. I could have exposed *John Bull* and
the *Sunday Express* as the most libellous scandal merchants,
and cleared the name of this Pimpernel. I would have done so
too, had that knock on the door at Boleskine never happened.
It was one of those supremely murky days by the loch, barely
able to see a hundred feet out to water. The rain had not
stopped all day, nor did it appear that it ever would. Just as an

ounce of cocaine and shutting up had once forced Frog and me into a forced state of creativity in that very same spot, then the similarly robust constraints of weather, exhaustion from the war, and relief to be free, allowed one to sit back in one's armchair, stare at the lake and appreciate the most simple of pleasures. Such was the feeling of contentment and a true sense of achievement that I was prompted to pull myself upright in order to walk to the soggy gardens in my untied dressing gown and my bare feet, while holding a very large and lit reefer. I opened the vast door of the southern arch, out to the lake and stood underneath its shelter, and put my feet into the mud. I smoked the rest of the hashish, and felt the effects ameliorate my spirit in all regards. I continued to experience this euphoria uniformly without any faltering sensation. The roach became soggy in my mouth as I stepped out into the torrents from above. There was a squelch underfoot on the lawns, and I took care not to slip on my backside as I tackled the low-gradient slope down to the water's edge. Somewhere across there, Urquhart Castle maintained her poise, as she had for centuries.

I was now very high. I thought of how much I missed Leah. Long gone were the days when we were able to enjoy the intensity of a tantric separation from one another. I thought of how we would not see each other – nor manhandle ourselves in private – for three months or so, if, say, I was on a mission overseas. These self-imposed conditions were strict, and just like those that dear Frog and I had once imposed to write and paint prodigiously there at Boleskine. But instead of those wayward powders in those hip-high Ottoman vases, hashish had helped Leah and me meditate and practise yoga from a grand distance apart. Even at my age (I was soon to be seventy), to deny oneself could still spark the brain, be its very own hallucinogen. If I were to abstain, I would see melting colours after the ten-day period as if on a mediocre acid trip. And in the spirit of the Rasta man whose dreadlocks become clean after six weeks without a wash, then so the sexual abstainer may also break on through to a higher consciousness. Prodigious smoking of pacific weed aids both processes equally by mauling each and every cell to attain the elevated spiritual plane.

These were the doped-up thoughts that bashed around my mind as I sat down into a lotus pose in the mud, my hands within reach of the minute grey breakers, frothing lightly and at very close quarters. It was hardly the bow's mast on that boat from Ceylon in the last days of that tinged century or on the *Duchess of Cumbria* mid-ocean, but there was a hint of it as I began to think how nice, even now, it would be to bend my Monster over and spank her; our faces in the storm. I relished the lapping of the water, and the rain dripping from my happy brow. The rolled hashish soaked and fell to the ground.

We had trained ourselves quite adequately in astral projection, and it was truly surprising for this old cynic to discover how well we were to achieve this glorious feat without the use of drugs. That is, if one does not count the slightest drop of ether as a true aid. Hashish was equally as effective and yet not really considered a major narcotic either.

I sensed a presence in my meditation that came to me, like Rasputin had in the Urals and by that frothing cesspool in Sicily, but without the stench. It was not in my immediate vicinity. Then I heard the rhythm of a fist on the front door on the other side of the house, a fist that seemed to wish urgently to come in from the storm.

I rose, careful to keep my balance. I walked around the house, towards the front. Two tall-ish, well-dressed men stood there, an elderly man and a younger one, it seemed. The younger fellow wore a deerstalker on his head and he looked towards the earth, rain cascading from his hat. The elderly chap, swarthy in appearance, a youthfulness and engaging honesty to him, looked straight ahead at me as I trudged around the side of the old place with my dressing gown open and mud up to my ankles. I noticed the raggedy dog collar around his neck, as he skilfully avoided glancing down at the exposed honesty below.

The elder chap turned on his heel and walked towards me, leaving his friend in an almost meditative state himself. I calculated that they must have walked the eight miles and a quarter from the nearest station, the poor souls. Not everyone is blessed with an adoration of the rain.

He came close to me and stopped, looking at me with a revered intensity. This continued for several seconds, while I waited for him to reveal his intention or his identity. Were they lost? I would gladly invite them in. I made an attempt finally to cover my groin with my dressing gown.

'You are Aleister Crowley,' he told me. And he then remained silent.

'Yes, I am. And I may be the world's greatest magician but I need *some* facts to go on as to who you are.'

'All in good time.'

He looked up at the skies and opened his mouth to catch some rainwater. And he laughed loudly.

'I am sorry to disturb you. We have travelled a long way to see you,' he said.

'Not at all, my friend. Come,' and I led him back to the door, which I opened and gestured them over the threshold.

I presumed them to be acolytes, for they were often known to turn up at odd times, or even to answer the author's note in several of my books that encouraged them to communicate with me. I found it always an enthralling encounter when it happened. These were some of those people I mentioned just earlier, whom I was delighted to have pleased with my canon.

The young man said, 'We are already soaked to the bone, it is not an unpleasant sensation now. May we sit by the lake, please?'

As he said this, he lifted his head to look at me.

'I *know* who you are!'

This may have taken some time for me to say.

There was no mistaking Robbie's dominant but petite and engaging features. I saw myself in there too. Each detail was part her and part me.

Equally as slowly, he replied, 'My name is Edward Crowley.'

And yes, it indeed rhymed with holy.

He too spoke the precise same inflection of English with the slightest Germanic clip as the elder gentleman.

'This man has been my father for almost twenty-seven years. This is Zealand, the army chaplain who saw my birth and my mother's death.'

I babbled quite involuntarily under my breath from the Book of Revelations. I did not mean to, but I know in that moment how my own father must have seen me.

'I saw another mighty angel come down from heaven, clothed with a cloud: and a rainbow was upon his head, and his face was as if it were the sun, and his feet as pillars of fire.'

I looked up and fixed my stare on him.

'Oh Christ. I never knew you that you lived. I am so sorry. You are your mother's son. She was the love of my life.'

These were not ordered thoughts.

I buckled, and crashed onto my backside in a quite unmanly and ungodly fashion. The stuff I had smoked smacked me in the centre of my brain, and the blood rushed from my face. I dropped my face onto my knees and I then crashed back onto my elbows, all in some visceral attempt to compute this. My nethers exposed themselves again, and I was swifter to cover them this time, as I then told myself of the known facts.

I knew his birthday already. He must have been taken from her guts as she died. He had survived all THAT. He was a stubborn and strong boy, as pride swept over where remorse had held ground. He must know that I did not know of him. This was bound to help our union. They both helped me up, seemingly concerned about my health, and rightly presumed that I was in shock and unstable in bare feet on a muddy slope, but unaware that I was really very high, a state that then vaulted my confusion into true bliss.

I held out my arms to him. What else could one do? Our son stepped forward with a manly grace and an elegance that again had both his mother's and father's thumbprint, but surely more of hers.

We met as equals, arms at an angle of twenty minutes to two of the clock that allowed for one of his to dominate and one of mine to. It also seemed right. It seemed well-measured and appropriate.

I sobbed, 'Our boy, our boy. Our darling boy.'

I believed that the rain on my face masked at least some of the torrents of my own droplets, though there was to be no shame in weeping here and now.

The elder man walked slightly away from us, and seemed to observe the lake quite politely, while carrying the shape and shuffled gait of a chap whose magnum opus had just been completed. Mine would have to wait yet again. Not only would this development put the next immediate volumes of *Hag* on hold, but any thought of revealing myself as the Pimpernel would now need further consideration. I could not compute why or how the arrival of these strangers impacted on all of that, but I felt that to free myself from pernicious name-calling became once again of zero consequence. I was holding our son, our boy, a man, of whose existence ten minutes ago I did not even know. Glorious confusion and rapture reigned. The empty-headedness I felt was a proximity to the Godhead, a blissful inability to think as a transcendent human being. I had neared this in narcotic, meditative, yogic and tantric highs, but never with this precision and virtue. I held the feeling as I clenched our son, and this god, this Beast, resolved to never let this feeling of ecstasy escape.

That night, I smoked much more hashish, and dreamed of him as a boy. In my dream, I bade farewell to him as I left on the boat train to climb Everest and K2 in the most perilous season. He was a lad of six, and he wept in a browned meadow, as I said, 'Chin up, my boy. I shall see you in the spring.' When I awoke, I recalled to the word the letter* I had penned to him in my mind and in the night as I slept. I immediately walked to my bureau and transcribed the whole thing. There was much of my father in my words, as I felt compelled to arm him with my soul, should I not return. The words had been those of a soldier going to the trenches, leaving his confused lad. I would never desert my family again. I would draw them close as a seamstress pulls on the thread to knit and bind, wrapping the cotton a dozen times around the stitch, before checking its tension, pleased with her work. I resolved to be now a family man. If I worked for England or for a revolution, it would be from the comfort of my dotage with my loved ones close. It was indeed time to ebb, to recede to the idyllic and the pastoral.

12.2 ESCAPE

Taken from his own kind, Mowgli was raised as a cub amid the magical benevolence of the wolves. There would be snakes

---

* *The letter I wrote sits in the Yorke Collection to this day.*

to avoid, as well as the bayonet claws of perilous killer tigers that put the bowels of almost all in the jungle on edge. He found life as tough as every other creature in that world, but the curious outsider, a survivor against the most unreasonable odds, was protected by a fearsome love among many brothers and sisters. One day, there was talk among the elders of his returning to his own kind. One day.

Zealand knew some German from his wandering childhood with the gypsies. He was a quick learner too, as the widows of the town of Halle* took him to their loving breasts, generously teaching him more than grammar, prepositions and the very specific Prussian word order. They enjoyed precision and efficiency. They were good like that, and the utter revulsion of the war changed the perspectives of many a religious man, now simply keen to bask in a woman's embrace. This he did with several of them, all community-minded and more than happy to share him. Zealand had heard young boys and tough bastards scream for their mothers with their dying breaths, so he felt it only right to do his polite best to bridge some unbridgeable and unendingly sad void on their behalves.

The perilously weak boy grew, and shook off those rudimentary ailments of a premature baby with a remarkable robustness. He walked by six months, was writing by the age of three, reading shortly afterwards and addicted to the cinema by the age of seven. He possessed a mild manner, yet showed a spiky determination were one to scratch his serene surface. He suffered from the familial girthy neck, rotund and bloated ankles and chesty curvature.

Zealand spoke to him of his mother, with whom he had spoken on her deathbed. The lad knew of her towering

---

* To the north-east of Leipzig and Dresden, in what would become East Germany.

courage, intrigue and mischief from an early age. The chaplain knew of the antics of his father, and many of these elements were filtered by him. It is one thing fostering a violently perverse public image as a Satanist and a black magician to save one's country and provoke fascists for decades, it is another thing altogether when that whole sham of a façade keeps one's own son across a sea, never truly knowing if it were better to step forward and speak. I had done this to myself, but had I have known, well then, everything might have been different. I was quite capable of being a good father *and* a prancing Pimpernel of vicious intent. If *only* I had fucking known.

He would have been exposed to no peril from me, his father. For him, the real and present danger would come in the second war, for there was a disease of the mind far more concerning to all who neared it; far more pernicious than cocking around with grubby-ish and leverageable magick.

And when that horror rose, Zealand and Edward were once again encouraged to wanderlust. This time they were pushed to leave not only by a general viciousness and a sweeping fascism, but also, as the son of a gypsy, Edward had been presented with an order to appear at 3.20 p.m. on the following Tuesday (in the same hospital that had allowed him to flourish as a small boy in short trousers). According to the paperwork, he was to be checked for head lice, but was actually, so the nurses said, booked in for his sterilisation. His father had a similar appointment at 4.30 p.m. They packed an almost comically small case between them, embraced several widows and left in the night three days before their expected appearance. The young man, Edward Crowley carried also a chess set, for this was his true passion.

They were both tall chaps of marginally over six feet, and lean-jawed from the austere years. Edward seemed to have mimicked several of Zealand's characteristics, like his smooth and engaging gait and the way he lifted his shirt to pick at his belly button when he felt relaxed. They chuckled a lot in each other's company, sometimes without muttering a word, such was their apparent telepathy. It was not unusual for them to hold hands in the most inoffensive, innocent and adoring of fashions.

It was May of 1938, and again the path of least resistance meant they had made it to the Czech borders on a motorbike, given to them by a widow as a final gift of benevolence and once the property of a master baker, father of fifteen and high-jump champion who had perished in the Battle of the Marne. This was only five months before that same Sudetenland would be overrun by Nazis. The journey was still a tricky one. They were fortunate that their *schedulas* did not indicate the precise minority status of gypsy, tinker or other undesirable. The papers were not stamped with a Star of David, and they both wore donated wedding bands in case they were perceived as homosexuals. They were both sure to urinate quite boldly at the border crossing, in full view of the guards, a gesture that, in itself, would have hinted at the presence of a foreskin. If the guards had cared to glance, they would indeed have seen two of them. Edward might quite reasonably have been within his rights to announce that his birth father was gallivanting with the Führer, but then that may have also complicated things quite nastily. The guard, of course, wanted to know the reason for the journey.

'*Mein Sohn spielt in einer Schach-Herausforderung gegen den Großmeister, Achilles Frydman in Venedig.*'*

---

* '*My son is playing in a chess challenge in Venice against the grandmaster, Achilles Frydman.*'

'*Wirklich! Der Jude! Gut, du musst ihn für Deutschland schlagen.*'*

Zealand and Edward were unsure whether the ensuing challenge for a game from the captain came as a test to corroborate their alibi or whether the men on the border were supremely bored, or both, but they threw forward their best player, a fresh-faced, barely pubescent boy, who seemed so young that he should have been cycling and diving naked into warm lakes with sound school chums. He was, however, a formidable opponent, but soon beaten by Edward with a close-ish discomfort, considering that defeat might have had them both shot.

'*Das beste von fünf Spielen?*'†

Edward Crowley played those games, and he even did so blindfolded. The victories came more easily than they had in the first game. He was relaxed now, for the threat of an immediate bullet was reduced. There was a sage method to his madness, for at least if he lost while blindfolded and his back to the board (just like in the Waldorf by Central Park between the imposter Svareff and me), there would have been a reasonable excuse. Of course, he won. And then audaciously suggested they play the best of nine. The soldiers lined up to play, and all were vanquished.‡ Edward was plied with a rough moonshine, but this just seemed to facilitate victory upon victory. Zealand took some grog out of politeness.

They woke up on scrubland, yards from the border crossing with several thousand marks (worth less than bugger all) shoved in the boy's top pocket, and to the sight of some young lads filling the bike with gasoline. They were brought icy

---

* '*Really! The Jew! Good, you must win for Germany.*'
† '*Best of five games?*'
‡ *I tingle with pride. Robbie would have too, I know.*

water from a nearby stream, as well as putrid and gritty coffee and magnificent bratwurst. They sat around with the soldiers, joked about the run of forty-three games unbeaten, and then slipped off as soon as it appeared to be a comfortable *auf wiedersehen*. They did not speak until they were twenty miles out of sight.

In Edward's inner top pocket was the single possession that they had guarded together for nineteen and a half years. It would remain close to the boy's heart throughout their journey that would bring them to Loch Ness seven years later. It was the letter from a dying mother to her child (written with the almost absolute certainty that that foetus would rot in French dirt) and one to the love of her life, a burgeoning Pimpernel, who would crumple when he would one day absorb the impact of its contents.

It is quite reasonable to think that either Zealand or Edward may have destroyed the letter, once they knew that I was now being regularly photographed with high-ranking SS and Gestapo* officials, and even with Göring, Goebbels, Speer, Hess, Hühnerbein and Adolf Hitler himself. Whenever Zealand and Edward had considered my current acquaintances, they each time came back to Roberta's sound sense of judgement, and her own status of agent provocateuse behind enemy lines, that the gypsy priest had himself witnessed. They lived on the prayer that I was precisely who I ended up being, a renegade of the most remarkable and dangerous mischief in the closest inner ring of Nazism. Such a keen and accurate sense of character, from afar and with minimal clues, well, this thrills me to the core to this day.

The pair rode on through Czechoslovakia, into Hungary

---

* *Schutzstaffel (SS) and the Geheimnis Staats Polizei (Secret State Police) or Ge-Sta-Po, two of the most brutal sets of Hitler's thugs.*

and to the Dalmatian coast. It was slow going on the old bike, but when faced with the alternative of a forced sterilisation and then perhaps a concentration camp, the men were euphoric and free. They took a fishing boat from the magical citadel of Rovinj in Croatia, and set to sea aiming at Rimini on the Adriatic coast of Eastern Italy. From there, the plan was to head to Tunis. They had read one of my books, seen on the dustjacket that I had written it in North Africa, and hoped I was still there. They intended to skirt past Sicily. Perhaps they might find me there too or, at least, validate their wishes that I was the man they had wanted me to be. One might question the wisdom of entering another fascist country, but they planned to remain less than one week, their papers were in order, and there was no war on yet.

All was indeed going to plan until they landed in Italy, where twenty-year-old Wanted posters* of a chap by the name of Crowley with an uncanny resemblance to the youth with the same name – as well as quite appalling artist impressions of Rasputin – were in railway stations, town halls and ports. The busybody official on a small desk in Rimini, clearly bored out of his skull and spotting an opportunity for a promotion, pulled Edward to one side and fetched the scabby old photograph of me, taken on Cefalù, looking imposing and, even in the picture, a threat to Il Duce.

The men were both held in a cell in Rimini until a thoroughly shoddy and unmotivated native with a camera arrived and took several mug shots of them both. An equally unprofessional police captain had two young *carabinieri* search the

---

* *Edward believed the photograph in the Wanted poster was from one of the images that I had mailed to Mussolini to taunt him when I showed him several old snaps. I still cannot linger too long on the pending impact on my own son at the hands of that bullying Fat Head, but how the hell was I to know?*

small suitcase and all of their pockets for the proof they really needed, presumably false beards, massive crucifixes and truly stinky robes, the kind worn by someone attempting to impersonate a dead Russian holy man. The silly bastards didn't even find the letters from Roberta. Another suited chap entered from time to time and spoke in what appeared to be Russian or Romanian in an attempt to engage Zealand and Edward for some unknown reason.

The following day they were charged with sedition in front of a kangaroo court and with no legal representation. They were found guilty within five minutes, cuffed and thrown in a van. They were driven eighty miles to Bologna, where they served seven years in Casa Circondariale, a penitentiary of appalling standards of cleanliness, space and thuggery, but where the food remained remarkably wholesome and plentiful. They were permitted to keep their chess set and Zealand's Bible. Both stood them in good stead, as the elder fellow gave absolution to sodomites, fellaters and even guilt-ridden self-stimulators, while Edward spent days blindfolded barking coordinates, first in English and German and then in Italian, to stun the inmates with his party trick.

Had Mussolini become more brazen with two decades of power? For, if he had known the identity of the prisoner, the names of Satan and Aleister Crowley were perhaps not so much of a threat anymore? Such is the dizzying effect of power. I could only presume in the maelstrom of combat, he knew fuck all about my boy. In my eyes, he would always remain an unmitigated coward regardless.

Zealand and Edward were in there until the American 5th Army, the British Eighth Army and the Polish II Corps spanked the 26th Panzer Division in the fortnight-long Battle of Bologna in April 1945. It was the Poles who captured the jail and liberated the poor bastards therein. The pair left with their Bible, the chess set and a supremely healthy wedge of cash won – and concealed – over seven years of chess. They slipped south-west to Rome to sit out the war until the inevitable ceasefire. It would, however, all be over by the time they reached the city limits in the back of a farm truck. Then it would be on to their next stop, Dulwich. Or, perhaps, Cambridge. Or even a dignified spot of majestic loneliness by Loch Ness.

12.3 WINSTON THE GENIE

When I found out what that flouncing cunt had done to our boy, I even pondered forgetting any consideration of retirement. He had confined him. He had locked up our boy. Our son. For years.

Upon receipt of a pair of letters from me, Dandylyon, Prudence and Winston came to visit us (Violet, Edward, Zealand, Frog and me) at Boleskine. It was the first day of September 1945. It was six years to the day since Poland had been invaded. Dandylyon and Prudence had barely aged, but spoke rarely, as if telepathy between us all was now adequate. They moved slowly, deliberately, relied on occasional glances and half-smiles, and held hands with each other and with me. It was an ecstatic state. Prudence looked as if she could still charm a man or boy.

As we elders (that is, all minus my children and Frog) sat by the back lawns on comfortable chairs, I told them that I had read of the details of how Mussolini had been executed in Mezzegra on the shores of Lake Como three days after our boy had been liberated. Had I been able to administer some slow spiritual torture and that bullet myself, perhaps I would have extinguished that lustful desire for revenge, but it seemed that some fortunate partisan peasant beat me to it and, according to the confused and vague-ish reports, shot and killed Benito. They all shut up and let me ramble.

'I must tell you all. And I fear the words like I have feared nothing – not even fucking Nazis – since school. The bald and blatant truth is that I am now a tired old man. I am too well known now in Los Angeles, New York, London, Paris, Rome, Munich, Berlin and Moscow to be of any real use any more, and there are hundreds still lurking out there who would slit my throat as I walked for a pint of milk and a paper.'

The words I dreaded were, 'I am done, my friends. Finished.'

They all remained silent. Winston stood, chuckled briefly and then shut up again, as he shuffled, rotund and elderly himself.

'But what will you do, old boy?'

He looked out across the waters, squinting to see Urquhart.

'Oh, I don't really know. Maybe I am going to sit down to write now in Cambridge and here. A lot has happened since *Hag*. And I want to spend time with my children. Perhaps we shall have term-times in Cambridge and holidays here.'

Winston seemed delighted with the plan, as we toasted our victory with newly lit hashish.

'Cheers,' all round.

Winston sat back, puffed on the spicy fag, and appeared to struggle to choose his words. 'If you write your memoirs, you might need to keep your trap shut on a lot of stuff.'

'Ha ha ha! Do you mean the Russians? Do you mean Grigori?'

'Yes, that is precisely, whom I mean. The Russians. Grigori. And, I am afraid, much, much more. You could disappear for a while. Go to the mountains, all of you,' Churchill said.

'Perhaps we shall. Perhaps let the buggers think that I have finally died,' I said, mocking my enemies, myself and the path I had chosen.

'Well, perhaps it is finally time for Shangri-La.'

'Leah should be most pleased,' said Prudence.

'Oh fuck. Yes, Leah.'

I knew immediately that this was the perfect idea. Of course it was.

'My Monster. My sweet, forgotten Monster.'

We decided that it would be a quite lovely idea if I did indeed fake my death. And if I could not fully and for now reveal the Pimpernel, then at least I could put my family first for a while. For once. This meant removing myself from all circulation in the near future. Perhaps it was time to resurrect Count Svareff, a chap who, if seen around Dulwich or St James, only bore a passing resemblance to the wicked man from the newspapers. A broad hat, a cape and a face for a foggy night should offer enough latitude for doubt and gossip.

That night, as we picnicked by the loch, Winston Churchill took on the role of the magic genie and granted me three wishes.

1. His own publisher would take *Hag II*. He had just spoken with London on the telephone. Terms as I decreed, though, he insisted, no mention of the Pimpernel.
2. I could take retirement in Shangri-La, as a demigod and halfway to heaven, and we could leave as soon as the death business was looked after. Violet, Frog, Zealand and Edward were, of course, welcome.
3. And he had certainly saved the best until last. The Fat Head Il Duce, Benito Mussolini was still alive, and Churchill had him imprisoned. He was all mine, and a thank-you gift for decades of service from the King of England and the British Empire.

And so, I now learned some new truths. Here I hold one of Winston's letters to Benito from 1940. Churchill had negotiated with the coward before and then in the early days of the war. There was a cunning and far-sighted madness to his method.

For when thousands wanted to murder him in 1945, Il Duce had thought it infinitely safer to be placed in Winston's hands were Italy to fall. He had surrendered to an English officer on the sands of Como, in order to prevent a lynching from his compatriots. Winston was a good man, but not a fool.*

Oh! what joy!

Benito was mine! He was, at that very moment, being transferred to his new home in a Sicilian abbey. For safekeeping.

12.4 HASTINGS AND ALL THAT

Meanwhile, the plan for my demise was precise and measured. Of course it was.

In June of 1946, I took rooms in a retirement home, Netherwood House in Hastings, that town by the sea whose battle would define these islands for a thousand years and likely more. It was suitably comfortable, as one, like the bank robber who avoids the immediate purchase of diamonds and fast

---

* Mussolini's nephew, Vanni Teodorani – the founder and the director of the powerful Axis of Bastoni – claimed up until his death that Churchill killed Mussolini in order to erase the traces of his talks with Il Duce before the outbreak of war. He was close, but did not know the full story.

ROMA – Churchill fece uccidere Mussolini per cancellare le tracce delle sue trattative col Il Duce prima dello scoppio della Seconda guerra mondiale: questa la tesi dei figli di Vanni Teodorani, nipote di Mussolini, fondatore e direttore dell'Asso di Bastoni.

ROME – Churchill killed Mussolini in order to erase the traces of his talks with the Duce before the outbreak of World War II: this is the thesis of the sons of Vanni Teodorani, nephew of Mussolini, founder and director of the Axis of Bastoni.

cars, did not want to appear too extravagant. I feigned minor illnesses and the odd fall to make my demise seem plausible. I behaved myself and played the old eccentric to perfection. I practised yoga, read prodigiously and painted signs to hang around the place to keep me busy.

Guests are requested not to tease the Ghosts.

Guests are requested to be as quiet as possible while dying of fright.

Breakfast will be served at 9 a.m. to the survivors of the Night.

The Hastings Borough Cemetery is five minutes' walk away (ten minutes if carrying a corpse), but it is only one minute as the ghost flies.

Guests are requested not to dig the graves on lawns, but to make full use of newly filled graves under trees.

Guests are requested not to remove corpses from graves or to cut down bodies from trees.

The office has a certain amount of used clothing for sale, the property of guests who have no longer any use for earthly raiment.

The young girls chuckled at me and the saucy old matrons blushed at me and my mischief (*crikey! if only they knew*), and I had mauve thoughts of them all.

My death was a formality to fake. Sir Winston Churchill's own doctor signed the death certificate on December the first, 1947 and allowed for heavy weights in the coffin in my absence.

Dandylyon and Churchill's officialdom looked after the bureaucracy, while, for the optics of laying in wake, I was quite thrilled to try tetrodotoxin, the infamous Haitian zombie drug mixed with *Datura stramonium*, known also as jimson-weed or Devil's snare of the nightshade family.* This would put me to sleep and appear to stop my heart, as I astral projected and lived my seventy-two years again. (*Oh Father, I am sorry I wept when I saw you. I have been so much stronger than that, I promise! My darling daughters! Oh Robbie, you would tingle with joy at our boy! Oh Yeats, I have not finished with you yet! Look behind you, Benito! Fuck off, Adolf!*)

Chronic bronchitis with pleurisy is quite easy to counterfeit, it seems, as I allowed myself large amounts of prescription-standard heroin throughout the final months. Why not?

Heavily disguised in the large crowd, I dropped in on my own funeral, and was quite thrilled at the turn out, the sobs and the stories I overheard as I slipped through, disguised as a bearded, old Russian count, whom we had all encountered in St Petersburg in '98.

('Is that that Count Svareff chap?' 'He is a mysterious one, I hear.')

Our son spoke at my funeral. 'He was calm, composed and I was supremely proud, as he quoted me.

> Behold! the rituals of the old time are black. Let the evil ones be cast away; let the good ones be purged by the prophet! Then shall this Knowledge go aright. I am the flame that burns in every heart of man, and in the core of every star. I am Life, and the giver of Life, yet therefore is the knowledge of me the knowledge of death. I am the Magician and the Exorcist.

*

---

* *Also known by the marvellous names of hell's bells, Devil's trumpet, Devil's weed, tolguacha, Jamestown weed, stinkweed, locoweed, prickly burr, and the Devil's cucumber.*

Mourners interjected with 'Do what thou wilt' and 'Love shall be the whole of the Law'.

My renegade darling, Violet, even sang a few words. You shall soon learn of this rebellious daughter of mine. Her choice of ditty might give a fair barometer of her twisted mind. These were the lyrics of the bawdy and traditional folk song, 'Vanessa Picklegin'.

One night for a jar, I went to the bar
And I drunk the barrel dry.
And the thoughts in my head were very far from bad
'Til this harlot catch me eye.
She was withered and small, like a pickled wal(nut)
That her bones had rubbed her sore,
With her teeth in a box, she had got the pox
And her age was fifty-four.

I've made very bold with young and old
And I've fucked 'em thick and thin;
But I never, never straddled a whore so riddled
As Vanessa Picklegin.

Well, no man knows who soberly goes,
To what that man can sink;
How his brain gets spoiled and he sees the world
Through the rose-coloured specs of drink
So I gazed in her eye 'til beneath my fly
My Y-fronts shockedly rose;
And the stand-in hand grew so bloody grand
That it nearly blocked me nose.

So up comes she and she says to me,
Do you fancy a whore to screw?

I can take without fuss any double-decker bus
So I'll readily deal with you!
For the average fool with the average tool
I charge an inordinate fee;
But since you've got a hard, which is more than a yard
To you the admission is free.

So it's back to her flat, and we slung out the cat
And to bed without a word,
For she looked, and she felt, and she bloody nearly smelt
Like a week-old, white-washed turd.
But I maintained that horn from night 'til morn
And we fucked the dark hours through
'Til the bones went *crack* in the middle of her back
And Vanessa fell in two.

Now all you lads that drink ale, be cautioned by my tale
For as I scrambled free,
I loudly wailed, for my prick was left impaled
On Vanessa's vertibrae.
So, when you're in the pub, the harlots snub
Or you shall surely find,
Though you may get away and not be asked to pay
You'll leave a lot behind!

My acolytes hooted and applauded and whistled. As did a proud Svareff. The dozens of journalists frowned and rolled their eyes, and the single-fingered and laboured typing of their sub-editors was as impossibly dreary as usual, the following day.

BLACK MAGICIAN CROWLEY DIES

WORLD'S WORST MAN DIES[*]

AWFUL ALEISTER,[†]

UNHOLY DAUGHTER FAR WORSE THAN BEAST

RASCAL'S REGRESS[‡]

ALEISTER CROWLEY DIES;
ONCE THE 'INVISIBLE' MAN

MYSTIC'S POTION TO PROLONG LIFE FAILS

WORST MAN IN THE WORLD DIES,
LEAVES WEIRD PICTURES

Hundreds were there, but they were all outnumbered by the silent and respectful birds in the trees, whom I had fed every day for months. They knew my schedule well, my darlings. Like Eva's German shepherds who knew to hone in on the musky groin, they were all such remarkable judges of character.

Reporters harangued mourners outside, while one old friend yelled back, 'Beware what you write. Crowley may strike at you from wherever he is.' I chuckled in the background, as I heard this.

The rains began, and the same voice then added, 'See, I told you. Look out.'

The sot drinks, and is drunken: the coward drinks not, and shivers: the wise man, brave and free, drinks, and gives glory to the Most High God.

– from *Liber CL: De Lege Libellum*, Aleister Crowley

---

[*] *My favourite.*

[†] *Rich for a paper that spent years criticising my alliteration.*

12.5 THE MOUNTAINS AT LAST

That evening we spoke of the journey to Shangri-La, for it was not an easy one. I was, however, the greatest climber to ever slight the English Mountaineering Club in favour of the Scots, and no doctor (other than my own friends in on the whole scheme) had pulled back my sheets or loosened my shirt all the time that I was in Hastings. I was as fit as a lop.

We were all there, but it was Prudence who spoke alone and without interruption. She considered that Violet, Zealand and Edward knew nothing of the place, and had even, with her usual consideration, taken the train into Edinburgh to purchase half a dozen copies of *Lost Horizon.*

'Hilton's path to Shangri-La in the book is reasonably accurate, though key elements have been changed, of course. You shall take a plane to Yunnan Province in north-western China where it meets with Eastern Tibet. You shall land at an airstrip on a plateau twelve thousand feet up, with just a hut and a store of food left there by Sherpas, well informed by MI-1. It is the path most similar to that taken by the two French priests in 1844, Évariste Régis Huc and Joseph Gabet and described in the 1850 journals, published in Paris, and entitled *Souvenirs d'un Voyage.* They wrote of a place called *Shambha-La,* the summation of a core concept and ideal of Tibetan Buddhism and where harmony and peace flourishes between man and nature. It is one that is disconnected from our own concept of time. The place follows its very own selfless *Kalachakra.* * The final part of the journey there can be peril-ous in bad weather, even in the times of year that one is advised to attempt it. You shall hike high, with some of those same friendly Sherpas, into those old pals of yours, Aleister, the Himalayas. And there, an earthly heaven awaits you all.'

---

*   *Wheel of Time.*

'You? Why do you say, "You"?' I asked her.

'Because Dandylyon and I shall stay here, Aleister. It has been decided.'

'And we shall not unman each other with farewells when the time comes. I sense this is only *au revoir* and not an *adieu*,' said Dandylyon.

12.6 TORTURE

There was still the boyish excitement of torturing Benito first.

I had considered keeping this secret news of his capture from Zealand and Edward, for they may have been more principled than I, given all that time with the Bible. But blood is thicker than water or wine. I was so proud to see how thrilled our son was when I told him of Winston's gift. We kept no secrets from each other now, and I finally began to tell him more fully of my past.

He agreed to type up *Hag II* when we all arrived in Shangri La. How happy he was to continue to learn of my life, as we floated by Cascais, Gibraltar, Marseille and the Balearics. How thrilled to now know that his suspicions of my righteousness and brave sabotage of the Nazi party had been confirmed.

15 June 1948

We were obliged one last docking en route to those Silk Roads, as we landed once again on my darling Sicily. Mussolini was now in the old abbey, one apparently quite haunted (he thought). Did Etna welcome us with a smoke ring? Perhaps. I was too giddy with anticipation to know if it were a mirage or not. I recall the friendly faces greeting us in the town of Cefalù, the ice-cream parlour as welcoming as ever, the *gelato* unreasonably delicious. The mayor and many others seemed to know (with their smiles, winks, slaps on the back

and even hugs at the knees from small children) that Il Duce
was in my Abbey, still conveniently disused according to the
municipal paperwork, and our celebrity in the town was a
silent, harnessed but joyous one. No one spoke of it, but the
British soldiers were treated like lords, for the sashaying
clown-turned-prisoner now possessed no friends on the island.

Il Duce was scared of the dark, I recalled Amatore having
said. He was scared of sex, I recalled his having said. Oh goody.
This was going to be fun, as we were greeted on those familiar
slopes to the east and west of the Abbey, dappled in light, overgrown with lanky capweed, dandelions and wild jasmine envel-
oping the ancient stone walls, with a new mob of golden midges
there to dance and greet with boyish excitement. The water was
as crisp and clean as I recall, as I supped from the first well.
Zealand and Edward approved of the Abbey. She had aged well
and with grace. As had Amatore, who was now whistling a
lullaby, and dangling his legs over the ancient stone wall. His
smile, however, had only increased in beauty.

We said nothing. We embraced.

I walked inside. I stayed six months.

12.7 A Pervert and a Spy

As we ground and chugged through the hugging womb of
Suez, I daydreamed of how Winston and I had, many times in
those final days in London, walked down to the old fleapit
cinema in Waterloo over the river from Westminster. We had
watched Mitchum and Jane Greer in *Out of the Past*, Welles
and Hayworth in *The Lady from Shanghai* and my favourite,
Black Narcissus; Deborah Kerr as a scorching hot nun at a
mission high in the Himalayas. The owner of the Rialto had
greeted the former prime minister as if Winston had been
a regular, and had eyed me as if I were either a massive

pervert or a dangerous spy. He had been right, surely, on both counts.

Each time, we had chosen a Technicolor treat. Afterwards, we had headed north. My retinas had seemed scorched from the blue celluloid palettes of the movies, for the brown slow turd-sludge of the Thames had appeared to glint a Mediterranean azure making me think of a *Chateau d'Yquem* rosé with my imaginary pals on the screen; Niven and Olivier on the beach at *St-Jean-Cap-Ferrat* with a conveyor belt of *crevettes au beurre à l'ail* as they flounced and posed and postured in vintage sailing clobber and the finest deck shoes, all designed by Edith Head, art direction by Cedric Gibbons. My mind's eye had recreated the scene to perfection, though the usually fine pomp of the MGM Orchestra executing the score in my head had played as if they were all quite vilely hungover, especially the oboist. On cue, a farting barge had brought me abruptly back to Westminster Bridge.

As we passed the southern vulva of the canal at Port Tewfik and still in the afterglow of my time with Benito and my team of obedient brutes and cut-throats, I recalled the final time we had relished ninety such glorious minutes in that South London cinema. We had watched David Lean's *Oliver Twist*. I had been most impressed with how the director had not shown the scene where Bill Sykes beats poor Nancy, but instead had implied great horror by a marvellous device. Nancy's Jack Russell dog scratches at the thick wooden door, as the brutality occurs, and that is all we see as we presume the worst. The *very, very* worst.

Goodbye, England, old friend. But the reason I pondered the *Rialto* now is that I knew somehow that I would see that old cinema again.

12.8 A Few Loose Ends
4 December 1948

As we sailed on, Zealand, my Mowgli, Violet and I continued to speak eagerly and yet with measure of our lives, as the fleshy dog Hühnerbein was slumping and sweating in Nuremberg waiting for his noose. I smiled at the thought, and now I shall tell you, as I told my son on that sturdy boat, about England's princess, my daughter and me, and how I had kept the King in England during the war, and therefore the future of the world safe. For now.

For once, there were no storms. There was no having myself tied to the mast by reluctant cabin boys. No spilled seed, no heroin, no pacific rafts of smoked weed or aroused incantations to Poseidon. Just we few. Just my family.

> I was not content to believe in a personal devil and serve him, in the ordinary sense of the word.
>
> I wanted to get hold of him personally and become his chief of staff.
>
> – Aleister Crowley

PART THREE

If you want a happy ending, that depends, of course, on where you stop your story.

– Orson Welles

Chapter 13

Tales of Saving England and Her Princess

> And the woman (the Whore of Babylon) was arrayed in
> purple and scarlet colour, and decked with gold and
> precious stones and pearls, having a golden cup in
> her hand full of abominations and filthiness of her
> fornication.
>
> – Revelations 17

As a young man, the more I conquered those European peaks, the more I wanted to dominate the Himalayas. I shall miss this enveloped paradise. I read out loud a chiselled transcription on the whitest block of stone, with the most marvellous calligraphy that soothes the mind and convinces one that it is the whole truth. The words are credited to Father Perot, that transcendent pioneering priest, who became the High Lama here.

Our general belief is in moderation. We preach the virtue of avoiding excesses of all kind, even including excess of virtue itself. We find in the valley it leads to great happiness. We rule with moderate strictness and in return we are satisfied with moderate obedience. And so our people are moderately honest, moderately chaste, and somewhat more than moderately happy.

There can be no crime where there is a sufficiency of everything. A little courtesy all around can solve almost all problems.[*]

I now walk between the large stone white temples, symmetrical, both simple and ornate, and then along the lordly lawns and simple pathways.

Why is the world beyond here called civilisation? It seems ridiculously obvious to point out that this is as civilised as the human race has attained.

No more time to go.

13.1 CHASING THE DRAGON
10 December 1948

As the SS *Manchuria* sailed south between Mecca and Medina on our eastern flank, and as we crossed from Egypt into Anglo-Egyptian Sudan on our western banks, I sat in the early morning on the portside deck with my children. Edward embodied much of his mother and the influential Zealand. He was calm, serene and keen to listen. He comported himself like a young librarian, but was also lithe, handsome and athletic enough to be a tennis professional or a film noir extra. Violet, who might have doubled as the teenage Elizabeth Taylor, twitched with the impatience of her paternal line. Of course, it was not long before she sprang up to run off to flirt with the touring cricket team of schoolboys on board, en route to the finest colleges of Delhi, Madras and Bombay.

*

---

[*] From Lost Horizon *(1937), directed by Frank Capra, screenplay by Robert Riskin, based on the 1933 novel of the same name by James Hilton.*

I was protective in the sense that I wanted her near and I wished also to learn from the horrors of having lost two daughters already, but I allowed her full range to blossom and provoke mischief. Anything else would have been rank hypocrisy on my part.

Edward and Violet were now spending a lot of time together. Violet knew that her conception had been unorthodox, just as Edward recognised his birth and upbringing to be somewhat unusual. They were the happiest pair of runts around, lauding and celebrating in this status and bonding firmly through it.

I was adequately self-centred still to have started to tell Edward much of my life story to this point, but as Violet flounced off to spread gloriously her bouquet, to quartergyrate her hips at and to share her comely eye-flutterings with the drooling schoolboys, Edward asked to know more of his half-sister.

I chuckled.

'Violet has always been turquoise and fire, and is now a magnificent parvenue of bubbling oestrogen and poisonous lip gloss. She used to collect knives, you know. As a five-year-old. This is one of her first precious memories. Her second was her obsession with her teeth and her breath. She now rinses and gargles with hydrogen peroxide and brushes her teeth at least a dozen times a day. She will then pick between them with needles until her morning, afternoon and evening milk is laced with swirling ribbons of blood. Blanche then rouge. Purity and virginity followed by sex and death. The chance of having her breath questioned in one of her plentiful rows is simply not worth the risk, for proximity in these duels is one of her effective strategies. Her eyes seem to focus several yards behind the head of her opponent. My darling daughter, the merciless, gaudy crackpot, is, by this time, already ahead.'

Edward nodded. I sensed he had witnessed this already.

I went on, 'Those who relish such minor scraps are rarely active on a larger stage, but for her, all conflict is welcome. She grazes on insignificant brouhaha, and still maintains a ravishing hunger for the evening banquet of a major brawl. I have always been the kind not to really bother with insignificant, low grade conflict, but I was always an exception. She has learned the skill of high-end battle and lofty quarrel from me, but her appetite has surely gone further.'

I turned to look my son in the eyes.

'I once told her, when she was perhaps eleven, about the old bull who told the young bull not to rush down into the valley to ignite passion with a particularly astonishing cow. The old guy said, "We will stroll down, take our time and service them all." Well, Vi's spiky and youthful viciousness cannot be quelled by such a patient approach, though she does already appreciate, like her dad, the proclivity towards pansexuality.'

Edward's was a comfortable laugh.

'Son, I am quite proud that I have never grown out of the infantile belief that the universe was made for me – and now for her and for us all – to suck.'

13.2 YOUTHS

'Violet is able to read the heart of a man upon first encounter. For years, they say, I had cast spells of an emetically deviant nature from my ancient Scottish castle in the direction of some pious nemesis in Northern France or Tunisia or Mexico, hitting my jack-knifeable target with regularity and preternatural force.

'They claimed that only *I* would hear the response of a pained "Oooooof" roll around the valley like my favoured Scotch in an archaic tumbler. Apparently, I chuckled at the precise time I knew my enchantments would be landing for this might have been six or twelve hours after the dark magic had been sparked. I had, they misguidedly claimed, defined twentieth-century Satanism in the uplands of our heathen antecedents. "Fucking sick bastard," is how Violet always far more accurately described me with an excitable lustre and worrying vigour, and far closer to the truth. She is a great judge of character, lad. Always trust her.'

'I shall,' said Edward.

'Despite having spent several years away from each other, we are remarkably close. We are so similar in our desire for groins of any kind. They say that such delectations are able to skip heartbeats, but less so generations. Claims that the youths at Boleskine were strapped down and borrowed for a few hours by Vi or by me are just wrong. They were always consenting, and this is verified by the fact that they always came back for more. Bless them. Some came just for supper. I would fall on them between courses and begin humping them right on the floor.'

We looked at each other as the ship's chaplain passed us. We paused, maintained our gaze and then broke into what must have appeared to be the most false theatrical, synchronised and melodramatic laughter. It was the precise pitch and timing that Dandylyon, Prudence and I had executed a thousand times. And there was nothing fraudulent about it.

13.3 EARLY LESBIC TENDENCIES

'Son, there is one thing you really need to know about her. Between her and me, we kept the King in England during the Blitz. I think with very sound reason that *this* might have saved the war and, therefore, the world for us in the darkest days.'

'How?' he said. 'How on earth could you *both* have done it? You, perhaps. But Violet too?'

'Sit back, lad. I will tell you.'

He sat back. And I explained.

'Violet met her nemesis, Princess Margaret, at a reasonably early age. They had been born on the same day, and both in Scottish castles. Both of their families were flirting with Nazis. The girls attended the same Brownie camp, and it was here when the bother began, at least the physical manifestation of it.

'All week, the Princess had been detracting attention from the precocious Violet, which was only understandable in the circumstances. Margaret was second in line to the British throne, after all. And so Violet approached her from behind on the stage of the camp hall and lifted her petticoat for all to see the regal unmentionables and administered a sharp boot to the revealed nethers. Margaret's vengeful attack, a sharp push from behind during rehearsals of the annual show, had not been well measured, for the high drop from the stage was a considerable one. It was, however, perfectly timed for those of a crimson humour, for the end of verse one of the Brownie anthem was really a time for a concentrated team ethic, love and hope.'

I sat forward, and theatrically spoke the words.

> 'On the African plain,
> I was camping with a lion called Adam
> And he told me about a gent he'd eaten and his
> poisoned madam'

I sat back. 'Then there was an impromptu girl-shout of "Up yours!" followed by a soft kick, a half-second pause and sickening bone-on-hardwood thud.'

I finished the lyrics of the song for Edward.

'Team leaders such as I, full of chat and merriment
    What we could gather – what we might do
    These heroes of tomorrow, just like you.'

'Violet, who refused to cry of course, was lucky to escape with three broken ribs and a cracked kneecap. Her attempts to exact immediate revenge were prevented by her injuries and a trio of corpulent and commensurately salty and duly perspiring dinner ladies of stunning dimensions and turgid odour. Hostilities had so begun on August the twenty-first, 1937. It was their seventh birthdays.

'"She stinks," Vi had noted before pasting a pound note to the camp noticeboard with the words *Verfickter Deutscher Furz** over the King's profile.'

'For each birthday after the physical assaults of 1937, their greatest annual gift was the inflicting of the severest pain, physical or emotional, upon the other. Strategically leaked and supposed secrets of head lice, allegations of lesbic (this was Vi's word) inclinations, and rumours of disturbed and disturbing methods of masturbation were their touchés.

'Old Miss Trubshaw, their pugilist martinet of a Brownie Brown Owl, noted that their intertwined paths and mirrored lofty and lordly family backgrounds might have been one reason for the hostility. Opposites attract, and all that.

'Supposedly, Margaret and Violet's clans were both of Teutonic root, and given the fulcrum of the twentieth century that the Germans inhabited, mumbles, whispers and innuendo followed. It would soon be suspected by the well informed that both girls had Nazi sympathisers within their familial grasp; King Edward's dubious leanings were founded in the Saxe-Coburg bloodlust and ravenous military stance. It had already

---

* *Fucking German fart.*

been widely written by the mealy of mouth that I had been
accused of spying for Germany.'

Edward nodded, and smiled to himself.

'Well, on the warring girls' tenth birthdays, Margaret had
had a Balmoral servant purchase a classified advertisement in
The Times.

Violet Fagg ist der faulige Produkt von einer Orgie des
Satans. Ihr Atem ist der Beweis dafür.*

'Princess Margaret had then mysteriously contracted a procession of illnesses, one after the other: whooping cough,
mumps, influenza, common colds, tonsillitis, chickenpox,
pneumonia, foot-and-mouth and measles. She had remained
seriously ill for a full year, too unwell to travel to Canada to
take refuge from the war, as had been planned in secret. Her
father, who was now king, had allowed *The Times* and the
BBC to lead with a story about how they would never abandon Britain. The truth had been actually quite different, for
the Duchess of York refused to go without their children, and
he would, in turn, not go without her. Margaret's illness thus
had kept the King at home.

'Their pretence of courage and fortitude had been largely a
façade, for *I* had had the idea† to bring Margaret down with
her ailments, and had kept the Royals in Britain. This plan
was instrumental in propping up morale and therefore winning the war. If the Royals had gone in those flimsy days, the

---

* *Violet Fagg is the putrid product of an orgy of Satan. Her breath is the proof of this.*

† *I was in Germany and so the Princess was exposed to a series of bacteria and viruses by a friendly and bearded doctor, who smelt of brioche and had a strange French surname. Rasputin had also used his leverage on a regent's child, it might be noted.*

country might likely have folded. Keep that Margaret girl in England, and we might even win the war; *this* was my perversely simplified formula.'

I looked for my son's reaction, and he seemed only mildly impressed.

'I tell you, I was an oracle and a genius; a towering and magisterial *orcneas* to shame Beowulf, the Greek gods and all of their second-rate illegitimii.

'Vi and I had saved the world, and it was a habit that would become tough to break, for any drug addict worth his salt shall insist with absoluteness upon chasing that elusive dragon. I had become hooked on righteousness. I wanted more.'

He remained impassive again. We stared at each other, before once more synchronising that loud and (possibly) annoying laugh from that same old third-rate play and tired director, whom, by now, I simply adored.

13.4 A DAY AT THE RACES

We sat on the decks for days. He spoke for hours on end too. Sometimes Violet even deigned to join us and listen, though I knew the proximity of the schoolboys meant that she was driving them to distraction, and we were nothing more than handy bodyguards right now. As we neared Ceylon, I thought of how marvellous it would be to anchor there, hitch a ride to the ambassador's and march into the jungles to find the monastery and the resin. How ironic that a vicious civil war prevented us from reaching the second-most pacific spot on Earth. Instead, she passed us on our left one evening, as I spoke to Edward on the subject of British royalty.

'The Third Reich had fallen by the time the girls had turned fifteen; Japan had surrendered just days before their birthdays. Violet had developed an impressively burgeoning taste for laudanum, opium and cannabis. I had encouraged and then fed this hunger, while I successfully implicated Edward and that horror Wallis Simpson in many Nazi sideshows. Thanks to me, we all know now about the abdicator and his apologist stance towards Berlin and rampant homoerotic fondness for the Führer.

'Just after the war, at Royal Ascot, I approached Wallis in a false beard and my hooded cloak, which I wore as a metaphor as well as the obvious and perverse joy I took in being a mere cliché. "People are so unimaginative, Vi darling" I used to tell her.

'The usually officious clerk on the Royal Enclosure's gate allowed me to pass (of course he did) and the timing of my arrival, upon which I prided myself, was impeccable. Wallis and Edward were in the throes of one of their usual and very public spats, which she invariably dominated. She was just lifting her chin and peering down at the former king with a rank anger, when she said within earshot of all, 'I am a very large fish in a very small pond. You goddamned English think you are so superior."

'There was an embarrassed and awkward hush. Edward, the servile slug, cowered, as did most of English society present, though their reason was a silent politeness; his was either fear or tipsiness. I, the corpulent, heavily bearded stranger with the shifted shape in the sack cloth threw back the deep hessian hood to reveal a head of Scandinavian blond mop, pinkened and skewed eyes, and the obligatory fat neck, for this is harder to hide.

'As our noses almost touched, I said to her in the well-educated and Slavic accent of a St Petersburg count as she began to quiver, "Oh! I simply must disagree. Your gamy pond has long ago dried up, ma'am and you are sadly a fish which has irreversibly curdled and turned. You might go on with your little dinner parties and dances with people who don't count and who are doomed anyway to perish in their own stupidity. You are a feculent and noxious strumpet and would be vastly improved by sudden death, which I should be most pleased to arrange with either one amateur spell or a sharp blow to your wattled and brittle neck. Which should it be?"

'The regent-unelect whispered an almost inaudible *hurrah* as Mrs Simpson's head rouged to scarlet and her chiselled and famous fury gave her the mien of a well-carved beetroot, as mauve as my stratagem. There was no answer, and if there had have been, I would have vanquished regardless. Society chuckled over the scene for months with the vocal Lord Mountbatten most chuffed at this intriguing intruder's appearance and audacity. His *Find the Stranger* campaign in the *London Evening Standard* came to naught. Of course it did.

'Violet would borrow this quip of the putrid fish for Margaret, when, on my behalf, I had Dandylyon and Prudence induce a premature (yet temporary) menopause in the Princess for her seventeenth birthday. For a few months, they replaced her productive ovaries with a penchant for cheap-ish sherry. Such choice and ill-lit behaviour brought Violet such joy, when she was quoted, via an accomplice of an editor, in a weekend rag that Margaret was "rarely anything but diaphragm-deep in booze and syphilitic man phlegm". That Violet was behind both the dependency on grog and a lack of a need for a diaphragm forced the Princess to weep for the first time because of her nemesis. When the journalist had spluttered at her use of the term *man phlegm*, Vi had cruelly added. "Yes. She gargles it almost incessantly, in an attempt to be loved by some sentient creature; you know, a sailor . . . or someone." When pressed to continue, Vi mumbled, "That Prussian cowbag has never worn the same pair of knickers once."'

The confidence rattling around inside Violet was a torrid beast, which required harnessing, but once allied might be such an ebullient and vanquishing force . . .

Edward, it seemed, was quite pleased to watch Violet flourish in this vein, with not a hint of a sibling competition, while he sat back, studied and measured, breathed deeply, smiled at strangers and avoided conflict at almost any cost.

13.5 A Whiff of Fledged Wheat

We arrived in the port of Chittagong and then travelled on by small plane.

As my old foes likely imagined, with glee, my rotting and boxed corpse under some Hastings muck, we landed in Yunnan Province at night-time. We were told to rest for several hours there in the cabin, so we dutifully slept, and woke in the aircraft at dawn. Our troop of eleven (Violet, Edward, Zealand, seven Sherpas and I) then took a small truck for fifty miles over increasingly rough lands until we were told that the walking would begin. We stopped by a small clearing, where a sedan chair to be carried by four of the Sherpas was tilted against a white-bark pine, a spectacular plant made all the more alluring for her ability to thrive above the tree-line where most trees cannot. Perhaps the white-bark pine trees and I were kindred spirits. Was this chair for *me?* Not bloody likely, as I told them to 'Eff awwf.'

I even offered to carry the Sherpas. I knew their language well from the Scottish Mountaineering Club expeditions here, when, according to the English press, I was supposed to have buggered, murdered and then eaten those two coolies. And so our march to Shangri-La began. It took three days at a fair pace. There were moments when a lesser kind might have questioned the wisdom had one not been armed with a full assurance from the coolies that we were close, this next slope would be as tough as it got, and we would be quite thrilled with the destination.

Shortly after dawn on the third day, the first truly calm one of the three, we passed through a narrow hole in the ice, away from the cliff that dropped perhaps three thousand feet. It was barely five feet high and not easy for a chap with my bay-window girth, but this was the final barrier to our nirvana, for then we walked onto a high lea side that was temperate and green. We were greeted by a distant birdsong, and the whiff of fledged wheat.

And as I meditated out in the meadow before we reached the citadel, I again felt a presence nearby; one that entered my world as had a stinking Grigori in St Petersburg and a soaked Mowgli by Loch Ness. This sensation was far different to the hum of the Holy Man. It was the glowing aura of Orr. He was now slightly crooked, and he smiled at me from that perpetual wellspring of benevolence that may well have been a pre-requisite to fire and fuel that quite enormous frame of his. When I had wiped a tear from my eye, he held me and said, 'Welcome, my friend. Come, I know where your Leah and your La Gitana shall be at this time of day. They are quite inseparable, you'll be thrilled to see.'

And then time would lose all meaning. I thought of the future. If I had been truly prescient and clairvoyant, I would have seen myself recounting the future tale of Margaret. It is a tale called LOVE.

13.6 LOVE
In early April 1953, a message, passed by hand on the wet cobbles of Albemarle Street, was hand-delivered to Bucking-ham Palace. It read,

M.

It was Easter Sunday in the plumb line of that momentous and cardinal afternoon.

I saw you dancing at the Savoy.

You imposing and abstract marvel, I have to have you.

I shall molest you.

The note was unsigned, but held an aroma of a man in his prime. In her chambers, Margaret rouged and moved in her seat, as she peered with an adolescent thrill out over Green Park. The nefarious and wilful missives continued, always in the same assured and assuring hand, always addressed to M., always unsigned. Their tone remained polite-ish and complimentary, yet somewhat sexually unleashable and demanding, sparkish, capable and potent. They would come in violent and inflamed spurts. Then nothing for weeks. Then they would begin again. They followed the highly charged distribution of an aroused and kindled serial killer. On Christmas Day, 1953, hundreds of the most fragrant white Persian tuberoses, a gradient of zero at their true zenith of potency, were flung over the Palace garden walls, an envelope taped to the brick wall at the Hyde Park Corner end of Constitution Hill. Inside there was a note,

M.

Think of me always.

I have to go away, for there are wars to be fought, and I am a soldier of twisted and perverse fortune.

A thousand and one nights should, if I control my and our future as I believe I do, see my return.

I intend to appear and make myself known to you, for this to date has been forbidden by *them*.

I intend to love you and maul you, in a way that princesses desire but never experience, due to vicious custom.

You shall rise high above this, for ours shall be an ancient and bestial custom. You are my *transcendante*.

You should indeed be worried, for the fall from our love shall not be recoverable.

There are no security measures in such precipitous elevation.

This cannot be avoided. It is written. Here and by me, and my tenacious word is the Truth.

We shall however be the happiest of people, my exalted darling.

Three years were to pass and Margaret heard and received nothing. Her womanliness had been stirred by a non-conductor, for such motion had not prevented rampant simmering and brimming. Her appetite for men became well known to the plebs most Sundays it seemed, over deadly cooked breakfasts and full ashtrays and through steamed, rain-splattered café windows via seemingly endless exposés in the *News of the World* and the *Sunday Mirror*.

MAGS IN PARK SEX SCANDAL (August 1954)
ROYAL BOOZE BUNK-UP ORGY (November 1954)
THE PRINCESS AND THE PEE (January 1955)

The Palace had fought back, let's not kid ourselves. Theirs is a brutal and unforgiving propaganda mangle, which labelled me, yes *me*, as 'the wickedest man in world'. If only they had the nous to realise this tag would regularly crease me around my girthy centre until I could laugh no more, for sometimes I was (in which case, thanks for the nod) and sometimes I wasn't (in which case, they really were just exposing themselves as the viciously inbred mongoloids they really were/are). I love myself for many things, but my ability to stick my chest out, my chin up and my shoulders back, and to tell the goddamned world that it is not fit to sit in judgement on my preternatural exquisiteness shall stick with me to my dying day.

Then in the first week of 1957, the thaw in her iced romance finally arrived. In public, Margaret held back the instincts of an awakened and animated beast. In private, one might only guess at the bubbling agitation. The simple note read:

M.
    Meet me at the Savoy in suite 346.* At 9 p.m. Saturday. I shall be yours.

There was never any doubt in Margaret's mind that she would be there and at that time. Precisely and as requested, submission was inevitable. She left the Palace an hour early and drove herself to The Strand, already half-cut on sherry. She wore a headscarf and dark glasses, for, like the brazen runaways checking in as Mr and Mrs Smith, and I in my hooded cloth at the races, Margaret too knew the benefit of overt cliché. The car keys to her white Bentley were handed to the stunningly bored bell captain at the hotel who, smelling the booze on her breath, took it for a lengthy spin around the Royal parks, blaring its horn outside Knightsbridge mews houses and Kensington mansions of several easily pleased lasses he had recently explored. By the time he planned to pull back in to The Strand, Margaret ought to be about to meet

---

*   Suite 346 was one of Wilde and Lord Douglas' rooms, though this would turn out to be mere coincidence.

her deviant tormentor. But for now, she listened to the pianist in the ballroom play Rachmaninov's tricky third with remarkable aplomb on a white grand, a Grotrian-Steinweg, and she stroked the deep aqua-blue velvet twirls on the cerulean flock wallpaper by the bar. Was that Monroe in the lobby? Margaret lit another cigarette, and nodded her head to the barman to serve her one last sherry.

Who was up there? What was he doing at this very moment? What were his scarlet intentions? Was her life about to change? Would they soon instead be writing of the torridity of the love affair of the century in those tawdry and vulgar Sunday gimcrack rags? Such sweet and chilled revenge.

Her hands were steady, but she felt that her left knee may buckle when she began to walk towards the lobby and then the lift at 8:58 p.m. She clipped over the fairy-lit oak parquet flooring that, according to hotel lore, had been made famous by Dietrich having made love on it five times. Margaret had been well groomed in betraying no nerves in public, but this shadowy admirer of vast compulsion had exposed, to her own surprise, one or two viciously fragile and rankly irresolute links in her supposedly robust regal chains.

Margaret recalled her old music teacher's words on Rachmaninov's masterpiece, 'The second movement is opened by the orchestra and it consists of a number of variations around a single lush, heavily romantic melody following one another without a rigid scheme.' She now restructured his repeated instruction in her mind, and chuckled to herself, allowing her and her sherry to overrule the wobble in her knee. 'Around a single lush', 'heavily romantic', 'without a rigid scheme'.

The lights on the digits above the lift door indicated that it was stuck up on the sixth floor, and remained there longer than any normal or selfless person would require to pass through an open door. It eventually departed the sixth, stopped on the fifth for thirty more seconds of semi-pleasurable anticipation and semi-painful consternation, and then the third for a regulation stop. Were her bowels on edge? *Oh Margaret, get a grip, girl.*

The Princess concentrated instead on the concerto's third movement: its overt digression, its willing recapitulation and its astonishingly triumphant crescendo to an unrivalled visceral-rattling toccata climax. Her highly conductive centre stirred now for other reasons, and she felt a chilled bead of sweat squeeze through onto her inflamed temple.

Margaret welcomed the lift on the ground floor and stepped inside. She thought she could smell white Persian tuberoses, and indeed she could. Her watch showed a minute past the hour, as a young bellhop first looked shocked to be seeing a princess, and then asked, 'Which floor please, ma'am?' She told him. He pressed three, and as the elevator moved, the knee twinged once more. Her eye muscle twitched, her mouth dried. She bit the side of her mouth to create saliva, a trick once taught to her father when he had had trouble making speeches during the war. She thought she could smell the young boy's body odour now, and indeed she could. The frisky sapphire-blooded mare was highly and finely tuned that brisk January night in 1957. She was now third in line to the throne, but remained as bawdy and as thrummable as any young fox of her flowered age. Her doctors had even noted an increase in her gourmande libido, as her proximity to the real milieu of power allowed her to inhale its unmistakeable musk.

She did not knock.

She walked in to the room. And she stood. Caught in time. Processing each word of every penned letter she had received over the Palace walls for three years, computing the significance of each bellowed threat to love, while sniffing at the heavy scent of tuberoses, as the tic in her cheek abated and the tight gripped fist loosened, allowing whitened fingers to softly pinken, and her spine to relax, as rapture and joy neared. After several seconds that seemed like an age to her, she spoke, quite involuntarily, relieved to know of her immediate and passionate nights.

'Oh, it's *you!*'

There *she* sat, beneath a pair of twenty-four-light chandeliers. Behind *her,* an open fire waned, but still launched and spat out, with a comforting rhythm, potent embers of peril.

(Did the room hold an essence of brioche and green apples? And was a door to a connecting room just being pulled to?)

Her surprise at seeing Violet was drawn and coaxed from her, sucked out like a snake's toxin. It was not mesmerism as such, but it was a close relative.

Margaret lost all signs of nervousness in her eye and knee, and stood relieved by the side of the large bed.

She smiled, as if she had always known. Violet, too, smiled. There was a whiff of opium she thought, and the sound of a roaring Bentley through the open doors and windows which looked out onto Savoy Place, the Embankment and the Thames. The driver, who might have glanced up and into the palatial rooms of the Savoy, might have thought he saw two womanly shapes move towards each other, stroking the exposed skin on each other's neck, and embrace as if under a guiding and generous spell. The vast panes reached from the scarlet shag to the electric white ceiling via velvet curtains of wicked crimson, which moved in the evening chill, but the room remained warm. Of course it did.

My spies had noticed two old Royal Bedfordshires, as they slumped after dinner into two solid armchairs of teal in the deep blueness of the bar of the Savoy. One had commented on the tenderness of the beef, as the other shocked himself with the ferocity of his belch and looked embarrassed, but just for a second. They then discussed a Christmas Day just over forty-two years before, when the hard, hard men of the German *Wehrmacht* and the British Expeditionary Force had stepped out of the scabrous muddied trenches, compared guns, smoked tobacco and played football, and how they had stayed there far longer and with far more humanity than we have ever been allowed to know. The two had been officers, who should not have approved of such treasonous and perilous behaviour, but thoroughly out of character, found a common ground in the perverse adoration of those to be found at the jagged precipice of death. And love.

> In the absence of willpower, the most complete collection of virtues and talents is wholly worthless.
>
> – Aleister Crowley

Chapter 14

New Friends & Monkey Business

The ordinary man looking at a mountain is like an illiterate person confronted with a Greek manuscript.

– Aleister Crowley

*E*dward has been a fine companion as I dictated Hag II to him. He knew it was never going to be a will-he-get-the-girl? affair. It was always more than that. This is clearing the name of a Pimpernel, while having the impossible conflict of fighting a perpetual scrap against evil, never able to wriggle free to pursue my own calm. But I know my life has been my own True Will. This always mattered more than the hundreds of love stories and thousands of afternoon entanglements.

Edward asks me, purposefully and volubly, if I am truly ready. I must not delay any more.

My son takes two phalanges of my corpulent left paw and tugs me along. I defer to his encouragement. My steps are light and elevated. I seem to float. I have felt this unblemished ecstasy before in far less angelic, far more tarnished company.

I speak as I move towards my doom.

14.1 Shangri-La

After a lengthy embrace with Orr, which might have appeared minutely comically given his huge frame, we turned to the others. I still referred (quite fondly) to Edward (now almost thirty) and Violet (in her late teens) as 'Children' and Zealand as 'Dearest Papa', but in the tone of my calling Leah, 'Monster' or Frog, 'Frog'.

'Children, Dearest Papa. My dear old collaborator, Orr. Orr, my children and friend.'

For us, the pleasantries were tinged with a euphoric relief and exhaustion from the journey, while Orr exhibited the boyish excitement that those golden midges had shown us as we had crossed the threshold in to the grounds of that Sicilian abbey many years before.

We turned and began to walk towards the outer reaches of the citadel, of which we enjoyed a full panoramic view. I thought of that sage old bull's advice to the aroused young bull on the hillside, and I chuckled at volume. Violet nudged me in the ribs, for I sense she knew my precise thought.

Orr now seemed to truly revel in the role of welcomer and tour guide as we walked on. He threw his arms wide to announce the work of art and majesty before us. My initial inspiration was admittedly a mixed one, for Shangri-La appeared to speak of the sadness of man that such an oasis was required, but far, far more of the quite stirring determination of the hundreds and thousands who had brought the wood, the metals, the tools, the treasures, the books and the spirit of adoration up here. It was a large plateau that spread out before us, perhaps ten miles by five. Were it to be any broader or longer, it seemed that it would be unlikely to benefit from its sheltering high mountain walls. It started with this measured perfection and this good fortune of nature, and then seemed to have that same fine fluke permeate every aspect.

The results were the blessings of warmth, wind, fertility and calm onto each square foot of the place, as well as, according to Orr and everything I had read, each simultaneous second on every perfect pathway, in each chamber, on each lea or pasture and in every temple. In short, there was no hiding from bliss and serenity, the silent rapture and the beauty.

Orr's enthusiasm in showing us all around on that day and the days that followed, introducing us to grinning kids and wise old types, barely masked the thrill he seemed to exude at knowing we would be there for a long time.

He had been alerted to our arrival by a dropped consignment from the Royal Air Force, though such sorties remained rare and reasonably perilous in those early days. Orr carried an air of authority, comported himself so that others certainly seemed aware of his vast presence. The children's joyous pitch was lowered, almost to a hush, when they ran past us or we strolled through their outdoor classrooms. He seemed to be aware that I was noticing this deference in all we encountered.

'You all must know of the character, Chang, from the book.* I suppose I am his equivalent. So much of what Hilton wrote is quite accurate.'

'It suits you well, my friend,' I said, as we marched on along cobbled paths between tulip trees, weeping willows, trickling brooks and cultivated and encouraged weeds. We have much to catch up on. But, crikey, we now have plenty of time to do it.'

'Yes, Aleister. We do,' and he threw a lanky arm around my shoulder and yanked me close.

'And the High Lama?' asked Zealand.

Orr stopped and turned to look down benevolently and curiously at the old man. He then shifted his gaze down to me,

---

* *Chang was a trusted official of the High Lama in* Lost Horizon.

nestled between his armpit and bicep. Each comfortable regard lasted perhaps ten seconds. He then turned back to looking at Zealand, and a soft, guttural chortle left his throat as if he had seen the future and everything was going to be fucking marvellous.

As we continued at a comfortable stroll, I was aware that we were not meandering, but instead heading in a very meas-ured but quite determined straight line. I knew he was taking me, first and foremost, to my Scarlet Women.

We first heard their giggling through the trees, Then, as we were spewed out into four-foot daisies and half-a-dozen whor-ing sparrows of a voyeuristic bent enjoying a fine day, I found *them* on a warm meadow of soft gradient. Leah's head was on La Gitana's thigh. They were still *young*.

It was only when I was twenty feet away from them that I realised the others had withdrawn, leaving me to take the last few steps alone to my destiny. Never had solitude felt so bloody welcome.

My loves. My darlings. I am home.

And so, this old Beast, this Sir Percy Blakeney, would (sort of) now zip up his flies and take his berth in a mountain paradise, a halfway house to the heavens, free from the ravages of a mean world. My only responsibility was to enjoy my family and friends, old and new, and meditate myself towards the Godhead. I thrilled at the thought of my hours at the type-writer or dictating to my Thelemic children or pals from a fat hammock.

When one had first acclimatised there, one had adjusted to the elevated nature of the oasis. The air was thin, but as we were protected on all sides by mountains and ridges, the fair weather was almost perpetual. We were protected from winds, while receiving an adequate and well-measured rainfall. We were in an unceasingly cushioned springtime that reminded one of perfect boyhood days and also provided the finest grapes for excellent wine. The brain took a day or two to marry this most clement climate with the strong winds we had faced on those narrow ledges by thousand-foot ice-drops. Soon after having arrived there, it was quite easy to lose the concept that we were surrounded by precipitous danger. We were constantly at the gentle core of the most vicious maelstrom, but all we felt was the calm. The brain can play the most marvellous and welcome tricks, this much I had always known.

As with telling of Rasputin, Churchill, Adolf and me, it was always tough not to drift over into cliché when observing my new home. The fine Goan incense was never too strong or overpowering, the fat candles in the temples never seemed to drip wax or shrink, the white doves were persistently fluttering nearby, and the large stone Buddhas never felt a drop of their bird shit. The outdoor schoolrooms by splashing fountains aided learning of the keenest young minds behind grinning chops. After school, the scamps ran through the perennial blossoms of springtime to the hot springs and waterfalls. The knees below short trouser hems were muddied but never bloodied. The boys and girls knew no word for doctor, misery or servant.

The rare treasures from the modern world, which had been delivered by porters from below, were tokens of gratitude for the loving types the mountain loft had given to the towns and cities around there. Gold was in the earth, but carried no value.

Leah had healed quite magnificently, and we now spent our days enmeshed with La Gitana. It seemed only right.

'We put it down to diet, climate, mountain water and, more than anything, the absence of struggle,' Monster told me, as the three of us lit a potent reefer one dusk, still entwined.

414   The Deaths and Afterlife of Aleister Crowley

'Here we see the indirect suicide of our ways of life down there,' said La Gitana.

Leah spoke the words of the much-vaunted Father Perot. It seemed that each inhabitant knew these words as we would know the national anthem or the Lord's Prayer.

> I saw all the nations strengthening, not in wisdom but in the vulgar passion to destroy and exalting in the techniques of murder and rage. Look at the world today, is there anything more pitiful? What madness there is, and what blindness. A scurrying mass of bewildered humanity, crashing headlong against each other, propelled by an orgy of greed and brutality. The time must come, when this orgy will spend itself, when brutality and the lust for power must perish by its own sword. When that day comes the world must begin to look for a new life and it is our hope that they will find it here, with their books and their music and the way of life based on one simple rule. BE KIND. When that day comes, it is our hope that the brotherly love of Shangri-La shall spread throughout the world. Yes, my son, when the strong have devoured each other that pure and Christian ethic will finally be fulfilled and the Meek shall inherit the Earth.

My days and the passing of time were as clichéd as the setting. But the oft-maligned cliché is sometimes just a cliché for a very good reason. It is true.

I meditated, read, wrote, taught the unblemishable children, schooled them in languages, science and art and then, with Orr's assistance, blindfolded chess. I lectured them and took questions on the scriptures of all stripes, and lauded nature to them, not that they needed this; I just could not help myself. I walked barefoot, ate minimally from the crops of our fields, sat in shaded meadows, where I received daily visits from midges and sparrows. You know of my goats, and the presence of several old chums, with whom I would spend auspicious and shining hours, days and seasons. I was ecstatic in the knowledge that I had deserved my dotage and was able to extend it to demigod-like proportions. My stone chambers were sparse, but for the further cliché of legions of books and an unused pair of hand-woven sandals beneath a simple writing bureau of feather, sheet and ink. There were no clothes there, so the hessian sack on my back and to my knees was my sole robe.

Violet was twitchy, of course. But she was also youthful and sprightly and determined enough to visit me for six months of every year, as she challenged herself with the true familial spirit of bloody mindedness to suffer the cleanliness and the noble holiness of my lair. She was mastering that sensational bipolarity of, on the one hand, self-deprivation of one's own desires in Shangri-La (see Sir Percy Blakeney), followed by a feast of depravity down below (see Aleister Crowley, The Great Beast, 666, Perdurabo). My, how she adored Edward and Zealand, for they were quite the contrast to my marvellous poisoned spawn of delicious malintent, my Violet.

And those fine men and best friends – one from the obverse seed of the gentle and high-born Roberta – quite marvelled at Violet's persistent wickedness. I saw them watch her with the intrigue afforded a controlled scientific experiment or a transgressive chimp. Her impishness found favour, of course, even with or without the umbra of her father's vastness. I wondered whether in isolation, Violet would have been brawling even in Shangri-La, but I afforded her broad latitude to err with her measured crassness and her ignoble tendency to blaspheme, curse and eye the locals with a pansexual's glare. Forgiveness is a fine state.

But something quietly nagged at me. For decades, I had been missing my TRUE dreams by inches. I wondered now why, when in utter bliss, would this feeling persist?

14.2 Meanwhile . . . Here Comes Trouble

Winston, like I, had resurrected himself. With typical verve and ballsiness, he had won a general election and served another four-year term* as prime minister of Great Britain and Northern Ireland.

When he finally left office, he was left scratching himself in that big house by Hyde Park Corner, bored and in need of a pastime. He wrote to me, at length. The letter took two months to reach Shangri-La. Like that castaway with his single message from a lone bottle, I reread these words many times, laughing, twitching with excitement and verve. I could imagine his face as he penned it, determined and wicked.

> Should we have some fun, Beast? You and I put our
> aged minds to mischief? Recruit some like-minded
> renegades? This idea of mine, which I am about to
> outline, can be a fine vessel for Thelema, you know.
> Prudence is sitting opposite me as I scribble, and is
> purring at the prospect of it all. *They* both send their
> adoration, of course.

And so at my prompting, he and I from very different worlds of London and Shangri-La, on the fifteenth day – a Monday – of April 1957, launched the *London Review of Passion*, and therein was the editor's playful and devilish column called 'Six Fingers & Fat Thumbs'. For us, this general monkey business would be a new *époque* of perhaps sedentary, but yet quite

---

* *From 1951 to 1955.*

rogue behaviour. The Sherpas in-and-out of Shangri-La now left and arrived (with our communiqués) every three weeks, instead of every two years. These intrepid couriers and then the telegram (or vice versa) were our only link between HQ and this Himalayan bureau chief.

The *LRP*'s arrival was greeted with intrigue, for no one in England (well, no one who was not a keen Thelemite) knew the identity of any of the owners, publishers, editor or scribes. This spectre was elusive and like smoke to hold. In the spirit of Count Svareff prodding Manhattan in the Great War, it really got the buggers talking. Imagine if they only knew it was an ex-prime minister and a dead Satanist – and a small tight unit of wordy Thelemites, who dined with Winston twice weekly – writing to them fortnightly. I worked on more philosophical and less time-sensitive articles. Winston read all of the papers daily, had a busy satellite office in that library in his Hyde Park Corner mansion, and was the lightning rod and nerve centre for the operation. He provided me briefs for editorials that might be of interest six months later. We had so much fun, and I felt, as I wrote in my solitude, as if I was still seeing him every day.

THE NIGHT I SAW RASPUTIN FIGHT A BEAR
(15 April 1957)
ASTRAL PROJECTION – A GUIDE FOR CHILDREN
(24 June 1957)
W. B. YEATS – NEW RUMOURS OF RAMPANT
PLAGIARISM & LOW-LEVEL BESTIALITY
(9 December 1957)
REDEFINING OUR WORLD (A.K.A. ALL THE -*ISMS*
ARE NOW -*WASMS*) (20 January 1958)

*

In London, Winston set up and maintained a façade of mystery around the whole publication. Submissions were always delivered by hand to the magazine's perpetually empty head office (apart from one spotty fourteen-year-old messenger lad on five shillings) in Berners Street, W1 and generally by 3 p.m. on Wednesday afternoons, close to the paper's deadline. Of course, this was not necessary as they were sending them to themselves, but Winston reckoned that the more they could fuck with the minds of any competitors or nosy-types, the better. It worked, as column inches by the score were dedicated to us in *The Times,* the *Manchester Guardian,* the *Telegraph* and the *Evening Standard.*

The submitted articles were always typed on solid-stock and embossed paper. The Crowleyian and Churchillian missives often contained pencilled or green-inked amendments and margin notes, as well as red wine, cigarette burns and what the writers knew to be stains of the finest goulash outside of the Magyar kingdom,* while rivalling many from within. The battered but precious contents came in a fine veneer, a vellum envelope, meticulous calligraphy and a lilac wax stamp on the reverse. The seal was of a Hungarian cossack, that organisation of illiberal violence so well suited to and moulded by their wholly vicious terrain. In those days, they were always signed with a single lilac *T.*

The editor and the publisher claimed in their copy that they did not know the identity of the supplier(s) of the editorials. The reader did not know the identity of all three: journalist, editor, publisher.

---

* *The famous Hungarian restaurant, The Gay Hussar on Greek Street in Soho.*

COCAINE – A GUIDE FOR PROVINCIALS
(18 August 1958)

IS BENITO MUSSOLINI STILL ALIVE? – EXCLUSIVE &
HARROWING PICTURES (12 January 1959)

HIGH HITLER AND THE GAME HERMAPHRODITE
(9 March 1959)

All the publisher would reveal was that he/she did exactly as he/she was asked by the contributors, to deposit a cheque each week into the account of the Kensington Butterfly Zoo. The owners of the place had been pressed in each issue by the *LRP* to increase the size of its enclosures. Now they had the funds and would soon, they promised, possess the largest butterfly enclosure in the Western world. At that precise time, this had been the funniest thing that Sir Winston and I, just two of the new team of senior editors, had ever heard.

Yes, just two, because by the time the *London Review of Passion* celebrated its third birthday on April the fifteenth, 1960, in private of course and at The Gay Hussar, that number had increased. Three new executives were penning politically precise, rebellious-of-spirit and bawdy, jocular pieces in each edition. They were three pre-eminent names in the world of cinema. I really ought to thank that fine lad, Dibdin for his urgings and promptings in having delivered to Six Fingers, Marlene Dietrich, Alfred Hitchcock and Orson Welles. I began to think, for the first time, that I might even like to come down from my lair to join this renegade mob. But life up in Shangri-La was such a delight. Such a delight. The grass was literally greener up there.

And it stayed that way for over four years, during which from those leas of ragweed and grass, and the pastures of sunflowers and billy goats, I regularly told a thrumming Violet and the nodding boys of our new revolutionary front, catapulted into the consciousness by the columns of 'Six Fingers & Fat Thumbs'. Our fight, aided by three cineastes of true stature, was not, I always insisted, unleashed against the Soviets, but, through the brave types we had recruited in Hollywood, Greek Street, a resurgent UFA Film in Berlin, and Cinecittà Studios in Rome, we now were fighting instead the meanness of McCarthyism and Cold War paranoia, which was the *reaction* to our own meddling of seven decades earlier. This was a quiet and dignified revolution of the mind through the movies.

And I would have stayed there forever, but in the May of 1964, Violet touched my hand as I meditated, and kissed me tenderly on the forehead. I knew something was wrong. The newspaper in her hand had been dropped by the RAF, and had been intended for me. When I saw the formation of a tear in my unshakeable girl's eye, I knew it was as serious as it could be.

I read the headline.

CHURCHILL ON DEATHBED

At the age of eighty-nine but with the rejuvenated appearance of a fifty-year-old, heavily disguised as a lumbering and aristocratic Norseman of unquestionably sapphire-blooded lineage, and urged on by the undiminishable love of a challenge and of a mountainside, Violet and I resolved to return to London and to England to say farewell to my great friend.

14.3 OUR BLESSED VESSEL FOR THELEMA

The journey home was easy. We rolled down that mountain like gambolling goats, Chittagong welcomed us and spewed us out to sea. Winds were forgiving. There was no storm in which to sully myself, naked on a mast and in front of my daughter. Instead, I wrote by day and night for the magazine. The soft ocean air on one's face was so conducive to producing a vast output. We were in Deptford in less than two weeks, and I carried an armful of typed-up articles and features.

The diatribes in the *LRP* were often commentaries on many aspects of London life, but, given the curriculum vitae of the contributors, 'Six Fingers & Fat Thumbs', now a column of length that often seemed to be ingesting the magazine, soon revelled and relished in the cinematic and artistic review. When I finally met them all, the first impression I had of their literary intent was that the three of them seemed to enjoy discussing paedophobia, whenever feasible and appropriate. Stuff like *The Bad Seed* and *The Lord of the Flies*. They, like me, knew that all of life's wonders and horrors began in childhood.

To the average reader, the writing style seemed to change, as if the penman were schizophrenic or it were the work of criticism by committee. Both were perhaps correct as Orson and Alfred shared the joy of a direct and pedestalled platform to the citadel. And, of course, they were always polite enough to never change their bawdy ribaldry when Marlene breached their smoky and degenerate lair, bringing her unmatchable thoughts and unrivallable *cassoulette* to their tables at The Gay Hussar.

Our editorial, I liked to think, carried real merit to a readership that appreciated *sensation*; not in the cheap and tawdry and gratuitous sense of the word. Sensation*alism* was supremely unwelcome, for we were measured and disciplined artists. This was not to say that we were, by any stretch, conservative. I would hope this is clear by now. We were unafraid of shocking, we revelled in it, lived for it, but never without foundation and a truly deserving target. We meant *sensation* in the truest form of the word – whether it was the needle-like Sicilian raindrops of a summer storm on the face, the spiciest goulash at the Hussar, any part or action of that high priestess, that Marlene woman, or sitting on the Hillary Step with a young Sherpa, recently satisfied and smoking on a vast pipe of ecstatic hashish.

Hitch and I decided to expand on an old Mussolini article. We called it:

MUSSOLINI FROM BEYOND THE DUNGEON OR GRAVE

The concept was a simple one. Il Duce was still alive, being drip-fed utter malice and kept hostage somewhere in Europe by those whom he had slighted. His captors had allowed him a nib and some fine stationery once a week to beg for his tormented life and to describe his quite subhuman conditions as comfort to all those sisters, wives, daughters, sons, brothers and mothers who missed their brave Giuseppe or Benvenuto. Just what would the old Fat Head have to say to his mother, to Italy and to God? Well, the good folk of London town found out on a fortnightly basis.

We exposed oppressive governments, juntas, prime ministers and presidents, as well as pederasts and frauds of any kind. We shone a light on reactionary and turgid freemasonry, that rancid old pastime and practice from which we had syphoned off the selfish cuntery. Thelema had catapulted the finer, remaining aspects of it to marvelled heights of kindness, self-fulfilment, protest and transgression. We did all this over goulash in the Hussar, and in our own beds, from Hyde Park Corner to Dulwich, over buttered crumpets with Marmite and gut-warming Ovaltine.

Deep down, I knew that what we were doing was never going to ignite a revolution. It might provide fodder for the rebellious of spirit, but it was in those soggy Soho days that something started to take hold. It was a feeling that this might lead to something greater. Was this Samson yet again to test his biceps and take on the pillars of the temple?

And despite the sadness around Winston's pending death, it was otherwise a marvellous and celebratory time that year with those degenerates in Greek Street, and I know our continued plotting brought them great joy between the productions of their treasured movies.

They were such mauve days, such fun and treasured days, for I knew they would end as soon as Sir Winston Leonard Spencer-Churchill, KG OM CH TD PCc DL FRS RA passed away, and that day was surely coming. It was quite true that there was nothing like a funeral to concentrate the mind. Even more so with a best chum dying in a hospital bed, but my time in Shangri-La allowed for an even greater appreciation of time, down on the plane of mortals. It only went to underline Winston's true stature, with his unequivocal greatness and his highly evolved state, that he did not seek to prolong his life in the Himalayas.

And so, we treasured each day of that sparkling year, as I took my darling Violet on a tour of the seaside piers of England, to Cambridge, and back to the place of her conception and well-stewed birth by Loch Ness and my darling Boleskine. We watched cricket at Arundel, Scarborough and The Oval. Her aching princess, now sister to the Queen of England, would sometimes abruptly arrive on a country lane or in a first-class carriage to Eastbourne without announcement or warning. And I knew to leave them alone, as any gent or father would.

14.4 MARLENE AND ORSON

As keen cineastes gladly stuck in the mountain, Zealand and
Edward were keen to hear by tardy return courier of how our
days and nights were spent with these stars.

I wrote to them on August the fourth, 1964. Here is a sliver
of my dribble and gossip.

You know that I have been so inspired by my friend,
Orson. He might be the cleverest man I have ever met.
And having him on our side now shall thrust us
forward, but I am too long in the tooth and have too
much foresight to believe that cinema on its own can
bring the revolution of which I dream.

I think we ought to seek to morph, to swell and to
evolve from a basic and personal mantra of drugs, sex,
freedom and personal fulfilment into a mouthpiece of
the Revolution that would urge the peoples of the
world to rebel.

And for this, I would require more than pamphlets,
books, cumbersome newspapers and mountainside
orgies in front of intrigued and nodding wildlife. It
would all require even more than celluloid. And despite
this suitably motivated and intellectually capable team
of acolytes and mischief-makers, this is all just a
preparation. But it must happen soon, for I cannot last
forever down here in this gloried grime. I will have to
come back, and then the chance might be shot.

I SHALL have my world of peace and love! I
SHALL! I have not come this far, and foregone a
comfortable life of libraries, cricket pavilions, golden
retrievers, naps after breakfast, larking bairns, summers
at Lord's, eagerly fellatic weekend lads and top-notch
wives for it all to end without the greatest glory of a

truly transcendent planet Earth. What sort of fucking god would I be?

Lord, I love and miss you both, and all there in our treasured loft.

A month later, my beloved son quite admirably brushed off my bluster in an adorably brief letter.

Yes, Papa. But tell us of Orson? And of course, Marlene? The mothers and aunts in Halle so adored her.

On October the twenty-fifth, 1964, I indulged the nosy sods.

When I first met him, Orson had already revolutionised theatre, pulled the world's most marvellous and heralded radio stunt and completely baffled Senator McCarthy. Welles's whole life to date has been the most magnificent virtuoso performance. Not to mention masterpiece. He is a quite the actor too.

Citizen Kane is, after all in its simplest form, just a series of greys, but what intuitive divinity. No wonder Hayworth, Garland, Dietrich and vast squadrons of marvels have salivated over the joyously soaked hound. And he has had to put up with some of the most unlamentable and particularly uneducated louts Hollywood has ever mustered, and that is some feat. He is a colossus, who possesses, quite reluctantly, a philistine's doubt over philosophy. I once told him, 'You put your finger on a basic failing of all lazy people: they have to work too hard or they won't do anything at all. You know? Once I stretch out in a hammock, you'll

426 The Deaths and Afterlife of Aleister Crowley

never hear from me again, you know, because I like it that way.'

He has since adopted it, with my permission of course, and it seems equally applicable to us both, at the time and with hindsight. I wouldn't have it any other way. He neither, I am sure. Anyway, Hollywood is so fond of quoting itself. It is, after all, a mirage of frauds speaking other people's lines against false scenery with fake lighting, unless you do it all yourself like Welles does. Hollywood deals in derivatives. And death.

There is no coincidence that four of his great works have ended up with his execution in a sewer, with slaughter in a labyrinthine, mirrored funhouse, murder in a no man's land border town river and a great man fading away with secrets never to be told. He is a multitude of a man, I exalt him. He might be the most exaltable man of this pivotal century, and those studio heads, especially that primitive counterfeit scoundrel and fakery-meister Harry Cohn, simply cannot be excused for their filthy, bogus behaviour. The ever-generous Orson prefers to concentrate on those he admires: Cooper, Cagney and Garbo. General Marshall and Churchill.

I am now relishing the nostalgia. I do not move my arse as I write, nor do I give any clue that I am not luxuriating in my fondness for my friends.

We do not agree on everything. Bullfighting is a passion of his. Welles, not Churchill, you understand. (I just laughed out loud, son.)

But he is changing his mind eventually. The sign of a truly great man is one who evolves, you see. Yes, there's stubbornness and self-belief, but that can only ever get a man so far. To really elevate oneself and crush those

supernatural constraints, agility of spirit and of mind
and, sadly, of foot is so very vital. He tells me that
bullfighting is indefensible but irresistible. I am not
averse to or unfamiliar with such lures; I once had
published *The Diary of a Drug Fiend,* for heaven's sake.
And so, I have been very well acquainted with such
ritualistic behaviour as that of the toreador, but then
Orson hates that it has all become folkloric. These are
his words, not mine. I guess he looks up to that
matador Belmonte the way I look up to *him*. He has
slaughtered bulls, but, weirdly, he also loves them, like I
adore those perverse young goats of mine.

As for Marlene, well, she and I have become ace
chums, as we often stay up all night here in the Hussar,
and practise our German and smoke strong hashish.
The best nights and mornings are when Orson and
Hitch are here too.

Just this morning we were all so elegantly high on
cocaine that we each spoke of that which excited us
most, with almost little relevance to what the others
were saying. There were some egos on show, boosted
further by the powder, but we remained the soundest of
chums. Marlene spoke of her lighting, I spoke of
revolution, Orson spoke of bullying and scaring Senator
McCarthy and Hitch spouted on about murder. Of
course.

As a joyous and charged dawn of light drizzle broke
over Soho (Violet and Margaret had slipped away,
unable to keep their mitts off each other at the bar over
champagne cocktails, like strutting and moody
kangaroos) and three faithful Magyar waiters kept us
all topped up, comfortable and supremely welcome, I
could have kissed Marlene, as she leaned forward on

those elbows in her girlish thigh-high cotton, lemon-yellow frock, eyeing me closely, and breathed warm and womanly rafts, flavoured by wine and tinged by desirous hormones. 'You know, Aleister. I am able to know if my lighting needs an extra ten degrees of tilt, while I am under it. I know more than any director who has directed me, and that includes Josef.'*

'This is a skill,' I admitted to her.

I looked at Orson, with his handsome widow's peak and bold eyes of serenity masking a darting brilliance.

I should have known better, for Orson, after a brief pause and fingering the loosened and drooping white bow tie around his starched collar, could simply not help himself.

'Yes, my dear. But I am able to pull off a far trickier feat. I know when I have hit my mark and whether I am . . . in FOCUS!'

The head-butting of such heavyweights has been our joy for these months, as we cannot get enough of each other, all aided by hillocks of vigorous and full-bodied cocaine that allows for our hours to become days. Your father is unlikely to change now, son.

'You know that I shall have my revenge for that, don't you, my dear,' she said to Orson with a chilling camaraderie. This was clear to anyone who knew her. Only my Marlene, the finest of Valkyries and so unreasonably perfect as Mata Hari, could have got away with seductively and audaciously adjusting her stockings before the firing squad as she did in

---

* *Von Sternberg directed her in seven films, most famously the provocatively entitled* Blue Angel *(1930); the* Blonde Venus's *cheekbones were far more memorable than the plots.*

Dishonored, sending grown men and women – aroused, hollow, remorseful and envious – to bed across the world, nation by nation, crying into their pillows. What a girl she remains.

Her casting as the clairvoyant in Orson's *Touch of Evil* had been her own inspired off-the-cuff idea, as was being Orson's lover, for she had executed the real-life act for the first time just minutes before the rushes on day one of shooting. Seeing into the future is easy for such women, for they always get precisely what they want.

Her line to him, 'You should lay off those candy bars. You're a mess, honey,' was remarkable ad-libbing that even silenced Welles. It remains four seconds of utter genius (almost matched by Orson's defeated and quite perfect mumble) and was just a touché in their persistent and fond battling and bating, just as was evident here at dawn today in the Hussar.

Orson nodded, acknowledged his debt, smiled at Marlene, and then, despite many bottles of Pálinka,* spoke with an intent and measure that even I found impressive. He was in a reflective mood, as he softly crowed.

'I know what I am doing too,' he said, his hands quite still despite a monumental intake of powder. 'You know that I bated that ass, McCarthy, and his thugs so much that they dared not ask me to testify in front of the House Committee. This was probably because I was constantly asking to do just that. They suspected that I might outwit them as I had been doing every day for

---

* *A strong fruit brandy from the Carpathian Basin.*

years and for fun. Well, I clearly already had. I was the
only one who was never asked to give evidence. You
would have been so proud of this Thelemite, Beast.'

Son, I tingle at the thought. One can never have
something like the cinema which impacts on and
lectures and moulds and moralises to the population all
the time, rolling through the weeks and years and
decades, without it being of central interest to bastards
like that senator. But it is curious that in response to
those nasty malfeasants, more was done for our cause
than any one person or event ever could. The mean
arseholes galvanised us and mobilised us in the name of
those millions of dead boys and girls in Europe, Africa
and the Pacific, who fought for the freedom he
threatened. I propose a toast in their honour and name.

Freedom. And our Revolution.

I shall see you soon, boys.

Your father and friend,

Beast

14.5 HITCH

I suspected I knew what they would want to know of next. I
was right. They asked after that lardy barrow-boy we all knew
as Hitch.

The letter was dated January 17th, 1965.

I first met Hitch in the snug of The Crown pub in
WC2. He was sitting with a mob of actors, whom he
loved more than they would have you believe. I sat at
the end of the bar opposite to him, as I heard him say,
'That has never happened, but Aleister Crowley did
appear in my bathwater once.' The mob roared.

One of his firm, a gawky lad with veiny temples,

purple pimples and championly crossed eyes, recognised me beneath my favoured fedora of the age before I removed her. He whispered quite loudly that the Wickedest Man in the World was now over by the whisky gills. Hitch carried on chatting, but allowed his company to take over as he casually doodled on a hefty tablet of heavy stock. I eventually walked over and dropped a scrap of paper onto his sketch. The two images – both shocking in their detailed nature – were absolute facsimiles. I smiled at him, he at me, and we met at my end of the bar within the hour.

The pustulous urchin eyed me with worry. In an attempt to put the boy at ease, I walked back to him later in the evening and announced his star sign to the group.

'How did you guess?' he stammered.

'I didn't guess, silly lad.' I said. 'I knew.'

I suppose my well-intentioned attempt to put him at ease had gone quite awfully wrong.

Hitch, who had been observing with his calm and inimitable countenance, then spoke. One always knew when it was time for Hitch to speak, because of his recently tilted torso, ready to contribute, and the sharp suck on the air in his immediate environs, the pause and then the slow, deliberate monotone that only a Great might deliver. He had a way of saying almost anything and making it seem relevant to the conversation at hand. This, too, is the sign that one is in the company of authorial greatness.

'You are all adequately informed to know that one has to find murder funny, and execute it with a lushness. It has to be hilarious to me. There's a fine line between tragedy and comedy. For example, how many

times, years ago, have you seen the old-fashioned scene
of the man walking towards the open manhole cover.
Of course he has to wear a top hat, because that's
dignity, you see. That's the symbol of dignity. And you
watch him and he walks. He is reading a paper. And
he's missed seeing it and he suddenly disappears down
the hole. And everyone roars with laughter. But
supposing you took a second look and looked down the
hole. His head is cut, bleeding. And they send for an
ambulance. His wife and weeping children rush to the
hospital. Think how ashamed that audience is that they
laughed in the first place. And yet they do. Slipping on
a banana skin is very painful. So there's a streak of
cruelty among everyone. I call it dipping one's toe in the
cold water of fear.'

And Hitch stopped. His point had been made, as far
as he was concerned.

Our home is Soho. It is so marvellously mauve and grey
and dank. Finely fetid, she is. The inspirational rains
outside are there for us to dance in, when we need a
devious and deviant plot gradient to our own
immediate lives. Hitch often comes up with arcs,
dialogue and directions, after having sat on the kerb,
ankles deep in a brown puddle. He then walks back in
towards the table by the piano, and heralds himself, in
his slow and intoxicating drawl: 'I am back.'

He is a marvel. After he has announced himself, he
walks to the piano with the gusto of a broad man,
oblivious to the chairs he knocks over en route. He then
sits and plays, though he is, of course, quite awful. It is
always a distressing and interminable episode when he
approaches that abused device. But boy! He shows the

right spirit, such zeal, and that is what counts. I often stroll over the river and pay homage to him at that old fleapit, the Gaumont Rialto, in Waterloo. I will watch four films back to back.

He wants to write a screenplay with your old man, son. Ours, he reckons, is a simple story around two men, foremen at an automobile factory. I must write it, he says. He wants my twisted eye on it. I want us to do the longest dolly shot in cinema history. Longer than Orson's famous one in *Touch of Evil*. (By the way, Orson told me that his opening sequence, a single six-minute take, was all shot at night when he was making a different version of the film. His version would not be the dull affair that the studio execs, who clocked off at five, thought they were getting. This is the devious nature of a fine and allied Pimpernel.)

Anyway, the concept of my script with Hitch encapsulates the brilliance of the man, both technically and, through suspense and intrigue, narratively.

The idea is that the take begins with the very first stage of an assembly line, two men walking and talking. Then we gradually see the parts of the car added behind them, and all the while, the camera's dollying for an age along with the vehicle, and then eventually there's a completed motor, all built and it is driven off the ramp. One foreman then opens the passenger side door and out falls a dead body.

Just as Hitch explained this denouement to me, our waiter, a Hungarian lad with a face of magnificent roguishness, had come to stand by my shoulder. As I had once with Rasputin in the Urals, by the stinking well at the Abbey in Sicily, and with Edward by

Boleskine in the rain, I envisioned the weightiness of what was coming.

I turned and looked him in the eye.

'Sir, I have a message from Sir Winston. He wishes to see you.'

I rose and began to excuse myself.

'I am truly sorry if I was unclear, sir,' the boy said with impressive firmness. 'He wants to see you ALL.'

14.6 WINSTON

A large and luxurious car hummed outside by Hitch's favoured kerb, as the young Magyar held the door for us. Once we were all inside, he then closed it with sturdy reverence behind us. We set off to the south, left onto Shaftesbury Avenue and then down Charing Cross Road to Trafalgar Square, where the morning fruit sellers were squawking and ogling the exposed legs of office lasses, clipping their way to typewriters and sub-servience.

Not long now, my girls. I shall free you caged birds, I swear.

Whitehall was clear and free of the usual messy bustle. I stared at Parliament, pondering how my friend had ruled there.

I had presumed we were going to St Thomas's hospital on the southern banks of the Thames opposite the House of Commons, but our man drove straight past and continued south down towards Kennington Park Road, when I realised where he would be.

The foyer to the old fleapit, where we had spent many magically flecked hours, was as musty as always, as we were ushered in from the quiet side street. Marlene led us in. Of course, she did. Winston knew them all so well, and there he was in his hospital wheelchair three quarters towards the back in the central aisle in front of that tobacco'y screen. The projectionist must have switched off the reel, as the pictures and sound stuttered to a rough halt. We all moved in on him, each offering a lengthy hug of an old friend. He clung to Marlene noticeably longer, while she ditched her Teutonic tendency and clung back with ferocity and without any resort to acting. Winston's frame had diminished, yet his head was still a weighty bowling ball, able to express simultaneously an obsidian humour, larking boyish mischief and deep potential menace, while gently carrying the spicy and woody whiff of a quite marvellous *eau de cologne*. We all sat around him.

His voice was slow, deliberate and yet stirringly urgent. Only a Great can pull *this* off. By God, that old fleapit had never shown such illustrious company on its screen, as sat there that drizzly winter morning.

'My friends. Thank you for coming. I must keep this short, though it is against every fibre of my being. You all know that. I want you to come close to me one at a time, as I have something to say to each of you in private, though I know you buggers will reveal all to one another. I want each of you to know that he who reveals all later, is, of course, prone to exaggeration. She, less so.'

He chuckled to himself, and coughed uncomfortably for having done so. He spoke to the others for perhaps five minutes each, all with an exchange of love and benediction at the end. He ended each with a voluble 'Let us not unman each other,' even to Marlene, and thus, the parting was firm and lacking in all sentimentality. I stepped forward last, as the others moved to the curtains by the ice-cream and cigarette counter.

I moved my face close to his, and I saw eyes bold and lively, but then minutely afraid and tired.

'Two things, old friend.'

I nodded. He continued.

'I know I owe you a secret.'

'Yes, Hühnerbein. Why did he hate you so?'

'Well, he was an unmitigated arsehole. Of course. That was the foremost reason.'

He managed a chuckle that rattled in his clearly fading chest, and began to wave two pudgy fingers to the east.

'There were all the stories you have heard from our friends about our mistaken identities, and the times I robbed him of praise or riches or lasses. And my dear Clem, come to that. These are all true. But the summer's day he began to hate me rather than love me was one at Harrow in '91. We were both there. We were batting together in the annual Masters versus Boys match. He was given out, when it was I who should have walked, both stuck halfway down the track in no man's land.'

'That was enough for him to hate you as he did?'

'No. He was then buggered by four prefects in the cloisters, thinking they had grabbed me.'

'Well, that might do it.'

'But there is more, Aleister.'

Several seconds passed.

'He was my brother. Well, my half-brother. Mother always despised the poor runt. He was a decent lad as a little one. Maybe that day turned him into the evil twin in the tower. Shortly afterwards, he was shipped off to family in Bavaria. His real mother was some nouveau Munich strumpet. And so, Hühnerbein was never his real name. It was Bertram Church-ill. So, now you know.'

I held his girthy left paw. 'Well, I'll be damned.'

'You thought you were the only one with a lifelong secret, didn't you?'

There was a long pause as we stared at each other and then we exacted our synchronised and theatrical bellow. I saw Marlene, Orson and Hitch turn swiftly in unison to regard our joy from afar.

Winston then waved me back in.

'There is one last thing. You have a final mission. From me. Not from those fuckers down the road.'

He clearly meant MI-1, as all of his mirth and joy turned to earnestness.

'Aleister, the price I pay now in having to die is equal to the price you have paid over decades of serving England through your secrecy and the absolutely abysmal treatment you and yours have suffered for it. I did not give myself the luxury of going to Shangri-La, but then again, I was not called a peder-ast or a traitor or a Satanist for fifty years. I shall tell you something now, and just once. If you wish to save England for me, you must now work *against* Her. I beg you, I urge and implore you to do this. She is turning a dark corner. This is the tunnel at the end of the light, my friend. What I mean by this is you must now follow those instincts of yours to rebel, for only by doing this shall the England you and I adore be returned to us, though I shall not be here to relish Her. England is becoming governed by dark forces, and they will take us to Soviet horrors.'

He paused for breath, and touched the lapel of his grey-checked day suit, before resting his chilled paw on mine.

'We were always allies against the Germans and we won, my friend. We bloody won.'

He stopped now, and allowed himself to think about this, it seemed. If he was thinking the same as I, then it was the bizarre clash of the firmest ecstasy in having saved the world from True Evil, while the absolute misery in considering the millions of poor bastards, dead, maimed, orphaned and widowed.

'But I was a reactionary Englishman, Aleister – nothing more – while you were a revolutionary first and an Englishman second. Sometimes we must keep what we have by giving it all away. Go to Paris, for this is where your rebellion is most likely to spark. It may be time for me to say that yours is NOW the righteous and only way. Please, bring back my England. Those boys and girls who will always remember the nights in the bomb shelters, well, they want something different from their age. This is the unleashing of the most powerful energy we shall EVER have. Youth. I love you, Aleister. Let us not unman each other.'

I knew he had finished, and all I said in return was the same expression of adoration, 'I love you.'

I withdrew, moved inches higher and put my lips to the frowns of his forehead, which slackened under my manly kiss. And that was that. I turned on him, and walked, as if going for a piss in the intermission.

And so, leaving Marlene, Hitch and Orson in the foyer with a fond embrace and farewell, it was to Paris that Violet and I would go.

24 January 1965
Goodbye, you fucking beauty.

Chapter 15

The Brothers, *Les Frères, Les Soeurs* & the Hippies

Piss for peace. Smile for peace. Go to school for peace – or don't go to school for peace. Whatever you do, do it for peace.

– John Lennon

I will now go. It is time to save the world. Make Her truly free. Thelema shall take her place in the heavens. The people of this earth will be bullied no more. They shall inherit the lot if I have anything to do with it.

If I perish, Edward knows to complete this tale, and to write of Paris and London in the sixties. And of two countries, soon-to-be decumbent and twitching; brutalised, dank and on their bellies. Not so long ago.

15.1 PARIS 1965
After Winston's death, Violet and I took the boat train from Waterloo to Dover with the intent of planting seeds of disruption in Paris, as he himself had advised. Then I would return to Shangri-La, and hear of the harvest of the revolution from afar, like a cocky bastard waiting for his exam results.

As we left London for what I thought would be the last time (again), Violet asked me if I would miss London, I said to her, 'My darling, I have so enjoyed that Himalayan sense of liberation from the modern world, as well as the geographical distance from Whitehall. Even more so, I have adored having passed through the special vortex of that hole in the mountain ice-wall that you now know so well, and I have been so fond of the conjugation with a wholly new measure of time. The question I always felt nagging at me was if I were given the choice and knew that each year down here would grant me perhaps ten up there, would I have gone there earlier? I settled each time on a satisfaction that my timing had been perfect. So no, my love, I shall not miss London, for London is a place that one only truly misses when one is there, so magnificent is she. She is a forceful lover, who demands adoration. She is the best of both worlds.'

I now spoke to her my plan, for it was, with a true sense of joy at the end of the Ceylon civil war, that I finally sanctioned – personally, and with Winston's urgent and fading words in my ears – a large scale shipment of toffee resin and jungle floor goo from Colombo to California, New York and London. Let's add a dash of rainbow, hippy-dippy, flower power, acid-traced, turquoise, lilac and death-white to this dreary world. It was time, not just to stop wars or beat Nazis, but to go one step further, and propel boys and girls to a truly liberated state of mind and being.

Do what thou wilt. Love is the law.

And so began what I believe to be my masterpiece of mischief to date. The nineteen sixties. I was no Orson Welles, who could muster up his magnum opus at the age of twenty-five and change the world with it. He was truly the special talent.

No, I took my time. I was like that old bull at the top of the field – about whom I once spoke to Violet Ambrosia Fagg – the one who would take his time and slowly pollute them all. The toffee goo was harvested, shipped, processed, and micro-dropped onto sheets. It was distributed through frighteningly large numbers of Thelemites, and even their resourceful and mercenary pals, an army with numbers to thump Adolf and Benito, and a secret society to dwarf and shame Yeats and his lame, prancing pussycats. We would feed and fuel that rampant youth by the hundreds of millions, leaving *them* defenceless in the fight: thinking, dancing, smiling, laughing, uniting, fucking and when the first rush of the party was over, fighting and thinking and fucking some more. Ad infinitum, but never ad nauseam.

Stardust had been sprinkled across England in my final years there after the war. Rogues* from Dartford, Heston, Brixton and Liverpool were my friends before they were born. We priests executed similar generosity across the Deep South and California. Wizardry and enchantment were cultivated in Tupelo, Mississippi, Memphis, Tennessee, Seattle, Washington, and Melbourne, Florida. You gorgeous bad lads know who you are. Our seedlings were latent and crimson and they were now coming for your sons and daughters alike.

I now saw it as my social responsibility to spoon-feed acid or hashish or jungle goo to mankind, so that it could see the true magnetism and gentle sorcery of Mother Nature, release a consciousness that could change the world order of war and money into one of a true harmony. To deny the people this was tantamount to keeping them in a prison, and we all know

---

*	*Jagger, Page, Bowie and The Beatles. Elvis Presley, Arthur Lee, Hendrix and Morrison.*

how I react to such utter meanness. (*Dear Benito, Who said nec-romance was dead?*)

Do What Thou Wilt. Love Under Will. Love Is The law.

This time we meant business. Love would triumph if we were to have our way. The united front that had beaten Nazism now fractured and splintered in peacetime. This is also a law of nature. Poor Winston had been voted out eight weeks after VE Day, for heaven's sake, but he did not sulk. He was a real man, but who could forgive like a child. The fucker got back up and brawled and won.

And given Winston's public spat with Gandhi, he might have pretended to gag at the words of the Mahatma, but more insightful ones are hard to find.

When I despair, I remember that all through history the ways of truth and love have always won. There have been tyrants, and murderers, and for a time they can seem invincible, but in the end they always fall. Think of it – always.[*]

Paris was our first target of a *coup d'état* – they even had a word (or some words) for it. They got the whole revolution thing all right. 1789, 1830, 1848, even the Americans managed one, while England was always more sedate, and yet not to be omitted. A mere nation of shopkeepers could not have presided over many decades of revolution in literature, music,

---

[*] *Winston and Gandhi were actually begrudging chums in the end. I should know for I introduced them. There was never real enmity, more of a running joke for the newspapers. Mahatma wouldn't play his game, though Churchill did so try to rattle his cage. The minuscule Gandhi was always slight enough to slip through the bars of that cage however, while that plumper and fine First Lord of the Admiralty was not.*

art, fashion, film, television, thought, technology, cricket for heaven's sake, and throughout the above, attitude. A small rock, yes, but Britain has been a vastly potent generating station of swagger, verve and audacity for hundreds of years. And when the small Corsican with the large gob was floundering on his hairy arse like a buffoon on battlefield and snow, Arthur Wellesley and England were already steadily imbuing future generations with an evolved wish to dismiss politeness and shopkeepery in favour of a shoulders back, chest-out, chin-up 'Eff awff'. The potency of our revolutions is such that they transmute, replicate, and quite marvellously refuse to be adequate. Ever. Wave after wave after wave. *That* is the true trick of revolutions.

So while in Paris, Violet and I lived in Le Chat Blanc in Montparnasse, as I was surrounded by simultaneously euphoric, rhapsodic and empty memories of Leah and Somerset Maugham and a thousand lovers. I slept upstairs in a vacant apartment in what was now a quite scummy *arrondissement*, Violet across the hall. We shared that address, as well as our appetite for the groins of young French and North African types, who remained quite unaware of who we were.

Crucially, however, I was visited by a tiny troop of seasoned, yet excited Thelemic friends, the most trusted knot of allies, as we honed a plan for a global revolt. We started with just three dependable teenage boys. The whispers and the fairy stories of my presence would not begin for a while, so tight-lipped were they. Then later when, by necessity, more knew and more saw me, then the slivers of rumours were presumed to be ridiculous myth, less-than-cunning metaphors and wishful drooling, all helped by strong weed, hallucinogens and the excitability of youth. What treasured cover I found.

I suppose there is a nice parallel to be drawn between how I had once simultaneously thrilled and pissed off the readers of my canon, separated them into two distinct camps, and how all the lads and lasses, whom I needed and wanted to believe in me, would and did, and how those who should believe me dead, would do just that. The rest of the time, anonymity was easy to attain with a passport sourced by old friends, and an array of fine hats, false beards, spectacles, uniforms, dog collars and many European and Eastern languages. If any undesirable got close to the truth and eyed me too curiously, then I ruined their day with old man spit in their eye and baffled the bastards with Sanskrit and Mandarin, delivered in a phlegmy Bavarian bark; a tough trick to master, but one which seemed to neutralise quite perfectly any nosy arsehole's thought-process.

The insurgency would all be achieved through the righteousness and the purity of those students, the young, my youths. They received my instructions and indirectly we schooled thousands of Thelemites. Through a fizzing network, they spread the good and pious word, as Papa and I once had, leaping through nettles and embalmed in love. The city soon whirred, thrummed and bristled with anticipation. They all had much work to do to prepare, for we required a replacement system once the corrupt old one fell. Otherwise, it would be a destructive and pointless anarchy – nihilism was not to be encouraged. Those who accused the students of that were atrociously mistaken. It would take three years to prepare the troops, the leaders, and for all the conditions to align for a revolution to take hold.

And so, from that summer of 1965 for three years, I would relish playing a new kind of chess, with the blindfold of concrete, *pâtisseries, boulangeries, hotels de ville, boulevards* and traffic, and then across seas and oceans. I could not see the effects of each move. I had to trust in my brotherhood.

15.2 LONDON, 1968

I was in Paris in 1968, but back home the *London Review of Passion* was under attack by the threat of a dozen law suits for slander and defamation. We continued to publish, but they closed down the printer, bullied shopkeepers, and so forced us underground. Fine with me, you cunts. Winston had been right. Those dark forces were coming for us and our kind. As the turncoat bastards in Whitehall and Washington had opened up a new front against the Soviets, the self-righteous hypocrites were also oppressing their own populace, far more subtly, of course, than that portly thumbed Stalin. It was an overt attack on Thelema. I therefore resolved to take Paris *now*, in order to conquer my own darling, London.

15.3 *M'AIDEZ! M'AIDEZ!*

> To keep your secret is wisdom, but to expect others to keep it is folly.
>
> – Dr Johnson

As much as I worshipped Orson, Marlene and Hitch, a movie won't start a rebellion. It might help fester one, and it might help join some dots of like-minds. Cinema was a fine foundation for what we would encounter next. We now dreamed of physical attempts to remove leaders from power. This, Paris in the sixties, would be closer the mark. When it happened, this was going to be hundreds of thousands on the streets until we shifted the stain. This was going to be storming palaces, barracks and parliaments.

We had spent three years planning how to take charge. It had taken just a few phone calls to make sure the trucks of lemons would be there in time. The fruits were to be our only defence in nullifying the effects of the tear gas, while our weapons of attack were our hands and the stones beneath our feet. Citrus from Spain, Italy, Morocco and the Lebanon was shipped to and stockpiled in Montparnasse and to the streets behind the students' halls on *la Rive Gauche*. The street-sellers and owners of the *marchés* gladly diverted each piece of that fruit to our cause. Many wanted to know how they could be of most use when the fighting started. They would know. It was an animal instinct.

I dreamed of this rebellion of ours forcing soldiers and police to switch sides to be with those over the barricades, whom they loved and respected. This was a million Samsons all pushing like fuck. And then quickly, the rebellion would shift into the realm of legend, and be seen as a blueprint for eager anger around the continent and world, to be broadcast out from the tip of *Le Tour Eiffel*. This was Thelema's time. It was time for France to

Do Her Will. Love is the Law.

May Day – 1 May 1968, 10 a.m.
'M'Aidez! M'aidez!'

Perhaps three hundred stern brows gathered in, and out onto the pavement around Le Chat Blanc. There was intense talk between clusters of some enthusiastic, some furious types. Many were in their late teens and early twenties, but some were congregated around older and more considered men. The auras were scarlet, black but with perilous arrows and vicious shards of silver and turquoise light shooting outwards. There were beards on youthful faces, clean-shaven jaws ready to brawl, turtlenecks, well-chosen tweed jackets and well-cut trousers sitting above fine Italian desert footwear. When the union leaders' creased faces, dirty thumbs and unpolished boots pitched up, they looked out of place with the well-dressed mob I'd gathered, whose only stains were yellowy ones on nicotine fingers and thumb. They were already taking off their spectacles for the fight, so keen were they. Not even Violet (as Liz Taylor in season) could distract them. Maybe a couple of them growled guttural lyrics at the minx and seemed to promise themselves they would come back for her.

When they saw me, only then did they show any reverence, usually in the form of nudges and silence as I passed among them.

In their small knots of fevered chat and crude gestures, I urged many of them to shelve all such emotions, and then I addressed them all: '*Parce que c'est un putain de guerre, les gars.*'*

5 May 1968
The plan worked to perfection and the expulsions of forty students from the campus at Nanterre were announced by noon. We did not even need to publicise the protests for the next day. Their announcement was the only alert we required. My boys and girls all knew what to do next.

6 May 1968
An estimated 40,000 marched from the Sorbonne to the Arc.

7 May 1968
Rain. Heavy rain. Thousands of police. Those nasty CRS bastards.

---

* '*Because this is fucking war, lads.*'

Seventy thousand were there to face them and make it clear they would not be cowed.

8 May 1968
Thirty arrests. Sixty hospitalised. Ten of whom were in uniform. Two beaten to a pulp by their own large sticks. News reports told of close to 100,000 demonstrators.

9 May 1968
The first all-night protests with tense stand-offs around the Sorbonne and in Montparnasse. Police retribution, several feared dead.

10 May 1968
Many thousands marched through streets, strewn with lemon skins and stomped on kepis, between our honey hives of Montparnasse and the centre. These mobs were mainly my decoys to fox the cops who by now had called in the army.

Culture Minister André Malraux was on the television news, declaring this to be the *Death of God*. I bellowed, melodramatically of course. We were not the *Death of God*. We were the death of the three-minute pop song.

Violet hugged me, as the number of civilians on the streets was an estimated two million. *The Night of the Barricades – Our Time* – was hours away.

A Thelemite in the French police convinced the cops to take the Sorbonne and defend it, the silly bastards. The concept of the people of France fighting into their seats of learning and centuries-old libraries and lecture halls stirred more hearts and minds than had they been fighting outwards. It was a sleight of hand, a nuance and a trick of the mind that convinced the masses of a collective determination and solidarity against meanness, failed colonialisation and cuntery in general. The advance of our boys and girls *on them* romanticised that night for present and future generations by doing what most only chuntered and whispered about. We were no longer *taking it.* We were overtly and bravely *giving it out.*

With bare hands, they ripped away the cobblestones, bricks and paving slabs of the old bourgeois Paris and lobbed them with intent and malice at the brutality of the law, catapulted by adolescent hormones. Pissed-off kids who came in on the train, aroused lovers, students and blokes with jobs in nice clobber with saucy girlfriends they looked like they'd just finished fucking and may start again any minute. Violet appeared to wish to join them, as we watched, with citrus-soaked handkerchiefs, from an embarrassingly comfortable four-storey *terrasse* on the *Rue Gay-Lussac.*

The vinegary stink in the Parisian air was naturally very arousing to me, and it seemed to a million others as well. How could it not be? Like the distinctive scorched stink of hashish and cocaine, blended together and then burned, one knows that when one smells it that one is having the time of one's life. It is always good to note this when it happens, you know, bookmark it for contentedness at a later date.

It was still going at 6 a.m. as a series of general strikes were announced on the radio. The television stopped broadcasting for several hours. Trucks burned, torched cars were on their sides. It felt like the city was ours as Violet and I looked down on a mob of surrealists who appeared to be re-enacting *The Tale of the Golden Flasher,* of all things.

'Are you anything to do with this?' I asked Violet, pointing at the mime artists and the street players below.

'Good lord, no. But it looks the most marvellous fun, Papa.'

A single police officer was still face down at the end of the street. His foot now twitched marginally. At dawn, he had been knocked unconscious by a well-wielded wheelbarrow that had just been used to bring in a few hundred more lemons. The cunt had deserved it. Of that, there was little doubt.

15.4 *IL EST INTERDIT D'INTERDIRE*

We so nearly toppled Paris, it was so bloody close. The power of the military and the tanks and the guns was just too much. God, we had their bowels on edge. De Gaulle flew out of the country, the fucker. Pompidou had ordered the Special Forces to be ready.

And had Paris fallen to the students, dissent and disobedience would have spread and taken New York, San Francisco and London. This was not a juvenile grab at a spiteful and peevish anarchy, but a true *coup d'état* with a beautiful message of freedom, narcotics and fornication for all.

It was simple.

This is why we had fought the second war.

This is why millions had died.

Intolerance is evidence of impotence.

It is forbidden to forbid.

Il est interdit d'interdire.

Freedom, you fuckers.

And so, that following much-vaunted summer of '68 did not ratchet up or, in my mind, even equal the anticipated fizz of the previous year. Leary was now well known, the Beatles singing 'All You Need is Love' on *Our World* reached 400 million, they say, but the real thrust of true revolution had passed, I knew. Paris, and our Night of the Barricades had been the REAL moment. Yes, the rebellious and transgressive fight in the United States of America continued, but it was merely (according to the *Smithsonian*) 'a gauzy juxtaposition of armed force and flower child innocence'. It had been Paris or bust. And we had lost.

The moment had passed, though fierce intent in smaller numbers still made me proud. The determination of that Grateful Dead movement was a truly marvellous spectacle to behold. We had learned much, and for a first *real* effort, I felt confident the future would be ours. Samson would keep pushing. Our numbers had been truly phenomenal, and I always knew there had been an appetite for my message. Love, love, love. It is *that* bloody easy.

The British youth movement had been on the wane since Paris. They say that it had become a grisly time in England, gnarled souls flapped on wizened shoes, fraying bell bottoms damp from brown puddles. Sages in the side streets and in the high-rises also saw that the momentum towards revolution had ebbed prematurely, while the ascendency of cheap shampoo and the whip hand of random violence were on a conjugal rise. It had been the Year of the Monkey, and so trouble was assured, but we had not yet evolved enough to prevail. The wisdom of the Chinese, however, allows for another Year of the Monkey. And another. We would be back, this I promised. Smarter.

I was so very proud of Violet for the piece, an album review, she wrote as the final column for 'Six Fingers & Fat Thumbs' in the last ever edition of the *London Review of Passion*. And it was an act that, one day, would be proven to contain more prescience than anything she had ever done and certainly would rival how I had kept a King in England to save the world, for she had pin-pointed precisely the path forward, but one that sadly looked increasingly likely never to include me again.

THE FINAL LONDON *REVIEW OF PASSION*
LOVE – *FOREVER CHANGES*

Love's *Forever Changes* is a powerhouse constellation of the stars. She channels the finest psychedelia and shall make one sense and sniff the kaleidoscopic Los Angeles of the sixties across space and time. She speaks of tender love, free love, love of mankind and love of the planet. I guess the band's name has never been in doubt. Amid the astuteness (which the fool calls brooding paranoia) in calling out a creeping police state, there remains a truly vast space for a bubbling and rampant optimism that gives this contributor such a secure comfort. The mariachi-driven force of the album's opener, 'Alone Again Or' is a wonder.

'Old Man' resonates with us all, for we all know one.

A lovelier and more stirring cant I have yet to hear.

The trumpeted joy and unashamed energy of 'Maybe the People Would Be the Times (Or Between Clark and Hilldale)' is enough to send me on a tour of all their haunts in the city; their squat-cum-hippy-love-nest; like Cosmo's Alley that hosts outdoor carnivals for the tripping hundreds as they play the basement club inside every night; Arthur Lee's school; to Bido Lito's, the Sea Witch and Brave New World; the Capitol Records building (Arthur sought them out because Nat King Cole was on Capitol) and their spiritual homes on Sunset, where their acolytes revel and rub shoulders on the dance floor with The Doors and The Byrds, college kids, beatniks, art students, artists and hippies. Take a deep breath between cars, close your eyes and you can feel the rabid and quite ghostly magic. As Arthur himself says, as good as The Beatles are, they are just four white boys.

Listen intently to 'The Red Telephone', and try to decide if the man is a seer or a danger. Or indeed both.

The interracial brassiness of their stance remains a marvel. Arthur is Morrison and Hendrix in stovepipes. Their intellectualism is a warm invitation to a place where fools are not suffered; gladly or otherwise. There is a hint of Arthurian English folk music in 'Andmoreagain', as well as of hippy-dippy and reincarnated times in India ('Live and Let Live'). There is a rejection of materialism and, at its core, a dazzling sun and enormous beating heart.

'The Good Humor Man He Sees Everything Like This' might have girls thrown out of school for a June day not so much for the pigtails they will wear for Arthur, but for a daisy behind my ear and one painted on one cheek with a hummingbird on the other. The simple, rising and arousing melody and its verdant imagery of nature shall haunt me to my dotage.

They are expansive, leavened and magnificent in their spaced romanticism; a departure from didactic rock 'n' roll. Their songs possess a sensuous timelessness in their construction. Horns and strings of a symphony move us into a jazzed cosmology via a matadorian *corrida* trumpet, blistering guitar ripples and nutty flamenco that shall destroy only what one once thought music to be.

'You Set the Scene' rounds off the record with pomp and vigour. It is one of those songs that can inspire each new day and at provocative volume. Try it. It works. She is composed of what lazier, satisficing artists would use for three songs. Not my Arthur. This is a seven-minute riot of ultimate disturbance, rammed tight with life-affirming seconds of precipitous gradient. Don't look down? Of course, look down.

Stop music. Now.

If this masterpiece long player doesn't inspire a thousand albums of malicious subversion and potent revolution and be a cornerstone of modern music for a century or more, then I need some of that very strong acid. Here is a clairvoyant and tuned-in plea of benevolence for Mother Earth's survival, for, at the very least, we owe to her her requisite changes. Forever.

And just like THAT, all we were left with was the music. The music.

But it was music that would turn tens, if not hundreds, of millions into unwitting and latent Thelemites.

15.5 ADIOS, BADMAN

As I held Violet's hand in our hotel rooms by *la Gare de l'Est*, we burned vast stashes of hashish, turned our Tarot, sat for yoga and meditated. My mind wandered, taking hers with me, and it sparked with visions of the future as I had once seen in Ceylon. This spiky and delicious hashish dredged up what I had once seen with Robbie, but which had, at that time, made no sense to me. The images returned strong and potent and clear-edged. And I spoke to her of each prescient vision.

I told her of how I would be *there*, when the spirit of Thelema would one day fire hundreds of dry-run rebellions, joining the dots of anger, righteousness and sedition.

Of how the fight would go on in Prague that same year. Of how it would not end, it cannot ever *end!*

Of how I would haunt the soldiers from the Kent State murders. Of how I shall offer large rewards for information and then the capture of the twenty-eight Ohio National Guardsmen who opened fire, with sixty-seven rounds of machine-gun fire over thirteen seconds, into unarmed boys and girls on a college campus.

Oh how my spirit and my hunched and shuffling shape, led by my elderly daughter, would be witnessed at a thousand summer festivals for decades. Of how my name would be whispered, the legend extolled and extended. Of how I might be seen sitting beneath oak trees in Golden Gate Park as flower power raged. Of how my name and my voice might be heard bellowing down the hallways of Berkeley. *Rebel!*

Of how there shall be thousands of sightings of me at Woodstock ('69) and on the Isle of Wight ('71). Of how the industrial strength of the drugs might or might not have been to blame.

Of how I shall stand with the Panthers, coast to coast, when they bring down cunts with truncheons, hats and batons.

Of how I shall applaud and fund and reward the many sons and daughters of Dibdin, as they distribute acid to the millions. And of how they shall be the first drug lords and drug ladies of that fine land.

Of Kesey and The Merry Pranksters, Kerouac and Cassaday, each of whom shall mention my revered name many times a day for years, sparking youth to ask of me and demand to hear their favourite fairy story.

Of how my spirit shall be there, as they all pinball across America a thousand times with the Grateful Dead. Of how my face will be etched onto a billion acid tabs. Of plumes of hashish smoke that might even form visions of me above the heads of hippies and free, joyous and angry buggers.

Of recognisable images of my bullet-head and slogans of popular defiance, sprayed and stencilled in lilac onto the concrete walls of raised highways in Detroit ('Stoned Love'), New York City ('What's Going On') and San Francisco ('Do What Thou Wilt. Love is the Law, Crowley Lives').

Of how my spirit would be seen and felt in Manhattan in '73 and in an urgent, charged and pissed-off London in '76 and more motorway underpass graffiti work.

Of how I shall be there with that short-vowelled and succinct Northern father of six hungry kids and husband to a missus close to stringing herself up in an empty council house, all the furniture burned to get through January. Of how I shall be with him as he wants to cry at the sight of the grime under his thumbs from the pit, even after an eight-month-long strike, and he can feel the filth in his lungs now aggressively numbering his days and how to tell the children. Of how I shall help to catapult his one solid punch, and together we will fully open up that cunting London copper's cheekbone, the one on triple pay and with a well-used knife strapped to his ankle.

Of how I shall be watching, and over the shoulder of the buggered and the sodomisers in the Coleherne. Of how any and all such social statements shall always be welcome.

Of when a lone Chinese lad will, two decades from now, stand in front of a loaded tank. Of how we shall *all* be there.

Of how I shall become a righteous bogeyman to scare and inspire.

I shall tell my daughter of how I will always be there in some shape or form. I promise. I promise.

Of how now, in the middle of 1968, Violet and I, perhaps knowing temporary defeat, shall now drift back off and up to our mountain lair.

Of Paris whispering a respectful, '*Adieu, Violet.*'

Of how I sensed my own bespoke and loving farewell from the city, my sister-in-arms.

And of how I heard somewhere in this doped-up cloud that both Dandylyon and Prudence had passed away. Did they come to me and tell me themselves? Of how this seemed to fire me to a steelier determination than ever. Of how they seemed to tell me they would be back, they've been doing this for centuries. And only to rejoice.

Au revoir. Badman. Gone, and not to be heard of again for fifty years. Or more.

15.6 BUT . . .
But let us all be very clear.

For the record.

Samson *shall* come for you, you fuckers.

Paganism is wholesome because it faces the facts of life.

– Aleister Crowley

PART FOUR

A mistake is only an error; it becomes a mistake when you fail to correct it.

– John Lennon

PART FOUR

Chapter 16

Part I – While Blessed Were the Children

> I can imagine myself on my death-bed, spent utterly with lust to touch the next world, like a boy asking for his first kiss from a woman.
>
> – Aleister Crowley

There are three reasons I am leaving here.

One is a god's boredom, but I have told of that.

The second is I cannot help myself from joining in, for this might be that final victory for Thelema and the truly rebellious. Paris, 1968, Woodstock, the Isle of Wight, the American campuses were all mere apprenticeships. If we do not take victory AND NOW here early in this third decade of the twenty-first century, then Mankind shall undoubtedly lose all freedom. For ever. Freedom of speech, freedom of expression and freedom of movement shall soon be gone, if I do not move NOW. Is this why we fought Adolf? And so, I stir for all those lads and lasses who perished because of him.

The Thelemites left in Winston's immediate slipstream are naturally a theatrical and melodramatic lot with a sense of occasion. They seem to demand the flick of a Messiah's wrist to light the blue touchpaper, and of course, my ego and I are thrilled to accept. Think of Zapata and Pancho Villa liberating Mexico City to cheering hordes, or an aged Spartacus taking Rome – if they were to sit back and be carried in in a sedan chair as all the young guns brawled and windmilled their fists ahead of them in their name.

I receive regular communications from my chaps, a process made all the simpler now that the mountain trail thaws to brown earth at fourteen thousand feet, and consignments are dropped from the air with ease. It seems these renegades have a plan in place, and they assure me that I need not concern myself with details right now. Yes, they can instigate it all themselves, but they know of my life's work, and think it only right I lead the charge. I suspect they really just want to meet me. They regularly quote the Book of Revelations, knowing that this will poke and stir me. They rant about the fall of empires and the end of civilisation. 'Fuck it,' I say. 'I'm in. I am not going to waste a century of graft for nothing.'

And as much as our Thelemites seem to yearn, like adolescents, for a figurehead, I now take great comfort in telling myself, *I want to be there in London.* I actually want to see it when it happens. Surely I have earned my front-row seat? In the spirit of the old actor who gets an Oscar for the direst and sloppiest movie he makes as a ninety-year-old, for the award really honours a lifetime of sheer magnificence, I now shall take the plaudits for my canon.

And anyway, I have a plan to help me should I get confused like a normal old man. I shall stop by a Ceylon jungle, where I aim to restock, reacquaint myself with those monks, and have a proper peek into the future; the kind that only a five-day jag can inspire. Then I shall start to concern myself with details of this technological fight we are to enter. But what are these hacks and viruses I hear of, if not twenty-first-century versions of hexes, spells and invocations? And I am happy to be schooled by these sharp, young buggers, especially, of course, if I get to breathe in the rafts from their fresh necks and sniff their adolescent slipstreams. I feel momentary shame that conflict and war brings arousal.

There is a third reason. The persistent drone of Violet urging me to 'Fight, Papa. Fight' was a feature of her years here. When this voice was an almost precise copy of Winston's in that cinema, I began to realise my true destiny. It was always just a matter of time before my moment approached.

I am seen off by dear friends, in a manner that reminds me of how some other old pals once said goodbye to a fading prime minister.

To the eye, Orr still shows signs of a boxing champion's physique, and his grip around me confirms this.

Zealand stands forth next, and says nothing. He holds my shoulders, looks deep into my eyes, and we implore each other in silence to continue to shield our son from harm.

Leah and La Gitana step forward together, holding hands, as we form a small circle and acknowledge a true bond.

They stand back, as Marlene, Orson and Hitch did in that old Waterloo fleapit, to allow the main event.

Edward stands and with the look of a proud son, who shields no one from harm.

I move close to him. There is little need to speak.

'Do you wish me to say anything?' he says.

We are silent. He knows.

'Very well. Then claim your righteous place, Father. And tell Violet I love her when you see her.'

He speaks as if there is no chance of my demise. He touches my hand thus.

'We shall be here for when your mission is over. Violet must come to stay this time.'

And so to self-slaughter I shall stride, but not before an almighty brawl in an unseen sphere.

To distract this sad Beast, Zealand appears at my side, and ushers me away off the lea side and the slightest chance of sentimentality. He tells me how he adores my determination to find and to scrap my old foe tonight. This is odd talk for a High Lama, but the circumstances justify the bullish tone. He is stirred, and twitches with excitement and pride. I am *very* high right now. I am waving farewell to those I love. I am on the move.

'You shall go with two Sherpas who are waiting for you at the exit of the city,' Zealand says. 'If you see your foe, Death, you have my permission to bring him down.' He laughs.

I speak of fear, the impact of true fear, as we walk. Is the High Lama shooing me out like a tired pub landlord wanting to get to bed but for the gobby and gushing straggler?

'You know, old friend. My enemies were never really afraid of Crowley the ogre, of Aleister the brute. I never gave them any firm justification for this. They only ever feared the public or private exposure of *their own* cretinism, such was the flimsiness of their spirit. So, who was I to deny them this?'

He snorts.

I tickle the wattle of a spry young kid. It feels more velvety and youthful than anything I have ever encountered. This goat is quite likely to outlive me, I tell myself. I do not care right now. I am ready.

I have swallowed enough jungle goo to make this an easier, perhaps even a more fun, task. Conscience shall not make a coward of me.

We pass the goats. At least, I think we do, for my narcotic is spiky, nicely charged and potent. We seem to move in synchronicity past the ivied cherub, who now has rich greenery all across his torso. Was he grinning so yesterday? I see Zealand's hammering heart in his skeleton. And he is now gone too.

My robes fall open, and those nearby shy away, concerned for their well-being, it seems. I attempt to assuage and to calm them, but they scatter.

I am alone. Into the mazy passageways, I shall walk. As long as I head uphill, I shall reach the exit of the city. So, this is how it ends. I suppose. Quickly.

'Oh! balls.'

I am barefoot. I hear Christ. How could I not, as, like he did, I prepare to perish on a hillside, shove myself towards doom and summon a steely will to die.

I shall be forced to walk the narrow passages and steep alleys until I too am abandoned on a slope. The dark shall come quickly. I shall soon wish the end to come. I am flanked now by my Sherpas. They hold me on the high gradient and force me into suitable protective clothing, goggles, fur hat, gloves and warm boots onto my feet.

The pass into oblivion is revealed around the next corner. Enough is now enough. The Old Boy is near, I sense him. I know the tang of that fucking Thug.

I ask for my friends. They have forsaken me. I forgive them before it even becomes a question.

At least Christ suspected or pretended he was going somewhere, to another realm. It is gloried dust for me. I laugh and then turn to the pass. And I walk out to die. But I do so with a walk that suggests I shall win.

'Come on! Where are you? Show your shuddersome face! If you dare. Fight a real god for once.'

His first blow must come soon, but he is a mauve one, we know that.

In my goo haze, I discard my coats and the chill is intense, and I am not dressed for such natural viciousness. I was not expecting to be flesh at this point. I should be dust, and therefore apparel had appeared to be an irrelevance to me. He is going to make me suffer. I move away from the arch that signals the border between there and here. I put yards between us, tens of yards. I lose my sight. Here we go.

Another step barely made, as the boots I wear find no traction on the ice. I stumble onto my backside within a second, knowing I shall rise.

I sit out in the pass, and my body allows me to fight. I am stronger than I thought. I cannot bear this cold for long though. Deep within lies the rampant pervert, high on goo, who wishes to be reminded of the absolutes sensations of the groin; I laugh when I think of this being the final part of me to perish. And perish I soon shall. My laugh echoes in the pass, and this reverberation forces a sheet of ice from above to land on my neck and shoulder, slicing me viciously. I feel as if my head is half off.

Yet I stand and force one partially blinded eye open, for appearances, in the sight of the enemy, might still be pivotal. The wind knocks my head backwards and my robes open again. With this bitter temperature and an exposed nether, I cannot appear too impressive a foe. I'm fully aware of my cinematic bluster as I speak to Him, that slack and effete cad, Death, without the courage or decency to come.

'How dare you not show?' I yell. 'Perhaps you recoil at

what I know of you. I recall you unfondly, and you seem insistent on maintaining my disdain.'

He has centuries of practice in sending a proxy, which right now appears to be this incessant and pre-eminent glacial inclemency.

There is no answer. I breathe. I shout, studied and annunciated. I picture my words, forcing their print into history, memory and snow. I know that I am really doped up.

'Yes, *you*. I remember your awkward walk, and your expertise in pioneering unimpressive sexual lows.

'At least my nadirs were spoken of in high regard. Come and get me, you sloppy pest. You think you're in my league? Yours is a daily, if not hourly shame.

'You are a limp clod, who cannot even claim to possess the fanaticism of a neophyte nor the brackishness of an ex-wife. If you are watching as a coward watches, then you will see my auras scarlet and cerulean, and those are the shades of victory. This is my naked testimony to you, you prancing and farcical Vengefulist. Moriarty be damned.

'Let the record show that The Great Beast stands in the mountain pass alone on this night, does not turn to dust and might only be taken by the ice of my own nature. My Own Nature! I shall end my life, not you. That is unless I decide to skip on to Darjeeling and dine belligerently with your most putrid sister, before landing on her and improving vastly her mangy mood as only I know how. Now for the final time, where is this Troublesome Grip of yours that I am supposed to fear? WHERE?'

My heart stops.

I am on my back. And then I hear a voice that seems to answer me.

It is not the voice I expect. Silence leads to a soft whistle that holds its pitch. There is no white light as they say there is. A final imprint on a dead brain.

La Gitana and Leah come to me first. I see them as a vision in front of me, cursing me, telling me to rise. I am not sure if my eyesight has returned or whether I hallucinate. They light a candle, their small hands robust enough to fend off the cutting sheets of wind. And then, my sight blurs to see two, three, six lights. They multiply, as my eyes for a second time seem to be the first part of me to feel a looming defeat.

'Stand, Old Man. And walk on.'

The ferocity within this scream is felt in the wounded neck of the faded Beast. I am helpless not against the cold or the onset of Dust, but against the desire of these women.

'Stand, Old Man. And walk on.' This time from my son.

My senses are sharp enough to know that this is a crowd that urges me; its tone is juvenile and whistley, but steely and stronger than I. I stand and see a hundred candles, a hundred shaved heads, a hundred children in robes. I tingle. They all speak, as a hundred turns to thousands. The ageing air affects them not. They make elevated their hero, form an unbreachable mass around me and shove me further from the citadel. This throbbing agent of rough and tumble is still with them.

They lead me to a cave, where we shall rest, take cover, breathe, take strength from the knowledge that I might live beyond the mountain pass, and then sit out the night as they hold me a grinning captive.

'At dawn, we shall lead you from here.'

We sit and they ask me to tell tales of olden days, while Leah, La Gitana and Edward flank me.

And we laugh.

I appear to be back.

I am heard to gasp, 'You cursed, astonishing world, you!'

The children giggle and explain it to the smaller ones, who also chuckle. And nod.

'This is for you, Robbie my love. You would delight at this evening. Christ resurrected by his acolytes. Recall, they that sup with the Devil must own a long spoon. It takes the wickedest man in the world to be sound pals with both Jesus and Satan.'

I reach into my pocket and eat some more toffee'd resin from a jungle floor, somewhere in my past.

I stand and speak of my thanks to my saviours, my head still spinning with my overwrought bravado.

'Shamed was the Dark Fool. While blessed were the children. You shall always own a deep blue in your skies.'

I am very high, as they all stare, tilt their heads, shuffle, but do not blink, as they listen to my unnecessarily boisterous crowing. I'm not going to change for anyone now.

Chapter 16

Part II – In This Life, There Is *Only* Friendship

A Sherpa walks on in the morning sun. He shall make time ahead of us, and this shall allow for a small plane to be at the elevated basecamp landing strip for my arrival. I am a joyous slowcoach behind him, walking with one other coolie. I feel as if I have accepted the loan of youth and juvenation from Shangri-La as a permanent and transferable gift. I have aged not a day in that pass. *It is the strangest thing.*

The plane is indeed waiting for us, and I am told by the captain, a slight man of barely five feet in height with a magnificent and wicked smile, that we will fly to a landing strip by the Karnaphuli River in the City of Twelve Awliya, The Queen of the East, Chittagong.

Chittagong, now far filthier and noisier than I recall, was supposedly named by Arab traders in the ninth century (literal meaning Delta of the Ganges). Islamic scholars stake claims that a Muslim type lit a *chiti* (lamp) at the top of a hill in the city and called out (*agaan*) for people to come to prayer. Hence, *Chiti-agaan*. But I prefer the Burmese explanation for the name that an Arkanese king of almost wholly pacific tendencies and a proclivity to make love to hundreds of men and women gave the city the name *Tsit-ta-gung* (to make war is improper), while having the admirable fucking nerve to invade it. I see him not as a hypocrite, for sometimes situations are forced upon us to act for the greater good against our natural inertia and to bloody the bully's nostrils. Of course, to make war is improper, but it is also often absolutely obligatory and sage. It is therefore quite appropriate that I set sail for the island nation of Ceylon from such a spot, named for such a hypocritical but righteous reason (see, Sir Percy Blakeney).

I am warned by my contacts against air travel. It is a constricting business, I am told, quite likely to end in lots of questions and the glare of hot lights. We still control much of the seas, for not only does Winston's pull within the Admiralty remain strong and sturdy, but we have also always had a bit of the pirate about us.

Yes, magnificent Ceylon is en route. I am, in my dotage, an increasingly nostalgic type, and so I relish travelling by boat, even if it is a larger, smoother, swifter and better-lit beast than I last saw fifty years ago. The journey across the water is across a still and teal mill pond of an ocean. This same fondness for the olden days also demands that I stop off at the ambassador's residence there, and enquire of those amiable monks in the mountain jungles.

From there, the trek is a joy. I know what and who awaits. I find the monks with ease. It has been a while since I have been in such saucy company. All of them know of me, as it seems as if Robbie and I made quite an impression at the monastery well over a century ago, and since then when my allies and Thelemites have followed the path into the lushness to fill their pockets and satchels, we are always remembered so fondly. They bow and lower themselves in my presence. I am revered, and I recognise my youthful face in the paintings on the monastery wall. A soft murmur comforts me wherever I go there, and I am fed and given water, before being led to a comfortable single bed. This old man must rest now, for I shall

need all of my vigour for the latest renewal of my acquaintance with the goo and all the grubby beauty that shall
accompany it for several days.

There is nothing new in the process of the most welcome
orgy, but the content of the hallucinations lays out my immediate future with an apparent precision as clear and exact as
when Robbie and I were enlightened just before the turn of
that damned, confounding twentieth century and then, as if I
have only a short time left in my life, there is then a deep and
abrupt darkness in my vision; a flat-line that appears to indicate the end of my days on earth. Perhaps Death allowed me
through the mountain pass, only to then greet me, with its
dark allies of my next opponent in England; the British and
American governments, and their pals in the vicious and murderous regimes in Moscow, Peking and Constantinople; Rangoon, Buenos Aires and Damascus. I am not deterred.

As I sit for yoga and prepare to leave, the elder of the trippy
natives approaches me. He sits by me, and says, 'Are you ready?
Did you see what you needed to see?'

I respond, but speak more for my benefit than for his. He
seems comforted more by the steeliness of my words than by
their content. I appreciate both.

'I now know of what I must do in London. I will revisit a
place that once defined me, and there I shall commit an act
that will have global repercussions. If the Thelemites are right,
the revolution will take the world for us, at last. There will be
no near-miss like in Paris, because this revolt will not discriminate between stone-throwing Parisian lovers and bastards
with batons, shields, helmets, tear gas, guns and tanks. If my
pals are correct, no one will be immune from what we unleash.
It is them or us. If we do not grab our freedoms now, they will
be gone for ever. And *that* would be a crime.'

I turn to him.

'Thank you,' I say.

He says nothing and only touches my hand. I feel his comfort, friendship and strength, as they seem to bloat the molecules within with hope. And I leave.

I recall how Robbie and I once scrubbed each other's backs there in those blessed waterfalls and I consider these moments. My bravest darling.

I walk and then am taken on a cart pulled by a donkey to the sea. Time is a factor, but I know that I only need to be in London for the summer solstice, so precise are *some* of the goo-inspired instructions I am able to continually recall. Even the most conservative Phileas Fogg-types would have my feet outside the Reform Club by June the fifteenth, about a week early. So, I board a ship from Batticaloa on the eastern coast, and follow the advice of my vision to sail not through Suez but instead around the Cape, just as I deferred to Winston and went to Paris. Gods must listen too, for we can be fallible creatures.

Winston was so nearly right about Paris too. I gladly consent to the longer journey around the bulbousness of the continent of Africa and, of course, the violent seas of the Cape. I once again have myself tied to a lofty vantage point only minutes after a gourmand dose of jungle resin that might maim an amateur and leave him in a wheelchair. The storm is a beauty. Nature seems to have missed me, and she thrills and surges to see of my return, the frisky mare.

Our route hugs the western coast of Africa, and we are yet again joined by a hefty mob of aroused sea mammals in the caress and fondle of our slipstream, just as we were when we escaped with all that chunky Boer gold all those years ago. I wave to them in friendship as they eye their pal and contemporary, The Beast, on the ship.

I acknowledge, with a meditative posture, the fine lands on the yellowy coast, and I astral plane through the ports, bazaars and brothels as we make fine time towards Europe. On the latitude of Tunis, I relive a special sacrament, and honour lost and distant friends, winking and smiling to our right. In this life, there is *only* friendship.

Within days, we slow at my request to breathe in the Portuguese air approaching Boca do Inferno at Cascais, where I once faked my death.[*] We drop anchor for an hour, for the superstitious skipper is captivated by the caves, and appears to be at my mercy, since he believes I, personally, vanquished the storm as we rounded the Cape, offering myself as a sacrifice on high. I am happy to take his reverence, if it allows me to slip back in time to Portugal maybe a hundred years ago.

The progress north is then steady and firm as we leave France over our right shoulders, and slip into the ploughed furrow of the armada that faced the most ignominious of defeats when she moved on England. Adolf did not even make his move on Her, thanks to me. I now resolve to elevate myself above them all. Spain, Germany and now this new, putrid and mean England, for I made that promise to Winston.

Land is seen, and the bowels ought to be set on edge, but are not. I sit lotus on deck, breathing with marvelled malintent, and eye Her, the errant bitch of a sceptr'd isle, who needs to be tamed. England.

As I meditate, I consider the vital questions for my own clarity, and dismiss all other clutter.

One.

Who are the combatants? Whitehall and GCHQ, Washington DC, Russia, China, Turkey, the Saudis, for no one is

---

[*] *For the first time.*

innocent if they fuck with their own people. Government *or* people. Bullies *or* the bullied.

Two.

What might defeat look like?

Three.

What might victory look like?

Despair or ecstasy, we will all know by the looks on several billion faces that will reflect either Stalin's Moscow and Adolf's camps or London shall resemble the dappled and fragrant ragweed slopes of that Sicilian Abbey on a June morning in '22. It shall be clear who controls the future.

I then stir myself with the question of the consequences.

Four.

What will it all mean for the world?

There will be no cries of 'Best of three, you cheating fuckers.'

This is Glory or Bust. For eternity. There shall be no coming back from this one.

Five.

How shall I do this?

I still do not know fully, though my unreasonably generous Ceylon jungle visions seem to lead me by the hand, and appear to squeeze it softly as the elder monk's mitt had. I am assured each step will be made clear by the previous one. I shall do the rest, and relish each second until the darkness of that flat-line.

And there she is. London. In the late afternoon, I wish for her face to be in the same old frame. But crikey, she seems to have changed. The air seems filthier than fifty or sixty years ago, but still far cleaner than when I was a boy. There are hints of old Manhattan to the skyline, but these structures shimmer and shine like cheap shoes. I sense my London weeping at the dagger-blows and thrusts each of these edifices have struck, not so much into Her air, though that feels a travesty, but more into Her flesh at ground level and beneath. This is where the hurt must be felt. These monstrosities, however, are not so shiny so as to be seen to reflect in the Thames, for it looks browner and shittier than ever. It seems like the worst of both worlds.

We meet again. 'Oh, London, my love. Come back to me. I implore you.'

Chapter 16

Part III – It is the Strangest Thing

> Character is what you do when you
> think no one is looking.
>
> – FBI

The Book of Revelations told of it. An empire shall fall. Civilisation comes to an end. All of these things can be true and still be worthy of utter rejoicing. Like all religion, it is the skewing and interpretation that is all important. It all depends on who is destroyed and who prevails. It all depends on the identity of the Messiah, and the empire and the civilisation that fall.

The high commanders within Thelema have been warned that The Crackdown is coming. The President of the United States has spoken of limiting the power of the technology the world uses to shore up his own position of command. He has been brazen about suspending elections. The lapdog British will do the same, mimicking those African and Middle Eastern despots, against whom they used to so rail. We know this from our lads and lasses within GCHQ and the CIA. If we do not strike first, we are doomed. The human race will no longer be a free species. ('It will soon be a race against time,' one Thelemite tells me. 'The best form of defence is attack. We have our mission planned for the solstice,' says another.)

The Crackdown will be coordinated by an axis of governments in Constantinople, Moscow, Peking, Washington, Tokyo, Nairobi, Lagos, Buenos Aires, Paris and London.

These authorities have willing accomplices in charge in fifty, seventy, a hundred other capital cities. This is *precisely* how Orwell's world happens. And so, their hubris has sparked this Beast. This slightly confused, but determined and curious Messiah.

A rebellion has been simmering, as our types on the inside discover more and more about The Crackdown. They will now urge on this Spartacus. It seems my name and works carry much weight. I am not too old to bristle with pride. Remember that the ONLY thing we have is friendship. So, I shall add my personal touch to it. Swagger, style, danger and a dash of symmetry are so pivotal to making a plan worthwhile in its execution and, of course, in hindsight in the afterglow of victory. Defeat is not worth pondering. I am a happy pawn, but pawns are handy bastards and might end up wearing a crown if set free behind enemy lines.

London

The fawning, yet quite adorable captain of the ship is kind enough to find an old suit and some shoes for me. A hessian robe might have attracted unwanted attention even back then in the Notting Hill, Pimlico and Chelsea of the sixties; today for sure. I am tempted to welcome the spotlight of the eccentric, but remind myself, there is perhaps a benefit to anonymity in my quest for that grail of glory.

At the gangplank, I am met by Violet, who shall soon explain more to me of what we must do. If I marry her advice

to the visions from Ceylon and the directions of the Thelemites, then we might be on track. It is ten years since I have seen
her. It is almost ninety years since her birth, and yet she is
youthful for her age. This is possibly a genetic benefit from
this godly father of hers, but equally likely are the stalled
months from Shangri-La, and the lustre these mountain years
also seem to allow to spill over back into the real world. Perhaps both.

I tingle when I see her, and my steps towards her seem to
allow me to float. My love is here. Mischief appears to shelter
in the shallow and few lines on her face. Her aura is vibrant,
redolent, and ready for war. Her posture exhibits a straight
back and a raised chin, arrogantly tilted as if she has all of this
covered. I adore her. I have never stopped.

We do not unman each other, as Winston would have said.
We are purposeful, and she remains less likely, as ever, to tend
towards sentimentality than I.

'It is good to see you, Father.'

'It is great to see you, Vi.'

'Come, Old Man.'

'Yes, love. Let us walk, and I shall tell you of Ceylon and
the I Ching I performed as we eased onto the Thames.'

I walk with her, her arm through mine. I carry no luggage.
Violet smiles at a uniformed man who is checking passports,
and we pass unhindered. I sense that the fellow stands imper-
ceptibly to attention, as I walk past him. Does he mumble, 'Do
What Thou Wilt'? There is, without doubt, deference and reverence.

My shoe'd but sockless foot touches a paving slab of London, and I am bombarded by memories.

'It is fucking marvellous to be back,' I say without having
had any intention to utter a word. It begins a series of minor
events when my subconscious seems to be dictating my own

path, as if my actions were speaking in tongues. 'Is there a greater puppeteer than I?' I briefly wonder. Either way, I am comforted.

'I want to walk, Violet.'

'I know, Papa.'

'Where do we have to be and when? To meet them?'

'The Gay Hussar, of course. Two days from now, at noon.'

It is June the eighteenth. Three days from the solstice.

And so, over the next forty-eight hours, I renew my *flâneu-series* of this city. Much of London has prevailed, I have heard – the old iron bridges, the Tube, the pubs, the Victorian parks and some remnants of guts and balls for a fight – but it is still unnerving to see how people behave. I feel like an intruder. I have heard of how the telephone has creeped into pockets, purses and hands, but I am not prepared for the extent of it. It seems like a Technicolor version of one of those old science-fiction flicks Winston and I may have seen at the Rialto. Oh! how Orson would have marvelled at this, and how Hitch would have shuddered and seen the ramifications for good old-fashioned murder.

I have a map in my head of the places that I must visit to build up the courage to do what I must do. I know I have to go to a place where I may well be known, recognised, exposed and murdered. If this happens, my battle is lost, and the free-doms of the world might perish. For ever.

We are in Deptford and so it is logical, we should first visit my Dulwich mansion before the meandering tour begins.

Violet and I shall then stand on the spot where my father once fell silent at the burlesque madness of the summer circus on the northern gradients of the lush park hillocks below Alexan-dra Palace when the Maximus de Paris Rouge came to town.

Violet holds my hand, precisely as it has been held regularly of late by those I love. I feel a conspiracy of beauty, nudging me to my destiny.

It was here on February the fifteenth, 1881, where Father was struck down on a soapbox in the middle of Deuteronomy 7:15.

> And the Lord will take away from you all sickness,
> and none of the evil diseases of Egypt, which you
> knew, will he inflict on you,
> but he will lay them on all who hate you.

Later in the rear gardens of a Camden guest house, we are applauded and cheered by a similarly conspiratorial gang of chimpanzees. As I make eye contact with them, a calm serene wisdom apparently owns them briefly before their frenzied bouts of self-pleasure and turd-chucking begin once more.

The next day, on the steps of that Marylebone Station hotel where we overnight, where concrete meets marbled tiles, I stare at a yellowy-lit window, where the boys of The Legion once sat, injected, laughed and plotted. I sit on the step where my father once spoke to me. I think of him, and those dutiful boyhood days in the countryside, golden midges, nettles and all. These treasured spots have barely changed and if I squint my eyes, I can almost see the eighteen eighties.

Not only is Redhill far away, there is no point in a pilgrimage to misery. We do not go there.

By lunchtime, Violet and I stand on a Waterloo side street, where a fleapit cinema used to be, and where I was regularly viewed as a pre-eminent pervert. It is all now apartments and a kindergarten. A young mother, who passes with her two toddlers, seems to eye me thus, despite the presence of Violet. She pushes the young ones past me so as to avoid my sphere, while still being unable to avoid casting a curious glance back in my direction. Women do have the keenest of sensors.

We then sit in an otherwise empty stand at The Oval and watch an afternoon of cricket. Christ, but for the creaking pavilion, the old gasholder, Archbishop Tenison's school and of course, the velvety green baize, I would not have recognised it.

We then stroll over the river where we stay at another old favourite, the Savoy on The Strand. The following morning, Violet and I bellow with laughter, and then she sheds a tear for Margaret. I think how the regrettable but necessary meanness exacted towards Margaret as a girl saved England and allowed us to prevail. This is the precise strength I need to draw on for the evening ahead.

We stroll up and down the length of Greek Street several times, before we enter at noon and marvel at the unaltered odours of the Gay Hussar. I am nodded at, called 'sir', and appear to be known by one or two sage types. I still sense the brackishness and the unrivalled beauty of Hitch, Orson and Marlene in the air.

Then Violet nudges me as the three of them come in in fine synchronicity, one from the front door, one from the lounge and one from the WC. There is an old soldier in the garb of The Legion, as if plucked from the Leamington train, one spotty and cross-eyed lad, who reminds me of the poor bastard I terrorised that night when I first met Hitch in The Crown in WC2, and a middle-aged lady carrying a shopping bag, wearing a knitted cardigan, a beret tilted rebelliously on her head and a half-snooker-ball of a wart on her cheek that would have demanded all of my respectful attention had it not been for the seriousness of our chat to grab back our planet. I still struggle not to ogle it.

We rise to meet them, and they silently usher to sit, palms down, as they approach, either as if this were no longer required these days, but, I suspect, more in polite deference to us. I feel as if I should be paying the respect to them. They might pull off a victory without me, but I am unlikely to achieve it the other way around.

The old shuffling soldier, perhaps sixty years younger than me, explains with a pleasant authority a third rationale. 'No fuss, no fuss.' I think he might even have the gall to call me 'lad' or 'son'.

Five shots of Pálinka appear quickly, and are placed in front of us.

'*Köszönöm!*'* we all say together.

The lady takes charge.

'The swifter we can do this, the better. If you are hungry, stay after we have gone. We cannot tarry, and we will leave separately. This is for you.'

She pushes an envelope across the table, and we are all aware of the cliché.

'It is a phone. It is fully charged, and set to the page you need. When you get to where you are going, Violet has been instructed how to do the rest. This machine will listen only to her voice.'

'And where are we going?'

'36 Blythe Road. After that, you might receive a message on here,' and she nods back at the phone.

This confirms the accuracy of my jungle vision.

The spotty lad wants to chime in, he seems excited.

'What do we do with it afterwards?' Violet asks.

'Either way, it won't matter,' the boy gets his chance to chime in. I can see that he wishes to note this moment to retell

---

* *Hungarian for thank you.*

to his children and grandchildren long after he loses his virginity. He might even use this moment as leverage to do just that.

He gets up to leave, before he can make a mess of his big moment. He smiles at Violet and me. The blessed boy. He is shaking, and turns for the door. The lady and the soldier do the same, but far more measured and steady. The old boy whispers to himself. It could be either a vicarious pep talk or early dementia. The lady is determined, and is off as if she has left a shepherd's pie in the stove.

Violet and I stare at the package and she slips it into her purse. No one appears to look at us in an untoward manner, and there are no shifty eyeballs behind broadsheet newspapers, as there would have been in my day.

We drink more Pálinka, eat goulash and enjoy each other for the afternoon. Often we don't speak, but just look. Finally, our telepathy stretches to rising at the same moment to leave. Violet tries to pay, but the Hungarian maître d' waves us to the door.

Do I hear him say, '*Sok szerencsét, öregember*'?*

I look back at him, and he then says more audibly, '*Tedd amit tenned kell. A szeretet a törvény. Messiás.*'†

There is one more place to go before we shall rest. Blythe Road. I know the time for conflict is here. We walk in the early evening, and it is not a long walk. The city is puking up its office workers and bankers and shop staff and ad reps and traders. We stroll towards the dropping sun of the summer solstice.

There is gravel under foot as we approach a broad Georgian town house mansion, set back behind wrought-iron gates

---

* '*Good luck, old man.*'
† '*Do what thou wilt. Love is the law. Messiah.*'

in its own grounds. There are grotesques and gargoyles above the imposing second floor, majestic arched windows of stained glass and towers and turrets from far safer fairy tales. There is a soft butter-yellow light in the arched windows, and the large cars beneath a weeping willow in the driveway appear to hint at a family house, or the possible presence of a gathered enemy.

On a park bench opposite, I see a silhouette of an elderly couple sitting on a bench with two larking kids at their knee. He looks down and his incongruous top hat covers his features. Her maroon bonnet too.

Violet and I pause before we glance at each other, and I walk up the steps to the formidable front door.

I knock slowly and loudly. My mouth is dry.

The door is soon opened by a middle-aged lady, who tilts her head at the strangers on the third and top step.

'I am sorry to disturb you, madam. I truly am.'

'How may I help you?'

'I used to live on this street here many years ago. I was remembering with an old friend here. Fond memories, you know. And I became so very thirsty. Might I *please* ask for a glass of water? And the briefest* use of the WC, *please*?'

'Of course, you may,' the kind lady says. She asks me in over the threshold, an invitation in the style that Count Dracula might have required. And so it begins, as we slip off our shoes.

The same façade of a family home masked the ceremonies and rituals in the hallowed and roomy temples underneath in the cavernous basement. The Golden Dawn may still be active below – the expensive cars on the loose gravel suggest it – and any one of them would recognise my face from the literature.

---

* *There is a polite way to impart one's intentions to piss and not shit.*

I doubt any of them would hesitate in attempting to hold me until more fearsome allies are summoned.

I consider hypnosis on the lady of the house, but I believe we have adequately convinced our hostess of our genuine need for water and a bathroom. And in any case, I shall save the hypnosis for later, when it will be a nationwide and then an international and global affair before this sisterly planet takes one more revolution in the heavens.

I tell the old lass that I need the help of my daughter with my ablutions, and we are ushered towards a broad staircase. The lady turns her back on us as one of our Thelemites, with perfect and planned timing, shouts, bawls, and generally creates a disturbance outside. An old-style Chinese firecracker goes off too, then four, five, six more, and we shuffle quietly down the wooden steps instead of up to the WC. I hear our hostess, 'Those bloody yobs again. I am calling the police this time.'

The surroundings all now seem so familiar to me, for it is the route that Winston and I took in the second battle. I push open the large arched door that leads to the hall. It is empty, but for that old altar. Violet and I stride over to it.

She removes from her purse the envelope and then the small black device handed to her by our pals in the Hussar. She holds it close to my face, pushes on the small tablet's face, it lights up and she nods at me to speak. I cast a spell of Thelema.

Man, unable to solve the Riddle of Existence, takes counsel of Saturn, extreme old age. Such answers as he can get is the one word 'Despair'.

Is there more hope in the dignity and wisdom of Jupiter? No; for the noble senior lacks the vigour of Mars the warrior. Counsel is in vain without determination to carry it out.

Mars, thus invoked, is indeed capable of victory: but he has already lost the controlled wisdom of age; in a moment of conquest he wastes the fruits of it, in the arms of luxury.

It is through this weakness that the perfected man, the Sun, is of dual nature, and his evil twin slays him in his glory, and who shall mourn him but his Mother Nature, Venus, the lady of love and sorrow.

But even Venus owes all her charm to the swift messenger of the gods, Mercury, the joyous and ambiguous boy, whose tricks first scandalise, and then delight, Olympus.

But Mercury, too, is found wanting. Now in him alone is the secret cure for all the woe of the human race. Swift as ever, he passes, and gives place to the youngest of the gods, to the Virginal Moon.

Then she smiles, nods and from a folded piece of paper, she speaks to the machine to activate the rest of the plan.

'Double U, double U, double U, dot . . .'

While she does this, I replicate some of the mischief I executed on Yeats's tomb as I unbutton my flies, drop my trouser and crouch. I manage to micturate liberally on the step before their altar. I was hoping I might need to defecate too, but I do not feel the peril I was anticipating. I try, but it won't happen. I shrug, as if it may remain a small regret. Such is life. I stand and fix myself, as Violet continues to speak.

'S . . . I . . . X . . . F . . . I . . . N . . . G . . . E . . . R . . . S . . . dot . . . V . . . I . . . R . . . dot . . . U . . . S . . . Send.'

She pulls the phone back from her face and then after it chimes like the Empress Dowager's gong, she whispers, 'Password,' then goes on.

'R . . . O . . . B . . . B . . . I . . . E. Send.'

Gong.

I then sit and, for a brief minute, allow myself to drop into a trance and astral plane to a time when I forced an ankle-deep fecal and orgiastic fuckfest here in the majesty of 36 Blythe Road. I relish that second battle before I return to the present.

It is done. We return to the staircase and move back to the ground floor.

And, with our shoes back on, we walk to take our leave as the lady appears from what seems to be a kitchen producing delicious smells.

'Thank you, madam. You have made an old man very happy.'

Her smile has been replaced by a more inquisitive countenance. I turn towards the door, but my way is now blocked by a large man. He puts his arm out in front of me. He stares at me, and brings his face close to mine.

'Do I know you, sir?' he asks me.

I am silent. Sturdy and confident, I stare at him.

'Are you on the television?' he says.

'I think not. Perhaps one day,' I say, hoping to prompt a smile.

He pauses, as I see the oaf attempting to place my identity. He is not the sharpest fellow, but one would want his help in a dark alley brawl.

The lady joins him at his side, and looks at him, as if urging him to have that penny drop.

'Okay, fair do's. Are you sure we cannot order you a cab?'

'That is so kind, but you have no idea how much I cherish walking the streets of this city. Especially now I have relieved myself. Thank you all the same.'

We leave as rapidly as is possible before the invisible ink on my face – a contingency plan that has just proved unnecessary – reveals two solid pentagrams identical to the ones at that same address way back when, and then also at a notorious chess game in the Waldorf Astoria in New York City a long, long time ago.

Once outside of that vast old house, Violet and I howl and bay with joy and mirth at the unnecessary theatrics, melo-drama and danger we have just been through. I do not need to explain that style and panache in executing a plan to save Mankind is so very vital.

'Wait,' she says. 'Watch this.'

And she holds up the device, and I see myself urinating and then hear my own invocation, measured, urgent and proud. We watch and listen again. And now as we stagger and laugh and hold each other up, an old Packard sweeps past us in what appears to be slow motion. I sense two faces I know so very well, smiling from the back, while two children seem to listen to and stare at their elders. Both males, young and old, wear gargantuan and identical spectacles, the gent a large beard, while both females, young and old, are in matching maroon and cream bonnets. *I know who you are!* I tingle. They know I am safe. I, they.

This part is done. The ritual of the ceremony, however brief, was still a ceremony and did not lack any sacredness. The Third Battle of Blythe Road* ought now be fought in an unseen realm in the ether over the coming hours, as the reper-cussions of the third-millennium hex that Violet has set in motion might, we pray as atheists, be seen.

The plan is simple. My legion of Ceylon monks – who number 666 – are currently in several hundred cities around the world.

---

* *'Best of three, you fuckers?'*

Until noon today, they were each armed with nothing but a satchel of gooey toffee. There they met Thelemites with a) access to key water facilities and reservoirs and b) several hundred with small aircraft, helicopters and drones.

Throughout this day, their supplies were lobbed, dropped, catapulted and dissolved – with utter sanctity and righteousness – into the water source of major conurbations and metropolises to give my welcome home party a perpetual kick.

Meanwhile, the *SixFingers* spell should be spreading by the wonders of technology.

The virus is designed to warn against the purchase and libation of any canned or bottled drinks. Billions should be cautioned that all such products have been laced and spiked in an undiscriminating tilt at mass murder. Billions should be advised to drink only tap water until further notice. We hope that editors at news outlets will take the bait and spread our word. I can only hope that the marvellous leverage to be found in paranoia continues to win wars for me.

Now, only time will tell. Violet and I head to one final spot to witness our glory or our defeat. We shall walk to Highgate Cemetery, where I will visit an old and resting pal, who would be so thrilled at the audacity and thorough simplicity of our plan, should it work.

It is a long trek now. Violet and I are tired, but fuelled by the anticipation of our Glory. We are aware from the friends we met in the Hussar of the immediacy and swiftness of these modern-day spells. This increases our excitement to juvenile levels, as an old man and his elderly daughter trace a path across the city. We appear supremely innocuous, banal, barely worth a look, but, like the minuscule Spanish flu virus or the sparrow that hits an engine and brings down a jetliner, those evil bastards in power should ignore the seemingly bland and the apparently inoffensive at their peril.

There is no way The Crackdown could have happened, so swiftly. I think. But I know this spy game well, and if we have lads and lasses on the inside of them, those slippery fuckers might well know slivers of what we are up to. Whether they have activated their own plan of a curfew or not, Violet and I certainly get a glimpse of how it may appear on those empty streets, oddly deserted for the London I once knew. The pubs are closed, and lit windows become rarer as night closes in. When we do see a person, they do not stagger like imbeciles, staring at the lit screen in their hand, but instead they now scuttle from the Underground station to doorways, as sirens are heard across the citadel.

In an empty pub, a television screen has been left on. It shows the face of a newsreader for several minutes. There is no voice, but, instead, a wailing coming from the screen. Another bar is open, surreptitiously, in a back street, but, as Violet and I peer into the window of the snug, the lone chap in there, slouched at a table, appears to be on the point of weeping.

From London W14, Violet and I walk through the parks to the northern slopes; through the gas-lit paths of Holland Park and the splendour and the ducks of Kensington Gardens. Hyde Park is empty, so we borrow a row boat and I paddle from south-west to north-east across the Serpentine, where I once saw a young family killed by a Zeppelin. In the middle of the lake, we both take a handful of toffee.

From Marble Arch, we move through the silent and scary back streets of Mayfair and Fitzrovia to Regent's Park and finally the Heath. We will walk through the night. We appear to be the only ones.

*

I show Violet the way into the cemetery after dark, and then we walk unthreatened and free to the final resting place of my chum. His gravestone bears no name, but we were given precise instructions in the Hussar.

Had that old friend have been with us, I am sure he would speak of old times, how his days in London had been his happiest. He would tell of the camaraderie of the doss houses, and perhaps the loneliness of the packed taverns and trains. He would revel and exalt the beasts in the zoo, and the ecstasy of sailors stepping ashore and their thrill of leaving again, with a lonely lass's name and photograph, away to the oceans.

The goo is now hitting me. I hear my dead friend's voice from inside his tomb. He tells me, clearly and audibly in my mind, as Violet touches my hand again in that same manner of late, of the company of whores and bishops, spicy-gobbed fish wives of vile invective and calm spies who knew their days were numbered. He tells me of the lads and lasses he has seen there in the cemetery with needles in their arms, and those he has persuaded to turn their backs on suicide. He tells me of the young blokes with prams, who every day sit on the tombs, cry embarrassed words, and implore lost wives below in the muck for advice on how to be a good dad.

He tells me how he misses me and I hear his laugh.

My Grigori Yefimovich. My Rasputin. I stir back from my reverie, and write his name in the dirt with a stick.

Morning is almost here. Violet has closed her eyes, but I know she cannot sleep on our strong narcotic. Instead, I sense she is concentrating. The streets around the cemetery and across the city appear silent. The blue-ish tinge of first dawn touches the outline of the tombs.

Yet, this is not the shade of morning, for this is a turquoise.

And an almost imperceptible lilac. And then a flicker of death-white. I have seen the Auroras when far north at Boleskine, but never here in the glare of the south, though never have I seen London looking so unblanketed and exposed to the stars as this pre-dawn was.

But this light does not come from the Aurora's north or the dawn's east. This comes from the south, and the west. Then, the same flickers come from within the viscerals and the groins of the city itself that I look across. The rays of those colours shoot from bedrooms and salons, bedsits and hostels from as far as my soggying eyes can see. *This* is how it happens. *This* is what it looks like.

My visions from the goo are now immediate and close by. I speak of them to Violet.

Of mobs of graffiti artists with lilac stains on their fingers, already celebrating the moment they have waited for since they bought their first vinyl long player, and, in their lonely bedroom, wept with joy to themselves as they first heard the music.

Of the same turquoise, lilac and death-white lights shooting out from army barracks and police stations. Of how we have just eliminated the one obstacle that stopped us from prevailing in Paris in 1968. The law. Those fuckers get thirsty too, it seems. I speak of how they are now mine, copulating on bunk beds, sodomising on parade grounds, fellating in squad cars and on tanks. Of how the sparks and shards and blades and sprayed bullets of the goo cannot be avoided.

Of how victory feels and sounds. And of how still I have no yearning to reveal myself as the Scarlet Pimpernel of the Twentieth Century. Of how *this,* what I feel and see now, is enough. Of how *this* was always going to be enough for me.

Of how tens, hundreds, of thousands, perhaps millions, stand forward on this day. Of how they are the great-grandsons and great-granddaughters of tired and scared boys, who were shovelled, by the thousand, out from trenches and shipped from the Western Front of the Great War, and out to safe beaches, jungles and small villages by a soldier called Robbie and a man their forefathers only ever referred to in whispers as The Great Beast. Of how they were all helped to safety by a bearded doctor called Dandylyon and a benevolent nurse named Prudence Venus-Coshe. Of how there were Germans, Italians, French, Belgians, English, Welsh, Irish and Scots, who sobbed with simultaneous joy and guilt. Of how there is here now a mob of remarkable-looking lads and lasses with green eyes, mahogany faces and red hair from Ceylon itself, where we once shipped those white-skinned champs from County Wicklow. Of how they are all paying homage today, on this speckled and flecked dawn. Of how some feel to me as if they are here, just miles away, such is the reverence and determination to be in this town today to say thank you. Of how the clusters of their families and communities have always been on alert and ready to pay their simple debt, merely with their presence, and their boots and sandals on the ground at a municipal-wide, then global fuckfest.

Of how the people at this party, once they have sipped that glorious potion, will never be the same again. Of how there are simply some bells that cannot be unrung. Of how there are no hangovers to shake off. Of how the chasing of this dragon becomes a cyclical and unending joy.

Of how this is neither a parochial and local bender nor a neighbourhood and provincial jag, for right now that big bully, Uncle Sam across the ocean, is on his knees, his face in a soggy groin, and wholly reminiscent of a scene I now recall as a young boy with a King James Bible under my arm and holding my father's hand on a piping-hot Gloucestershire afternoon. It was the day I remember watching at length an over-keen bulldog licking porridge out of a bucket, as Papa chuckled at his enthusiasm. I knew it to be a boy by its broad, weighty, rhythmical and swinging scrotum. Well, this is the precise and purposeful gusto with which the United States is currently engaging in a nationwide analingus.

I speak to Vi of the America I once knew, and honour now the gloried spots that made me so happy in that land, the places that are now being submerged in the greatest revolt. I tell of that scrubby roof in Chelsea, where La Gitana and I summoned magickal hours to the pristine west coast towns now lorded over with generosity by young Dibdins. I tell of that exact spot in the park during the Great War, where Winston and I first met and started all of this astonishing nonsense, to the bubbling persistent rebellion that shall always be New Orleans. From the ballroom of the Waldorf Astoria where I once wooed Manhattan society over a century before, with inked pentagrams on my face and filthy talk, to that treasured spot on Esopus Island, high above the Hudson where my Scarlet Woman and I daubed vast letters and Thelemic slogans onto the rock face, taunting and confusing tourists and inspiring sailors alike. From the polished flamenco floor and the tables pockmarked by a thousand clipping heels in the Little Madrid Café to Naples, Oakland, Detroit, Boston, Chicago, Toledo, Memphis, Nashville, St Louis, San Antonio, San Jose, Seattle, Portland and El Paso. And into every nook in the dustbowls, coastal towns, bad-lands, swamps and mountains.

Of how nowhere is immune as biblical scholars and pious grandmas turn into premium degenerates and perverts of vast scale. Freaks and deviants now stroll across the land of our shimmering apocalypse.

Of Rangoon, China, India, Brazil and those thoroughly game Africans too.

Game over.

*

The beasts in London zoo now begin to wail and howl, for the smart buggers sense a metropolis in municipal-wide coitus. It is a populace with visions – just as Robbie and I had that first time – of the rain that now falls upwards to the skies, lovers as rampant skeletons with vermillion, pumping hearts, and clear images of the future, clear images that ignite further rapture and triumphant bellowing. And so *it begins*. The turquoise, lilac and death-white.

'Violet, Violet. Stir, my love. Open your eyes. *It is the strangest thing.*'

And my vicious and feisty daughter opens her eyes in the rain, touches my fat, damp paw again. Violet now knows of the greatest victory, as we add to the glory of walking on moons, and the sheer wonder of piano concertos, *this new day*.

And *this* is how I crown the lovers of this planet – and thus make billions of noble swines the permanent rulers of our great world. The one we shall now live in ecstatically, perpetually and for free.

And They shall write and speak of this Dawn, as Mankind finally takes Her rightful and righteous place, and She lights up the Skies. Forever.

Epilogue

Only those who fear shall fail. Those who have bent their backs to the yoke of slavery until they can no longer stand upright; them will I despise. But you who have defied the law; you who have conquered by subtlety or force; you will I take unto me, even I will take you unto me . . . Only if ye are sorrowful, or weary, or angry, or discomforted; then ye may know that ye have lost the golden thread, the thread wherewith I guide you to the heart of the groves of Eleusis. My disciples are proud and beautiful; they are strong and swift; they rule their way like mighty conquerors. The weak, the timid, the imperfect, the cowardly, the poor, the tearful — these are mine enemies, and I am come to destroy them. This also is compassion: an end to the sickness of earth. A rooting-out of the weeds: a watering of the flowers.

– *Liber Tzaddi vel Hamus Hermeticus sub figura XC*,
Aleister Crowley

In days, I shall be anonymous in Cambridge, walking among the youth in early summer.

'Good morning, sweet Prince,' they shall think, as I pass them or they go by me as I sit on a bench under a weeping willow and a girthy hat, while watching a punt or the cricket.

And I shall not miss my mountain retreat, for despite her magnificence she cloaked the most elegant and noble truth; that I am a god who does not require her generous preservative air, lovely as it seemed to be at the time.

I want it always to be clear that I never wanted to father a flock, to be the fetish of fools and fanatics, or founder of a faith whose followers are content to echo my opinions. I only ever wanted each man to cut his own way through the jungle. This should be my epitaph.

I proudly hide under the brim of my *chapeau* by the river, twiddling my cane, pondering mischief and degeneracy aforethought.

I think again of those pustulous boy twins, whom I enlightened that becurtained Cambridge afternoon as a youth between finals, and I consider a sherry in a tavern.

An old-ish lady sits next to me, and she fondly calls me 'Papa.'

Winston was right. We would, indeed, NEVER surrender.

The rays of the scorching sun are impinged upon by a gathering and relieving mist, leaving nothing more than a gnarled tangerine in the heavens. A small child passes and asks his father, 'But can lightning and thunder happen at the same time, Daddy? And without rain? And why did that thunder sound like an old man's laughter?'

Violet touches my fat fingers. She is a tender one at heart, and she knows by now that having to talk destroys the symphony of silence.

Yes, I think a sherry in a tavern. We stand.

'Come, Old Man.'

And Samson smiles. He is finally free. And he walks on.

Unbound is the world's first crowdfunding publisher, established in 2011.

We believe that wonderful things can happen when you clear a path for people who share a passion. That's why we've built a platform that brings together readers and authors to crowdfund books they believe in – and give fresh ideas that don't fit the traditional mould the chance they deserve.

This book is in your hands because readers made it possible. Everyone who pledged their support is listed below. Join them by visiting unbound.com and supporting a book today.

Diane McInerney
Martin Meyer
Dusan Mihajlovic
Dilyana Mincheva
John Mitchinson
Carlo Navato
Willow Nicholson
Scott Pack
Hugh Platt
Justin Pollard
Neil Rivington

Malcolm Sargent
Arild Stromsvag
Dominic Sweeting
Parvez Tehrani
Andrew Tuschak
Cara Usher
Monique Van Remortel
Mark Vent
Kirsty Waddell
Chris Wade-Evans